# Rosie's
# Curl and
# Weave

# Rosie's
# Curl and
# Weave

Rochelle Alers
Donna Hill
Felicia Mason
Francis Ray

St. Martin's Paperbacks

ROSIE'S CURL AND WEAVE

"In Love Again" copyright © 1999 by Felicia L. Mason.
"Just Like That" copyright © 1999 by Donna Hill.
"The Awakening" copyright © 1999 by Francis Ray.
"Special Delivery" copyright © 1999 by Rochelle Alers.

ISBN: 0-312-96828-0

Printed in the United States of America

St. Martin's Paperbacks edition / February 1999

St. Martin's Paperbacks are published by St. Martin's Press, 175 Fifth Avenue, New York, NY 10010.

10  9  8  7  6  5  4  3  2  1

# CONTENTS

# In Love Again

## Felicia Mason

# Chapter One

She walked in the door and set off Louis Sweet's personal earthquake alert. She appealed to him all at once and on so many levels that Louis could only stare and hope he didn't topple at her feet like an unsteady building straddling a fault line. Smiling a general greeting, she moved to the receptionist's desk to check in. Louis tracked her every movement.

"Hi, Ms. Webster. You're right on time," the receptionist told her. "A shampoo assistant will take you at station three."

"Thank you, Rebecca. It's busy today," the woman said, glancing around the shop.

"Prom season."

Louis's appreciative gaze stayed on the sway of the customer's full hips as she followed the receptionist to the salon's shampoo area. She walked with confidence, like a woman with a purpose. The honey of her voice carried a gentle softness and a refinement that made him take more than casual notice.

For more than three decades, Louis Sweet had earned a successful living by noticing the details others missed and by making women beautiful. About fifty, just a few years younger than his own fifty-seven, she had the fuller, rounded figure Louis had always admired on a woman. The electric blue suit and pearls added a gracefully feminine touch. Her Ferragamo shoes and handbag let him know she paid attention to detail and had a sense of style.

Her smile was as radiant as sunshine, her voice as melodious as a sweet song.

Something long dormant in Sweet's existence roared to life.

"That's a fine-looking woman."

"Mr. Sweet?"

"Huh?" He glanced at the two women standing beside him, one of whom had been harassing him about buying magazine subscriptions.

"We have several excellent choices that will enhance your customers' wait and relaxation experience in the salon."

His grunt, a noncommittal answer at best, couldn't be mistaken for interest. His attention was elsewhere. Louis still watched the woman named Ms. Webster. She settled in the shampoo chair, placed her handbag in her lap, and let the shampoo girl, someone he didn't recognize from here, drape a cape around her smart blue suit. She crossed her legs at the ankles and Louis strained his neck trying to get a better look.

"Mr. Sweet?"

Reluctantly he turned his full attention back to the saleswoman. "Look, we already get a bunch of hair books and about ten women's and men's magazines, including *Ebony*, *Essence*, *Jet*, *Today's Black Woman*, *Emerge*, and *Black Enterprise*. Right, Della? My customers have enough to read. Thanks anyway."

Without giving the spluttering saleswoman time to pitch anymore, Louis headed toward the shampoo area.

Della Frazier smiled as she watched his progress across the salon. "Well, it's about time," she said.

The saleswoman turned to Della. "Ms. Frazier . . ."

"I'm sorry," Della said as she turned the woman toward the door. "He's the boss and he's right. Our customers really do have lots of options. Good day."

Della ushered the saleswoman out the front door, then watched her dear friend beeline to Elaine Webster. "He's out of practice. I'd better check on him," she muttered to herself.

"Della, do you have a moment?"

She made her way toward Perry, the stylist who beckoned her.

"Mrs. Anderson is interested in details about Rosie's Ultimate Adventure," the stylist said.

Della turned a bright smile on the customer seated before Perry. Louis Sweet forgotten for the moment, Della pitched the salon's most expensive and exclusive pampering package. "It is divine. You'll love yourself for doing it and if you're giving it to a friend, he or she won't ever forget the experience—or you."

Feeling like a stranger in his own business, Louis hovered near the shampoo area. He didn't know half the people busy washing, conditioning, and coloring hair. Making a mental note to ask Della about the new hires, Louis zoomed in on the woman named Ms. Webster.

The black plastic cape covered most of her body, but he got a good view of her legs and the fine curve of her calves. Louis had always been a leg man. Hers were thick, shapely; just the way he liked them.

"Mr. Sweet, good to see you, man!"

Louis shook hands with a long-time customer. "Maurice, it's been a while."

A shampoo assistant tucked the man's long hair into a clear plastic cap, then stepped away.

"You just come in to collect the profits these days, huh? Living large."

Louis laughed. "No, it's not like that. I've been busy on some projects."

"Been so long I bet you forget how to handle a pair of clippers."

"It's like riding a bike and taking candy from a baby," Louis said. Without thinking, he checked his employee's work, then secured the cap around the man's ears. "I see you're sporting that old-school look."

Maurice touched the bag on his head. "The old school is the new school now. Good thing I saved some of those suits I was wearing back in '73. Had a brother offer me three hundred dollars for a powder blue leisure suit I had on one day."

"Yeah, and tell him what you did, Maurice," a shampoo assistant said.

"I told that fool 'just a minute,' then walked into Kmart, bought me some sweats for twenty bucks and handed him that suit. I had four of 'em just like it at home."

Everybody in the shampoo area laughed. Louis noticed the smile on Ms. Webster's face and remembered his original purpose. But before he could say or do anything, he found himself in the middle of greetings and well wishes from staff and customers. Some of the newer people, realizing he was the big boss, introduced themselves.

It had been a while since he'd been in the shop. Louis had almost forgotten the easy camaraderie that flowed all around. Cool jazz softly piped through the salon added a relaxed feel to a place where hustle and bustle was the norm.

Louis looked around his thriving business and realized how much he missed hearing the whirr of blow-dryers and the hum of the hood dryers. He got a kick out of the occasional moan of pleasure from a customer getting a good scalp massage during a hair wash. He loved the acrid smell of chemicals and the sweetness of the fruit-scented deep conditioners. Today a couple of televisions were on, as always, tuned to the soaps and the talk shows. The phone rang, the front door chimed as a customer walked in, and, above it all, a symphony of voices in conversation, easy debate, and the latest gossip welcomed him.

Louis Sweet stood in the middle of the floor and grinned.

It was good to be home.

"Mr. Sweet, would you take a look at this?"

A few stations down, a stylist and an assistant were taking a look at a customer's scalp. Louis joined them, secretly pleased that his opinion was still valued after all this time. Louis and his late wife Rosie had been doing hair longer than some of the shop's employees had been living.

He gave his approval to the work the two were doing and recommended fifteen minutes of deep conditioning.

"You can sit up, Ms. Webster," the shampoo girl at station three said.

Louis turned from his inspection of another customer's hair and toward Ms. Webster. "You're doing a great job, Mela," he told the assistant.

But he missed the shampoo girl's proud beaming smile because he was already headed to station three where Ms. Webster was getting a towel wrapped around her hair.

"Hello. I'm Louis Sweet."

She smiled at him. "I gathered as much. I'm Elaine Webster. Nice to meet you." She held a manicured hand out to him.

Louis shook her hand, then held it longer than necessary.

"Your hands are very soft."

"I get manicures done here. Pedicures too."

"Of course. We're a full-service salon."

"Is that a fact?"

Sweet's eyebrows rose. This was looking right promising.

The shampoo assistant patted the excess moisture from Elaine's head. "LaTonya can take you now."

Louis held out a hand to escort Elaine to her stylist.

"Have you been coming to the salon long? I don't remember seeing you," he said. She had to be a new customer. Louis knew he would have noticed her on one of his visits to check on things.

"Just about six months. Rosie's Curl and Weave was recommended to me by a friend."

"Good to hear. You know, we offer a gift certificate to customers who recommend others. How many have you earned in the six months you've been coming here?"

"None, I'm afraid."

Louis helped Elaine into the stylist's chair. Della, standing near the stylist, slyly smiled at him.

"What has you so amused, Della?"

"Oh, nothing," she told him. "Are you ready to take a look at those estimates now?"

"Sure," he said. "I'll meet you in the office in a moment."

Della exchanged a knowing smile with LaTonya, then made her way to the business office.

"It was a pleasure meeting you, Elaine Webster."

"Same here."

Elaine twisted the gold wedding ring on her left hand. Louis's eye, drawn to the nervous gesture, took in the sparkling gold and the glistening diamond. Disappointed, he took a step back.

She was married! Served him right for thinking the thoughts he'd been thinking.

With a quick word of departure he hastily made his way to the office, where Della sat on the edge of the desk, flipping through a trade magazine.

"I see something caught your interest out there. It's about time."

"What are you talking about?" he asked. Louis stomped around to Della's desk chair and plopped into it.

"Louis, it's me. You can fool some of the people most of the time, but never me. I know you too well. Her name's Elaine Webster."

"I know her name. She's married."

Della shook her head and closed the magazine. "She's actually a widow. Her husband died about a year or so ago."

Sweet's face lit up and he smiled. "Really?"

"That's supposed to be a sad thing."

He schooled his expression into a look of remorse. Della laughed.

"You're still a mess, Louis Sweet." She walked to a filing cabinet and pulled open the second drawer. "So, what do you want to know?"

"Everything."

Della sighed. "We're going to be here all night."

Louis rubbed his hands together. "Excellent."

Shaking her head, Della pulled out a thick file. "Okay, if the contractors complete the work by the end of July we could have . . ."

Looking puzzled, Louis stood. "Hold up, Della. What are you talking about?"

With the folder in hand, Della took a seat on the black leather sofa. She handed him a sheet of paper. Louis barely gave it a glance.

"You said you wanted to know everything about the construction project."

"Construction? No, no, stay with me, woman. I want to know everything about Elaine Webster."

Della closed the folder and arched one elegant eyebrow up at him. "I beg your pardon?"

"Tell me everything you know about Elaine Webster, the full-figured lady in the blue suit," he said, nodding his head toward the salon.

"You're serious?"

Louis thought about it for a moment, then bobbed his head in the affirmative. "Yes, I'm serious. You said she's a widow. What else do you know about her?"

Della folded her arms. "Louis Sweet, you old reprobate. I know that look."

"What look?"

"That 'love 'em and leave 'em look' of yours. Ms. Webster isn't like your passel of professional widows and lonely hearts."

"You injure me, Della."

"If the shoe fits," she said.

"Those nice ladies are simply friends."

"Well, you have a whole lot of friends. Too many if you ask me . . ."

"I didn't," he muttered.

". . . I don't want to see Mrs. Webster hurt. She's a nice lady, a good customer, and besides, she's still grieving."

Louis picked up the folder Della left on the desk. "You're acting like I've left a trail of broken hearts all over Harlem."

Della's lips pursed. "At least from 125th to 130th Streets."

"I'm practically a recluse!"

Della didn't look convinced. "I know your moves, Louis Sweet. I watched you when we were in school. I watched you put those moves on my best friend."

Louis's face fell at the reminder of his late wife. Della was suddenly sorry she'd evoked Rosie's memory.

She cocked her head and studied him. When she really thought about it, Louis hadn't done anything to attract the

women who'd descended on the salon like a plague of locusts
in heat. Word had gotten out that an eligible older widower
was available. The ladies gave him three months, what they
apparently decided was a suitable mourning period, then all
of a sudden the shop overflowed with apple pies and sweet
potato pies. Louis had had more dinner dates and home-
cooked meals than a single man should be allowed. Women
who weren't regulars and others that Della knew were long-
time customers at a rival salon down the street, constantly
found reasons to come to Rosie's Curl and Weave.

It got so bad at one point that a couple of the stylists suggested doubling the rates since Rosie's was the hottest ticket
in town.

It didn't take long for all the women Louis had casually
flirted with all those years with Rosie right at his side to realize that a good man was hard to find. Louis was not only a
good man, he had a thriving business, a couple of houses, a
boat, and all his own hair and teeth to boot. Louis Sweet *was*
a good catch.

Della eyed him as if she were inspecting a prime piece of
horseflesh. He squirmed under her perusal.

"What?"

"You miss her, don't you?"

Sweet looked away. "Every day, Della. Every day. What
Rosie and I had was special, one of a kind. We had twenty-
two good years together. But she's gone now. She's probably
looking down, wondering what's taking me so long to find a
new squeeze."

Della laughed out loud. "Yes, she would say something
like that. Rosie was as big a flirt as you used to be."

He pounced on the ammunition Della had provided. "*Used*
to be."

For a quiet moment, they studied each other. Louis and
Della knew each other too well to even consider the idea of
an affair. Their friendship and business partnership had
stretched too many years and had weathered too many storms
for them to contemplate that kind of foolishness.

"She's a retired schoolteacher. Lena recommended us to

her. She's a regular. One week is hair, the next week nails. She's always on time, and is always dressed like she just left a corporate boardroom. She tips well, doesn't gossip, and no check of hers has ever bounced.''

Louis grinned. ''You, Miss Della, are a treasure.''

''What are you going to do to her?''

For a moment, Louis didn't answer. Too many wicked ideas were running through his head. Della, liberal soul that she was, would be shocked. Then he smiled.

''Okay, I'm ready to hear the update on the renovation.''

''Louis!''

His response, a sly smile, didn't reassure Della.

# Chapter Two

Elaine Webster tried to get her whirling thoughts under control. Surely that man hadn't been flirting with her. Distinguished in a roguish sort of way, he looked as if he enjoyed every moment life had to offer. It had been a while since Elaine could lay claim to a similar *joie de vivre*.

She'd heard that the salon owner lost his wife some time ago. Elaine didn't know how long she'd continue missing Raymond. Maybe until she, too, was laid to rest next to him. She sighed.

Her stylist chuckled. "Yeah, that's the response from all the ladies when they see Mr. Sweet the first time. He can lay on the charm. But he's sincere about it."

Surprised that her sigh of loneliness had been interpreted another way, Elaine glanced back at LaTonya. "How long have you worked here?"

"Five years. Mr. Sweet hired me right out of school. I didn't even have a client base but he and Rosie gave me a chance. It's a good place to be. Della runs the shop well. And I couldn't imagine doing anything else for a living. How would you like your hair today?"

"The usual," Elaine murmured.

The stylist reached for a spray bottle of blue setting lotion.

Elaine settled back in the chair and smoothed the protective cape over her lap. Had he been staring at her legs? She raised her left leg out and inspected her ankles and shoes. Then a thought hit her: What if he saw her with a head full of green hair curlers? She might be a widow lady, but she was still woman enough to be self-conscious about a man, particularly an attractive one, seeing her all a mess.

"LaTonya, I've changed my mind. I'd like something different today, something new. Yes, that's it. A new look."

LaTonya rounded the salon chair and stood in front of Elaine. "Okay. What would you like?"

Elaine's small shrug gave credence to the fact that this desire for a new look had been a spur-of-the-moment decision. "I don't know. Something chic, hip."

One of the stylist's arched eyebrows rose. "Hip?"

Elaine smiled. "I'm showing my age?"

LaTonya smiled back then studied her face, tilting Elaine's head first to the left, then the right.

"How about a soft, feminine look?" Reaching up, the stylist pulled a few still-damp strands of hair down to frame Elaine's face. "Something that sets off your eyes and highlights your mouth."

"Hair can't work miracles," Elaine said with a small laugh.

"Yes, it can. But you don't need any miracles. You have excellent cheekbones and very expressive eyes. I've wanted to do something new on you for a while."

"Well, why didn't you say so?"

LaTonya smiled down at Elaine. "Now, Ms. Webster . . ."

Elaine nodded. "You're right. I've been stuck in a rut. Well, no more."

"Trust me?"

Elaine nodded.

"Okay, then, we'll start with a blow dry and then . . ."

Taking a deep, refreshing breath and slowly exhaling, Elaine tuned out the rest of LaTonya's plans for her hair makeover. LaTonya was the expert. It wasn't every day that Elaine did something as dramatic as change her look. But life had been stagnant for so long. In the weeks after Raymond's death, she'd barely functioned. Only recently had she realized that life continued. She could be a part of it or she could wither up and join her husband.

"I'm only fifty-six."

"Is that a fact?"

Elaine nodded, not realizing that she'd spoken aloud.

I'm fifty-six, she thought. Today, an attractive man flirted with me and here I am getting a new hairstyle for the first time in ten years. Elaine closed her eyes and smiled. Maybe things weren't so bad after all.

Louis opened the blinds at the office's two-way window. In the old days, he and Rosie liked to keep an eye on what was happening in the shop while they worked on the books. Now, Della spent so much time on the floor that the blinds were generally left down.

For a moment, he stared unseeing at the busy tableau, not noticing the frenetic pace of the stylists and assistants who waited on customers. Then he focused in on one chair.

Her smile would make an angel jealous. Louis wondered what thought had brought such joy to her face.

"It's time, Della," he said quietly.

She tucked the folder back in its spot and looked at him.

"I know. I just want you to have a care."

"I think I'll ask her to dinner."

Della folded her arms. "Isn't that a bit abrupt?"

"We're not eighteen anymore. All those preliminaries . . ."

"Are what matters," Della finished.

He turned to her. "You think so?"

"I know so."

He turned the slim guide that closed the black mini-blinds, then faced the woman who knew and kept his secrets. "So, wise one, what would you suggest?"

The following week, when she arrived for her appointment and manicure, Elaine paused at a dramatic display of white delphiniums and yellow roses. She'd never seen the two mixed together in such a startling arrangement. The tall graceful blooms of the delphinium clusters complimented the subtle yellows and the deep golds of the roses.

"This is beautiful," she said as she leaned forward to enjoy the scent of the flowers.

"Aren't they gorgeous?" the receptionist responded. "Della and Mr. Sweet decided that fresh flowers would be a nice touch today."

Elaine fingered a delicate rose and smiled. "The floral design is exquisite. Do you know which florist they used? I'm on the planning committee for my sorority's annual scholarship dinner. I'd love to use the people who did this."

"I'd be happy to oblige."

Elaine turned and came face-to-face with Louis Sweet. Today he wore a blue double-breasted jacket and gray trousers. The clothes accented his tall form. With his easy smile and salt-and-pepper hair, he reminded her of Harry Belafonte. Louis Sweet was quite dashing. A man shouldn't be allowed to look that good. Louis Sweet appeared to be a man who enjoyed the good life.

Then she gazed into his eyes and forgot what it was she'd been thinking and assessing. She wondered what it might be like to be held in his arms, to laugh with him, to dance with him. She also wondered why her heart beat so fast, why her hands—hands that a moment ago had been perfectly fine—now trembled just so.

"Hello again." Elaine hated the fact that her voice seemed to have gone the way of her hands. To her ears, her usually calm voice sounded much more like a breathless sigh.

"It's wonderful to see you again, Mrs. Webster."

"Please, call me Elaine," she said. Then, wondering if that was too forward, she quickly added, "Everyone in the salon seems to be on a first-name basis."

"Elaine it is. Would you like me to show you some of my floral arrangements? I have photos. But this is the grandest one to date."

Elaine stared at him and then pointed at the flowers. "You? You did this?"

Louis nodded. "Flowers are a hobby of mine, particularly roses. I've been experimenting a bit in planting and cutting."

She didn't realize her mouth hung open until he reached over and with a gentle touch, stroked her chin.

"Don't look so surprised," he said. Then, leaning close to

her, he added in a conspiratorial whisper, "I've always appreciated beauty. And no, I'm not gay."

Elaine's mouth snapped shut and she drew herself up to her full five feet seven. "Well, I . . ." she sputtered.

"That's what lots of people assume about men who play with flowers. Couple that with the fact that I've been doing hair since I was about ten years old . . ." he said with a shrug, "Let's just say I've been called a lot of things in my years."

Her dour expression told him it was past time to change the subject.

"Do you garden?" he asked.

Before Elaine could answer, she was summoned to the shampoo area. Grateful for the interruption, she sent a weak smile in Louis's direction, then quickly followed the assistant whose high heels clicked on the pink-and-blue marble floor. Elaine concentrated on the sound and not on the fact that her brief conversation with Louis Sweet left her cheeks warm with equal parts embarrassment and feminine awareness.

Louis watched her hasty escape. "Well, that didn't go very well," he muttered.

"Sweet, my friend, *that* was pitiful."

Louis turned and faced Mitchell Forbes, owner of Style by Forbes, a smaller hair salon just down the street. Mitchell and Louis had been not-so-friendly rivals for more than twenty years.

"You're supposed to be the smooth operator with the ladies, Sweet. At least," he added, "that's the rep that's been on the street all these years. Looks like the sweet talk is growing a bit sour in your old age."

Louis eyed Mitchell Forbes wondering what the man knew for fact and what he guessed.

"Just a little rusty. What brings you in here snooping around?"

Despite the man's winning smile—won by a mouthful of caps—the slick Armani suit, and the savvy ponytail, Louis knew he couldn't trust Mitchell Forbes. Sweet's memory was long and Mitchell's treachery legendary among salon owners and operators.

Mitchell smiled and spread out his hands, encompassing the salon. "Well, with all the work being done over here, I thought I'd just come over and see what you've been up to. But now that I see just how fine things are," he said, glancing the way Elaine Webster had gone, "I might stop in more often."

Louis's eyes narrowed.

Della, spying the two and hoping to avoid bloodshed, quickly made her way to the two men.

"Mitchell Forbes, to what do we owe the honor today?" she said as she coolly and efficiently stepped between the two men.

Mitchell brought her hand up and pressed a light kiss on her smooth skin. "Ah, Della. Always the diplomat. You're looking beautiful as ever."

Not at all impressed, Della shook her hand free from his light embrace. "If you've come to steal a stylist, you're wasting your time."

"The two of you do me a grave injustice."

"Cry me a river," Louis muttered.

"Actually," Mitchell said, "I came over to tell you about the merchants' meeting planned for next Tuesday. It's been moved to the Adam Clayton Powell, Jr. Building. You'll see the sign for our room." He glanced in the direction of the shampoo and nail area. "Pity it couldn't be held here. I sure like the view."

Louis took an aggressive step forward. Della carefully slid a little closer to Mitchell, creating a small but significant barrier between the men.

"Yes," she said. "The addition makes things nice."

"Mmm-hmm, it sure does." Then, with another glance around the shop, Mitchell smoothed his thin moustache, then gave a small two-finger salute to Louis and a slight tip of the head to Della. "Seven o'clock. Hope to see you there."

After Mitchell left, Della herded Louis into the office, shooed out a stylist who'd dropped off the mail, and shut the door.

"I don't understand what you ever saw in that man," Louis grumbled.

"It's ancient history, dead and buried, Louis. Leave it that way."

He harrumphed and picked up the stack of the day's mail. "What do you think he was really here about?"

"Maybe to tell us about the merchants' meeting."

Louis rolled his eyes. "Yeah, right."

"Well," Della said. "If I were to wager a guess, I'd say it was Andre. Since he gave that workshop and won first place at that hair show, the offers have been pouring in from all over the place. A shop from Chicago called yesterday."

"Is he going to leave?"

Della shrugged. "He seems content. We pay him premium and his partner is based in Manhattan."

Louis nodded. He had a pretty good idea of what Mitchell was after . . . or would be after soon. And it wasn't a hairstylist. Forbes may have come in with the bold intent of luring away his top employee, but Louis was well aware of Mitchell's penchant for lovely and lonely grieving widows.

"I still don't understand why women are always lined up to throw their panties at his feet."

"Must you be so crude? It's bad enough that I have to monitor the talk on the floor without having to hear it from you, too. Besides, you were just as big a scoundrel in your day."

"In my day? You make me sound like I have one foot in the grave."

Della raised one elegant eyebrow at him. "I thought you did."

Louis's glower didn't even faze her. "Since you don't want to do it my way, go ahead and give it your best Mack Daddy shot."

"What are you talking about now?" he grumbled.

"You sound like a big, old grizzly bear who hasn't eaten in about three months. That's no way to woo a lady."

He turned his back to her and dropped the mail on the desk. "I'm not wooing anyone."

Della grinned at his back, then marched around the desk to face him. "And I suppose you just happened in here today dressed up like you have an appointment with the governor. Maybe you planned to do some work?" The Saccharine sweetness of her voice dripped sarcasm.

"I'm the boss. I don't have to do any work. That's what I have you for."

"Yes, I know. You just up and walked out one day and said, 'Della, take care of things.' And I haven't had a rest since. I need a vacation."

"So take one."

She touched his arm. "Louis, look at me."

For a moment, he resisted, then apparently realized he'd lose every round with Della. He glanced at her, their eyes level.

"If you're interested in her, let her know. But remember, she's the high-maintenance, kid-gloves type. Amateur night at the Apollo isn't going to appeal to her."

"How do you know? Are you implying that I have no couth, no culture?"

Della hit him and smiled. "You know what I mean."

She tugged on his arm until he rose. Then, waving him toward the door, Della returned to her desk. "Go give her your best, Lothario. I have a salon to run."

A few minutes later, Louis found himself in a chair next to the manicure station where Elaine sat.

"Hello, Mr. Sweet," greeted a manicurist whose name Louis couldn't quite recall. The flap of her black salon jacket covered the nameplate on the jacket pocket.

"Hi. Make sure this lady gets extra tender loving care. She's pretty special."

Elaine felt her cheeks warm again. "That's not necessary," she demurred.

The manicurist cast curious glances between her employer and her customer. Elaine noticed and quickly added, "We just met last week. Here at the salon."

"And I've counted the days since," Louis said.

The manicurist's eyes widened. Louis glanced at her and winked.

"I'll finish up here," he said. "Why don't you take a break now?"

The startled employee looked at him and then at Elaine. "But . . ."

"No need to worry. I'm very good."

Elaine gasped. "Of course, you mean at doing nails . . . as the shop owner I mean." *Open mouth, insert foot,* she thought to herself.

The quiet laughter in his eyes and the twitch of a smile at his mouth let Elaine know her awareness of this man had been duly noted.

With a final curious glance between the two, the manicurist vacated the chair that Louis slipped into.

The warmth in Elaine's cheeks escalated to a full-scale blush and her hands trembled when he took hers and began to file her nails. She had no doubt that Louis Sweet was very, very good at everything.

Louis smiled and Elaine was lost. Sweet temptation beckoned in Louis Sweet's smile. Elaine noted the laugh lines at his eyes. Here was a man born to laugh often and well.

The sexy salt-and-pepper of his close-cropped hair called to her. She wanted to stroke those tiny curls as his head lay nestled in the pillowy comfort of . . .

Elaine took a deep breath and fanned herself with her free hand.

"Warm?" he asked.

Elaine nodded.

"Would you like me to turn up the air conditioner a bit?"

Her breathing seemed to come in short gasps. "That . . . that won't be necessary."

She'd spent a full week thinking about this man, wondering if his flirtation had been casual or deliberate, general or specific. All of a sudden, she seemed to be getting a pretty clear answer. Elaine just wasn't sure if she could handle the heat of a deliberately specific flirtation.

For the first time in a long time, Elaine let herself fantasize about what it would be like to be intimate with another man. She'd loved Raymond dearly, but in the last few years before his illness, they'd fallen into something of a rut. The routine became just another part of their weekly existence, sort of like taking out the trash or washing the car. Everything was done by rote, as if they followed some outdated script neither felt like rewriting. Eventually, the diabetes claimed even that part.

Elaine longed for romance, courtship, and magic. She wanted to be appreciated for being a woman. Since Raymond's death, she'd fallen into even more of a routine: church, volunteer work, sorority. Church, volunteer, go to a meeting.

She groaned and closed her eyes. When had life become one boring obligation after another?

Louis smiled. The tension in Elaine Webster radiated right down to her fingertips. He had a remedy for what ailed her. In his large hands, he warmed a musk-scented oil. Then, with slow strokes and gentle pressure, he began to massage her hands and her wrists.

Elaine moaned her satisfaction and leaned forward. Louis smiled.

"Feel good?"

"Heavenly."

With his thumb he traced the inner line of her arm, then applied a bit of pressure. His warm touch grew even warmer on her pliant skin. The earthy scent of the massage oil hovered between them, enveloping them in a soft cocoon. He worked with a deliberate sensuousness, stroking, retreating, brushing, kneading.

"Ohhh." The sound drifted from Elaine in a slow exhale of pleasure. "You're very gentle."

"It pays to have a slow hand."

Elaine opened her eyes and stared at him. Her eyes widened at the same moment her breathing stopped. Louis continued to slowly, meticulously and oh-so-expertly massage her arms. No manicure had ever made her feel like this, as if she wanted to just melt or curl up in Louis's lap and purr.

Her brain took a moment to register exactly where her

thoughts had drifted. Elaine snatched her hand away and quickly fanned herself.

"Still warm?" Louis asked. "People usually complain about it being too cool in here."

"Hot flash," she fired back.

"You hardly seem old enough for that," he said.

A devilish smile, the very one that transformed his face, told Elaine he knew that she knew her sudden hot flash had little to do with menopause and a lot to do with the man sitting across from her.

"You're not going to wash my hair, are you?" Elaine didn't think she'd survive a moment of Louis's ministration if those strong hands massaged her scalp the way they worked over her hands. She was already putty.

Louis's own breathing deepened and slowed. He read the awareness in her eyes and cursed himself a fool for starting something he couldn't finish.

So wrapped up in their own world were Elaine and Louis that neither noticed they were the center of attention in the shop. The busy chatter had fallen off one voice at a time until all that remained was the hum of the air conditioner and the low hum of hood hair dryers. A few amused glances were exchanged across the floor.

After a moment, Elaine and Louis realized something was amiss. Elaine glanced around. Knowing smiles and not-so-kind smirks greeted her. A shudder of humiliation rippled through her. Someone cleared a throat.

"Oh, dear."

Della clapped her hands together, breaking the awkward silence. "People, people, we are running a business here. Get busy."

Instantly, sound filled the salon.

Satisfied that all was well again, Della looked toward Louis and Elaine. Then, shaking her head, she returned to her duties.

"You embarrassed me," Elaine whispered to Louis.

"Have dinner with me," he said.

# Chapter Three

"Did you hear what I said?" Elaine glanced around, positive that curious ears and eyes were again focused in her direction.

"I heard," he said. "Let me make it up to you. Have dinner with me."

She sat so straight in the chair that a board could have been tucked down her dress. "I don't think that's proper."

"Walk on the wild side. Throw propriety to the wind."

"Are you wild, Mr. Sweet?"

"I can be," he said.

"I don't care for wild men."

"But usually I'm as gentle as a lamb."

Elaine smiled, and then laughed. "You're a mess."

Taking pleasure in her joy, Louis sat back. He wiped his hands on a soft cloth and then stroked Elaine's hands with the cloth. But before he could respond to her, Della approached.

"Louis, there's an important call for you in the office."

"I'll be right there," he said without taking his eyes off Elaine.

But Della stood her ground and called for Elaine's original manicurist. "Mei-Mei, please finish up for Mr. Sweet. It looks like buff and polish is all that remains."

The young woman glanced at Della and Louis, hesitant to displease either of her bosses. After a tense moment, a moment charged with anticipation and unfulfilled need, Louis rose. He leaned down and for Elaine's ears only said, "I'll talk with you later."

She nodded before realizing that that meant their conversation hadn't been completed. "I don't think . . ." she began.

"Don't think. Feel." And then, with an "Excuse me" to all three women, Louis walked away.

Elaine watched him leave, then turned embarrassed eyes on the manicurist. The woman smiled shyly and picked up a bottle of Burnt Redwood nail enamel. "I'll have you finished in just a moment."

Elaine asked for the quick-dry spray, overtipped the girl, then dashed out of the salon before anything else happened.

Not sure she'd be able to withstand the temptation of Louis Sweet, Elaine took the coward's way out: She changed her appointment to Tuesday morning instead of afternoon. She wanted to get in and get out without encountering Louis.

"I just need some time to sort through my feelings," she told her friend, Lena. The two, friends for more than thirty years, talked every morning on the phone. "He asked me out to dinner, you know."

"So you told me. Dinner is a meal, Elaine, not a marriage. Go. You need to keep a bit of company besides the work you do at Abyssinia."

"I live a perfectly fulfilled life, thank you very much. As a matter of fact, I've been thinking maybe I should buy that house in South Carolina. I'm tired of New York."

"Elaine Webster, don't you dare start that South Carolina talk again. You're a city girl, born and bred. Running away won't do you a bit of good."

"Buying a retirement home in Charleston is not running away."

"Right. Every time you have a new challenge in front of you, you start talking about heading south. The only thing you'll find down there is yourself. You can't run away from you. Stop being afraid. Step out and enjoy life."

"I do not run away from challenges."

"Elaine, I'm not going to argue with you about this. When

you think about it, you'll know it's the truth. Now Louis
Sweet, he's a bird in the hand. If you've snagged his attention,
you've done better than a whole lot who have deliberately
tried over the years.''

Like a hungry fish, Elaine took the bait. ''What do you
know about him?''

''Enough to know that if he's asked you out, he's serious.
Louis Sweet was a flirt when he came out of his mother's
womb. It's just not very often, if at all, that his flirting is
followed by an invitation. And to dinner at that. Do you have
any idea how long and hard some women have angled for
less, only to be turned away with a smile and then good-
bye?''

''Well, I am not 'some women.' And if he's such a
charmer, why is he still single?''

''His choice. Men have it like that, you know. As a widower and business owner, he'll be an eligible bachelor until
the day he dies. A woman in the same circumstances, however, is either a lonely widow or hot to trot.''

They'd had this discussion many times before. Not in the
mood to debate feminist ideology, Elaine changed the subject.

''Are you going to volunteer for the tutorial group at
church? We need some more professional teachers.''

''I'm wise to your games, Elaine Webster. The question on
the table is: Are you going to dinner with Louis Sweet?''

Elaine, silent for a long moment, finally voiced her fears.
''I could never fall in love again. Not the way Raymond and
I loved.''

''You're going out to dinner, for goodness' sake. What's
love got to do with a steak or some lobster?''

''But Raymond . . .''

''Is gone, Elaine,'' Lena said gently. ''You're still here and
you have to live your life.''

''It's too soon. I miss him so much.''

''I know, Elaine. You're supposed to miss him. You two
shared a lot of years together. And you have a lot of years in
front of you.''

''Maybe I should go back to work.''

Lena sighed. "There you go again. Retirement suits you, Elaine. You have time to do all the things you've always wanted to do. And you have time to have a meal with an attractive man."

Despite all the years between them, Elaine was too embarrassed to tell her friend that she found Louis *very* attractive, in a carnal sort of way.

"And here's something I bet you haven't considered," Lena continued. "You miss Raymond, and Louis misses his Rosie. That gives the two of you something in common. If nothing else, you'll get to talk with someone who knows exactly what you're going through."

That thought hadn't occurred to Elaine. "You think so?"

"I know so," Lena assured her. "Listen, are you going to the sorority meeting Saturday? I'm not going to be able to make it and I wondered if you could give my committee report."

With that, the conversation shifted. By the time Elaine finished with Lena and completed her errands for the day, she'd made up her mind about Louis Sweet and his dinner invitation. She couldn't go. It would be a date. She hadn't been on a date since . . . since forever.

Unfortunately, her mind had other ideas. Throughout the day, Louis was never very far from her thoughts. Standing in line at the grocery store, she recalled with bold clarity the sensual feel of his hands on hers.

Waiting in the dentist's office, she trembled with just the thought of the electric sparks that bounced between them. Elaine fanned herself with the *Black Enterprise* magazine she'd been thumbing through.

The day before her next appointment at Rosie's Curl and Weave, Elaine gathered her courage and called Louis. When the line connected and Della answered, Elaine breathed a sigh. Whether it was of disappointment or relief she didn't examine too closely. Thankful that Della, a woman closer to her own age, had answered instead of one of those twentysomething receptionists, Elaine identified herself and asked to speak with Louis.

Elaine held her breath.

"I'm sorry," Della said.

Elaine's breath whooshed out in a disappointed sigh.

"He's not in right now. May I leave a message?"

"No. I just . . . On second thought, yes." Elaine left her home and cellular phone numbers with the salon manager. Then, with shaky hands, placed the cordless receiver on her dining room table.

"That was worse than calling a boy for the first time when I was a teenager," Elaine said out loud.

And being honest with herself, she had to admit to the same giddy rush she'd felt then. But this time, she was fifty-six, not fifteen. She'd taken the first tentative step. The rest was up to him.

Before she could get her thoughts together and figure out what to do next, the telephone rang.

"Hello?"

"Elaine, this is Louis Sweet."

"Oh!" Elaine's mouth dropped open and she gripped the receiver. "That was fast. I just called."

"Della's quite efficient. She caught me in the car. How are things with you?"

"Just fine."

"That's good to hear. Have you given any more thought to what we talked about? What I asked you?"

"As a matter of fact, yes. That's why I called. I'd like to have dinner with you if the invitation is still open."

"You bet it is."

After that, their conversation was easy. They settled on a day, time, and place, then talked about gardening for a while. Forty minutes later, Elaine realized she was late for her shift at a soup kitchen where she volunteered.

"Will I see you in the shop tomorrow?" Louis asked.

"Yes, that's my appointment day."

"I know. Tuesday is the highlight of my week."

Elaine smiled. Later she found herself smiling at odd times throughout the day.

That night, as she prepared for bed, she was still smiling. Lena had been right. Attention from an attractive man did wonders for the soul.

Elaine didn't see Louis the next day, but she did pick up peculiar vibes at the salon. Being respectful and kind to customers was one thing, but the deference paid her Tuesday was something else. Elaine suffered through what seemed like hours of overly solicitous scrutiny.

After her wash and blow dry, Della discreetly told Elaine that Louis sent his apologies. An emergency had come up and he was stuck in midtown Manhattan.

Despite the queen's treatment at the salon, Elaine found herself in an odd mood. She'd been looking forward to seeing Louis. The feeling of disappointment surprised her in ways that made her wonder just where this attraction might lead. Not really ready to consider all *those* avenues of thought, she paid her bill, tipped the appropriate people, and made her way out the front door where she promptly bumped into a man.

"Pardon me. I wasn't watching where I was going," she apologized.

"It's entirely my fault," he said. "Mitchell Forbes at your service."

Elaine nodded and moved on. When she stepped around him and headed to her car, the man fell into step beside her. Elaine clutched her purse a little tighter to her body.

"Your hair is lovely."

"Thank you." Elaine gave him the once-over and found him attractive in a disarming sort of way. Maybe it was the ponytail. She'd never seen a man her age with that kind of hairstyle. Where Louis seemed to have an inherent sense of style, this man's seemed forced.

"I own Style by Forbes down the street," he said. "I saw you last week when I came to see Della and Sweet. I didn't get a chance to introduce myself then and tell you how delighted we'd be if you stopped in at Style by Forbes one day. You won't be disappointed.''

Elaine relaxed a little. He was obviously harmless.

''I'm perfectly fine where I am.''

Mitchell first smoothed his slick ponytail and then his thin moustache.

''Yes, I must say you *are* perfectly fine.''

Compliments seemed to be coming from every direction these days. But something about this man made Elaine's skin crawl. Despite his words, intuitively, she picked up something from him that wasn't quite pleasant. She wanted to put distance between them, quickly.

''Excuse me,'' she said as she attempted to step by him to get to her car.

''I didn't catch your name,'' he said.

''That's because I didn't give it to you.'' Elaine turned and took the long way around her car. She quickly unlocked the door and slipped inside. Mitchell Forbes closed the door for her and with a smirk, tipped his head to her.

Elaine wasted no time pulling out. She shuddered. Glancing in her rearview mirror, she saw him still standing in the street.

''This city is full of weirdos.''

# Chapter Four

The next night, Elaine couldn't remember the last time she'd been so nervous. Louis Sweet was to pick her up at her house at six-thirty.

"It's just dinner," she told her reflection as she put a touch of Crimson Joy blush on her cheeks. Her hand hovered near the slim tube of mascara. She applied it, then a muted eye shadow. Next came perfume. Elaine studied the assorted bottles and atomizers on her bureau top, then selected an earthy scent. She dabbed a bit on her wrists and behind her ears. She paused and checked her reflection in the mirror. The thin straps of her slip gave way to two inches of pale gray lace, some of which would peek out and serve as a décolletage for the red figure-hugging suit she planned to wear that evening.

A slightly devilish grin spread across her mouth. "Of course, there's nothing wrong with a little flirtation." With that, she dabbed the stopper between her breasts. Then, with a secret smile, she finished dressing for her dinner date with Louis Sweet.

He was late.

Elaine waited and waited. At seven-fifteen, she got angry.

"This is beyond even CP time, Louis Sweet."

She sank into one of the upholstered chairs at her dining room table. He had her phone number. If he was going to be late, he could have called.

At seven forty-five, Elaine took off her shoes and shrugged out of the suit jacket. In her slip and skirt, she made her way to the kitchen and put together a chicken sandwich from Sunday dinner leftovers. Her gaze kept straying to the telephone. Twice she checked all of the sockets to make sure the telephones were plugged in.

At eight-thirty, Elaine changed into a lounger and settled in her den for a night of bad sitcoms. The cordless phone sat within reach . . . just in case Louis called to say he'd been in a car accident or something.

She tried to pretend she didn't care. She desperately wanted to be nonchalant about the entire thing. But she couldn't quite pull it off. She'd been stood up. His flirtation hadn't been deliberate and specific. It had been for kicks . . . his.

As a laugh track played on the television comedy, Elaine cried herself to sleep on her sofa.

The shrill ring of the telephone woke her much later. Elaine sat up and glanced at the television. A late-night host hammed it up for his studio audience. The clock above the fireplace said eleven thirty-five. The telephone rang again.

She reached for it, and tugged up the antenna. "Hello?"

"I'm sorry," Louis began.

"I have nothing to say to you. Good night."

Elaine punched the END button and slammed the phone down. With her arms folded and a mutinous expression on her face, she sat back on the sofa.

Hanging up on him made her feel good for about thirty seconds. Then she felt silly. What if he had had a really good excuse?

The telephone rang again.

She snatched it up. "I'm sorry. That was childish of me."

"What are you talking about, Mom?"

Elaine sighed. "Oh, Belinda, it's you."

Elaine's daughter laughed. "Well, that's a fine how-do-you-do. I won't keep you, since you're obviously waiting for a call. I was just calling to say hello."

"I'm sorry, sweetheart. I haven't had a good evening."

"Want me to call back tomorrow?"

"That would be fine."

Elaine ended the call and sat on the sofa with the phone in her hand.

Feeling sorry for herself, she made her way to bed. "Well, so much for your attempt at dating."

The next morning, a beautiful arrangement of flowers arrived. Elaine tipped the delivery guy and plucked the card from the plastic greeting stem.

> *I could offer an excuse, but it wouldn't make up for missing our date. Please give me another chance.*
> > *L. Sweet*

"I'll think about it," she said.

Then she smiled; she couldn't help it. The flowers, a colorful riot of lilacs, tulips, and a bold plant Elaine couldn't identify, filled the foyer with the sweet scent of spring.

Elaine placed the arrangement in the middle of her dining room table, then went in search of a telephone book. She scanned down a short list of Sweets. There, *Sweet, Louis & Rosie*. Elaine felt a stab of . . . she frowned. Hurt? Jealousy?

Then, remembering that her own telephone number was still listed under her husband's name, she shrugged and called him. He picked up on the third ring.

"Louis? This is Elaine Webster."

"Well, hello. How are you? I wasn't sure if you'd talk to me again."

"The flowers are beautiful."

"Elaine, can you forgive me? I got stuck someplace and couldn't get away."

"Will you call next time?"

"You're giving me a next time?"

Elaine, silent for a moment, thought about her answer. A "yes" would mean crossing an important threshold, one that would lead to an unknown place—possibly a future with Louis Sweet. A "no" would mean she was still afraid of stepping out beyond the fear that gripped her at unexpected moments and at inconvenient times.

She closed her eyes, clutched the phone receiver with two hands, and took a deep breath.

"Elaine? Are you still there?"

"Yes, Louis. I mean, yes, I want there to be a next time for us."

Suddenly, Elaine's world didn't seem so dark around the edges. Lena had been right.

"Thank you," he said softly.

Elaine wondered if he, too, had been holding his breath awaiting her answer. "Louis, I'm sorry I hung up on you. That was childish."

He chuckled. "No, it wasn't. I deserved that. I deserve worse. Listen, there's a garden show coming up. I'm not exhibiting, but I think you'll enjoy it. Would you like to go with me?"

"I'd love to."

Louis dressed carefully. Today was important—in more than one way. Elaine had granted him another chance and he didn't want to blow it. For the first time in four years he had a reason to feel like a king, a conquerer. She put a new spring in his step as he faced each new day. It had taken time, lots of time, for him to reconcile that Rosie was gone and not coming back. He sensed in Elaine a lingering sadness, despite her smile and her cheery disposition. From his own experience, he knew he could help Elaine . . . if she'd let him close enough.

"Standing her up didn't help the cause," he told himself.

But it couldn't be avoided. He had an unresolved issue to deal with. Until it was straightened out, Louis wasn't going to be able to give Elaine one hundred percent. Sometimes he wondered if Della knew. Louis was pretty sure she suspected. Della knew too much about him, but at least he knew she had his best interests at heart.

Louis made the last loop of a Windsor knot in his tie, tugged it to straighten it up, then surveyed his handiwork.

"Outstanding." He grinned at his image in his bathroom mirror. Then frowned as he took a closer look at his hair. "Lotta gray up there." Making a mental note to ask Della if she thought there was more salt than pepper in his hair, he smiled at his reflection.

On more than one occasion and by more than one so-called expert, he'd been told that a positive attitude would go a long way toward getting him out of the mental and physical abyss that had haunted him since Rosie's death. On the recommendation of one of those experts, Louis had taken up gardening. The roses brought him so much pleasure, he couldn't recall when he *hadn't* found a measure of peace and contentment as he worked the soil, and pruned and cared for the delicate flowers.

And now there was Elaine, another delicate flower in need of some tender loving care. Something in Louis had awakened and stirred the moment he first saw her. It was time to face life and living again.

More than ready for the challenge, Louis smiled.

Outside, he carefully snipped one perfect Artistry rose from a bush near the front door. He dropped his gardening shears in a basket on the stoop, and paused to inspect, then smell, the coral bloom.

"Exquisite. Just like Elaine."


The moment Louis walked in the salon door he knew something was wrong.

"Oh, dear. Hello, Mr. Sweet," the receptionist squeaked when she saw him.

Louis barely gave the girl a second glance. His gaze darted around the salon. Dryers whirred, televisions hummed, stylists worked. He didn't see any physical damage to the salon, no cars through the windows, no leaking roof. But something felt wrong.

"Where's Della?"

"In the color and shampoo area, sir."

Louis made haste to that part of the shop.

The salon manager, two stylists, and two assistants he didn't know hovered over a customer.

"Della?"

As one, the group turned. Elaine sat in the middle, a grimace on her face as she gripped the armrests of the chair.

For a single tension-filled moment, no one spoke. Then everyone started at once.

"What happened?" Louis demanded.

"I'm sure it's not that bad," someone consoled Elaine.

"Wash and rinse her again," Della directed. "Use the Cholesterol shampoo. And don't use a scrubbing motion. Be very gentle."

"I'm sorry. I thought . . ."

"What you *thought* isn't important," a stylist snapped at an assistant.

Louis's glare should have petrified the whimpering woman on the spot. "Are you responsible for this?"

In the face of his anger, the woman stepped back quickly. "I'm sorry, Mr. Sweet. I just . . ."

"Please, just get it out," Elaine said.

Louis's attention was immediately on Elaine. "Let me see."

He concurred with Della, who added orders for a hot oil treatment and then ten minutes under the hair dryer.

After overseeing the damage, Della turned toward the assistant who'd caused the problem. "Deneen, please wait for me in the office."

"But . . ."

Della shot the young woman a look that sent her scurrying. "Ms. Webster, how are you doing?"

"It still burns."

"LaTonya is going to wash you again to make sure all the chemical is out. Then she'll do a deep conditioning. The burning and tingling you're still feeling should subside as she washes your hair. Then we'll get you dried."

"Is my hair going to fall out?"

"I don't think so. Your scalp will be tender for a little while, though. You let Deneen know something was wrong pretty quickly."

"And she didn't believe me," Elaine fired back.

Della nodded. "I'm going to go take care of that right now.

And I'll take a look at your scalp before you go under the dryer.''

Elaine nodded. Louis squeezed her hand.

"Ms. Webster, I'm going to get everything straight," LaTonya assured. "I'm sorry this happened to you." The stylist settled a clean cape around Elaine's purple suit jacket.

Since Louis didn't look like he was going to leave Ms. Webster's side, Della turned to head to the office.

"Della," he called.

The manager turned questioning eyes toward Louis.

"Fire her."

Della nodded, then went to deal with the color assistant.

Forty minutes later, Elaine sat in the salon office with Della and Louis.

"Ms. Webster, please accept my apologies for what happened here today. Deneen has been appropriately disciplined.''

Elaine cast a wary glance between Louis and Della. "What does that mean, 'appropriately disciplined'?''

"That means she's looking for another job," Louis said flatly.

Della nodded, confirming the girl's fate. "This wasn't the first problem. Some people aren't cut out to be in customer service.''

Elaine nodded.

"As I said earlier, everything seems fine," Della said. "We'd still like you to go to a doctor, a dermatologist. At the salon's expense, of course. I'd just like to be sure you have the all-clear. Remember now, if you have any discomfort, any sores or scabs, the dermatologist will be able to give you an antibiotic cream.''

"You seem to know a lot about this sort of thing," Elaine observed.

Della smiled. "I spent a little time as an LPN before Louis lured me here. Some customers have allergic reactions to chemicals. That's why there are different strengths and different products. Deneen didn't read your card or consult anyone. And she ignored your alert that something was wrong.''

"I hope she finds a more suitable line of work," Elaine said.

"I hope she gets hit by a cab," Louis mumbled.

"Louis!" Della and Elaine chided simultaneously.

"Violence isn't necessary," Elaine added.

Della rose, and so did Louis.

"I'd like you to come back in seven days for a deep conditioner. We'll take it from there, okay?"

Elaine nodded. "Okay." She and Della shook hands.

"I'll see you to your car," Louis offered.

With a final word of farewell to Della and her stylist, Elaine left the salon with Louis. When they got to her car, she winced and touched a tender spot on her head.

"That's it. Come with me." Louis clutched her arm and steered her to his silver Cadillac DeVille.

"Louis Sweet, where are you taking me?"

"We're going to a doctor's office right now. I want to make sure you're okay."

"I'm fine. Della said my scalp would be tender for a day or so."

"Della isn't a doctor. I want to be sure."

"Louis, really. This isn't necessary." A part of her was thrilled at his concern. Another part thought he was being more than a tad excessive. Elaine had never had anyone fired. That didn't sit very well with her either.

He handed her into the smooth leather seat and shut her door. When he got behind the wheel, he pulled a small address book from the glove compartment and looked up a number.

"Louis, you don't have to do this."

Plucking his cell phone from its cradle rest, he looked at her. "I want to."

That silenced her. She watched as he punched in a number on the telephone and then started the car.

"Clyde, it's Lou. I need the name of a good dermatologist who can see someone right now."

He paused a moment, listening. "Right now means just as soon as you give me a name and directions." He glanced at Elaine. "Yes, it's an emergency."

"Louis."

He jotted down a name and street address.

"Thanks. I owe you one."

"Who is Clyde?" Elaine asked when he replaced the phone.

"My brother-in-law. He's a GP. We're headed to his complex. He's calling a buddy and telling him we're on the way."

"Louis, I said this isn't necessary."

He pulled on his seat belt and turned to her. "Yes, it is. You're important to me. This happened to you in my shop. That makes me doubly responsible."

Elaine realized she wasn't going to change his mind on this. "Did Della really fire that girl?"

Louis nodded as he handled the big car. "It wasn't the first time she'd been reprimanded. Her customer service skills are nil. And this is a business where the customer always *has* to be right, or at least pleased. I'm sorry this happened to you."

"If you or Della apologize one more time I'm going to launch a boycott of the shop."

He sent a small smile her way. Then, with nothing left to talk about, they fell silent the rest of the trip to the dermatologist's office. Elaine was seen. The doctor confirmed Della's prognosis and gave her a small tube of ointment to apply to tender spots.

Louis, finally assured that Elaine would indeed be all right, escorted her back to his car. They'd just settled in when Elaine's stomach rumbled loud and long.

She covered her face with one hand and her stomach with the other. "I could die of embarrassment."

"No need," he said. "I have just the cure for what ails you."

Elaine glanced at him. He sure did. But she didn't think he had the same thing in mind that she did. She smiled, more to herself than him. It was amazing, but here she was, attracted to someone. It had been a long time since someone wanted to be her protector, since she had someone to lean on. She relaxed into the supple leather and decided to enjoy the moment.

"Should I ask or just let it ride?"

Louis made a right turn and chuckled. "Enjoy the ride."

Several minutes later, he handed his keys over to a red-jacketed parking valet and ushered Elaine into an elegant restaurant for an early dinner. After reviewing the menu and placing their orders for wine and dinner, Louis leaned forward.

"So, tell me about yourself."

# Chapter Five

Elaine smiled as she leaned forward, resting her elbows on the table and her chin in the groove of her clasped hands. "What do you want to know?"

"Everything."

She smiled. "Everything?"

He nodded.

She leaned back and began in a bluesy drawl. "Well, I was born in a small town in upstate New York."

Louis chuckled. "Okay. Okay. Start with your fabulous sense of style. You're gorgeous and everything you wear just accents all that natural beauty."

Elaine's breath caught. "My . . . I, that's . . . Thank you," she finally got out.

He leaned forward and reached for her hand. "It's true. I'm enchanted by the sparkle in your eyes. You know the first thing I noticed about you?"

Temporarily without the power of speech, Elaine just stared at him and shook her head.

"Your sassy and sexy walk. You walked into the salon like a woman with a purpose. And then there was the sweet honey of your voice when I heard you talk. All you said was 'hello' and I was hooked."

"Uh . . ." She quickly reached for her goblet of water and took a cooling sip. A moment later she'd regained her mental equilibrium. "And how many degrees do you hold in po-etry?"

"Not a one. But I'll enroll if you want me to."

Elaine sat back. "Oh, my."

"I'm serious. I want to know about you."

"What do you want to know?"

He sat back and regarded her with unabashed appreciation. "Whatever you want to share."

"I always thought that a rather complicated concept."

"What?"

"This 'sharing' that's so popular these days. In the old days, people just talked to each other. Now, 'they share their feelings and emotions.'" She shrugged, the motion an unconscious, elegant lift of her shoulders. "I guess I haven't bought into that particular concept. 'Sharing' seems so much more complicated than simply talking. Do you remember the days when people could converse without making an emotional commitment?"

"Guilty as charged," he said. "That's what I get for watching *Oprah* every day."

"You watch *Oprah*?"

He nodded. "I tape it if I'm not home."

Elaine leaned forward. "I never miss it either, and I tape it, too."

That led into a discussion of other favorite programs and talk show themes. Through dinner, they talked about books and music, food and flowers. They lingered over coffee, neither one quite ready to call it a night.

Louis floundered for a way to keep her talking. He could listen to her read the obituary pages and still be enchanted. The combination of silky huskiness and brisk efficiency in Elaine's voice never failed to send a comforting ripple of awareness through Louis. He'd spent the last several years without sexual contact and had grown resigned and accustomed to the fact that it could no longer be a part of his life. So his attraction to Elaine always took him by surprise.

When Elaine talked, her entire body joined the conversation: her hands, her shoulders, a tilt of her head, it all coordinated in ladylike and sensual precision. Louis considered himself a bit rough around the edges. The last few years of solitude had mellowed him enough to appreciate, to be really cognizant of, all the little things in life. That awareness included Elaine, the essence of her, the heat that radiated from her, the touch of nervousness in her smile, the hint of musky fragrance that lured him closer.

"Louis, it is getting late."

He glanced at his watch, surprised to find three hours had passed since they'd entered the restaurant. The night was just beginning. Maybe she'd consider a movie. Before he convinced himself he was being too eager, he asked her.

"Would you like to go see a movie?"

"Right now?"

He nodded.

"Louis, I . . ." Elaine paused in midsentence. She'd been about to turn him down out of hand. But she was a grown woman. She enjoyed his company. No one waited for her at home, not even a dog needing a walk or fresh water. She didn't have to follow anyone's rules. At fifty-six, she could make her own rules. Surely she'd earned that right by now.

Tamping down a recalcitrant twinge of guilt, Elaine nodded. "I'd love to."

They agreed on a comedy, shared a bucket of popcorn, and laughed through the two-hour film. Now, Louis parked the big DeVille next to Elaine's Volvo, the only other car in the small lot. He cut the engine but left Nancy Wilson's husky melodies to quietly play on the CD.

"Louis, this day has been terrific, even with what happened earlier," she said. "I'm glad we spent this time together."

Unbuckling his seat belt, he faced her. "I am, too. But, Elaine, I have a confession to make."

The content smile fell off Elaine's face as she came to a horrible but very real conclusion: He'd been charming her all day, not because he enjoyed her company, as she did his. He'd seen to her injury, wined, dined, and romanced her, all just to save his shop. Louis and Della were afraid she'd sue the salon. They'd probably decided together that Louis had best dispense with the problem.

Elaine sat erect in her seat, the handbag in her lap clutched tightly by tense hands. He had a confession to make.

"I see," she said.

"Do you?"

He sounded relieved. It *had* been too good to be true. Elaine took a deep breath and willed the tension out of her body. She could handle this like a grown-up. Reaching to her left for her seat-belt clasp, she pressed the button to free herself from the constraint. All her life, including the years with Raymond, she'd been constrained and restricted, careful in how she comported herself; always a lady even when she didn't want to be.

Well, she mutinously thought. No more. I can break something off as well as the next woman.

Elaine reached for the door handle. "It's been a lovely day. There is no need to end it on a sour note. I understand completely."

"Whoa. Hold up," Louis said. He stayed her with a hand on her arm. Elaine kept her gaze fixed out the tinted window.

She felt him push up the armrest that divided the wide front seat, then heard him scoot over. When his body heat flowed around her, Elaine realized how close he'd gotten.

"I don't think you understand at all, Elaine. Don't you want to hear my confession?"

"I already know why you did what you did today."

"You do? It was that obvious, huh?"

Elaine sniffed. Her feelings and her pride had taken a beating in the last few minutes. He'd seemed like such a pleasant man. Why did he now insist on the slow torture?

"Elaine?"

When she finally turned to him, his nearness startled her even though she'd known he was there. They sat face-to-face, so close she could see the tiny lines at his mouth, a mouth she found herself more than a little curious about.

"If I've been so obvious all day, then this won't come as a surprise," he said.

In the next moment, his lips covered hers.

Elaine's eyes widened in surprise, then drifted closed on a

soft sigh. She gave herself up to the sensations coursing through her: curiosity, tenderness, eager impatience. His kiss sang through her veins. She met him with equal ardor. Louis's claim on her mouth was total. Elaine was thrilled at how much she enjoyed it.

Too soon, they broke apart.

"Thank you," Louis finally said.

"For what?" she breathed, surprised to find that her voice still worked.

"For granting me one of the best days in my life. All day long, I kept trying to figure out how to keep you with me. When I'm with you, I just . . . I don't know. You're special and I like spending time with you. That's my confession."

Her mouth dropped open. "You mean . . ."

"I mean, I didn't intend to hog your entire day. But . . ." He shrugged. "I didn't want our time together to end. Pretty selfish, huh?"

"I thought . . ." Elaine's voice drifted off.

"What?" he asked. An indulgent smile tilted the corners of his mouth.

"Maybe I better not say."

He traced a finger along her hairline from her temple, down to her check. "You tempt me, Elaine Webster."

"No one's ever accused me of being a temptress."

He chuckled softly. "Good. I want to be the first."

She thrilled at his words, at his touch. It had been a long time, too long since she'd been in a man's company, particularly like this when she enjoyed being treated like a goddess. A temptress, for goodness' sakes!

This time when his lips covered hers, Elaine was ready and willing. A shiver of awareness coursed through her as she savored every moment, every touch, every thrust and sweep of his tongue.

He pulled away and tugged on his door handle before she was ready to end the sweet seduction. Her entire being tingled with wanting.

"Come on before you tempt me into thinking the backseat of a car is a good place for people our age."

Elaine giggled and glanced at the wide backseat.

She caught at the sound. She hadn't giggled in ... well, ages. At least a lifetime, maybe two. As Louis opened the door for her, Elaine wondered when she started thinking of herself as old, too old for things like romance or giggling or making out in the backseat of a car.

This day spent with Louis Sweet made her realize that she still had a lot of life to live. As for love to give, that was still up in the air. Dinner and a movie did not a lifetime commitment make, yet, for some inexplicable reason, she found herself thinking about Louis with words that had more to do with forever than now.

"Thank you again for spending the day with me," Louis said. He turned toward the salon. "I've ..."

His sudden frown alarmed Elaine. "What's wrong?" Her gaze swept the area, but she saw nothing out of the ordinary.

"There's a light on that shouldn't be on."

"Is that a problem?"

His frown didn't bode well.

"I don't know. I'm going to check it out though. Stay here. I'll be right back."

Elaine glanced around. This area was fine during the day, but she had no intention of standing around in the dark looking like a potential victim. She quickly fell into step beside Louis. Without thinking about it, she slipped her hand into his.

He gently squeezed hers, but didn't break his stride toward the salon.

At the front of the shop, Louis peered in the windows, then inserted a key in the lock. Once inside, he disengaged the alarm, then, in the dark, he and Elaine inspected the interior.

"What is it?" she whispered.

Louis shook his head. "It looks like someone just forgot to turn off all the correct lights."

Leaving Elaine standing in the middle of the floor, Louis went to the nearest switch and flipped it. Light flooded the interior of the salon. She watched him do another visual search of the shop. He plucked a few dried leaves from a floral arrangement, then fiddled with and straightened a couple of the silk wall hangings at two of the stations.

He looked like he was going to be a while, so Elaine settled into a stylist's chair. She draped the slim strap of her handbag along the chair back, then resumed her study of Louis. She liked watching him and enjoyed the simple pleasure of his smooth but efficient movement as he inspected each station.

Louis shrugged out of his jacket and placed it over a chair. She wondered if the woodsy scent of his cologne remained on his suit jacket.

"In the old days," Louis said, "we left no light on. We couldn't afford the extra money for the utility bill. Now, if there's anything even slightly out of whack, we notice. With some of the equipment and the addition, Della is even more careful."

Elaine twirled her chair around and stared at her reflection in the mirror. When she smiled at her reflection, she watched her face light up. She was fifty-six. Without remorse or regret she could say she looked her age. The twinkle evident in her eyes added depth, as well as light and youth. In the mirror, she watched Louis approach. Without speaking, he stood behind her.

She smiled at him. And for a few quiet moments, they simply stared at their reflections. His eyes were sharp and assessing, hers filled with wonder and a soft vulnerability. Louis lifted a hand and placed it on her shoulder. Her gaze tracked the movement.

She clasped his hand in hers and he read both the question and the answer in her eyes. The tension shifted from expectancy to certainty.

A dozing part of Louis woke up and took notice. He squelched his surprise and cleared his throat.

"It will be all right," he said, more to himself than to her.

"What?"

He glanced away from her gaze for a moment, then nodded to her head. "Your hair."

"Oh." Elaine cleared her throat and she felt heat in her cheeks.

She'd been so caught up in Louis that she'd forgotten about that. She wanted more of his gentle kisses. Letting his hand go, she touched the soft curls that framed her face, then smoothed a wayward strand.

Louis leaned forward. Elaine's breathing deepened. He lifted his own hand as if he were going to stroke her. Elaine's breathing stopped.

Then, suddenly, with a jerk, as if he'd thought better of it, he stopped and rested his hands on the back of her chair.

Elaine's breath whooshed out; the soft sigh was the only sound between them.

When the silence grew uncomfortable, she met his gaze in the mirror. "That's not what I was thinking about," she said quietly.

"What were you thinking about?"

She dared not speak the whole truth. Or did she?

"That I'm still young," she said. "That I've been without companionship." She glanced away for a shy moment. "I've been without companionship and other things for a while. I took early retirement because my husband and I planned to travel, to finally see the world together. He was several years older and had been retired after putting in forty-three years at the post office."

Louis moved and sat on the edge of the swivel seat at the station next to Elaine.

"We had big plans," she said, turning to face him. "We were going to do all the things we'd never taken the time to do. Our daughter was grown and out of the house. We thought we had nothing but time and years in front of us."

"What happened?"

Her thoughts far away, Elaine sat silent for a moment, staring past him. Then her mouth trembled a bit and she blinked back the sudden moisture at her eyes.

"He had a heart attack. He died two days before his sixty-seventh birthday. We were supposed to leave on a month-long cruise the next week."

A few tears escaped. Elaine swallowed, then quickly wiped

at her eyes. "I'm sorry. It just hits me at odd times."

Louis plucked three tissues from a box on the stylist's station and handed them to her. "I know what that's like. When Rosie died, I was bereft. I felt so . . . I don't know how to describe it. It was worse than alone. Lost, kind of helpless in ways I'd never known existed. I didn't realize until she was gone just how close we'd been and how special what we shared really was. We were yin and yang together. Alpha and omega."

"How long has it been?" Elaine asked.

"Three years. Sometimes, just out of the blue, it feels like yesterday."

Elaine nodded, understanding completely. "How do you cope with the pain?"

"Time. It's the only thing that works. You keep going through the motions of living. Then, one day you look up and realize that the motions are all there is. You never forget, though. You ask why a lot. At least I did. Then the days become weeks and months and years. Just when you're sure you're okay, you hear a song or see something that reminds you and it'll be like yesterday again with the pain slapping you in the face."

Elaine dabbed at her eyes again. "Yes, that's exactly how it feels."

Louis watched her for a moment, then reached for her hand and gave it a gentle squeeze.

"One of the things that helps a lot," he said, "is realizing that what you had was very, very special. Never forget the good times."

She nodded again, then balled up the tissue and tossed it in a wastepaper basket. "I'm not usually given to public displays of grief."

Louis looked around the shop. "I don't see any public here."

Elaine smiled and relaxed. She had nothing to be embarrassed about in front of him.

"How do you feel about what happened in the car?" he asked quietly.

She met his gaze head on. "A little frightened. Intimidated. Exhilarated."

His amused chuckle warmed her.

"And did the fear and intimidation parts outweigh the exhilaration or vice versa?"

"You're asking a lot of questions, Mr. Sweet."

His expression turned contemplative. "This one is serious," he said. "I like you a lot, Elaine Webster. I want to get to know you better, a lot better."

His searing gaze lingered at her mouth, then traveled lower. Elaine's heart skipped a beat. She didn't pretend to misunderstand him. She flushed all over and wondered why hot flashes were so similar to the heat of passion.

Louis waited.

"I'm intrigued," she finally said.

His smile widened in male approval. Elaine was suddenly reminded of the Big Bad Wolf's wicked smile and wondered if Louis Sweet wanted to eat her for dinner.

He leaned forward, drawing even closer to her.

"I'm a bit overwhelmed," she said.

He sat back.

"But mighty interested," she quickly added.

Louis's chuckle echoed through the salon. "I think I'm getting the picture. Interested but wary?"

"Something like that. My husband, Raymond, he was the only man I ever . . ." Elaine blushed and looked at her hands.

Louis cleared his throat. It was his turn to look a little embarrassed. "Well, uh, let's just take things slow, one step at a time."

She nodded. "I like that plan."

Elaine sat back. Then, like a child in a toy store, she whirled her chair around. "Tell me how you and Rosie got started doing hair."

Louis smiled at her whimsy in the chair, then settled comfortably in his own.

"We met in beautician's school. I grew up with a house full of little sisters. My mother worked third shift. So I had to get everybody up, fed, and dressed. I learned how to cook, sew, clean, and do hair pretty early on. Survival skills, I guess. I was good at hair. In junior high, word got around and I used to make extra money doing hair for high school girls' proms and whatnot. Fridays after school and Saturday mornings, my mama's kitchen sink turned into a beauty salon. One thing led to another and I went to school for it.''

Louis told Elaine about his and Rosie's first shop in the basement of the apartment building where they lived. He told her about their dreams of having children, dreams which never came true, and how they'd become surrogate parents to a number of young people and stylists just starting out.

Elaine shared the story of how she met Raymond in junior high school study hall, their steady romance, the birth of their daughter, and the death of their only son.

They laughed together as they shared stories about nosy neighbors and of being young and in love. Louis made a pot of coffee and their conversation shifted to tales of vacation misadventures and the discovery that they both had a fondness for Jamaica.

One topic led to another and time passed quickly.

Elaine yawned. Then she smiled. "It's not the company."

"I've had you sitting here like it was early in the day."

She glanced at her watch. "Louis?"

He looked at her.

"It *is* early in the day."

He peered at a clock on a far end wall then snapped his head back and jumped out of the chair. "Oh, Elaine. I'm so sorry. I had no idea. Time just seemed . . . I didn't realize."

Elaine stood and shook out her full skirt. "Don't apologize. I've had a ball."

Louis made fast work of the coffee machine, the lights, the alarm system, and the locking up of the salon. When he walked her to her car, the faint glow of dawn edged its way over the horizon.

"I had no idea it was so late," he apologized again.

With two fingers over his mouth, Elaine shushed him.

The light physical contact got both of their attention. Elaine grew bold and traced his lips. He wrapped an arm around her waist and pulled her closer as they leaned against her white Volvo.

"I love the feel of you," he said.

"I'd feel better minus about fifty pounds."

"Don't get rid of a single ounce. I like a woman I can hold on to."

She pressed closer. "You do?"

He nuzzled her neck. "Mmm-hmm. A lot."

Sweet nibbled on her neck and worked his way up. "I'm going to kiss you, Elaine Webster."

"No, you're not."

He leaned back and looked at her.

Elaine smiled and cupped his face in her hands. "That's because I'm going to kiss you."

She did. Thoroughly.

The horn from a passing car reminded them that they stood outside.

"We're acting like a couple of teenagers," Elaine said.

"Age is nothing but a number."

With that, he kissed her on the cheek and opened her car door for her. "I'll call you." Louis watched her settle behind the wheel, start the car, and then, with a wave, drive away.

Louis smiled to himself, then grinned from ear to ear.

# Chapter Six

The next morning, Elaine slept late but doubt came early. She'd spent the night with Louis Sweet. The time zipped by so quickly with him, the hours seemed like mere minutes.

She touched her lips. The memory of Louis's kisses still warmed her. The cool cotton sheet seemed heavy on her body. Elaine's breathing deepened and she wondered what it might be like to sleep with someone else. She'd come to Raymond a virgin and had never so much as kissed another man.

Louis's mouth was firm, insistent. He was a wonderful kisser, Elaine realized. She didn't know if Louis's skill was an uncommon one. She just knew she liked being the recipient of that particular talent.

The last few years of her marriage with Raymond had been platonic. The effects of his diabetes had stifled their sex life, and soon after, Elaine stopped longing for what she couldn't have. Now, however, long-forgotten urges sprang forth from an unfamiliar place.

Her legs stirred beneath the sheet. She turned onto her stomach and clutched a plump pillow under her arms as she pressed her body into the firm mattress. It had been so long . . . so very long.

With a deep sigh, Elaine sat up in bed. Tucking the sheet patterned in sunflowers around her bosom, she glanced around the bedroom she and Raymond had shared for twenty-five years. The house, nestled in a good neighborhood with good schools, had been their five-year anniversary present to each other. They'd scrimped and saved, invested wisely and doubled up on mortgage payments until they'd burned their thirty-year mortgage ten years early.

Raymond had been proud of that fact, but Elaine had wanted to spend the money on family vacations. Instead of traveling with her husband, Elaine spent the years with her daughter, Belinda, as her travel companion. By the time Raymond finally acquiesced on a big vacation, it was too late.

"Louis would have taken me."

As soon as the ornery words escaped her mouth, Elaine regretted the blasphemy. With a vicious kick, guilt came knocking.

Repentant, Elaine got up and walked to her dresser where an eight-by-ten frame portrait rested. The photograph had been taken for their thirtieth anniversary. Elaine reached for the frame and ran a finger down the side of Raymond's image.

"I didn't mean to dishonor you," she apologized. *Even though you had your faults,* she added to herself. She quickly glanced over her shoulder as if expecting a scowling Raymond to be standing there.

She smiled at her whimsy, and carefully replaced the photograph on the dresser. Then, with a naughty thought about Louis Sweet and a not-quite-guilty peek at her tumbled bed, Elaine made her way to the bathroom.

Louis slammed a fist on his doctor's desk. "I got a tingle, but nothing happened, Doc! Nothing, dammit. She's everything I want. She has a figure that makes me want to hold her close and never let go."

"That's a start, Louis."

He paced the short area between the door and the desk. "I'm not a whole man. She was there, right there in my arms," he said, holding his arms out as if Elaine stood in front of him. "She was right there, and nothing."

The doctor sighed and pushed his half glasses up a bit on his nose. "We have had this conversation at least fifty times, Louis. There's nothing wrong with you that time and patience can't cure."

"What about another test?"

"You've had every test there is to have. For a man your age, you're healthy as a horse. No diabetes, no hypertension, no kidney disease. You don't smoke, you drink in moderation. You don't do any drugs that I know of. You have no history of anything, no symptoms of anything. You're perfectly fine."

"Then why can't I get and keep a hard-on?"

Shaking his head, the doctor pulled off his glasses and tossed them on the desk. "I don't know, Louis. Performance anxiety, maybe?"

Louis's derisive snort made the physician sigh again. He sat on the edge of his desk and contemplated Louis.

"What you and Rosie had was very special. The impotence you experienced after her death is fairly common, Louis. That may have just been your head and heart telling your body it wasn't time yet to let go. You ran in here a few weeks ago all excited about meeting this woman Elaine. Give it time. Give her some time and give yourself some time. Go slow. Male impotence, especially the instances like yours where no physical cause is to blame, can't be cured overnight. There is, however, the new drug . . ."

Louis cut him off. "No, drugs, Doc. Not even that one."

Louis sighed and slumped into the chair in front of the desk. He ran his hands over his face. "So what am I supposed to do now?"

"You and this Elaine need to talk. Tell her. You can work on this together. I have a video . . ."

Louis slammed his hand on the desk. "I don't want a video. I want to be able to make love to my woman."

A model of patience, the doctor simply nodded. "I know that. And you said you're attracted to her?"

"Very much so."

"Since Rosie died, have you been attracted to any other woman like this?"

"After that first fiasco with Helen, no. I haven't even looked at anybody hard."

A smile tugged at the physician's mouth, but he let Louis'

choice of words go without comment. "But there's something about Elaine?"

Louis' grin flashed briefly as he sat up. "Like chocolate I just want to eat up all day."

Dr. Shelton's eyebrow rose at that. "Well, I think I have the perfect solution for you."

"You've been holding out on something that'll make me work?"

The doctor reached for a prescription pad on his desk and made a few scribbles. "I think this will do the trick."

More than a week passed before Elaine saw Louis again. She'd expected him to call, had waited for him to stop by—but he didn't. He was nowhere to be seen when she'd arrived at the salon for a deep conditioning. LaTonya and Della fretted over her. And on more than one occasion, Elaine thought she caught a sly glance exchanged as she passed through the salon's corridor. Her steps had even faltered as she passed the place where she'd spent the night talking to Louis.

Doubt assailed her. Guilt consumed her. And Mitchell Forbes wooed her.

She'd run into him as she left a florist's shop next to his salon.

"So we meet again," he said.

Elaine smiled at him. "Hello, Mr. Forbes."

"Please, call me Mitchell. Those flowers are as beautiful as you are."

Charmed, Elaine murmured a thank you as she glanced at the centerpiece she'd picked up. Then she looked at the man. Today he seemed, well, nice. Maybe it had just been nerves the day she bumped into him at Rosie's.

"Have you seen Sweet lately?" he asked.

"No. Not in about a week or so."

Mitchell tsk-tsked, even as his appreciative gaze roamed over Elaine. "If we were more than casual acquaintances, Elaine Webster, I can assure you I wouldn't let a full week go by without seeing you."

Elaine thrilled at the words, words that she should have

been hearing from Louis Sweet. After all the time they'd spent together, she'd expected more than abandonment from Louis. Mitchell Forbes did have style, an élan that escaped Louis. He'd even done a little homework.

"How'd you get my name?" she asked.

"Inquiring minds get answers."

Elaine smiled and Mitchell fell into an easy step beside her as she headed to her car. "You know, Sweet has a reputation with the ladies. He's known around here as a big flirt. I'm sure you've encountered the type, love-'em-then-leave-'em."

"And what about you?"

He paused in his walk. Elaine turned to face him. Mitchell reached for her hand.

"The flowers!" But Elaine's worry was unnecessary. Mitchell took and balanced the centerpiece in one of his hands and lifted her right hand to his mouth. He bestowed a gallant kiss there, then released her.

"I know how to treat a beautiful lady."

"It seems you do."

"Have lunch with me," he said.

Did she dare? Seems she'd turned into a femme fatale overnight. A grin lit up her face and a giggle escaped. "It's after three, going on four, Mitchell."

"Then we'll be just in time for tea, maybe an early dinner."

Elaine hesitated as myriad excuses popped into her head. Then, throwing caution to the wind, she accepted. She'd heard the talk about Louis. Mitchell simply had confirmed what she already knew about him. Louis Sweet thought he was the only game in town. Two could play by his rules.

"What about the flowers? I don't want to leave them in the car."

"Not a problem. We can put them on the front desk in the salon and pick them up when we return." Mitchell's smile was just the encouragement Elaine needed.

He crooked his free elbow out. Elaine draped a hand through and let him lead her first into his shop, then to tea.

\*     \*     \*

Hours later though, she regretted the impulsive move. Mitchell Forbes led her in witty conversation. They shared many things in common. He complimented her on her suit, her jewelry, her knowledge about gourmet tea and coffee. As nice as he'd been, Elaine felt more than a twinge of guilt about going out with him, particularly on such a spur-of-the-moment decision.

She missed Louis the entire time she'd spent with Mitchell.

Maybe something *had* come up with him. Maybe he'd had second thoughts about a woman who was so available she could spend all day and night with him on a first date. Maybe after kissing her, he'd decided he didn't *really* like her all that much. Maybe . . .

"Stop it this minute."

Elaine yanked the vacuum cleaner cord from the wall socket and started winding up the cord. "Just get a grip, Elaine Webster. You're acting like a schoolgirl."

And just like a schoolgirl, she'd glanced at the silent telephone each time she passed it as she'd vacuumed. Facing the fact that the affair was apparently over before it had begun, Elaine shoved the appliance toward the closet and glared at the telephone again.

The sudden shrill ring made her jump.

Her heart pounded as she stared at the white cordless. Clutching her chest in surprise, Elaine stood mute. Was it really ringing or was she having an audio hallucination?

On the fourth ring, she snatched up the phone and punched TALK.

"Hello?"

"I've been out of town for a few days. I missed you."

Elaine smiled at the sound of Louis's voice. She pulled a chair from the table and sat down. "I missed you, too."

Over the telephone line she heard his sigh of relief. So, he'd been nervous, too.

"I thought I'd bored you so much you decided to cut and run."

"Elaine Webster, let me tell you something. You do a lot of things to me. Boring me isn't one of them."

She smiled and clutched the phone tighter. Later on she might chide herself for acting like a sixteen-year-old in the midst of a full-blown crush. For now, though, this was too good, too heady and sweet. Elaine felt younger than she had in years.

"Would you like to come over for dinner?"

"You bet."

They set a date for the following night.

Over the next few weeks, Elaine and Louis fell into a courting routine. They went to lunch and to flower shows. Sometimes Elaine cooked dinner, other nights they went out. They watched hospital and police dramas on television and they saw the occasional movie on a Friday or Saturday night. They hugged and cuddled and kissed, but Louis never pressed her for sex.

Elaine was too relieved and too embarrassed to ask. She enjoyed their easy relationship and liked Louis's company too much to mess things up with a complicated sexual relationship. From Louis Sweet she got more romance and tenderness than she'd gotten from Raymond in their last ten years together.

Then, one night, Louis arrived at her door for dinner. The gleam in his eye let her know that tonight would somehow be different.

"What are you up to, Louis Sweet?" she asked as she let him in.

"I have a surprise for you."

Elaine smiled. "I love surprises."

"Change clothes first."

Elaine glanced at the neatly pressed and coordinating slacks, vest, and blouse she wore. "What's wrong with this?"

"Too casual. We're going out."

"But I made a roast and your favorite double-mashed potatoes."

For a moment, Louis wavered. Elaine could put a hurtin' on a kitchen. In the time they'd been keeping company, he'd gained about five pounds from pulling up to her table.

"A roast, huh? With those chunks of vegetables?"

Elaine nodded and smiled.

He reached for her. With a hand at her waist, Louis pulled Elaine into his embrace. "You tempt me, woman. But I think you'll enjoy this surprise."

A kiss that held lots of promise swayed Elaine.

"I'll put the food away while you change."

Knowing his game, Elaine chuckled as she headed to the stairs. "All right. Just make sure you leave enough for my dinner tomorrow."

She paused at the stairwell. "What look am I aiming for?"

Already on his way to the kitchen, Louis glanced over his shoulder. "Casual elegance."

Elaine did a quick mental tally of her closet. "So, where are we going?"

"It's a surprise," he called from the kitchen. "You'll find out when we get there."

A little while later, Elaine let Louis lead her to their destination. She'd changed into a silk pantsuit with a red, sequined, flowing top.

"No peeking," he said.

"I'm not cheating."

Elaine kept her eyes closed and reveled in the heightened awareness of Louis's hand at her waist.

"I smell water. Are we at a dock, Louis?"

"No peeking. Just a little farther."

"Louis?"

"Almost there," he replied.

True to his word, a few moments later he told her to pause. She felt his nearness. Then his mouth settled over hers and Elaine's arms circled his waist. Pressing her open lips to his, she quivered at the sweet tenderness of the embrace.

Louis ended the brief liaison and stepped away. Elaine's murmur of disappointment encouraged him.

"Open your eyes, Elaine."

Her soft gasp of surprise and pleasure pleased him.

The boat was large enough to be a house, but small enough

for a couple of people to manage on their own. Small white lights twinkled all along the boat and railings. In the early evening, the vessel beckoned like a fantasy island of romance.

Louis helped her aboard.

"Welcome to *La Dolce Vita*. This is my retirement home."

"You live here? But I thought . . ."

"I spend so much time here, it's like I live here. Watch your step."

Elaine stepped around the rigging. He led her into a nice-sized cabin. "What would you like to drink?"

Elaine took in the table set for two, the wine chilling in an ice bucket.

"How about a glass of wine?"

Louis's eyebrows rose; she didn't usually drink. But he didn't say anything. Making his way to a small wet bar, he poured a glass of chardonnay for her and sparkling water for himself. He joined her on the built-in sofa and handed her her glass.

"To friendship and more."

Elaine smiled and clicked glasses with him. "To friendship and more," she repeated.

Her heart tripped as she sipped her wine. Louis had never done anything untoward. But tonight . . . well, tonight the mood was romance. Maybe their relationship was about to take a turn, one she wanted but wasn't quite ready to navigate. Things had been progressing nicely between them. Her daughter had encouraged her to go for it.

But now . . .

Elaine drained her glass and held it out to him.

Louis smiled and got up. He refilled her glass with the light, dry wine.

"I'll get us underway. We'll go out a ways and anchor to just enjoy the evening."

Elaine nodded and watched him walk away. She sipped from her glass, then decided to join him.

"Anything I can do to help?"

"Just relax."

She watched as he pulled up the anchor and went about his business in an efficient manner, as if he'd done this a thousand times. Elaine had been on cruise ships, but never a personal craft like this one. Before long, they were underway.

She enjoyed the cool breeze on her face as they cruised through the waterways. She watched the marina and then the city slowly fade from view. Together they watched the sun's final descent. The red-gold light fired the horizon in magnificent splendor. Louis wrapped an arm around Elaine's shoulders as she circled his waist and leaned her head on his shoulder.

"This is perfect," she said. "Beautiful."

"Um-hmm." But Louis's gaze was on Elaine as he concurred.

Her soft smile of contentment stirred something in Louis. He'd carefully followed his doctor's instructions. The unconventional prescription called for touching, hugging, and kissing, followed by more touching, hugging, and kissing. Tonight, he'd take them to the next level. Without a doubt, Louis knew he was ready. He'd been ready for some time now. Elaine's hesitancy held him in check. But tonight . . .

With his free hand he turned her face to him and lifted her chin. Questioning eyes met his, and then they were one. Their bodies shifted so they faced each other.

Elaine's arms draped around his neck. The lingering doubt about her desirability evaporated. His erection pressed hard against her. Elaine reveled in the heat of desire. He moaned and deepened the kiss.

Her senses reeled. This was so right.

Then Elaine lost herself in the moment, and the man she'd fallen in love with.

Louis surprised her with a four-course meal on museum-quality porcelain dinner plates. They sipped champagne from crystal glasses as Billy Eckstine, Nancy Wilson, and Nat King Cole serenaded them with longing love songs of days past.

The white lights along the boat and the candles lit throughout the cabin added to the sweet romance of the evening.

After dinner they settled themselves on deck and watched the stars in the night sky.

"This is living," Louis said.

Elaine nodded. "The sweet life. I've often wondered what it would be like to live life without a care in the world. This is what it's like."

"What cares keep you away from enjoying the sweet life?"

Elaine glanced at him and shrugged. "I don't know. The pressures of the world, I suppose."

She stared up at the stars. "Before Raymond died, my life was content, even while there were times when I wondered if there was more. Not more financially. Except in our early years, money was never the issue."

"What was the issue?"

She shrugged again. "More. I wanted more, and Raymond didn't understand. I'm not sure I understood."

"More contentment, more peace?"

"Yes." She nodded. "But something else, too. This," she said, waving a hand around them. "Raymond was a good man, but he never understood the seeking part of me. I've always strived for total control and balance in my life. Somewhere along the way, the pursuit of those things cancelled out or negated the purpose of the search. Does that make any sense to you?"

"More than you know. I dropped out of life after Rosie died. With no one to share it all with, what was the point?"

He stood and held a hand out to her. Together they went and stood at the railing to gaze at the still, starry night and the calm water.

"Elaine, have you found what you've been searching for?"

Their gazes met.

"I've found it in you," she said.

He caressed her face with a gentle hand. "I'm glad. I feel the same way."

For a long moment, they remained quiet, lost in the sureness and the depth of their feelings.

"Elaine, I need to tell you something."

"What is it, Louis?"

He took her hands in his and pressed a kiss to them.

"I want to make love to you."

# Chapter Seven

"I . . ." she started.

He placed a finger across her lips. "Let me finish."

When she nodded, he removed his finger, but didn't let her out of his embrace.

"I want to make love to you, but I'm not entirely sure I can."

"But what about . . . ?" she said, pressing herself against him and feeling his response.

Louis nodded and took a shaky breath. "My doctor says everything checks out. That I—we—can do whatever we want to."

"But?" she asked.

He glanced away for a moment, then faced her. "Most people think I lost interest in the salon when Rosie died. But that's not it."

He loosened himself from their embrace and walked a few feet clear of her. Elaine, standing alone, leaned back against the seat rail, then sank into the cushioned seat.

"What's wrong?"

"Apparently nothing. I've had every test that's available. Not long after Rosie passed, I got involved with a woman. When it came time to . . . you know, between the sheets, I couldn't do it. My doctor said the impotence was psychological, not physical."

"Was?"

He nodded and met her gaze. "Until I met you, until just

a few weeks ago, I couldn't even get an erection.''

Elaine's gaze immediately fell to his crotch. "But . . .''

Louis grinned. "Yeah, you do that to me."

"I don't understand," she said.

He sighed. Dr. Shelton didn't say how difficult the explaining part would be.

"I want to make love to you, but I don't want to disappoint you," he said. "You're too special to me."

Filled with sudden assurance, Elaine's smile dazzled him. She got up and took one of his hands. Entwining their fingers, she lifted his hand to her heart.

"Louis, there's more to a relationship than sex. I've enjoyed, immensely, the romance of being in . . ." She paused, not quite ready to admit that to him. "Of being romantic," she finished. "And there's something you should know."

Embarrassed, he stared at his feet. "What?"

Elaine brought his face up so she could look in his eyes, so he would hear and believe.

"Raymond had diabetes. The sugar affected his ability to have intercourse. I know all about male impotence."

"I might not be able to give you what you need."

"You've already given me what I need."

His questioning look made her explain. "You've given me intimacy. You've given me tenderness. A man isn't defined by his sexual prowess. It's what's in here that counts," she said, tapping his heart.

"Don't give me that. I've seen you looking at me," he said.

Elaine smiled and traced a finger along his hairline. "You're an attractive man."

"But not necessarily a whole man. That was the problem a few years ago. Women were coming at me from every direction. When things didn't work, I laughed it off with the lady I was seeing at the time. Then I broke things off between us before she could spread the word."

Elaine's eyes narrowed. "You sound like you were dating every woman in Harlem."

Louis laughed.

"It seemed like it," he said. "They were all chasing me. And that's not conceit talking either."

Something about his offhand comment rubbed Elaine the wrong way. But she couldn't quite put her finger on it. Not willing to spoil the evening with a quibble, she let it go.

"Single men in our age group are few and far between," she said.

"Oh, is that what it was?"

Her smile was indulgent. "Women tend to outlive their men. I bet you got invited to a lot of dinners and a lot of church services."

"I couldn't figure out if they thought I was too skinny or if they thought I needed to mend my ways with some religion."

She sidled closer to him. "They just wanted to show you off at church."

"And all those dinner invitations?"

"Well, dinner sometimes leads to other things."

Louis sighed. "Elaine, that's what I'm trying to tell you. I'm not sure that the 'other' part works."

She hugged him. "Louis, just being with you, having you kiss me, is more than I thought I'd ever have in my life again."

"Because your husband died?" he asked as his hands slid up and stroked her back.

She shook her head no. "Because we had a peaceful life together, but it wasn't a perfect life. His diabetes cancelled all the intimacy between us. Unfortunately, Raymond didn't realize that intimacy means more than sex. When he could no longer have sex, he shut me out completely. I tried to tell him it didn't matter, but he never believed that I could be content with hugs. He didn't understand that I liked being held and stroked and kissed."

Elaine saw the flare of awareness in his eyes. His hands moved lower and caressed her behind.

For a long time, Louis didn't say anything. They held each other. And then he hugged her close.

The hug turned into a gentle sway. Before long, they were

dancing in the small open space on the deck. A faint Sinatra tune drifted over them and Louis hummed "The Way You Look Tonight" in Elaine's ear. They slow danced long after the music faded away.

"It's been a long time, a long, long time since a man set up a seduction scene for me. You're quite accomplished."

He chuckled. "Hell, Elaine. I'm fifty-seven years old. I think I ought to know how to seduce a woman by now."

"Well, I'm impressed by your skill."

"You're supposed to be."

"You've done this quite often, I take it. I'd heard that about you."

Elaine noticed the shrill note in her voice, but she couldn't help it. Not when his own words stirred the doubt she'd harbored just beneath the sunny smiles she sent his way.

"Don't believe any of those nasty rumors," Louis quipped as he tried to pull her closer.

But Elaine turned away from his embrace. Impotent or not, she wondered just how many women he'd seduced like this.

"There's even some chocolate for dessert," he said. "Godiva, of course."

Obviously a lot of women, the militant part of Elaine answered to herself.

"How did you know to get Godiva?"

Louis didn't miss a beat of the tune he hummed. "Can't miss with it. Most women love it. Rosie did. She always . . ."

Elaine's eyes widened and she stopped hearing his words of rhapsody about his former wife. Something in her died in that instant. After what had seemed like a perfect evening— too perfect, she now realized—he had to go and spoil it. He hadn't been spending a romantic night with her. Louis had wined and dined her, romanced her and wooed her as a substitute for his precious Rosie. This wasn't a special evening just for her benefit and enjoyment, she concluded. Everything came back to Rosie.

How many times had he planned and carried out this very seduction scene with Rosie—or with another woman he used as a replacement for his dead wife?

Elaine wanted to cry but she was too angry to shed any tears. She stood still on deck.

"What?" he asked as he nuzzled her neck.

"I'd like to go home now."

Louis's head popped up. "Home? Now? Why?"

Elaine pushed at his chest. He didn't even realize he'd hurt her.

"Elaine? Wait. What happened? What did I say?"

She stomped away from him and went to stand at the rail. Looking out over the water, she realized how alone they were, and how far from shore they'd put out. Elaine closed her eyes and willed both the tears and the hurt away. It didn't work.

Louis came up behind her.

"Why are you mad?"

"I'm angry, not mad."

"Then why are you angry? I'm not a mind reader, Elaine. You've got to help me out here. What happened?"

"How could you stand there and compare me to her?" she lashed out.

"Her who?"

"Rosie. Rosie. It all comes back to Rosie. At the salon, I've heard a lot about your fabled love affair. She sounds like a saint. And then you stand there and compare me to her. How many times did you run this romantic evening by her?"

Frustrated tears fell from Elaine's eyes.

Louis clasped her shoulders. "Elaine, I bought this boat after she died. Rosie didn't like water unless it was in a tub. How could something like that even cross your mind?"

"I'd like to go home, please."

"Elaine."

She wouldn't respond. Louis sighed and dropped his hands. "This is crazy, Elaine. I don't understand why you're so upset."

For a moment, she didn't say anything. Too many conflicting emotions ran through her head. Was she really jealous or was she just overreacting?

"I'm the one you're supposed to be dating," she finally

told him. "I thought *we* had something special, but I can see now that I'm just the widow of the week."

"Widow of the week? What are you talking about? You're my woman."

Truly angry now, the words poured from Elaine. "Well, you have a funny way of showing it. You've been ignoring me. You say you were out of town, but I'm pretty sure most of the country is wired for telephone service. You didn't even call."

"Ah, Elaine, I'm sorry," he said, lifting a hand to run the back of a finger along her face. "I didn't even think about calling."

Elaine sniffed. "That's exactly what I mean. Some men are willing to pay attention to me."

"I pay attention to you, baby," he said while tracing curlicues on her palm. Then, "Some men like who?"

Elaine snatched her hand away. "Like Mitchell Forbes, for instance. He knows how to treat a lady. We had a lovely afternoon the other day. It was spontaneous and delightful."

And oh, so stupid to blurt out, she realized a strained heartbeat later as his face closed. She was acting like a jealous shrew.

Louis stood perfectly still. He could have been a statue in a Roman garden or Lot's wife after turning around. He looked as if she'd slapped him. It was too late to take back the words she'd thrown at him in anger.

"I didn't mean . . . Louis, Mitchell and I aren't . . ."

He turned away from her.

"Louis . . ."

Elaine glanced around, looking for some sort of assistance. But her companions, the quiet night and the water, offered no solace.

"I'll take you back now," he said.

Elaine heard a strain in his voice that hadn't been there before. She quickly followed behind him, leaving a trail of words and apologies along the way. Louis ignored every one.

"Elaine, we're cool. You wanted to go home, we're going home."

She took exception to the patronizing tone. Her obstinate streak kicked in. *She* was the one who had the right to be angry.

On the way back, Louis tried to make small talk. But the mood of their date had been altered. Elaine wasn't talking to him, and he was sick of trying to get her to open up, particularly about Mitchell Forbes.

Back at the marina, Elaine stood at the dock while Louis secured the boat. After two more unsuccessful attempts to get her to open up, he admitted defeat and a perennial inability to understand women.

The drive to Elaine's house was done in silence. But at her front door, Louis again tried to get through to her. A foot in the door kept her from closing it in his face.

"Elaine, I'm a good gardener, a pretty decent business owner, and a damn good hairdresser. I can look at a woman's hair and face and instinctively know how to make her natural beauty shine through. But I can't see inside her head. It doesn't work like that. And I'm too old to learn how to be a psychic."

A shadow of a smile crossed her face and Louis was encouraged.

"I know I said something out there that upset you. Whatever it was, I'm sorry."

"You don't get it, do you?"

"No, Elaine. That's just it. I don't. And unless you tell me, I'll probably end up doing it again. Help a brother out, will you?"

"I'm not Rosie," she said.

"I know that. What does Rosie—"

She cut him off with a curt "Good night, Louis."

He sighed, then shifted his weight from one foot to the other. Elaine took the opening.

"Good-bye."

The door shut in his face before he could get another word in.

\*    \*    \*

It didn't take Elaine long to realize she'd acted foolishly. She figured that out long before her best friend lit into her about "messing up a good thing."

Folding her arms across her ample bosom, Elaine patiently listened to Lena's whispered tirade in the middle of a sorority meeting.

"I don't believe you could do something like that. Do you know how many women have wanted that man? Here he lays out the red carpet for you and what do you do? You fling it back in his face and toss in some ancient history to help rub salt in the wound. Mitchell Forbes of all people. Do you know how much they hate each other? Really, Elaine . . ."

"Soror Lena, was there something you wanted to tell the entire group?" the sorority president asked.

Elaine snickered. "Now you've gotten us in trouble."

"Uh, no, Soror Ellen," Lena said aloud. Under her breath, for Elaine's ears, she added, "Does she think we're her fourth-graders or something?"

"Shh," Elaine shushed.

Lena pouted. "We'll take this up later, Elaine Webster."

Elaine knew her friend would do just that. But in the meantime, Elaine still had to sort through her own reaction. Yes, she'd been hasty in her conclusions. But Louis had been too suave, too smooth. Everything on *La Dolce Vita* had been perfect, from the lights and music that set a romantic tone to the champagne and dancing. Like a well-oiled machine or a tried-and-true cliche, every moment seemed practiced, perfected, and precise. He knew which buttons to push because he'd run that scene with Rosie and countless other women.

*And what about his confession?* a little voice asked. Designed to gain my sympathy, the stubborn part of her answered.

*What are you really afraid of, Elaine?* Risking my heart again. It's too late for that, you know. Somewhere along the way, Louis Sweet strolled in and stole it.

Elaine wasn't quite sure when it happened. She'd fallen in love with Louis. She shook her head. It was too soon, just too soon. What would Raymond think?

*Raymond is dead, Elaine. You're still here. Don't you think he'd want you to be happy?*

The sorority president announced something that made all the other women applaud. Elaine glanced around, not sure what had transpired while she argued with herself.

As the business meeting ended and the ladies headed toward the tables for a repast, Elaine remained in her chair.

"What's wrong?" Lena asked.

Elaine glanced up and shook her head. "Nothing."

"Well, we need to talk about Louis some more."

Elaine's attention was elsewhere. "Okay," she absently answered.

Carefully, she considered the women who were her friends and sorority sisters. The graduate chapter was filled with women from all walks of life. A few were singles who had never married. Several widows were counted in the number. Others had or would soon celebrate silver and golden anniversaries. And still a few others, like Mary Rose, had been married several times.

Elaine watched the flamboyant Mary Rose gesticulate as she talked with a soror. Mary Rose had buried two husbands, divorced another, and had just walked down the aisle for the fourth time with a new mate fifteen years her junior. Soror Mary Rose didn't care what people said about her, she aimed to get the most out of life. Elaine remembered the talk when, less than five months after her third husband was buried, Mary Rose announced she was engaged.

Would people talk if she married Louis Sweet?

Elaine's eyes widened. Married! Where had that come from?

"Lena, if you don't mind, I'm going to skip out now. There are some things I need to do. I'll call you."

"You don't look so hot. Are you all right?"

"Fine. I'll be just fine," Elaine said. *As soon as I get crazy thoughts about Louis Sweet off my mind,* she added to herself.

\*     \*     \*

She called, but never caught him at home.

She went to the shop but was told he hadn't been in.

Three weeks after the night he'd surprised her with a romantic date on his boat, Elaine still hadn't seen or heard from Louis Sweet. Taking her pride in hand, she went to Della Frazier. Della and Louis had been friends for a long time. Maybe the other woman could give Elaine some insight.

Della took one look at Elaine and decided that their conversation shouldn't be in the salon where eager ears tuned in all around. The two women walked along 125th Street, taking in the sights and enjoying the summer afternoon.

"I've tried to contact him, but he seems to have disappeared."

"Your rejection hurt him, Mrs. Webster."

Elaine turned to Della. "Please, call me Elaine. I'm feeling old enough as it is."

"Elaine, Louis is very vulnerable. I know he comes across as Mr. In Control. But this is the first time since Rosie died that he's shown a real interest in anything—the salon, a relationship. He cares about you a lot, but he's not going to beg, particularly if there's something between you and Mitchell Forbes."

Elaine shook her head. "No, Mitchell means nothing to me. Our dinner was a spur-of-the-moment thing. I was angry with Louis. If I'd thought about it longer than a second, I never would have gone out with him. Louis is the one I love. He's the only man I want."

Remembering the time when he'd told her he wasn't too proud to beg, Elaine wondered if she'd pushed him away so far that the damage was permanent. "I don't want him to beg. I want to do the begging," she said. "But if he won't answer his phone or come to his door and he's not at the hair salon, how am I supposed to tell him I'm sorry?"

Della didn't have an answer for that.

Three hours later, Della and Louis sat in the salon office with the door shut and the blinds closed. Louis, indolently sprawled across the sofa, studied Della, who sat prim and proper at her desk.

"Okay, so how did it go? Does she miss me?" he asked.

"Louis, this is really juvenile."

"No, it's not. Look, Della, Elaine is the woman for me. I know it right here," he said, pointing to his heart. "I need to know she knows it, too."

"How do I let you drag me into these things?" Della said. "I felt like a fraud today. That women is wracked with guilt. She was pouring her heart out to me and you're playing games."

"I'm not playing games," Louis defended.

Della's hand landed on her hips and she cocked a brow at him. "Then what do you call peeking out the window when she comes to your house, not answering your calls, and sneaking into the salon when you're sure she's not here?"

"Strategy. It's strategy, woman. Now come on. Tell me what happened."

Della sighed. She wasn't going to win this game.

"I did like you asked," she said. "We went for a walk. I told her you were vulnerable."

Louis grinned. "And what'd she say to that?"

The salon manager was losing her patience. "Louis."

"Come on, Della. I love this woman."

Della looked at him and decided to turn the tables on him. "Mitchell Forbes stopped by today."

The curl of his lip spoke volumes about Louis's distaste for the rival salon owner. "Yeah? And?"

Della shrugged. "He came in. Elaine happened to be here, too. An off day for her, you know. She usually sticks to her schedule."

"Yeah, yeah. And?" Louis prompted.

"And they chatted for a few minutes."

"And?"

Della innocently looked at Louis. "And then Elaine and I went for our walk."

She picked up a magazine and absently thumbed through

it. "Do you want to send anyone to the hair show in Memphis?"

Louis hopped off the sofa. "No. I want to know what he said to her. I thought he didn't mean anything to her. That's what she said. That's what you said."

Della shrugged, the movement an elegant motion in nonchalance. "So maybe he wants to change her mind."

"What did he tell her? What did he say?"

"I don't know. I was with a customer. She was smiling when he left."

Louis cussed and muttered as he paced the office. "I should have known."

Della hid a smile behind her hand. "Anything else, Louis? I do have a salon to run."

"When is Elaine's next appointment?"

"Her usual. She'll be in tomorrow to get her nails done."

"Fine."

Louis stomped out of the office and slammed the door.

Amused, Della chuckled. "That ought to keep him busy for a while."


But Della's plan backfired.

Louis showed up the next day but was told Ms. Webster had cancelled her appointment. When he saw Elaine's Volvo parked in front of Style by Forbes, he knew he'd lost her.

Louis slid into a depression and couldn't be consoled. He ignored the salon and wouldn't even talk to Della.

A week later, Elaine kept her regular hair appointment, but when she walked into the salon, she was unusually quiet.

"Is anything wrong, Ms. Webster?" the receptionist asked.

Red-rimmed eyes with circles underneath them told the story, but Elaine simply shook her head and followed the receptionist to the shampoo area. The usually relaxing wash didn't revive her. Neither did the chatter from her stylist.

"Today isn't very good for me, LaTonya," Elaine said. "I'd like something that's fast."

The stylist got the hint and fell quiet. But she handed Elaine a tissue when tears fell from the woman's eyes.

"Tell me what I can do for you, Ms. Webster. Is it Mr. Sweet? I'm sure things will eventually work out with the two of you."

Elaine's face crumpled as more silent tears fell. She twisted the rings she now wore on her right hand.

"How soon will you be finished?" she choked out.

Looking distressed, the stylist apologized. "I'm sorry. I'll be done in just a few minutes."

LaTonya made haste getting Elaine's hair curled. Clutching her purse and the wadded-up tissue, Elaine paid her bill and hurried out of the beauty salon.

"What was that all about?" Della said as she approached LaTonya's station.

"I don't know. I was just coming to tell you."

The stylist quickly relayed Elaine's uncharacteristic behavior and her concern. "I think I made it worse when I mentioned Mr. Sweet. I'm sorry, Della."

"It's not your fault. What in the world has Louis done now?" Della muttered.

"Line three for you, Della," the receptionist called.

"Excuse me," she told LaTonya.

Della picked up a cordless phone and walked to the supply area where the music and conversations wouldn't interfere.

"This is Della Frazier. How may I help you?"

"Ma'am, are you the manager of Rosie's Curl and Weave?"

"Yes, I am."

Della handed a shampoo assistant a stack of clean towels and nodded when the girl thanked her.

"My name is Belinda Webster. My mother is a customer at the salon. I haven't been able to reach her and I think this is her regular day. Is she there? I'm very worried about her."

"I'm sorry. She left about ten minutes ago. You said you're worried about her. Is something wrong?"

"Yes," Belinda said. "I've tried to reach Mr. Sweet, but I can't seem to locate him either. Are you able to get a message to him? It's very important."

Della shooed another assistant away. "What's wrong?"

The woman's heavy sigh came through on the telephone. "Ms. Frazier, today is my mother's wedding anniversary. My father died more than a year ago. They would have been married thirty-five years today. She's liable to be very depressed or despondent. She was last year and I'm very worried about her. I thought maybe she was there. I know she and Mr. Sweet have been seeing each other. Maybe she's with him."

Della rubbed her brows. If she knew Louis like she believed she did, he was holed up in his house sulking and feeling sorry for himself.

"No, he's not here. But I'll get the message to him."

"Thank you so much."

After farewells with Elaine's daughter, Della called Sweet's house as she made her way through the salon. When she didn't get an answer, she handed the cordless phone to the receptionist.

"I'll be out for a while. Take any messages."

"Yes, ma'am."

From the back of her desk, Della retrieved a key that she hadn't used in years. She grabbed her purse and went to talk some sense into Louis Sweet.

# Chapter Eight

Louis knocked on the door, not expecting an answer but ready to wait until Elaine let him in. Her car was in the driveway, so he knew she was home.

His persistence eventually paid off. Almost five minutes after he started knocking and ringing her bell, Elaine opened the door a sliver.

"Hello, Elaine. May I come in?"

"No," she sniffled.

Louis ignored her, pushed the door open wider and stepped into the house. "These are for you," he said, handing her a bouquet of freshly cut roses.

"Thank you," she mumbled.

Elaine looked like hell, but Louis was too much of a gentleman to tell her. The curls on one side of her head were squashed, as if she'd been fighting with a pillow . . . and the pillow won. Bags under her eyes and that frumpy housedress made her look twenty years older.

He hadn't known what to expect when he saw her again. The one thing he did anticipate was the hitch in his heart. No matter what she looked like, he loved Elaine Webster. And before he left her house today, she would know it.

Della made it sound like Elaine was about to jump off a bridge or something. But Louis recognized grief when he saw it. With her shoulders bent and a linen handkerchief twisted in her hands, Elaine just stood there looking pitiful.

Since she hadn't taken the roses, Louis placed them on a

chair in the foyer and closed the front door. Then he folded his arms around her.

"I know it's your anniversary."

For a long time, she just stood there.

"Today would have been thirty-five years," she said in a trembly voice.

Then the real tears came. Louis rocked her and cooed comforting words. Elaine's shoulders shook and she snuffled on choked tears.

"It's okay. I know. I understand," Louis told her.

Eventually, Elaine's tears dried up. She wiped her eyes and apologized.

"I messed up your shirt."

"I'll never wash it again."

A smile curved her mouth.

"That's what I like to see," he said. He pressed a gentle kiss to her lips.

"I must look awful."

"You're beautiful."

"You're a lousy liar," she said.

"I love you."

Elaine lifted wide eyes to his. "I beg your pardon."

Louis slipped a hand around her waist. "I love you, Elaine Webster. I've missed you something terrible."

"But what about Rosie? What about Raymond?"

"I'm sure they've met each other by now."

Stricken, Elaine's hurt gaze lowered.

Louis sighed. "I'm sorry. I didn't mean to make light of your feelings." He reached for her and turned her chin up. "But they are both gone now. What we have is real, it's right now."

"I know," she said quietly. "That doesn't make the pain any less."

Elaine picked up the flowers he'd placed on the chair. The strong, sweet smell of Medallion roses greeted her. The color of the exquisite apricot blooms reminded her of juicy nectarines.

"These are beautiful. From your garden?"

Louis nodded.

Elaine sniffed and wiped her nose with the hankie. Then she glanced in the mirror above the chair.

"Oh, Lord."

She dropped the roses, clutched the housedress to her and mumbled, "Excuse me," as she dashed upstairs.

Louis chuckled as he watched her flight. He gathered the flowers and went to the kitchen in search of a vase.

Fifteen minutes later, Elaine emerged looking cool and confident again. She'd brushed her hair up and back in a quick, easy style. A pair of hunter green slacks and a scoop-neck blouse were a marked improvement over the rumpled housedress. Her makeup, while flawless, couldn't quite conceal the shadows under her eyes. She'd taken an extra moment to spritz on an earthy perfume, a fact that didn't escape Louis.

He'd made a pot of coffee and now poured for them.

"You're comfortable in my kitchen."

Louis answered with a smile.

"I'm sorry," she said.

"No apology is necessary."

"The roses really are beautiful."

"I'm glad you like them."

Elaine twisted the gold band and diamond on her right hand. The nervous gesture didn't escape Louis. Neither did the fact that she'd finally taken her wedding rings off her left ring finger.

"About what you said," she began, then paused.

"Would you like coffee in here or the dining room?" he asked.

Elaine glanced around as if she were a stranger in her own house. "In there."

Louis reached for a tray and placed the two cups and saucers on it. Elaine lifted the top of a clear glass cake plate and cut two slices of coconut cake. With coffee, cake, and forks, they settled at Elaine's dining room table, Louis at the head chair and Elaine sitting next to him.

"I meant what I said, Elaine. I've come to care for you a great deal. I know this probably isn't the best day to declare myself, but you need to know how I feel." He paused, swallowed, and then looked her in the eyes. "And I need to know how you feel about Mitchell Forbes."

"Oh, Louis. Mitchell means nothing to me. He's just been trying to use me to get back at you. I figured that out pretty fast. What I said out on the water that night, I said all of that out of anger and frustration. I went to his shop the other day to tell him to stop dropping in at Rosie's and to stop trying to see me."

"Need a protective order? I have some friends . . ."

She smiled and shook her head. "No. He got the idea."

"So did I," Louis said. "Even if I was a little late figuring it out. I'm sorry I upset you on the boat. I wasn't deliberately ignoring you or comparing you to Rosie."

Elaine's smile was trembly. "I know."

"Will you forgive me?"

Elaine nodded, but kept her hands primly folded in her lap. "Only if you'll forgive me. I'm the one who flew off the handle. After Raymond died, I never thought I'd fall in love again. I never thought anyone would be interested. I sure wasn't. The very idea of loving someone else as much as I loved him seemed repulsive."

She glanced at him. "Then you came along."

Louis grinned. "Oh, yeah?"

Elaine's schoolgirl giggle brought a smile to his face.

"And after I came along?" he prompted.

*This is it*, Elaine thought. She'd spent the last few weeks moping about Raymond leaving her and Louis frustrating her. What she said next would define her future, their future.

Elaine took her time answering, so long that Louis began to worry. She couldn't possibly be forming a polite rejection. Could she?

He watched her swallow and glance over at him.

"Louis, I . . ." She paused.

He sighed, and his shoulders slumped. He put down his cup and pushed away his chair, and rose. "I understand Elaine. It's still too early for you."

Her hand quickly covered his and stayed his movement.

"No, Louis. You don't understand. Sit down and please, hear me out."

His eyes met hers.

Slowly, he took his seat again. Elaine released his hand only when she felt assured he wouldn't bolt.

"I realized pretty quickly that I was being silly. I wouldn't want you ever to forget your time with Rosie, just like I'll always cherish and remember Raymond. He had his faults, but he was a good man."

"And?"

Elaine swallowed. This was the hard part. Walking way out on the ledge and letting go of the security of familiarity frightened her. But her course was set.

"And he's gone. I'm not quite sure when it happened, but I looked up one day and realized I'd fallen in love with you."

Louis let loose a tremulous sigh of relief. Then he grabbed her hands and kissed them.

"You just made me a very happy man."

He hopped up and grabbed Elaine. Her squeal of alarm turned into a moan when his lips pressed against hers, then gently covered her mouth.

Before it turned into something more, Louis broke off the kiss and hugged Elaine close.

"Elaine Webster, I want you to hear me out. I don't want any confusion on this."

She leaned back. "On what?"

He let her go just enough to put space between their bodies, but his hands still curved at her sides.

"Yes, I loved Rosie. We had twenty-two years together, God rest her soul. I loved Rosie just like you loved Raymond. But there's no ghost on my boat or in my heart making me feel like this."

"Like what?"

He took her hand and placed it over his heart. "Do you feel that?"

Lifting her brown eyes to his, she nodded.

"That's my heart racing a mile a minute for you."

"I don't know what to say."

"Say you love me."

"I love you, Louis Sweet."

"Say, 'Kiss me, Sweet.' "

Elaine smiled even as she lifted her hand to caress his mouth.

"Kiss me, Sweet."

"I thought you'd never ask."

# Epilogue

The wedding took place two months later. The scent of rose petals filled the church chapel where Elaine and Louis vowed to love and honor each other. Gazing into each other's eyes, they recognized friendship and more, the factors that would enrich their lives together.

The wedding night took place aboard *La Dolce Vita*. Any trepidation they felt about being intimate for the first time vanished under a starry sky. They sipped champagne and danced to soft music.

In Louis's arms, Elaine was introduced to the passion of sweet and tender lovemaking. And Louis discovered the ultimate and lasting turn-on was being in love with the woman he called his own.

# Just Like That

## Donna Hill

# This Isn't Funny

"What!" Chauncie shot up from the edge of her mother's bed as if she'd been an opened can of shaken soda. "You can't be serious."

"Oh, I'm very serious," her mother, Della, said, moving with practiced grace around her bedroom, as she took item after expensive item from her closet and deposited them neatly in her Louis Vuitton suitcases.

Chauncie's light brown eyes, the color of pure honey some folks said, followed her mother's movements in disbelief. Okay, her mother was obviously going through the change or some other midlife crisis thing. What other explanation could there be? Nobody up and leaves their business, just like that, with no warning, no nothing. Her mother couldn't have thought this through. Even though she had to admit Della had mentioned it several weeks earlier, she hadn't taken her mother seriously. Or maybe she just didn't want to.

"Ma, for heaven's sake," she said in her what-is-wrong-with-you? voice. "Would you just tell me how in the world the shop is supposed to function with you gone?"

Della spun around to face her daughter, her hands planted firmly on her hips. Della's normally wide, expressive eyes squinted—the first sign before she let loose with one of the tirades for which she was famous. Inwardly Chauncie cringed, bracing herself.

"You've been my 'alleged' assistant manager for more than a year, Chauncie Frazier. I—and the whole shop—car-

ried you while you *pursued* your craft as an actress,'' she said
with plenty of theatrical sarcasm—or so Chauncie thought.
''Well, honey, this is your first big break; *act* like a manager.
I've dedicated more than ten years of my life to running Rosie's Curl and Weave, God rest her soul.'' She made a quick
sign of the cross. ''And thirty years to you. It's my time.''

''But, ma—''

''Don't 'but, ma,' me, Chauncie.'' She held up a slender,
soft-as-butter hand, a hand that Chauncie wished would just
stroke her cheek like it had done for years and make the
twirling sensation in her stomach go away. '' 'Cause I know
you're gonna try to give me a million reasons why you can't
do it,'' Della went on. ''I don't want to hear it. For once
you're going to do something for someone else for a change.''
She zipped her bags and snatched up both from the bed. ''I'll
be back in six weeks.'' She started walking toward the door.

''Six weeks!'' Chauncie practically ran behind her.

''Maybe longer.'' Della opened the door, then turned and
stared at her daughter's panic-stricken face. She wanted to do
what she'd always done. Take Chauncie in her arms and tell
her she'd fix it. Or give her the money she needed to cover
her rent or her bills because she'd overspent her paycheck.
She had even made up excuses to her staff as to why Chauncie
didn't show up for work on time, or sometimes not at all. And
if she stood there a moment longer, looking into those eyes
that always had the power to twist her heartstrings, she would.
So she didn't. ''My cab is waiting.'' She kissed her daughter's
cheek. ''You can do this, Chauncie. And you'll have help.
The staff knows what to do.''

''The staff!'' she wailed. ''They can't stand me.''

''Deal with it, Chauncie.'' She smiled tightly, turned, and
shut the door behind her.

Chauncie suddenly had the wild impulse to pull the door
open, run screaming and wailing down the hallway, grab the
hem of her mother's Versace dress, and beg her not to leave,
like in *Gone With the Wind* or something. She knew she could
turn on the tears at the drop of a hat. And Della would be so
overcome with guilt at having done such an awful thing to

her one and only child that she'd give up this crazy notion and take herself right on over to Rosie's first thing Tuesday morning. But she couldn't seem to move, even as she envisioned herself performing in her greatest role to date, the distraught and desperate daughter.

Instead she stood in front of the closed door, staring at it for a good five minutes as if by sheer will she could turn her mother around and make her walk back through the door.

Nothing happening.

Shaking herself out of her malaise, she looked around, spotted her money-green linen jacket and the spare set of keys to her mother's house, took both, and walked out.

It was only Sunday morning, she reasoned, taking each step down the mahogany staircase as if she were in a funeral march. Della could have an attack of good sense any minute now and come home.

She opened one of the double wood-and-beveled-glass doors leading to the stoop, then locked it behind her. She stood on the top step, the grip of the early July heat—more potent than three quick drinks of rum and Coke—wrapped around her with no intention of letting go. She slid her shades onto the bridge of her short, sharp nose, giving her body a minute to adjust to the up-close-and-personal touch of the sun. She looked up and down the tree-lined block, at the stately brownstones that had been meticulously restored to their original glory.

There was a time no one wanted to live in this part of Harlem, New York, she mused, so all the black families were able to buy these homes at a steal. Now this once-forgotten neighborhood was the hub of the city. The brownstones on Shriver's Row could easily sell for a quarter of a million dollars each. If her mother would just sell the house, she wouldn't have to work at Rosie's with those gossip-spreading employees of hers and *she* wouldn't be in this predicament.

Slowly she walked down the limestone steps and got behind the wheel of her leased Lexus. How in the world was she going to run the shop? Those evil wenches in the shop hated her inside out. She knew they were just jealous. Jealous of

her looks, jealous of her clothes, jealous of the close relationship she had with her mother, the kind she knew they wished
they had with their own children. Della gave her everything
she wanted, and she knew they resented the coddling and
exceptions her mother made for her.

Why wouldn't her stomach stop spinning? Damn, she
wished she'd been paying more attention to what her mother
had been trying to teach her this past year. What in the world
was she going to do?

The weekend was too damn short, Chauncie fumed. She
hadn't even had a chance to get her program together and
Tuesday morning was already cresting over the Manhattan
skyline, streaking orange and gold along the panes of her windows.

That old, unwanted, sinking sensation gained momentum
in her stomach like the rush of wind that builds seconds before
the storm hits, pummeling with pellets of rain.

She rolled over in bed and curled on her side. She knew
what her rain was going to be—those fast-talking, hair-
pressing-weaving-curling sisters at Rosie's whose wagging
tongues were sharper than their hair-cutting shears. Yeah, they
would pummel her with their catty remarks, and slice-you-up
glances from the corners of their eyes and no umbrella in the
world would protect her from the downpour.

She groaned at the prospect and forced herself out of bed,
her bare feet slapping across the wood floors in an uneven
rhythm, just the way she felt—out of step.

Chauncie peered at her reflection in the bathroom mirror.
She was definitely good-looking. No two ways about it.
Everyone always said she took her looks from her mother,
who could have been a television double for Diahann Carroll.
The resemblance was startling. She remembered growing up
and walking along the streets of Harlem with her mother and
their constantly being stopped because people thought her
mother was the famous actress.

She recalled the first time Della had taken her to the renowned Apollo Theatre on 125th Street for an amateur night

performance, and her mother had been besieged by theater-goers demanding an autograph.

Well, Ms. Della Frazier-slash-Diahann Carroll had played it to the max, and had even signed a few autographs. The memory made her smile. Yeah, her mother was ''somethin' else.''

She blinked and her reflection boldly stared back at her. She might look like her mother, maybe even act like her on the surface. But she knew underneath she didn't have what Della had: determination and focus—two major qualities that she was sorely lacking.

And right about now, she was more pissed off at her mother than she'd ever been in her natural-born life!

Chauncie was parked out in front of Rosie's nearly an hour before the shop was scheduled to open at ten. She wanted to get out, just march right on in there and act like she knew what the deal was. Truth was she didn't have a clue. And she sure couldn't ask any of *them* to help her. They'd love to see her fall on her face anyway. How could her mother have done this to her? she asked herself for the nth time.

She bit down on her bottom lip and stared at the closed gates of the shop. Folks were already walking up and down the avenue, heading to wherever they were going, and she was just sitting in her car like a bump on a log. Maybe she could get Reggie to help her sort things out. He had a flamboyant personality and never held his tongue, but he'd always treated her nice. Yeah, that's what she'd do. First chance she got, she'd pull him aside and find out what was what.

Taking a breath, she grabbed her purse from the passenger seat, turned off the CD player, and stepped out. A passing car nearly rammed into the back of the one ahead of it, coming to a screeching halt because the driver was staring so hard at Chauncie, who was decked to the nines in a form-fitting, lemon yellow linen and rayon jacket and matching micro-miniskirt. Her shoulder-length auburn hair tumbled to her shoulders in a cascade of waves, which she absently flipped with a toss of her head. If she'd learned nothing else in the years that Della had managed Rosie's it was how to hook up her hair.

She was so used to all the horn-blowing, hey-baby-lemme-walk-with-you-talk-with-yous, that she didn't even pay the brief commotion any attention. She clicked on the car alarm, waited for the telltale beep, and then, rounding the car, she approached the locked shop, dug in her purse, and pulled out the keys. Della had left her a slip of paper with the alarm code on it. "You have about thirty seconds to deactivate the alarm once the gate is opened," she'd warned. "Don't get it done in time, all hell will break loose."

Her heart thumped as she twisted the key in the lock and pushed open the gates. *Ten seconds.* She unlocked the door to the shop and closed it behind her as she'd seen her mother do, and quickly crossed the room behind the reception desk to the alarm box. The red light was flashing. She dug in her purse again for her wallet, where she'd stuck the paper with the code. She guesstimated that she had about fifteen seconds to deactivate the alarm. She pulled open her wallet and the slip of paper floated to the floor. When she bent to retrieve it, the contents of her purse spilled, right on top of the paper. *Five seconds.*

Frantic, and with her heart really pumping now, she scrambled through the debris of her emptied purse for the number. Just as she picked it up and stood, the blaring sound of the alarm bounced off the high-gloss walls, reverberated up, down, and in between the stylists' chairs, twisted around the blow-dryers, zipped up to the high-arching ceiling, then settled right in the center of her chest. The classy decor of Rosie's seemed to turn into a glaring, blaring ball of red.

"Damn!"

She looked around, ready for the sirens of the police to add to the melee. Quickly, she punched in the numbers, hoping to still the wailing of the alarm. She nearly jumped out of her skin when Ruthie, the head operator, pushed through the door, raced around the desk, nearly pushing her out of the way in the process, and pressed the green light on the alarm box.

Without a word she turned to the phone on the desk and punched in seven numbers.

"Yes. This is Ruthie, over at Rosie's Curl and Weave. Yeah, I know, sugah. Wasn't quick enough this morning. You know how Tuesdays can be sometimes. Yeah. Everything's fine. No need to send the troops. Yes. Hot to trot," she added, giving the alarm company rep the password. "Thanks a lot, hon." She hung up the phone and turned to Chauncie. She blew out a disgusted breath and sashayed across the room to her booth, depositing her big, black, worn, and overflowing pocketbook—you couldn't call it a purse, Chauncie thought— into the drawer beneath her table. Ruthie slipped on a black smock over her stark white blouse and black slacks, the *de rigueur* uniform for the shop, and secured the belt as tight as it would go around her waist. She peered into the mirror, checked her bloodred lipstick and patted her lacquered French roll. Then turned to Chauncie.

"Your mama catch her flight okay?"

"Yes," Chauncie mumbled, then straightened her shoulders. "Thanks."

Ruthie waved her hand. "Ain't nothing. Happened to me more times than I can count. Just got to be more careful. They charge us if they have to come over here." She started organizing her supplies on the counter and began humming to herself. "Need to get these lights and air turned on," she added off-handedly, not looking at Chauncie.

"Oh, right." Chauncie took a breath and walked across the pink-and-blue marble floors to the back of the shop where the electrical closet was, her heels clicking all along the way. Ruthie shook her head. Won't last long in those shoes, she thought, chuckling.

Chauncie opened the gray metal box and stared at the rows and rows of switches, trying to remember what she'd seen her mother do at least a million times.

"Just flip everything from one through thirty-six to the right," Ruthie shouted.

Chauncie did as she was instructed and immediately heard the hum of the air conditioner kick on. The shop was bathed in a soft, iridescent light. Jazz music from the hidden speakers in the ceiling drifted through the trendy interior.

Closing the box, she walked back into the center of the shop. Ruthie was still humming. The rest of the crew had yet to arrive. *What to do next?* What would Della do?

First thing Della would do was *act* like she knew what she was doing even if she didn't. Well, her mother had spent enough money on her for acting lessons, so how much "motivation" would it take for her to *act* like she knew the deal? How hard could it be?

She took a breath and strutted, with what she thought was purpose, across the room and eased behind the black lacquer reception desk, assuming an air of superiority.

Ruthie watched the one-woman parade from the corner of her eye and bit back a smile. She just kept humming.

"Is Reggie coming in today?" Chauncie asked, taking a seat on the high-back black leather chair. She crossed her legs.

Ruthie swiveled her chair in Chauncie's direction, extending her arm, a long, manicured nail pointing toward the desk. "Schedules and appointments are in the desk, bottom left-hand drawer." She turned back around and began to slowly file her nails, periodically holding her long, slender hands out in front of her for examination.

"Thanks," she mumbled again, and realized with growing ire that "thanks" was going to be the key word in her vocabulary around Rosie's. She retrieved the books from the drawer and flipped the page to the current date. Running her finger down the list of operators who were scheduled for the week, she exhaled a silent sigh of relief when she saw Reggie's name. Unfortunately, he wasn't due in the shop until one o'clock. She could certainly wing it until then.

She scanned the list again. Jewel, the weave-tress; Melody, the precision-cut queen; and Blaize, who specialized in African braiding, were all scheduled to arrive at ten, and their day was full from the moment they walked in the door. Then there was Tricia, the masseuse, and Holly the manicurist. They would arrive at noon. But, of course, Reggie had more customers than all the others and was usually in the shop well into the evening. Folks just loved his stories and his flamboyant personality, not to mention the fashion statement he made each time he strutted through the door.

But all in all, Rosie's was as classy as they come. The decor was top-notch, the operators had talent down to the bone, and customers came from all over the city to be coifed, rubbed, wined, and dined. And they never complained about the wait, especially when Della descended among them, flitting from one to the other like an uptown social butterfly—a talent which had garnered her a legion of devoted fans—dropping a compliment here, a soft reprimand there, entertaining, smiling, accommodating. If Chauncie didn't know better, she'd think that half the customers came to Rosie's just to watch Della Frazier do her thing. She'd seen more stars walk through the doors of Rosie's to get their hair done, or enjoy a quick massage while they were in town, than she'd ever seen during her stream of acting auditions. And they all loved Della.

She closed the books and sighed. How was she going to step into her mother's shoes for six weeks and deal with the deluge of customers who frequented Rosie's, not to mention the staff, who could be as irascible as irritated two-year-olds deprived of a nap? *Artistes!* Her mother would always remind her, with a French accent. "You must pamper them to bring out their best."

She checked her watch and sighed. *Nine-forty.* She felt like she'd been there for hours already. The soft chime over the door made her look up as Jewel and Melody sauntered in, followed by Blaize. All three turned "oh-you're-here" looks in her direction.

She forced herself to smile. "Good morning."

"Did Della leave?" Blaize practically demanded, eyebrows squeezing together as if being pulled by a string.

Chauncie sat up straighter in the chair. "Yes, on a long-overdue vacation. I'll be running the shop until she gets back," she said with what she thought was the perfect combination of authority and sympathy.

Well, one would have thought she had told them to get out and not come back.

Blaize started shaking her head and rolling her neck. "Awww, hell no. You!"

"I don't believe this mess," Melody said, stomping across the room to her booth. She threw her bag in the chair and turned mean, squinted eyes on Chauncie. "You lyin', right? You don't know nothin' 'bout nothin'."

"All I have to say is don't mess with my check," Jewel threw in with a hard roll of her eyes.

"How come Della didn't say anything to us about leaving *you* in charge?" Melody added, suspicion making her already deep voice drop to a new low.

"Now y'all know Chauncie's been learning about managing the shop," Ruthie cut in.

Chauncie could have hugged her. Instead she gave her a wan smile, which Ruthie seemed to ignore.

A round of "humphs" and "yeah, rights" bounced from one woman to the next, as they went to their individual stations.

Chauncie tried to catch what they were mumbling as they slapped the tools of their trade on tabletops, but she couldn't.

Then, quick as you please, they seemed to have completely forgotten she was there as they chatted among themselves, sharing stories of their weekends and anecdotes about their customers.

Chauncie sighed, feeling totally out of place. She'd never developed a rapport with these women. She'd never believed she had anything in common with them. So she couldn't very well add any little tidbit to the chatter.

She came from behind the desk and walked over to the refreshment table. At some point—she didn't know when—Ruthie must have turned on the coffee and set out the cups and condiments. Chauncie opened the fridge, took out the half gallon of orange juice, and poured herself a cup, just at the moment the delivery boy from the bakery up the street brought in the daily carton of bagels and Danish.

Now this was something she could handle. She straightened her jacket and click-clicked across the floor.

"Hey, Jimmy," the women chorused.

"What ya got good?" Blaize asked, giving him a wink.

He seemed to turn a dozen shades of red beneath his barely tanned peaches-and-cream complexion at Blaize's boldness.

"Same old thing, Ms. Blaize," he mumbled, setting the carton on the front desk.

"How much do I owe you?" Chauncie asked in her most I'm-in-charge voice.

Jimmy blinked as if he were trying to get her into focus, or as if by blinking he could better make out what she'd just asked.

" 'Scuse me, Ms. Chauncie?"

The entire room grew quiet as a graveyard on a rainy day. Even the music seemed to have slipped to the pause mode.

Chauncie's gaze quickly darted around the room, seeing the women fighting to hide their smirks.

"How much?" she asked in a voice barely above a whisper.

"Everything's paid for. Ms. Della takes care of that first of the month like clockwork."

Chauncie heard the snickers pelting her in the back, trying to make her bend. She swallowed, tossed her hair, and put on her camera close-up smile. "You're right. I completely forgot. Thanks, Jimmy."

"No problem. See you ladies tomorrow morning," he said in his still–straight-off-the-bus Southern drawl.

Chauncie watched him walk out and felt the burn of embarrassed tears sear her eyes. "I'll be back," she said to no one in particular, not that anyone would care, she realized. She took her purse from beneath the desk and walked out, refusing—unable—to meet the eyes of the women who reveled in her angst.

"Where she think she's going?" Blaize asked.

"I sure as hell ain't answering no phones. That's the least she could do, 'til Annie gets in," fumed Jewel.

"Got that right," Melody added.

"Y'all just need to shut up. We'll take turns till she gets back," Ruthie said with authority. "If she comes back," she mumbled under her breath.

Chauncie stepped into the blazing morning sunshine, moving aside as the first stream of customers began to filter in. She should be inside greeting the customers, making conversation and seeing to their needs like her mother was famous for. But she couldn't. Couldn't stand another catastrophe today, or at least right now. She'd probably make a mess of that, too.

She started walking down 125th Street, sidestepping strollers, joggers, street vendors, and local residents. Oh God, how was she going to get through the next six weeks if she couldn't do something as simple as deactivate the alarm or turn on the lights without instruction? And who knew what other responsibilities lay in the cut for her, ready to strike. And those women! Nothing would make them happier than to see her fall on her face. *Ma! How could you do this to me?* she screamed in her head.

The tempting scents of brewing coffee, hash browns, and grilled bacon wafted out of the doorway right under her nose. She slowed her pace and stopped, looking up at the faded letters over the open door. *Briffins.* Her stomach gave a little shout and she realized she hadn't eaten. She hadn't been inside the local coffee shop-slash-restaurant in ages. But if memory served her, Briffins made the best home fries and eggs this side of the Harlem River. Maybe some food was just what she needed. At least she'd be able to kill some time and try to think.

She walked through the door. The place was as busy as usual—nearly every booth was occupied and there were no vacancies at the counter. She started to leave when she spotted a lone seat in the back.

Ignoring the usual barrage of "Hey, sweet thang" and "Hmmm, baby," she headed for the empty seat, passing a noisy bunch of what looked like construction workers who took up two booths.

Now she remembered why she'd stopped coming here. The

clientele. She picked up the menu and pretended to read it, in the hope that the Bawdy Bunch would realize they were being ignored.

"Whaddya havin', hon?"

Chauncie looked up from the menu into the face of a waitress who appeared bored witless. She hadn't known it was truly possible to look completely expressionless. She'd have to practice that look. Never know when it would come in handy.

The waitress popped her gum and blew out a Doublemint breath. "If you're not ready I can come back."

"No. I'm ready. I'll have the breakfast special."

"That with home fries or grits?"

"Home fries."

"Something to drink?"

"Orange juice, please."

The waitress jotted it down on her frayed, green pad and snatched up the menu like she thought Chauncie might run off with it.

Yes. It was all coming back to her now, she mused. Great food, but no class. She pursed her lips as she watched Attila the Hun walk off.

She was just about to begin studying the red-and-white design on her placemat or start counting the packs of sugar in the little clear plastic holder, when her gaze ran smack into Mr. Should-Be-on-the-Cover-of-Somebody's Magazine.

Her heart did a quick giddyup until she pulled on the reins with a sharp inhale. The brother was f-i-n-e. He reminded her of that actor Ving Rhames from the movie *Rosewood*. A brother that didn't take no mess and had a body that could give you grief.

He had on a white T-shirt that looked liked its sole purpose in being made was to define the muscles in this man's chest. He was the kind of brown that a penny turned when it wasn't quite shiny anymore, but still had that deep russet undertone. But it was mostly his eyes. Those light brown Michael Jordan eyes that looked right at you, then sank a little deeper.

She almost licked her lips.

• • •

Drew sipped the last of his coffee, casually eyeing the woman in yellow over the rim. He'd always liked yellow, but he hadn't run across many women who looked as good in it as she did. And that hair just set it off.

He could tell she had a lot going on. Probably had money, a flashy car, and a man. He just knew by looking at her that she'd never go for a guy like him, someone who got his hands dirty for a living—when he *could* make a living, that is. He knew her type, and wondered why she was slumming in this neck of the woods.

Drew finished his coffee and looked away. "Come on, fellas. We have a full day ahead of us."

There were a few mumbled comments as the men pulled their wallets from dingy denim pockets and slapped bills on the table like a hand of spades.

One by one they filed out. Drew was the last to leave. He gave her one last look and walked out.

When Chauncie picked up her glass of orange juice, her hand was shaking. She took a breath and set the glass down on the table, the contents sloshing over the top. That man had really unnerved her the way he was looking at her as if she were sitting there in her birthday suit. Or maybe she was just imagining him looking at her in her birthday suit. A shiver scurried up her spine.

She shook her head. *Get it together, girl.* Must be the stress. She reached for her glass again as the waitress appeared with her food. But all of a sudden she didn't feel hungry and she was sure she couldn't keep anything down with her stomach doing a serious tap dance.

She picked over her breakfast, finally pushing the half-eaten food aside, then got up and paid her bill at the counter. When she walked back out into the light of day, she had a good mind to just keep going. They'd probably never miss her at the shop anyway. But "better-sense-than-that" stepped in and she reluctantly headed back to Rosie's.

By the time she returned, the shop was jumping. There

were already about ten customers in the shop in various stages of beautification. Music was playing; the operators were chatting with their customers; coffee, tea, juice, and bagels were flowing; and amidst it all she heard the underlying rumble of male voices and distant hammering.

No one seemed to notice her return, or if they did, they paid her no attention.

The hammering grew louder. She frowned. The noise was coming from the back of the shop. Just as she was about to head in the direction of the offending ruckus, the door opened behind her and in strolled two grungy, but Adonis-like men carrying toolboxes and what looked like wood beams.

" 'Scuse me, Ms."

Instinct made her step aside to avoid getting whacked in the head, but then a swift dose of "what do you think you're doing?" kicked in.

"No. You excuse me. Where are you going and what are you doing?"

The two men looked from one to the other, and shrugged.

"Our job, Ms. Got any questions, you should take it up with the boss."

"The boss! I am the boss."

"Hey, didn't I see you in the coffee shop up the street?" one of the men asked.

"I really wouldn't know. And I'm asking the questions," she added, her voice and hip-holding stance geared for a confrontation.

"No disrespect, Ms., but if you're the boss, then you should know why we're here," said the second man, giving her a long look.

"Where's your supervisor . . . boss . . . whoever?" she demanded.

"You mean foreman? That would be me."

The voice sounded like distant thunder, low and rumbling. Chauncie turned and would have fallen flat on her face when she looked into those honey-brown eyes—if she hadn't taken ten years of ballet lessons. Her heart made a mad dash up to her throat and kept pounding, making it hard for her to talk.

She swallowed and jutted her chin, hoping she appeared more confident than she felt.

"You want to tell me what's going on?" she asked, trying to sound forceful, but thinking her voice sounded more like an invitation than a threat.

Her eyes locked in on his mouth and she watched the corner of it curl slightly upward as if he thought she was amusing. Her temper rose. She hated it when people didn't take her seriously. And he obviously didn't.

He stepped closer and she had the urge to move back to keep from having to look up at him, but she couldn't seem to move.

Drew kept his gaze locked on the woman in yellow. He couldn't believe how twisted fate could be. But he still wasn't sure what was going on and where she fit into the picture. One thing he *was* sure of, though, she was even more gorgeous close up. That wasn't good.

"Cliff, Jake, go on and take those beams in the back," he instructed, tipping his head in the direction of all the noise. "I'll take care of this."

"Sure thing, boss." They moved toward the back, and Chauncie distinctly heard the appreciative murmurs from the female audience.

"Now, Ms . . ." His right eyebrow arched as he folded his arms across his chest and stood with his legs apart.

"Frazier," she supplied. "Chauncie Frazier. And you are . . . ?"

"Drew Lennox." He grinned, and that smooth russet-brown cheek dimpled. "Della's daughter?"

"That's right and I'm taking over for her while she's away." She planted her hand on her hip, knowing that the operators were watching the exchange from their mirrors.

Then those damned eyes rolled up and down her body as if she were up for auction, and she almost forgot what they were supposed to be talking about.

"Guess Della didn't tell you about the construction."

*Was he snickering?* How would Angela Bassett handle this?

When he wasn't looking, she'd set his stuff on fire, that's what she'd do.

"No, she didn't. So you will," she said with authority. "We'll talk in the back. I want to see for myself what you're doing."

Drew bit back a smile, lowered his head, and said, "After you."

She brushed by him, half expecting to catch a whiff of musk, but instead was pleasantly greeted by the scent of aftershave and soap and water. She made a mental note.

Strutting to the back of the store, she took inventory of the sidelong glances she received from the employees. Their expressions were a bit too amused for her tastes. She had the distinct feeling that they knew exactly what was going on, but no one would say a word.

When she reached the back room, all of the hammering ceased. A half dozen pairs of eyes landed on her.

"This is the *other* Ms. Frazier," Drew said by way of introduction.

A round of deep hellos and good mornings danced around the room.

"Good morning," she returned, trying to make heads or tails of what was going on. She turned toward Drew, waiting for an explanation.

"Your mother contracted with me to add an addition to the shop."

Chauncie frowned. Not once had Della said a word to her. Or maybe she had, and as usual, Chauncie wasn't paying attention. She took a breath. "How long is it going to take?"

"At least a month."

"So my clients have to be subjected to the noise and dust for a month?"

"Looks that way."

She tried to think. There had to be another way. Once again she asked herself what was on her mother's mind.

"We'll have to work out some arrangements that suit all of our needs," Chauncie said.

"And what might that be?" Drew asked with a bit too

much sarcasm, Chauncie thought. She didn't like his attitude, no matter how good he looked.

"Do what you need to do today. I'll discuss it with you before you leave." She turned on her heel and walked out.

Drew frowned. He wanted to grab her sophisticated little neck and squeeze it. She'd tried to embarrass him in front of his men, something he wouldn't tolerate. He ran a tight ship, and didn't give more than an inch. Some of his crew thought he was a real S.O.B. and he knew it, but he got the job done, on time and on budget. And he'd be damned if he let some prima donna with an attitude ruin his track record.

"Don't just stand there gaping, get to work!" he bellowed. "Get those beams up against that far wall. Jake, get me the blueprints." He clenched his jaw, anger bubbling through his veins. Yes, Ms. Chauncie Frazier had put him in a real foul mood.

"Get everything straight, Chauncie?" Blaize asked with a smirk.

Chauncie cut her eyes in Blaize's direction. "As a matter of fact, I did. And there may be a few more things I'll have to straighten out before it's all over." She gave Blaize a cool stare and could have sworn she saw big, bad Blaize cringe.

Ruthie watched the exchange, quietly pleased.

Annie, the part-time receptionist, finally arrived at noon instead of eleven and hadn't bothered to call to say she'd be late. Chauncie had been forced to take calls, setting up and canceling appointments, until Annie-come-lately finally showed up. Chauncie was furious and she had a raging headache. For a heartbeat she understood the frustration her mother must have felt when she strolled in when she was good and ready without explanation.

"Annie, as soon as you get settled, I want to talk with you," Chauncie said, doing an Oscar-caliber job of keeping her voice saccharine sweet, as she slid from behind the receptionist's desk.

Annie gave Chauncie a pinched look. "About what?" she

asked, placing her bag beneath the desk and putting on a black smock.

"We'll discuss it later."

"Where's Della?" she wanted to know, as if Della's appearance would set Chauncie straight.

"She's not here, as I'm sure you already know, and won't be for the next six weeks. I'll be running the shop."

Annie's eyes widened. She'd completely forgotten.

Chauncie smiled and headed toward her mother's office. Well, that was two discussions she had to have before the day was over. Now all she had to figure out was what she was going to say.

# The Day That Never Ends

Chauncie entered her mother's small but neat office, took a seat behind the desk, and covered her face with her hands. Her entire body was vibrating. How was she going to manage for the next six weeks? It was impossible. She felt like Caesar moments before being stabbed by Brutus—everyone was turning on her, not to mention Mr. Universe and his crew. She couldn't even remember her name when he was looking at her with those eyes. *And that body!* However, she was going to have to figure something out so that they could all work together and not run the customers out of the shop in the process. "You can do this, Chauncie," she heard her mother say. And she could. She would.

She raised her head and looked around. Her mother had to keep notes and records around somewhere: timesheets, inventory. She pushed away from the desk and walked over to the file cabinet and tugged. Locked.

*Figures.*

She went back to the desk and hunted around for a key. Then she remembered that Della kept the key taped to the bottom of the chair. She reached beneath the chair and pulled the key free. She smiled. Her first victory for the day.

Once the drawers were unlocked, she began going through them. There were files of personnel records, vendor records, payroll, ADT information, licenses, and a dozen others. She found the file for Lennox Construction, Inc. and pulled it out. Taking it back to the desk, she sat down and flipped it open.

The first thing she saw was the contract which outlined the job to expand the back of the shop to accommodate a small cafe. The job was estimated to cost fifty thousand dollars. Della had given Drew a deposit of twenty-five thousand with the balance to be paid upon completion. The canceled check was photocopied in the file and stapled to the contract.

Chauncie blew out a breath and rifled through the balance of the papers. The rest was information from the bank about the loan Della had taken out for renovations and reference letters from former clients of Lennox Construction, Inc.

She flipped through some of the letters, all of which were glowing accolades for Drew Lennox and his crew. She shut the folder and clasped her hands beneath her chin. *Think, Chauncie. Think.*

There was one thing that Della had instilled in her since she was old enough to understand, a dictum that translated well into her fledgling acting career—appearances. With the right appearance you could make people believe anything. Rosie's always gave the appearance of being upper crust, top of the line in the way of salons, even though it was in the heart of Harlem. But the staff and her mother worked hard at it. So hard that everyone believed it. Now, with her mother gone, she had to keep up appearances. She couldn't have those gorgeous, grubby construction men traipsing in and out, tracking dust and dirt through the shop, no matter how many oohs and ahhs they generated. She had to manufacture the appearance that she was in total control of the shop and the staff or else there would be chaos. "*Act* like a manager," her mother had said.

That's exactly what Melanie Griffith had done to Harrison Ford in *Working Girl*. She had him believing she was the boss. And she did it by believing in herself and doing her homework.

Chauncie let out a long breath, feeling a bit better. Her mother had to have notes, records, something that she could go through. Maybe she'd even rent the movie on her way home and take some notes of her own.

But first things first. She needed to deal with Annie. She

**Donna Hill**

reached for the phone and punched in the two digits for the front desk.

"Rosie's Curl and Weave," Annie greeted.

"Annie, it's Chauncie. Would you come into the office please?"

"I have a customer on hold and one at the desk."

"Take care of them and come back here. Is Reggie in yet?"

"Yes."

"Let Reggie handle the front. I'd like to see you now." Chauncie clicked off without another word.

The countless conversations that Della'd had with her about lateness and absenteeism ran through her head as clear as a memorized script. Chauncie smiled. She could do this.

Moments later there was a light knock on the door.

"Come in."

Annie sauntered in, her micro-braids fanning around her heart-shaped face. Annie was stunning to look at, which was one of the main reasons Della had her up front, and overall she had an engaging personality. But business was business as her mother had told her more times than she'd wanted to hear.

Chauncie cleared her throat, and tried to ignore the banging and hammering coming from the adjoining space and the vision of hard-packed bodies doing their thing.

"Have a seat, Annie."

Annie looked uncomfortable. Her eyes kept darting around the room and she was fidgeting with her braids. At least she didn't appear to be on the defensive like the rest of the staff, Chauncie thought.

"You want to tell me why you were so late this morning?"

Annie swallowed, cast her gaze down, then looked across at Chauncie, who was forcing herself to look stern and detached like Vanessa L. Williams did in *Soul Food*, when she busted her husband. She folded her hands atop the desk.

"I . . . I had an interview this morning."

*Uh-oh.* "An interview? For another job?"

"Well . . . not exactly. It was a modeling interview."

Chauncie's brows shot up in surprise and excitement. She

knew what it felt like to be in the business and maybe have that one chance.

"Really?" she said, forgetting her real reason for calling Annie into the office. She leaned forward. "So . . . what happened?"

Annie's anxiety seemed to slip away. That drop-dead smile that greeted countless customers spread across her mouth like a ray of sunshine. "They want me to come back for a photo shoot, do some test shots."

"Get out!"

Annie grinned and bobbed her head.

"That's fabulous, Annie. Congratulations."

"Thanks."

"What agency?"

"Ford."

"Ford! *The* Ford Agency?"

"Yep."

"Well, you're on your way, girl."

"I hope so. This is something that I've wanted for so long," she confessed.

"You just have to stick with it, Annie."

"How is your acting coming?" she asked.

Chauncie shrugged. "I get bit parts here and there." *Like this one.* "I'm still hoping for my big break."

"You'll get it. Your mother talks about how good you are all the time."

Chauncie felt her heart tumble in her chest. "She does?"

"Yeah. Every chance she gets. 'Chauncie this, Chauncie that,' " she said in a playful singsong.

Chauncie wanted to beam all over. She never knew her mother thought much of her acting pursuit. She took a breath. "Anyway, how is this going to affect your job here, Annie?"

"I'm not sure. I really like it here. But . . ."

"If opportunity strikes, you'll take it," she said, finishing Annie's sentence.

Annie nodded.

"Okay. I know I'm not the best role model, but I still have a business to run in Della's absence. What I need is cooperation. So . . . let's make a deal. You let me know up front whenever you have auditions, interviews, whatever, and we'll work it out. If you're going to be late, I need to know so your spot can be covered. Fair enough?"

"Thanks, Chauncie. I really appreciate this. And . . . I'm sorry about this morning. It won't happen again."

"Good."

Annie stood up. "I'd better get back out there. You know Reggie, he'll have talked the clients half to death. And you should see what he's wearing today." She shook her braided head and slapped her thigh.

Chauncie chuckled just imagining the flamboyant Reggie.

"Thanks again, Chauncie."

"No problem. And congratulations."

Chauncie leaned back in her chair and smiled. She had handled it. Really handled it. And it felt good.

Now, if the rest of her day could just follow the same storyline.


The morning crowd had thinned out somewhat by the time she returned to the front of the shop. But that incessant banging, hacking, and drilling continued. However, no one seemed to mind. Maybe it was because Reggie was holding court—with his own shock of carrot-colored twists, wrist-to-elbow bangles, and a neon jumpsuit the same color as his hair that could stop Times Square traffic—while he colorized a client's hair an interesting shade of wine. When Reggie told a story, he put his whole body into it, with dips and head-rolling and plenty of finger-popping. He was a one-man show if she ever saw one and the clients loved him. At the moment he was regaling the shop with a tale about a nightclub he'd visited over the weekend.

She stopped in front of several clients who were under dryers to say hello. Then she checked with Blaize, Melody, Jewel, and Ruthie to remind them to take their lunch breaks, and was pleased to see that they seemed to appreciate her concern. She even got a smile out of Melody.

As she approached the front desk, she noticed something

different. She stopped and realized that the banging had halted. She turned toward the back of the shop just as Drew, followed by his crew, emerged and trooped toward the front door, dirty boots and all, making distinctive tracks on the pink-and-blue marble.

She watched the mess they were making and her temper rose with each footfall. She leaned against the reception desk, awaiting foreman Drew Lennox's approach.

"We're heading out to lunch. Be back in an hour," he said when he reached her. He made a move toward the door.

"We need to talk, Mr. Lennox." She folded her arms beneath her breasts, feeling her heart race against them when he turned those honey-brown eyes on her.

He turned completely around. "You guys go on ahead. I'll catch up with you," he commanded like an army general. "I'm listening."

"Can you come into the office?"

"You're cutting into my lunch hour, Ms. Frazier. That means extra time away from the job. Is that what you want?"

"Of course not. But this can't wait."

He looked at her for a moment and she got that fluttering feeling in her stomach again.

"Have you had lunch yet?"

She swallowed. "No."

"Then why don't we talk about whatever's on your mind over lunch?"

She wasn't sure if his question was an invitation or a threat, not with his eyes burning into her and that river-deep voice rumbling like an impending storm.

She angled her head to the side. "Preferably someplace quiet."

"Fine. Lead the way."

She turned toward Annie. "I'll be back in an hour."

Annie was staring so hard at Drew, Chauncie had to repeat herself.

"Oh, sure," Annie finally mumbled. She reached beneath the desk and handed Chauncie her purse.

"Thanks."

Chauncie and Drew stepped out into the afternoon heat. "Where to?"

Chauncie looked up at him, shielding her eyes from the sun with a cupped hand. "What do you like to eat?"

"Whatever's filling."

She cleared her throat and tried to shake off the feeling that his response wasn't an erotic suggestion, but a simple answer to a simple question. "There's a pretty good soul food restaurant about two blocks down."

He shrugged. "My time is your dollar."

She chose to ignore his sarcasm and headed off in the direction of the restaurant. Walking down 125th Street, she thought about what an incongruous pair they must be; she with her designer suit and Revlon hair, and he with grit and grime covering every exposed inch of that incredible body. She wondered what he'd look like all cleaned up and in a suit and tie. How would he behave in the type of company she kept? Was he as vulgar and crude as other construction men she'd run across as they perched outside of construction sites catcalling every woman who walked by?

Drew strolled along, absorbed in his own train of thought. Periodically, he checked Chauncie out from the corner of his eye. She had a haughtiness about her that on most women would be annoying, but on her it was kind of cute because it seemed as if she were working at it, not that it was her natural personality. He got the sense that she'd been saddled with the job of running the shop, wasn't pleased about it, and was learning the ropes as she went along. Chauncie Frazier didn't appear to be the kind of woman who was cut out for working *any* kind of job. She was one to be taken care of. She was accustomed to being the center of attention, getting what she wanted. Probably always had, with her looks.

He clenched his jaw. *Another Gloria.* His two-year marriage to Miss Cover Girl had been the worst two years of his life. Nothing he ever did pleased her. All Gloria did was want ... more and more. He thought he'd hit pay dirt when the beautiful Gloria Neal said yes to being his wife, a high-school-educated laborer, trying to build a business. He couldn't believe his luck. But he soon learned the difference between love and lust.

So he'd turned all his anger and hurt into building his business and he ran it like a military installation. But he never asked for more from his crew than he was willing to give himself. He didn't take no mess from any of his men or they were out. Never again would he subject himself to being run over in business or in love.

"This is it," Chauncie announced, halting his thoughts.

He frowned down at her as if she were the source of his ire. Then slowly the storm clouds cleared and his thick, black brows smoothed. He reached out and opened the door, standing aside to let her pass. He caught a gentle hint of her perfume, and it settled somewhere deep inside him.

A shudder wiggled through her when she looked at him, and she wondered what she'd done to cause the dangerous glare that laser-beamed out of his eyes.

They were quickly seated and a waitress took their orders. Chauncie had to hold back comment when she heard the amount of food that Drew ordered. *Guess it would take a lot to fill that body, though.*

Drew leaned slightly forward, bracing his forearms on the table. "So, what's on your mind, Ms. Frazier?" he began without any preamble.

Chauncie blinked. "Well, it's about the traffic in the shop," she began, hesitating along the way. *Damn, this man upset her nerves.* "What I mean is, my mother, Della, has a thing about appearances and . . . it doesn't look good to have dust and dirt tracked back and forth through the shop, especially when the customers are there."

"So what do you suggest? If we work before or after hours it's going to cost you twice as much."

She pressed her lips together. "I know this may sound like slave talk but, could you and your men use the back entrance, so that you won't have to come through the shop during business hours?"

The right corner of Drew's mouth curved up and then he suddenly broke out laughing, a deep, soul-stirring laugh that made his eyes crinkle and her heart flutter. "I appreciate your intro to your request," he said, slowly regaining his composure. "I don't see that as being a problem. All the property behind the shop belongs to it, correct?"

She nodded, unable to say much since she was still caught up in the magic memory of his laughter. *Get a grip, girl.*

"Then that's what we'll do. Anything else?"

"Well, actually, I was wondering, since the shop is closed on Mondays, maybe you could do the bulk of the work—the hammering and banging—on Mondays."

He half smiled. "I'll see what can be done about that. No promises."

"I understand."

"Anything else?"

"That's it for now."

He nodded, then looked around. "Nice place."

"It's been here forever," she said with a smile. "My mother used to bring me here when I was a kid."

"Live around here?"

"On Sugar Hill."

"I always thought that was just the name of the Wesley Snipes movie."

Chauncie laughed and he liked the sound. "It's quite real. Where do you live?"

"Queens. St. Albans."

"I don't go out to Queens much. It's a very confusing borough. I think whoever designed it was on drugs."

"Yeah, it takes a lot of getting used to," he agreed. "But I've lived out there all my life."

"Hmmm." She took a sip of water. She wanted to ask him a million questions: if he had a girlfriend, wife, or significant other, what he did after work. But she couldn't do that. At the very least, she was his employer and she certainly didn't want him getting any ideas. Besides, he wasn't her type. She went for the clean-cut *GQ* kind of man, one with polish and style.

"So . . . what did you do *before* you started running the

shop?'' he asked with a tad bit too much humor in his voice, she thought.

''I'm an actress,'' she said with that haughtiness he thought was kind of cute.

''Is that right? What have you been in?''

She took a sip of water. ''Nothing major. Small stuff, mostly.''

''Been at it long?''

''Sometimes I think too long.''

''Stick with it. I'm sure you'll get your break when the time is right.''

She looked at him for a moment, seeing the sincerity in his eyes, hearing it in his voice. ''Do you really think so?'' She wasn't sure why, at that moment, his opinion mattered, but it did.

''Anything worth having is worth working for, Ms. Frazier. That's the only way I built my business up. We're still struggling, but I'm a long way from where I was five years ago.''

Their food arrived at that moment, halting conversation.

''Can I get you both anything else?'' the waitress asked.

Drew looked at Chauncie, who shook her head. ''No, thanks. That's it for now,'' he said, answering for them both.

Drew had ordered the fried seafood and chicken combination with mashed potatoes, a huge salad, and a side order of chopped barbecue. Chauncie looked down, comparing it to her puny meal of grilled chicken and salad.

They ate in silence.

''How long have you been in the construction business?'' Chauncie asked after the lengthy pause.

''Since I was about sixteen. Started as a summer job.'' He jabbed a shrimp with his fork and dipped it into the bowl of tartar sauce. ''Kept it up after I graduated and went to work full-time for a crew in New Jersey.''

No mention of college, she noted. ''So when did you go into business for yourself?''

''About the time I realized I needed to call the shots for myself and not live and work on the whim of someone else.''

His voice had taken on a bitter, almost resentful tone, and

Chauncie wondered what had happened to Drew Lennox.

He waved his fork in the air, tossing the thoughts aside. "That was about five years ago."

"You seem to be doing all right for yourself."

"Like your mom said, *appearances*." He gave her a half smile. "I don't do bad, but I can do better." He shrugged. "But with anything it takes time. Bad thing about construction is that a lot of work is seasonal. Hard on a man with a family to support."

She suddenly felt bold. "Is it hard on your . . . family?" She brought the glass of lemonade to her mouth.

"Don't have one to worry about." He put his fork down and stared at her. "Doesn't your man find your running from one audition to the next, meeting handsome actors a problem?"

Her breath rushed and lodged in her throat. "It's not a problem." She kept her gaze focused on the contents of her glass.

"Is that because he doesn't mind, or because there's no one who *does*?"

Her eyes flashed. "That's a little personal, don't you think, Mr. Lennox?"

He shrugged his broad shoulders. "Depends. I always try to be direct. If there's something I want to know, I ask. It avoids confusion down the line."

"Down what line?"

"Whatever line I choose to take."

Her eyebrow arched. "I see. And what line do you see yourself taking now?"

He ran his tongue thoughtfully across his lips. "Let's put it this way, Ms. Frazier, we have to work together for at least the next month. Given time, a lot of things can happen between people who are around each other a lot. If that should happen, I'd like to know well in advance what and who I'm dealing with."

"What makes you think anything *will* happen?" she challenged.

"Didn't say it would. Let's just say I'm a cautious man."

She had no comeback, so she finished off her salad instead.

Where was all this coming from? he wondered. He was practically coming on to the boss's daughter in the middle of a job. That wasn't his style and he'd already decided she wasn't his type. At least he had thought she wasn't until they actually started talking. She wasn't at all what he'd imagined she'd be. And he was probably exactly what she'd imagined. In a mindless act of loose lips and male bravado, he'd just epitomized every stereotype ever associated with construction workers. And for some reason he didn't want this Ms. Frazier to toss him in the barrel with the all the others who actually belonged there. Even though he knew he'd stand a better chance of winning the lottery than getting next to Chauncie Frazier, he didn't want her to walk away with a bad taste in her mouth.

Slowly he chewed his food, wishing he could drill himself a hole to crawl in, at least long enough for him to think of something appropriate to say to her.

Well, she'd rarely, if ever, been in the company of a man who actually said what was on his mind. She wasn't sure if she should be insulted by his bluntness or intrigued by it.

She chose intrigued.

This self-made man didn't get to be where he was without a lot of gut instinct and determination. Hmmm.

He really should say something. He didn't want their lunch date . . . meeting . . . whatever you wanted to call it, to end with her thinking who-knows-what about him.

Drew opened his mouth to say something, but Chauncie didn't give him a chance.

"Drew . . . Can I call you Drew?"

*Uh-oh. What was with the voice and that come-hither look in her eyes?* "Sure."

"I have a proposition for you."

*Well, knock me down.*

Chauncie leaned forward a bit, daintily placing her fork alongside her plate. *How would Lynn Whitfield play this one?* Sultry but straight. "Drew, I'm going to confide something to you because I get a sense that you're an honest man and would give me an honest answer.''

He frowned, bracing himself for what, he wasn't sure.

"I'm listening.''

She blew out a breath. "I'm supposed to be running the shop in my mother's absence for the next six weeks. I've never had to run a business in my life.''

"Why did she leave it to you to take care of then?''

"It's becoming painfully clear that her reason was to teach me a lesson.''

The corner of his mouth turned up in a grin. "She's taking a mighty risky chance. Suppose you blow it. Then what?''

"That's exactly what I've been thinking. My mother has worked too hard and too long for me to mess things up.''

"How do you think I can help?''

*Oooh, this was easier than I thought.* "I was hoping you'd be able to give me some . . . assistance, a few tips on managing a staff, business things I need to know.'' She angled her head, giving him that vulnerable Halle Berry look.

He stared at her for a moment. She was good. Almost had him fooled with that "please-help-me-I'm-just-a-defenseless-woman'' routine. But hey, why not? He didn't have anything to lose and in the meantime he could further his own agenda. "Sure, why not.'' He checked his watch. "I've got to be heading back. Why don't we talk later? After work. We knock off at four.''

She bit down on her bottom lip for a moment. "I have to stay at the shop until closing. We take the last customer at six. I probably won't be out before eight.''

"We could always wait until tomorrow. Or I could swing by and pick you up after you close up.''

"Didn't you say you lived in Queens?''

"It's no problem. I'll go home, change, and come back. While I give you the inside scoop on management, you can give me a tour of Harlem. Then we can find someplace to have dinner.''

*Dinner.* "If you're sure. I don't want to put you out.''

"It's no problem.''

"Great."

Drew signaled for the waitress, who brought their check.

Chauncie's pulse beat with an erratic rhythm all afternoon. In between trying to keep up with the goings-on in the shop, her thoughts kept drifting back to Drew Lennox, their informative lunch, and their evening rendezvous. Things had worked out much better than she'd expected. The tiny thrill of expectation ran through her, keeping her energy level up—although her feet were killing her—and her good humor in place, even as the staff seemed intent on pretty much ignoring her.

It was just the first day, she consoled herself, as she sat behind the desk in her mother's office and massaged her aching feet. She knew she needed to get her point across with more authority. A perfect example was Melody, who was busy gossiping with Blaize while working on a customer's hair. Definitely a no-no. Even she knew that. But when she spoke to Melody about it, the stylist acted as if Chauncie had just descended from the moon.

Since Chauncie didn't want to cause a scene in the middle of the shop, she let it go, but she knew she'd have to speak with Melody before she left for the day. Not to mention Tricia, who decided to take two hours for lunch and had a backlog of grumbling customers upon her return. If she didn't know better, she'd believe the staff was in cahoots to sabotage her.

To top that off, she'd been so busy trying to soothe the customers, she'd never gotten a chance to talk with Reggie as she'd planned. Hopefully, her meeting with Drew would help.

*Drew*. She was actually looking forward to seeing him later, and it had nothing to do with work.

"Okay, fellas," Drew announced. "Let's call it a day. We're gonna start at seven tomorrow morning, try to get some of this work done before the shop opens."

"That's what the lady said over lunch?" Jake quizzed from the back of the room. The group of tired, grimy men chuckled.

"That's what *I* said," Drew grumbled. "And as long as I

write the checks, don't question me. Got it?'' He glared at each of the men, who one by one averted their gazes. ''See you all in the morning. Out front. On time.''

Amidst low grumbles, they tossed aside sweat rags, closed up toolboxes, and filed out, leaving in pairs and threes.

Drew watched them leave and was hit once again by the stark reality; all he had was himself. He didn't have a good buddy to toss back a few beers with after work. He'd always believed in keeping his business life separate from his personal life. But his business was his life. As a result he'd isolated himself from everyone and everything else. Sure he had lunch with them from time to time, but was never included in after-work activities, like backyard barbecues. He'd wanted it that way. Kept a distance between himself and his workers. He'd wanted their respect and maybe their fear. Never their friendship.

Watching the guys laugh and joke with each other only reinforced his self-imposed exile from society. Even outside work, he couldn't count a single real friend. He'd cut everyone off. Burned his bridges.

He heaved a sigh, looked around, and gathered his belongings. Truth be told, his ''appointment'' tonight with Chauncie would be the first time he'd been out with a woman in months. Not that he hadn't had the opportunity or the offers. He just hadn't been interested.

His divorce had taken a real toll on his self-esteem and his level of trust in women was at an all-time low. As a result, he steered clear of any possibility of intimacy, preferring brief liaisons with no expectations. All of his energy went into building his business. His marriage might have crumbled, but he had no intention of letting his business fall apart. So he drove his men, would take no less than one hundred and fifty percent from anyone on his crew. And anyone who didn't like, or couldn't meet, his standards was out. Plain and simple.

He grabbed his toolbox and wiped his forehead with a damp handkerchief, then stuck it in his back pocket and walked out.

''Good night,'' he mumbled as he passed each of the

women, receiving an array of approving glances and coy smiles. He stopped at the front desk. "Is Ms. Frazier around?" he asked Annie.

"She's in the office. I'll buzz her."

"Thanks." He leaned against the counter and surveyed the space. It was perfect for what the senior Ms. Frazier had envisioned. Women spent tons of time in a beauty salon, so why not include a cafe for them to relax in, to have a snack and chat while they waited their turn? He thought the idea was brilliant. If it was marketed properly, she might even be able to turn her little cafe into a nightspot after closing.

"She said to come in," Annie said, cutting off his train of thought.

He nodded and walked to the back of the shop. He knocked once on the partially closed door and went in.

Chauncie turned from the files she was going through and closed the drawer. "Still trying to feel my way through things," she said, overcome once again by the sudden drumming of her heart.

Drew sympathized. "It takes time."

"More time than I have, unfortunately." She smiled at him.

"I was checking on this evening. I'm getting ready to leave. Do you want to meet somewhere, or would you like me to pick you up?"

"Uh, I guess you could meet me back here."

He nodded, suddenly feeling like an awkward teen. "So I'll see you about eight, eight-thirty."

"Sounds fine." She wanted to ask him if he was going to pick her up in that truck that was parked out front and if he wanted to go casual or dress up. But she didn't. There was just something about Drew Lennox that subtly spoke class and good judgment, even underneath all the grit and grime. She'd take her chances.

"You pick the place, but dinner's on me," Drew announced as he walked to the door.

She opened her mouth to protest. He held up his hand.

"Consider it the first step in solidifying our working arrangement."

She angled her chin and looked up at him from beneath her lashes. "You drive a hard bargain, Mr. Lennox. Consider my arm twisted."

He smiled. "See you later."

Chauncie watched him walk out the door, noticing his long-legged stroll and the way his faded jeans hugged his thighs and defined his rear end, and she couldn't help but lick her lips. She took a peek over her shoulder and checked her own. She conceded that his looked better.

Returning to her seat behind the desk, she tucked her hands beneath her chin and tried to imagine what a night out with Mr. Drew Lennox would be like. Originally, her agenda had been purely professional—well, almost, but the more she thought about it and mulled over the possibilities, the more she wanted to find out just how far things could go between the two of them. Of course, she'd glean whatever information she could about operating a business, but even the hardest worker's day had to come to an end sometime.

She checked her watch. Five o'clock. Three more hours and she'd be able to see for herself.

Or so she thought.

When she walked back out into the center of the shop, all conversation seemed to come to an abrupt halt. The only sounds were the hum of the dryers and the underlying beat of the music. She was obviously the center of the aborted discussion and suddenly she felt as if she were on display. All of the operators guiltily averted their gazes, focusing unusually hard on the heads beneath their talented fingers.

Chauncie cleared her throat. "Melody, I'd like to see you in the office before you leave," she said, then quickly turned around and headed back to the sanctuary of the office.

Generally she didn't mind being the center of attention. Most of the time she strived for it. She leaned against the closed door, feeling that sinking sensation sucking her down. She'd bet money they weren't discussing her fabulous outfit, her bouncy hair, or traffic-stopping walk. No. They were talking about what a fool she'd made of herself today, her inability to run the shop and how they were just waiting around to see her fall flat on her perfect little face.

She blew out a breath. Well, she wouldn't give them the satisfaction. She was going to pull this off, no matter what it took. She was going to prove them wrong and make her mother proud.

Somehow.

The knocking on the door pulled her away from her master plan. "Come in."

Melody strolled in, full of attitude.

"Have a seat, Melody," Chauncie offered in a controlled voice, playing the magnanimous boss rather well, she thought.

Melody frowned slightly, eased her defensive stance and slowly sat down. "You wanted to see me," she challenged. "I have one more customer, and . . ."

"This won't take long. I wanted to remind you of store policy regarding gossip during working hours, especially in the presence of our customers. It's not good business."

"I wasn't saying anything that everyone didn't know," she snapped, folding her arms and angling her head.

"I'm sure. But that's not the point. Ma . . . I mean Della has clear standards that she wants followed." She took a breath. "Is that clear?"

Melody just stared at her, trying really hard not to roll her eyes.

"Thanks."

Melody stood, then paused for a moment. "It's kind of hard taking orders from someone who never paid attention to any of the rules before." Her eyebrow cocked upward at an arrogant angle. "Know what I mean?" She spun away and stomped out, leaving the door standing open.

Chauncie's heart pounded. She knew Melody was right. And it was probably what all of them were thinking and obviously saying. But the deal was, *she* was in charge until Della returned and like it or not, *they* were going to have to live with it.

But could she?

# Good Things Come

There was only one customer left in the shop when Chauncie finally emerged from the back room. Ruthie was working on her hair. Melody, Blaize, and Jewel were packing up and heading out. Holly and Tricia had already gone for the day and Reggie was primping in the mirror.

He turned upon Chauncie's approach. "Hey, Ms. Chauncie," he said, giving her a long up and down look. "Love that suit, girl."

Chauncie grinned. "Thanks, Reggie. I got it from that shop in the Village you told me about."

He flicked his wrist and rolled his eyes upward. "The clothes in there are slammin'. Filled my closet." He walked over to her and examined her hair. "Looks good. I'll touch it up for you in about two weeks."

"Thanks, Reggie."

"Where's Della?" the customer asked Ruthie.

"She's on vacation."

"Well, I'll be. I've been coming in here for about five years. I can't ever remember a time that I didn't see Della."

Ruthie angled her head in Chauncie's direction. "Her daughter is running things while Della's away."

The woman eyed Chauncie from the reflection in the mirror and Chauncie would have sworn she saw the woman turn up her nose.

"Hmmm," was all the woman said, before getting out of her seat. "Didn't even introduce herself," she said under her breath, but loud enough for Chauncie to hear. "Della never would have done that. She had a word for everyone."

Chauncie felt her stomach shift as she pretended not to hear what was being said about her and continued on to the front of the store. The woman gave her something that couldn't possibly pass for a smile as she left.

"See you tomorrow," Reggie said, blowing Chauncie a kiss on his way out. Ruthie was right behind him.

"You didn't do too bad today. Folks are just used to Della, that's all. Just do the best you can. Don't forget to tally the receipts and put the money together for the bank deposit. The slips are in the bottom drawer. And set the alarm before you leave. Good night." Ruthie opened and closed the door before Chauncie had a chance to scream.

Receipts, tallies, bank! Her head started to pound. She didn't know anything about the bank deposits or tallying receipts. She covered her face with her hands. What was she going to do?

She checked her watch. Drew would show up anytime now and she didn't have a clue about what needed to be done.

"Mo-ther!"

Drew was nervous. Actually nervous. His palms were sweaty as he gripped the wheel of his BMW, turning onto 125th Street.

It wasn't really a date, he reminded himself. It was a business meeting—with a beautiful, sexy woman who unwittingly resurrected emotions he hadn't felt in a long time.

The shop was up ahead. His stomach knotted. He scanned the long stretch of 125th Street for a legal parking space, his eyes stopping briefly on the rows of stores that supported apartments above, the occasional street vendors—though banned from the famous strip by a mayoral ruling—still played the catch-me-if-you-can game with the police as they hawked their tables of oils, incense, Black soap, Shea Butter, African fabrics, and ten-dollar telephones.

Many of the buildings that he passed were in disrepair and could use a good dose of what Lennox Construction had to offer. Maybe he could pick up a few more accounts after the job at Rosie's was completed.

*Then you'll still be close enough to see Chauncie from time to time,* his subconscious whispered.

He finally pulled into a spot that was being vacated. Since it was well on the far side of seven o'clock he didn't have to worry about a meter.

Checking his reflection in the rearview mirror, he took a breath, turned off the engine, and stepped out into the balmy summer night.

The sights, smells, and sounds of the inner city gathered around him like curious tribesmen with a stranger in their midst, touching, testing, clinging, pulsing. He let them all settle around him, became one with them as he moved with the rhythm.

Up on the next block he saw the stream of people standing on line to get into the Apollo. Funny, he'd heard about the famous theater all his life, but he'd never been inside. The closest he'd ever come was watching the antics of the amateurs on television during *Showtime at the Apollo.* Maybe one day, he thought, heading up the block to Rosie's.

New Yorkers generally took so much for granted. People came from all over the world to see the Empire State Building, the Statue of Liberty, the World Trade Center, and hit Broadway plays. They would walk down Fifth Avenue or visit Rockefeller Center, while its inhabitants barely paid the sights and sounds of New York much attention. He could count himself among the guilty.

Passing a homeless man, who appeared very comfortable in the doorway of an abandoned building, his grandmother's favorite saying, *"There but for the grace of God go I,"* ran through his head. He turned back around and gave the man a ten-dollar bill. "Get yourself something to eat," he said to the startled, toothless man.

Drew kept walking toward the shop, knowing that the old man would probably just drink up the money, but there was always the possibility that he wouldn't. He stopped in front of Rosie's and had another attack of nerves. He blew out a long breath and knocked on the door.

The sudden banging snapped Chauncie out of her lethargy. Her heart raced. It had to be Drew. What was she going to do? She couldn't very well leave the money in the shop. And she didn't want him to think she was a complete idiot, not knowing how to tally the day's receipts and make a bank deposit.

She jumped straight up when he banged again.

Pulling herself together, she patted her hair, adjusted her skirt and slid from behind the reception desk. Straightening her shoulders and putting on her best ''got-it-together look,'' she pulled open the door.

What she expected to see on the other side was not what she found. Who was this *Fine*, with a capital F, man standing on the other side of the door, smiling down at her as if she were the only one for him?

She blinked.

He was still there.

"Drew?"

He grinned. And for the first time she noticed he had the cutest dimple in his right cheek.

"Weren't you expecting me? Or am I early?"

"Uh . . . Yes . . . No . . . Come in. I'm sorry." She stepped aside, and wondered when the Babbling Idiot had stolen the lead role from Ms. Got-It-Together.

"Everything okay? You seem a little preoccupied."

"I was just trying to . . ." The lightbulb went off. "This is my first deposit for the store. It's been taking me longer than I thought."

He closed the door and bit back a smile. "Need some help?"

"Oh, no. I couldn't ask you to do that. I mean . . . unless you really want to."

"It's not a problem. I could show you what to do in no time. Been doing this for years."

She beamed.

"Where do you keep your deposit slips?"

At least she knew that much. "I'll get them. They're in the office."

"We might as well work back there. Not a good idea to count money in the front of your store."

"You're right."

He followed her to the back of the shop, trying to keep his eyes off her legs and swaying hips. But it was hard. *Really* hard.

Once inside, Chauncie scurried around as if she knew what she was doing. She pulled the deposit tickets out from the file cabinet, feeling momentarily triumphant.

"Do the staff write up receipts for each customer?" he asked.

"Yes."

"We'll need them to compare with what's in the register."

"Right." She hurried out to the front to get the receipts.

"Bring the whole cash drawer. It'll be easier that way," he yelled.

"No problem."

She went to the front of the store and took the receipts from the box where Annie kept them, then took the cash drawer out of the register and returned to the office.

"First add up the receipts," he instructed.

Chauncie took a seat, pulled the adding machine toward her, and began adding.

He watched her intent expression as she tap-tapped in the numbers, her eyebrows knitted together in concentration, and suddenly he had the overwhelming desire to take care of Chauncie Frazier. But at the same moment, he also realized that was Chauncie's biggest problem—always being taken care of. He didn't think she'd ever seen a hard day's work in her beautiful life, had never known what it meant to be hurt, not to have to struggle. Yet it didn't make him think any less of her. It's just the way things were. There was something about Chauncie that made you want to do for her.

She knew he was watching her, which made it very difficult to concentrate on hitting the right numbers on the calculator. *Wonder what he's thinking?* Does he know how good he looks—smells? It was hard to believe it was the same man she'd seen earlier. Yeah, he looked good then, too, but now . . .

His close-cut hair sparkled, inky black against smooth russet-brown skin. The cream-colored shirt and hunter green slacks flowed along his body in lazy-river fashion. She couldn't name the cologne he was wearing, but it floated around her like a comforting cocoon, and she wanted to wrap herself in it. *Oh boy, this is not good.*

"I can start counting up the money. If you want me to," Drew said, cutting off her wandering thoughts.

"That would be a big help." She hit the TOTAL button and pulled the long white tape from the machine.

"It'll be a lot faster if we do this together," he said, in a tone that sounded more like an invitation than a suggestion to Chauncie.

"Sure." She came around to his side of the desk.

"Largest bills first," he instructed, and peeked at her from the corner of his eye. "I'll count, you double-check. We'll need two tapes."

"Fine." She wasn't sure why, but he obviously knew what he was doing.

His fingers flew through the bills and he ran a tape, then passed the bills to her and she did the same thing, then entered the numbers on the deposit slip.

Intermittently their fingers brushed as they worked and they'd toss apologetic glances in each other's direction.

The whole process took about twenty minutes and they balanced out to the penny. Chauncie couldn't have been happier. She felt like her body was on fire.

Drew turned to Chauncie and smiled. "All done. Where's your deposit bag?"

She went to the file cabinet, pulled out the blue deposit bag and handed it to him. He wrapped each denomination in a rubber band, separated the change into their respective paper sleeves, and put everything into the bag along with the deposit ticket.

"Do you do a night deposit, or does someone pick this up in the morning?"

She searched her mind trying to remember. "We do a night drop. At Chase," she said, recalling the evenings she'd accompanied her mother to the bank.

Drew frowned. "That really isn't such a good idea. Especially a woman making a bank deposit alone, at night." He shook his head. "You really should check into having a bonded company come and pick up your deposits."

"Is that what you do?"

He nodded. "It's just as rough out there for a man, believe me." He laughed lightly. "But in the meantime, let's take care of this."

"Could you recommend a company?"

He looked down into her questioning eyes, and his insides shifted. He swallowed. "I'll bring the information in the morning."

She smiled. "Thanks."

For a moment they stood there, staring at each other.

She thought he was going to kiss her.

He wanted to kiss her.

He stepped closer.

She didn't move. Her heart began to race.

The phone rang and they both jumped as if they'd been caught doing something they didn't want anyone to see.

Chauncie blinked, mumbled something, then picked up the phone, hoping that her voice didn't sound as shaky as she felt.

"Hello? Yes, Ruthie, I'm fine. Yes, the deposit is done. No problem. Yes. Well, thanks for calling. See you tomorrow."

She hung up, but the moment was gone.

"Ready?" Drew asked.

"Yes." But not to leave, she thought, surprising herself with a wicked little image that ran through her head.

She picked up the deposit bag and locked the office door and they headed for the front of the shop. She stopped, remembering to turn out the lights, flipping all the switches to the left, then headed up front where Drew was waiting.

"You can go outside. I need to set the alarm."

He nodded.

Chauncie gave the shop a quick once-over. Everything looked fine for opening tomorrow. She let out a relieved breath. She'd actually gotten through her first day. With a little help, but she'd done it. She punched in the numbers to set the alarm and rushed out, locking the door behind her.

When she stepped outside, she stopped short when she saw Drew standing there, hands in his pockets, gazing out toward the horizon, his profile set against the backdrop of summer twilight—and a wave of staggering desire rocketed through her.

This wasn't like her at all. To be so taken by a man. Not her style. She was used to toying with men, never showing her hand, playing the elusive one.

But every part of her wanted to walk right up to him and tell him, like Marvin told his listening audience, "Let's Get It On." And that scared her, made her vulnerable.

This was definitely not good.

He turned toward her and a slow smile spread across his mouth.

When he looked at her, he wished that this was a real date, that he could wine and dine Chauncie Frazier, see what made her tick and if they could tick-tock together. But it wasn't. She was his client's daughter and what they were headed for was a business dinner. Nothing more. "All set?"

She nodded because the sudden knot in her throat wouldn't move out of the way so that she could talk.

"We can take my car," he offered. "I'm parked up the street."

They started walking down the block together and she had no doubts about how they looked together: good.

"So, did you decide where I'm taking you for dinner?" Drew asked, liking the way he felt walking next to her and the way people looked at them as they passed.

"I thought we could go to the Motown Cafe. They have great soul food and entertainment." She looked across and up at him and felt her heart jump in her chest. *Get a grip.*

Motown Cafe. He'd met his ex-wife there. She was having

dinner with a few women from her sorority and they'd passed each other coming and going from the restrooms. The rest—he didn't want to think about.

Chauncie noticed the sudden change in his demeanor. If it was one thing she was good at, it was reading people's body language, a skill that came in very handy in her acting jaunts. His loose, long stride seemed to have stiffened, and the open look on his face, the half smile were gone, replaced by the beginnings of thunderclouds around his eyes.

"Is something wrong?" she ventured, as they came to a stop in front of a fly BMW. Her eyebrows slightly rose in approval.

He disengaged the alarm and opened the door on her side. "No."

Chauncie watched him round the front of the car as she slid into the smooth black leather seat. *Mmmm, smells good in here. Like Drew*, she thought.

Drew got behind the wheel, not daring to look at Chauncie. He knew he had to get his act together. But it was almost like an evil omen or something, her suggesting that they go to the Motown Cafe. Chauncie had no way of knowing that the restaurant held unpleasant memories for him.

He turned the key in the ignition and the car hummed to life.

"We could go someplace else," she offered. "I just thought—"

He shook his head. "It's fine. Really." He turned to her and forced a smile, then pulled off. "But first, to the bank."

It was a few minutes before they were seated at the restaurant, and during the wait the memories came rushing back to Drew.

Gloria had been beautiful too, like Chauncie. But Gloria's beauty, he discovered soon after their whirlwind romance and marriage, was purely superficial. Gloria was a gold digger to her core. All she ever wanted was *more*. It should have been her middle name. And with the type of work he did, more was not always a possibility. Bad went to worst and then it was over.

"What happened to you here?" Chauncie asked, seeming to reach down into his thoughts.

He blinked, bringing himself back to the present. He pressed his lips together. "At the time I thought it was the start of something good."

"And it wasn't," she stated more than asked.

"Yeah, I guess you could say that."

She wanted to reach out and touch him, stroke away the look that saddened his eyes. Instead, she let out a short breath and put a smile on her face. "Maybe it can be this time."

He looked down at her, searching her face, and started to ask her what she meant.

"Your table is ready," the waitress said, stepping up to them, cutting off his almost question.

Once they were seated, they both buried their noses in the menus, as if it would camouflage the array of emotions that ran through them.

Chauncie couldn't read the words in front of her; all she could see was Drew's face, the soft expression in his eyes when he looked at her. She would listen if he would talk to her, tell her what was haunting him, what memories were hidden in the walls, behind the pillars, waiting to strike. She'd played the role of a counselor once, in an off-off-off-Broadway play. She remembered how consoling she'd had to be, nodding and gently prodding her "client" into talking about what was troubling her. Maybe she could reenact the role.

He probably should just tell her what was bothering him, he thought. It really was no big deal, and it had happened a long time ago. Then why did it still pinch his insides when he looked around and saw the same decor, smelled the same smells?

"I met my wife here," he said suddenly.

Her eyes widened in alarm as she lowered her menu from in front of her face. *Well, there goes any chance of anything.* "Oh," was all she could find to say.

He cleared his throat. "About ten years ago. We're divorced."

Her stomach settled back down. "Sorry." *Yahoo!*

"I'm not." He chuckled halfheartedly. "The divorce was the best part of the marriage."

"It couldn't have been that bad." She took a sip of water.

He shrugged. "Probably not. Just seemed like it sometimes."

"How long were you married?"

"Two years. Divorced for eight. What about you?"

"Never married, engaged, or otherwise connected."

"Is that the way you want it?"

She didn't want to read anything into his question. But what was he really asking her? "What do you mean?"

"Is it in the grand plan to be unattached?"

"I hadn't really thought about it. It's just the way it's been. I've been trying to pursue an acting career."

He grinned. "Really? So how did you wind up working in a beauty salon?"

"I keep asking myself the same question." She chuckled. "My mother has her own plans for me, it seems. She thinks my desire to be an actress is just a lark, something that will pass."

"Is it?"

"No." She leaned forward and her eyes seemed to brighten. "I really love it. I get such a charge out of being in front of a camera, or onstage."

"I bet you're good at it."

"I think so. I just need a break."

"But in the meantime, you have to run the shop. Something you have no inclination to do. Right?"

"On target." She smiled.

"How much do you really know about the business?"

She toyed with her water glass. "To be honest, little to nothing. I've been 'in training' for the past year. But I never took it seriously because my goals and thoughts were always on acting. And having a good time," she added sheepishly.

Drew took a sip of his water. "I got the sense that the staff isn't too helpful," he hedged.

"Oh, you got that sense, did you? That's an understatement. They hate me."

"I doubt that. It's difficult for anyone to accept change. And you happen to be it for them. Apparently they've been used to your mother and the way she does things."

"But I'm not my mother."

"Exactly. But you have to be somebody to them. Let them know that even though Della isn't there, you're responsible for managing the shop and in order to do that you need their help. The success of the shop isn't ultimately to your benefit, but to theirs. Once they understand that they have a stake in the business it'll no longer be them against you."

She looked at him for a moment, digesting what he'd said. "So what do I do?"

"Act like a manager." He grinned.

She twisted her lips. "My mother said the same thing to me on her way out the door."

"Then do it."

"It's the one role I've never played," she said.

"Then I guess I'll need to give you a crash course."

"Mr. Lennox, I didn't know you were in the acting coach business."

"One of my many talents, Ms. Frazier."

*Hmmm. I can only imagine what some of your others are.* "When did you want to start?"

"How about over dinner, in a restaurant named the Motown Cafe, where memories are made?"

"This time good ones," she said.

"Is that a promise?"

She looked deep into his eyes. "Yes."

During their dinner of shared barbecued baby back ribs, cole slaw, sweet collard greens, and candied yams, and a stage performance by a trio doing an excellent imitation of the Supremes, they shared stories of their lives. Drew reminisced about growing up in the residential district of St. Albans, Queens, pretty much sheltered from the rough-and-tough world of the surrounding areas, then surprised her with the declaration that he had attended Catholic school for eight years, which he swore jaded his thinking about life and relationships. "They made everything sound like a sin," he confessed. "It was years after I finally got out that I could even look at a woman with any kind of desire and not think I was going straight to hell." It was hard for him to really enjoy life or pleasure, for that matter; he'd been brainwashed into believing that frivolity was tantamount to being sacrilegious and that hard work and dedication were the only road to the afterlife. "I guess looking back at it now, it really wasn't so bad. It did instill a lot of values in me that many of the guys I grew up with didn't have. But as a kid . . ." He shook his head. "It was rough. I suppose that's why I still work so hard, and I'm sometimes hard on my men."

"I can just see you now in your school uniform, marching off to class." She grinned. "I bet you were adorable."

"Adorable, huh? I guess I forgot to mention, that one of the side benefits of Catholic schooling was that you learned how to defend yourself. With all the teasing and tormenting we got from the other kids, about us being so *adorable*, you had to know how to take care of yourself."

"Is that why you really got into construction? Because it presents that rough exterior?"

He thought about it for a moment. "You know, it never really occurred to me before. But you're probably right." He smiled. "You'd make a great counselor."

She almost choked on her wine. "You think so?"

"Absolutely. You have a natural way of getting people to open up to you. I mean, I've known you what—a day?—and I've said things to you I don't think I ever told my wife. Not that she ever asked, but . . ."

Chauncie lowered her gaze. "My life was entirely different," she began, gently moving away from the subject that seemed to cause him so much pain. She told him about her hell-raising high school years when her mother swore she'd send her to boarding school if she got suspended one more time. "I developed cutting class down to a fine art," she confessed. "But it wasn't because I wasn't smart, or couldn't handle the classes—it was probably just the opposite. School bored me. I learned everything so quickly that I'd get turned off and cut class looking for something to stimulate my imagination. I partied hard, even dabbled in drugs for a while. Nothing hard, just weed. But one day, in my senior year of high school, I snuck into a theater up on Amsterdam Avenue. They were rehearsing *A Raisin in the Sun,* and I was never so enthralled with anything in my life. From that moment I was hooked. I still like to hang out and have a good time, though, but acting . . . Wow, it really turns me on.''

As he listened to her talk, he felt himself being drawn into her essence, falling under her spell. He could easily see how she could mesmerize an audience. There was a fire that burned inside Chauncie Frazier and anyone who dared to come too close and not know how to handle her would get burned.

''Seems we have some things in common. We're both passionate . . . about what we do,'' Drew said.

She swallowed. ''I know I am,'' she countered with a look full of challenge.

Drew tossed his head back and laughed. ''I just bet you are, Ms. Chauncie Frazier. I bet you are.''

They finished their meal while Drew shared some tips with Chauncie about how to handle her staff while she learned the ropes. ''Always be there early. Be willing to do just as much as they do and even more, but you should demand their loyalty.''

''But what about being friends with them?''

Drew looked away. ''Do you want to be their friend or their boss?''

''I'd like to be both. I'd like to know that the people who work for me like me.''

''It's not about liking you, Chauncie. It's about respect.''

''I think it can be both,'' she tossed back. ''Don't your employees like you?''

''It doesn't matter if they do, as long as they get the job done.'' He couldn't meet her eyes.

She propped her chin up on her fist. ''Tell you what. You

teach me how to run a business, and I'll teach you how to win friends and have some fun.''

Drew looked at her a moment. "You have a deal."

"How far do you live from here?" he asked when they'd stepped outside the restaurant.

"About ten minutes away. But my car is parked by the shop."

"Oh."

They started to walk toward his car. "So I guess I'll just take you to pick it up." His statement hung in the air like an unanswered question.

"You could follow me home. Make sure I arrive safely," she said coyly.

"Maybe I'll just do that."

When they arrived in front of her apartment building, Drew got out and opened Chauncie's car door for her. She stepped out with barely a breath between them. For an awkward moment they stared at each other, unsure of what to do next.

Finally Chauncie spoke. "I should be getting upstairs, get some rest if I'm going to start my second day on the job on the right foot."

"I had a great time tonight, Chauncie," he said, not ready to let the night end.

"So did I."

"Think we could . . . do this again?"

She smiled. "I thought you'd never ask. I'll even let you pick the place."

His stomach finally settled. "I might even pick Motown. I think I like the new memories."

Her heart thumped. "See you tomorrow?"

"We'll be there at seven." His eyes grazed her face. "Can I kiss you good night, Chauncie?"

"I thought I was going to have to ask you," she whispered, stepping closer.

Drew tilted her chin upward with the tip of his finger and lowered his head until his mouth was a whisper away from hers. He brushed his lips lightly against hers and felt her sudden intake of breath. His other hand slipped behind her head, his fingers threading through her hair. *It was so soft*. The thought rushed through his head like a sudden breeze, as his mouth pressed more urgently against hers.

The scent of him rushed through her senses and she suddenly felt light-headed, wanting to cling to him for support. Her fingers grasped the front of his shirt, sure that she would simply slip away if she didn't. So sweet, she thought, the faint taste of wine still lingering on his lips. And then he moved away.

She blinked. Shaken.

"If we stand out here much longer, we just might cause a scene," he said in a deep, gravelly voice she recognized as desire.

At the moment, the way she was feeling she didn't care who was looking. Maybe they'd see what they were missing if they did. But she knew he was right.

"I . . . better get upstairs."

"Yeah."

Reluctantly she moved away, turned, and started for the stairs to her building.

"Chauncie."

She turned around. If he asked her if he could come upstairs, *yes* was already on her lips.

"How about Friday night? After work."

She angled her head to the side. "Suppose I don't want to wait that long?"

He grinned, looked down at the pavement, then up at her. She appeared like a ray of sunshine against the night sky. "You have a better idea?"

"Thursday. I have a rehearsal at eight at a theater in the Village. You could get a chance to see me do my thing."

"Sure."

"And I won't even bring my car." She turned without another word and trotted up the steps.

Drew watched her disappear behind the heavy oak doors. Thursday seemed like a lifetime away.

But there was always tomorrow.

# Those Who Wait

Chauncie awoke before the sun streaked across the horizon, but this time without the sinking sensation of dread floating around in her stomach. Today she was filled with expectation mixed with a healthy dose of excitement.

She sighed and looked up at the ceiling, recalling her evening with Drew. It was the first time in longer than she cared to remember that she'd enjoyed an evening so much with a man and was not just going through the motions. All the men she'd dated over the years always had an agenda: A short way to her bedroom. And as shameful as it was to admit, more often than not, she had the same agenda.

But Drew was different. For all the animal magnetism that he exuded like an expensive cologne, he was reserved, almost shy in his approach to her. Maybe it was that Catholic school upbringing. Or perhaps, as he said, he was still gun-shy from his divorce. Cautious. But whatever it was, it was endearing. It made her want him even more.

And to think, she'd started out planning to use him to her benefit . . . and look at her now, practically drooling at the mouth. The tables had certainly turned.

She peeked at the bedside clock. Five-thirty. If she got up now, did a half hour of her daily exercise routine, showered and dressed, she could be at the shop by seven. She smiled. Maybe she could even get a few early-morning pointers from Drew to start her day.

\*   \*   \*

Drew rolled over in his bed, and the first image that popped into his head was Chauncie. He smiled, thinking of how she believed she was pulling a fast one on him. He'd known all along what she was trying to do. Funny, he didn't mind. In fact, he rather enjoyed all of her little performances, her subtle cries for help without really asking. But he'd never let her know that.

Sitting up, he took a look around and wondered what his refurbished two-story house would feel like with Chauncie moving around in it, bringing her energy, and warmth.

"Whoa, buddy, you're getting way ahead of yourself." Was he really willing to take the risk of getting involved again, especially with someone like Chauncie Frazier, a girl who was used to having whatever she wanted? It had been one simple kiss.

*It wasn't that simple.*

He got up and plodded into the bathroom, hoping to temporarily wash Chauncie out of his system with the beat of the shower. As the water poured over him, he made a pledge to himself to back up before he took this thing between them further than it should go.


Chauncie arrived at Rosie's early enough to get the shop open, deactivate the alarm without mishap, and turn on the coffeemaker. Yeah, she was feeling good. As she sipped her first glass of OJ for the morning, she heard the rumble of Drew's truck pulling up to the back of the shop.

Her heart pumped a bit faster. With a mirror every which way she turned, she was able to take both front, side, and back views of herself. Every inch was in place. With about all the casualness she could summon, she strolled to the back of the shop as the crew was coming through the door.

"Good morning, gentlemen," she greeted.

The men looked at her with surprise, then pure male appraisal. A round of "mornings" floated around the space. Drew stepped through the group.

"Bright and early," he said, fighting back his smile.

"Quick learner."

He nodded in approval. "We're going to get started."

"I have some coffee on if you guys want some before you get going."

"Sure," Drew said, answering for the group. He followed Chauncie out. "You look great," he whispered.

She almost tripped, but kept her composure. She could feel his eyes burning into her back. "Thank you, Mr. Lennox," she whispered in return, a smile tugging the corners of her mouth.

"Smell good, too," he added, totally forgetting his promise to himself to take it light with Chauncie.

"What happened to the shy Catholic school boy I met last night?" she said, turning to him when they reached the refreshment table. Her gaze rose to lock with his.

"I think he's under renovation."

"Don't modernize him too much. I was kind of getting to like the take-it-slow guy."

"I'll keep that in mind." He filled his cup and was about to walk away.

"Think we could have lunch?" She swallowed, knowing she was really putting herself on the line. "I don't think I can wait until Thursday."

His stomach tightened. Looking at her looking at him like she wanted *him* for lunch, he wasn't sure if *he* could wait that long. "Sure. About one o'clock?"

"I'll meet you outside."

He nodded and walked to the back and she immediately heard his voice barking out instructions to his crew. In an instant, he seemed like an entirely different person. With her, he was soft-spoken, gentle, had a sense of humor. With his men, he was almost abrasive.

She frowned. Was that the real Drew Lennox, the one she heard commanding grown men as if they were children? Or was the real Drew the man she'd had dinner with the night before? She pushed the thought aside. She had her own business to run.

If there was one thing that could be said about Chauncie, she was a quick study when the situation called for it. By the time Ruthie arrived at nine-thirty, the air conditioner was on, soft jazz played in the background, a fresh pot of coffee was perking, and the juices were chilled. She'd checked the work schedule and knew who was due in at what time.

Ruthie watched Chauncie fill in for Annie at the reception desk until Annie arrived at eleven. Della's daughter had a smile and an anecdote for every customer who walked in. She just might make it, Ruthie thought.

The morning progressed smoothly, and as the hours ticked by, Chauncie was feeling better about herself. This was definitely a role she could handle, she mused, as she reviewed the work schedule for the rest of the week in her mother's office. Just when she thought everything was fine, Annie knocked on the door.

"Come in."

Annie eased in and shut the door behind her.

"Hi, Annie. What can I do for you?"

"Well, you did say to let you know in advance if I needed to take some time off."

"Sure. What day do you need?"

"Actually, it's more than a day."

Chauncie's eyebrow arched. "Oh."

Annie cleared her throat as if the words had suddenly become stuck, and Chauncie wished they had. She knew from enough of her own throat-clearing that something not good was up.

"More like three months."

"Three months!" She knew she was screeching, but she couldn't help it. Her stomach did a quick flip. She couldn't think as half a dozen thoughts raced through her head at once, pushing and shoving each other aside in a serious game of poor sportsmanship. She couldn't seem to get one of them to make it to the finish line. And after all that she could only mumble, "Why?"

Annie helped herself to a seat and a sudden smile bloomed across her face. "I got a modeling assignment. *The* modeling assignment. The agency called me last night. I leave for Paris on Monday. The show opens at the end of the month. Isn't that exciting?'' She beamed, totally oblivious to Chauncie's distress.

Chauncie took a breath. "Yes, that's great, Annie. I'm glad for you. Will you be able to finish out the week?"

"Sure. Listen, Chauncie, I'm really sorry about the short notice, but there's really nothing I can do."

Chauncie forced a smile. "That's show biz."

Left alone in the office, Chauncie tried to figure out what to do about Annie. What did one do to find employees? She knew about casting calls, and figured other job opportunities were done the same way. But since she'd never answered, or cared to look at a help wanted ad in her life, she was totally unfamiliar with what they looked like, or what they should say. Maybe she could just put a sign in the window. She'd seen plenty of those. She blew out a breath.

Is this what her mother went through every day—spending all of her time and energy making the shop work? Not to mention soothing the egos of the eclectic staff. Yet Della always seemed to have a smile.

And so would she. She slapped her palms down on the desk. This thing with Annie would work out. Maybe she'd talk to Drew about it over lunch, see what he suggested.

Drew. Just thinking about him make her stomach flutter. But like a bird in flight, her momentary euphoria landed with a dull thump. The sound of his voice talking with his men earlier reverberated in her head.

Maybe it was a onetime thing, she thought. She couldn't imagine that the warm, soft-spoken man she'd gotten a glimpse of could be so callous and indifferent to the feelings of the men who worked for him. At least she hoped not.

She sighed. If she could get through the rest of the morning without any more surprises, she'd be a happy camper.

When Chauncie returned to the front of the shop, she nearly stopped dead in her tracks. It looked like a bargain basement sale day. Women were everywhere: standing, sitting, leaning. She couldn't believe it. Where in the world had all these women come from, and didn't they have anything else to do at eleven A.M. on a Wednesday? She eased her way through the milling throng, smiling all along the way until she reached Annie at the reception desk.

"What's going on, Annie?" she hissed under her breath. "All these women have appointments?"

Annie put her hand to her mouth to stifle a giggle. "Most of them don't," she said.

Chauncie frowned. "Walk-ins?"

"You could say that. They 'walked-in' to see if they could get a peek at the men in the back and the fine brother running the construction crew in particular."

"What!" There was that squeaky voice again that she'd promised herself she'd work on. "What do you mean? They're here to see Drew? I mean, Mr. Lennox . . . and the crew?"

"That's the word, Chauncie. It seems to have spread like wildfire. I asked them if they had appointments, or what they wanted done." She shrugged. "At least I got all of them to either get a manicure or have their eyebrows waxed. They can't just stand around taking up space, you know."

Chauncie almost laughed. She could just imagine nineteen-year-old Annie telling those grown women to pay for something or leave.

"You should have told them to get a body massage." She chuckled. "That's where the money is."

"I'm way ahead of you. Got a few of those, too."

Chauncie shook her head as she looked around the expanse of the shop. Every woman was dressed to impress, and those who weren't having their hair done looked as if they'd stepped off the pages of *Black Hair Digest*. Then it really hit her. All these women in various stages of drooling were here because of Drew Lennox.

It would be amusing if she didn't feel the sudden stirring of something green rumbling around in her stomach and snaking through her veins.

Her eyes narrowed and she pursed her lips. She had a good mind to tell them all to beat it, to hit the street, but she knew that was totally out of the question. The reality was that there wasn't much she could do. They were paying customers. Yeah, paying for a sideshow. Humph. She could play the game, too. She adjusted the sleeveless cinnamon sweater over her hips and smoothed the matching linen pants. She checked her watch. Twelve-thirty. She smiled and strutted through the congregation of designing women, smiling, asking a question here, dropping a compliment there, until she reached the rear of the shop. She opened the door that separated the salon from the construction area and stepped inside. The noise was almost deafening. She took a second to adjust to the dust-filled light before she could make out Drew straddling a sawhorse as he labored over a thick plank of wood.

Her breath got trapped somewhere in her throat as she watched the thick muscles of his arms expand and contract with his every movement. A thin line of sweat traced his hairline, and his smooth brown complexion seemed to glow as if heated by an inner flame. The man was gorgeous. There was no other way to put it. Dressed up. Dressed down. Just plain ole fine.

His gaze slowly rose from the task in front of him and landed smack on her face. A slow smile spread across his face as if he knew she'd been standing there staring at him.

She took a breath and click-clicked across the concrete floor.

"Hi."

"Hi, yourself." He pulled a plaid handkerchief from the back pocket of his jeans and wiped his brow. "One o'clock already?"

"Not quite. I was hoping . . . if you could get away . . . that maybe we could leave now."

He took a quick look around. "Sure."

He unplugged the power saw, crossed the room, and spoke briefly to one of his men, who quickly stole a glance across Drew's shoulder at her, then returned to her side. "Let me just wash up and I'll be right with you. You can wait up front if you want. It's kind of dusty back here."

"Oh, I'm fine. Watching the men work is fascinating."

He shrugged. "Be right back."

When she stepped back out front, she fully intended to be walking right alongside Drew. That would give them something to look at.

Drew returned shortly, looking refreshed. He'd taken off his white T-shirt and changed into a pale blue cotton shirt.

"Ready?"

"Yep."

They strolled out front and Chauncie derived supreme pleasure from the open-mouthed expressions on everyone's face. Drew, however, seemed unaware of the stir his appearance caused.

"I'll be back in an hour," Chauncie told Annie on her way out.

"Enjoy," she replied, giving Chauncie a wink.

"Have anyplace in mind?" Drew asked when they got outside. He slid on a pair of dark shades against the glare and Chauncie wished she'd brought hers.

"I thought we could walk up Lenox Avenue and see if there was anyplace you liked," she said, shielding her eyes with a cupped palm when she looked up at him.

"I'm not particular, you know. Burger and fries are fine with me."

"In that case Jo-Jo's would be perfect. It's up on Amsterdam Avenue. Best burgers on this side of town."

"Lead the way."

They began walking down 125th Street toward Amsterdam Avenue, the midday sun seeming to have every intention of cooking everything in its path, with them as the main course.

"Shop seemed mighty crowded today," Drew said. "Is it always that busy?"

Chauncie almost choked on her Juicy Fruit. "No. Not that I can ever remember."

"Running some kind of special or something?"

She looked at him from the corner of her eye to see if he was pulling her leg, but his expression was a portrait of innocence. "No. Not exactly."

He looked at her. "What's that mean?"

She angled her head to look up at him. "I'll tell you about it over lunch."

By the time they'd walked the few blocks to the restaurant, Chauncie felt like she wanted to take a shower—or like she had been in one and hadn't dried off. The blast of icy-cold air was a welcome relief.

While they waited for their food to arrive, Chauncie told Drew about her dilemma with Annie and the need to get someone to replace her as soon as possible.

"I have no idea how to go about it, to be honest."

"The easiest thing, I would think, would just be to ask the staff if they know anyone looking for a job." He shrugged. "At least that way it would be someone who was referred. Is it full- or part-time?"

"Full-time."

"Check with the staff first. If that doesn't pan out, then put the sign in the window. I can't see running an ad unless you exhaust your options."

Chauncie nodded. "Thanks. I'll work on that as soon as we get back."

"Oh, before I forget." He slid back in his seat a bit and pulled a piece of paper out of his pants pocket. "Here's the information I was telling you about for the service to pick up your nightly deposits."

She took the paper, looked at it quickly, then stuck it in her purse. "Thanks. I'll give them a call. How's the work progressing?" she asked just as the waitress approached with their meal.

"Pretty quickly, actually. I have a great crew. They know what needs to be done and they do it."

She hesitated a moment, debating whether she should broach the subject, then decided, why not? "Drew, this morning, when I heard you talking to your men, it kind of bothered me."

He frowned. "Bothered you? Why?"

She swallowed. "It wasn't so much what you said, it was just the way you spoke to them. On the one hand, you say that they're experienced and know what they're doing, then on the other, you talk to them as if they were idiots.''

Her statement caught him completely off guard. His first reaction was to go on the defensive. ''They're grown men. They can take it. It's just shop talk.''

She looked at him for a long moment. ''Really?''

''Yes. Really. They don't need to be coddled like a bunch of women.''

''Maybe not. But they do need to be respected.''

''Are you saying I don't respect my men?''

''No. What I'm saying is I can't see any reason why you have to speak to them that way. I'm sure they'd work just as hard for you without you cussing them out, especially if they're as good as you say they are. And even if they're not, for that matter. Listen, just forget it. I was only trying to help.''

He clenched his jaw, stabbing a french fry with his fork. She didn't know what she was talking about. He'd been running his business long enough to know what worked and what didn't. Any man on his crew who didn't like how they were treated could find something else to do. Simple. Briefly he looked across at her, seeing her almost-hurt expression. He took a breath. Suppose she was right?

''I don't think you're in much of a position to tell me how to run my business, or talk to my men.''

Chauncie's gaze snapped up from her glass of iced tea. She held on to her temper. ''I may not know a lot about business. I'll admit that. But one thing I did learn from watching my mother is that you can get more bees with honey than with vinegar. There's nothing wrong with being cordial, nice, friendly, and interested in your staff beyond their just being your staff. Think of them as people. After I got over the shock of having to run things in my mother's absence, I've seen how much her personality drives the shop and brings in the customers. They love being treated as if they're someone special.''

''That sounds fine for a bunch of women, Chauncie. But I'm dealing with a group of hard-core men, who don't always work under the best conditions, and their tempers can flare at the drop of a hat.''

''Don't you think that's even more of a reason to treat them with some more consideration?''

''No,'' he mumbled, still unwilling to concede. How could he explain to her that the only way he was able to deal with them was to be tough? Maybe more than necessary, but tough. How could he explain that he didn't want to get attached, or care about them or their lives? He had to stay in control. His work was all he had and he wouldn't lose that by being soft. When you cared, people took it as a weakness.

She eyed his stern profile, unwilling simply to give up. ''Anyway, I thought we had a deal. You'd teach me how to run a business, and I'd teach you how to make friends.''

He frowned.

''As a matter of fact, I have a great idea,'' she said, not dissuaded by his scowling expression. ''Let's have an after-work party next Friday. Your staff and mine. We close the shop, order some food, turn on the music, and really get to know each other.''

''A party! You must be kidding,'' he grumbled. He slowly shook his head. He'd never socialized with his men before. He just . . .

''Don't even think about saying no. It would be perfect.''

''Chauncie—''

''A deal is a deal, Drew.''

She leaned forward, her eyes sparkling, her smile inviting, and he knew resistance was futile.

On the walk back, Chauncie told him the reason for the overflow of women in the shop, and Drew cracked up laughing for almost the entire trip. Then something that had started down in the pit of her stomach found its way upward and out.

''The real reason I wanted to leave early was because I wanted each and every one of them to see me with you.'' She looked boldly at him.

He stopped walking, slipped off his shades and looked into

her eyes. "Why?" he asked softly, almost as if he were afraid of the answer.

Chauncie's heart started to pound. She knew she'd crossed the line and hadn't even seen it coming. "I'm not good with the competition thing," she admitted. "I wanted to keep the playing field clear for a minute."

All of a sudden the last of his reasons why not crumbled like a crushed Ritz cracker. "What if I told you the field was clear?"

Her mouth curved ever so slowly. "Then I'd say, let the games begin."

# Making Moves

As promised, Drew attended her rehearsal on Thursday and was simply enthralled watching her perform. If he had any doubts about her ability to mesmerize, she erased them. He could truly see that acting was her calling. All she needed was a break. Afterward, they had a late dinner, talked about her rehearsal and strolled along the avenues of Harlem, enjoying the light breeze that blew gently around them before returning to Drew's car. After a day and a half of badgering from Chauncie, and hearing the enthusiasm over the idea from both staff, Drew had grudgingly agreed to the after-work party. It seemed as though everyone was really looking forward to it except him. He wouldn't even know how to act around his men. And he had serious doubts about wanting them to see him un-bosslike. To him it just spelled trouble.

"The party is going to be great," Chauncie said when they neared her apartment.

"So you keep telling me," he mumbled, sounding gruff.

She elbowed him in the side. "You know you're looking forward to partying. When was the last time you really hung out and had a good time?"

"I'm sure a lot longer than you have," he admitted. He blew out a breath and gazed up toward the stars.

She angled her body in the seat and reached out to him. She cupped his chin and turned his head to face her. "Are you in a hurry to go home?" she whispered.

He looked into her eyes, to see if he could see what it was

she was really asking. "Not if you don't want me to."

Chauncie took a breath. "I'm not sure what I want. Right now, I don't want you to leave. What all that means I don't know."

"It needs to mean something, Chauncie. That much I'm sure of. Otherwise there's no point." He took her hand. "I don't want to get into anything just for the sake of availability. I really like you, Chauncie. More than I realized. I don't want to take it too fast and miss something really important."

She smiled, partly because what he said was so incredible and partly because she was honored. When was the last time she'd been with a man who would turn down a chance? Humph. She couldn't remember. And here was a man who actually had some substance and was looking for something more than just the moment. Whatever feelings were brewing for Drew Lennox just reached another level.

"Well, how about if you come up for a while and we continue to get to know each other over an old movie, some popcorn, and into-the-night conversation, just to make sure we don't miss anything?"

"I like the sound of that."

Drew couldn't remember the last time he'd been in such a foul mood. But if he wanted to be honest with himself, he'd admit that his real problem was nerves. Pure and simple. He'd long-since forgotten how to socialize and didn't know if he wanted to remember. Socializing reminded him of his married days. A time best forgotten.

All he'd heard about all week was the party. *The party.* All the men were bringing their wives or girlfriends and from Chauncie's nonstop conversation about the shindig, all of her employees were coming and bringing their significant others.

He slammed his toolbox shut, snatched a handkerchief from his back pocket, and swiped it across his brow. He needed some air. The banging, dust, noise, and chatter about the party that night was giving him a major headache and his stomach was one big knot. He stalked toward the door and went out to the front.

As usual, the salon was packed. He shook his head in amazement. *If a woman didn't do anything else, she would spend some money to have her hair done*. He kept going past the booths toward the exit, barely acknowledging the hellos and finger waves from the stylists. He opened the door and stepped outside.

"Drew."

Any other time the sound of Chauncie's voice would have been a balm to his soul, but not today. For a hot minute he wanted to ignore her and just keep going. Reluctantly, he stopped and turned.

Chauncie hurried across the pink-and-blue marble floor, her heels click-clicking, as usual. He clenched his jaw and frowned.

"Hi. Heading out to lunch?" She walked out beside him, her smile bright and inviting.

"Yeah. Why?"

It was Chauncie's turn to frown. She angled her head to the side and planted her hand on her right hip. "What is wrong with you?" she asked, enunciating every word.

"Tired. Can't I be tired?"

She stared at him for a moment, taken aback by his tone and realizing that he wasn't actually looking at her, but through her. "I didn't say that, Drew," she responded softly. She wanted to reach out and rub away the deep furrows on his brow. "I thought if you were going out to lunch we could go together," she said instead.

"Maybe some other time, Chauncie."

She blinked and tried to swallow down the hurt that suddenly hung in her throat. She forced a smile. "Sure. We'll see each other tonight at the party anyway."

"Uh." He shook his head. "I'm not too sure about that. Something came up and I doubt if I'll be able to get away."

"Something came up? Just like that?" She popped her fingers for emphasis. "Why don't you be honest with yourself, Drew, and with me? You were never too keen on the idea in the first place and you never wanted to come."

"That's right. I wasn't and I'm still not. So you shouldn't

be surprised if you don't see me.'' He turned away.

"What *would* surprise me is you coming down off of that employer pedestal of yours and showing your men that you're a human being!'' she shot at his back with a little neck roll for emphasis, before spinning on her heels and storming back inside the shop.

The words hit him like daggers, momentarily faltering his step, but he kept walking. To nowhere in particular. Just walking.

Chauncie couldn't figure out if she was angry, hurt, or just plain old disappointed. She knew Drew had some doubts and some personal issues about mingling with his staff, but she'd thought that with her coaxing and all the excitement of the employees and the preparations going on, he would have eased into the idea by now. Obviously she was wrong.

The balance of the day flew by and the stylists worked at lightning speed to get their customers out as soon as possible. By seven-thirty the shop was empty and party preparations were underway.

While everyone buzzed around, setting out food, sweeping floors, and decorating, Chauncie wondered where Drew was. She hadn't seen him since he'd walked out at lunchtime and she refused to ask any of his men where he was.

She sighed as she mixed the bowl of punch.

The music was going full blast, the guests were beginning to filter in and there was still no sign of Drew. Maybe this wasn't such a good idea in the first place, Chauncie thought, taking surreptitious glances around in the hope of spotting Drew coming through the door. She'd always been a people person, loved to be the belle of the ball, the center of attention. And to her there was nothing like having a good time. It was hard for her to imagine that there were those who found socializing something to turn your nose up at.

She filled a cup with punch and took a small sip. *Not bad.* She poured in a bottle of seltzer to give it a little kick and stirred some more.

"Where's Drew?" Ruthie asked, easing up alongside her.

Chauncie's stomach tightened. She turned and plastered a smile on her face. "He told me he may not be able to make it. Something came up," she said as casually as she could.

Ruthie arched a brow. "Oh." Then she patted Chauncie's shoulder. "Well, whether he comes or not, I just wanted to tell you this was a great idea. And even if the others haven't said anything, you've done a damn good job of running the shop over the past two weeks. Your mama would be proud."

Chauncie felt warm all over. "Thanks, Ruthie, that means a lot."

Ruthie waved her thanks away with a shake of her hand. "Just have a good time." She turned and walked away.

Chauncie refilled her cup, took a breath of determination, and did what she did best—charmed everyone who she came into contact with. Before she knew it, the tightness in her chest was slowly easing as she talked with the wives, girl-friends, and boyfriends, saw to it that everyone had what they needed and that they were having a good time. The center of the shop had been cleared out and couples were on the floor dancing to "My Way" by Usher. But it was Reggie who captured everyone's attention with his skintight jumpsuit in gold lamé with splashes of iridescent color as he gyrated across the floor.

Chauncie was so busy hand-clapping and foot-stomping at Reggie's antics that she didn't see Drew when he first walked in the door, until her attention was drawn to his tall, handsome figure striding across the room.

Her heart thumped. His gaze was fixed on her face until he stood right in front of her.

"Hi," she whispered.

He slung his hands into the pockets of his pants. "Hi."

"Fixed that thing that came up?" She gave him a soft smile.

"Yeah. Something like that." He looked around. "Quite a turnout."

She nodded. "Why don't I introduce you around? Everyone has been asking for you.'' She took his arm and felt him tense, then slowly relax.

''Chauncie . . .''

She looked up at him.

''I—this is hard for me. For a lot of reasons. Crossing the line from employer to hang-out partner is one. I worked too hard to rebuild my life and I never wanted to jeopardize it by letting my men think I was one of them, and then lose their respect as a result. All my experiences of getting close to people, and letting them get close to me, have turned out to be disasters.'' He swallowed, looked down, then back at her. ''I always associated being part of the party crowd with my ex-wife. Memories I'd just as soon forget.'' He took a breath. ''The reason why I'm here, the only reason why I'm here, is because of you. I realized that there was something more than my pride and my ego at stake. I didn't want to disappoint you. And—I want to take a chance again. Live again.''

Chauncie released a long sigh, rose slightly on her toes and touched his lips with hers. ''Then, hey, baby, let's party.'' She grinned.

She knew it was hard for him, and her chest swelled with pride and admiration as Drew slowly, tentatively, began to interact with the group. For the most part she stayed by his side, giving him support, adding sparks to the conversations, laughing at the jokes. And little by little, without him noticing, she began to ease back, give him some space as he became more comfortable.

They danced together, laughed, and gorged themselves on the food. Drew even danced with Ruthie and Blaize to the delight of everyone. And before anyone knew it, it was nearly two A.M.

Chauncie insisted that everyone go on home and she would clean up—and they were more than happy to agree. Drew hung behind and locked the door behind the final straggler, who, of course, was Reggie.

''Well, Mr. Lennox, you actually survived,'' Chauncie grinned with her hands on her hips.

"Looks like I did." He crossed the room to stand in front of her. "Thanks to you."

"You did it, Drew. You gave yourself a chance and it worked out. *And* you had a good time." She rolled her eyes up and down his tight, muscular body. "I saw you out there, working out Ruthie and Blaize."

He tossed his head back and laughed. "With those two, I would definitely say it was the other way around."

"Your crew really likes you, Drew," she said softly. "As a boss and a friend. Tonight didn't change that—it only made it better."

He put his arm around her shoulder, drawing her close. "You know what, Ms. Assistant Manager? I think you're right." He kissed her forehead. "Let's get this place in shape and get out of here."

"Ooh, back to giving orders again." She chuckled.


Drew and Chauncie continued to spend all of their evenings and free time together. It was as if they couldn't get enough of each other. At the shop Chauncie always found an excuse to take a trip to the back, "just to check on things." Or Drew would find a reason to seek Chauncie out to ask her opinion about whatever came into his head, just so he could see her. Everyone thought it was so cute.

They talked about everything, and day by day, Chauncie became more adept at running the shop—she'd even found an excellent replacement for Annie, one of Blaize's references. And Drew actually could be heard in the back laughing with his men. Her staff slowly had begun to accept her and she even went to them for advice or input and they came to her with little confidences that they hadn't previously shared.

The renovations were nearly completed and the job should be finished in about another week, Drew told her one evening as they sat curled on her couch.

Her heart thumped. "Another week?"

"Looks that way. It's all touch-ups now and painting."

Her thoughts began to run amok. Would that mean that *they* would be finished, too? Even though they spent all of their free time together, they never really talked about anything beyond tomorrow, as if to discuss it would make whatever was happening between them real.

She swallowed. "Oh," was all she could say.

Drew curved his arm around her shoulder and pulled her close. He tilted her chin up with the tip of his finger. "Don't go there, Chauncie. I may not see you every day, like I do now, but that's not going to stop me from being with you every chance I get. If it's what you want." His heart raced. Suppose this was just something for her to do? Something to occupy her summer? What if she didn't want the *more* that he did?

"Drew, I knew a long time ago that I wanted to make this work out between us. That I wanted to be with you. I've just never been really sure what you wanted, except to wait." She grinned mischievously. "We talk about everything except where we want to go—together."

"I've been taking my time because I wanted *you* to be sure. I went through a lot in my relationship with my ex-wife, Chauncie. It turned me away from getting seriously involved with anyone, until I met you. I don't think I could take that kind of hurt again."

"I'd never hurt you, Drew," she whispered, stroking his cheek. "Can't you see that I'm in love with you?"

The air rushed to his chest, filling his lungs. His eyes roved over her face. "Chauncie—"

"Sssh." She put her finger to his lips, then replaced it with her own. "Don't talk," she said against his mouth.

And he didn't, at least not with words. He let his body, his hands, his mouth do his talking for him and Chauncie responded in kind with the roll of her hips, the swell of her breasts, the stroke of her fingertips along his bare back.

Their conversation was a symphony of perfect harmony, finishing each other's sentences, responding to all the questions that their bodies craved answers to. They spoke with damp flesh and shaken moans of pleasure, melding together, rising in tempo, matching each rise and fall, each rock and roll, until finally their voices could no longer be contained and erupted in unified cries of their names in a shuddering exclamation point of complete satisfaction.

He held her close, needing to assure himself that what they'd just experienced, what he'd felt as he moved within her, was real. That what they had was real. He knew he was still afraid. But crossing the line with Chauncie could be so easy. She filled him, made him feel whole, feel human, feel needed and wanted. His heart knocked in his chest and his throat tightened. She loved him. She'd said it. He believed her because he felt the same way.

About a week later, Drew tapped on the office door.

"Come in."

"Hi." He closed the door behind him and crossed the room. Leaning down, he pressed his lips to her upturned mouth and took a long, slow kiss.

"Hi, yourself," she whispered when he eased back.

He pulled up a chair and straddled it. "We're all done. I wanted you to come and take a look."

Her heart thumped. *This was it.* She put on a bright smile. "Sure."

She followed him to the back and stepped into what had once been a dingy storage room. Although she'd been watching the progress over the past month and a half, it was still incredible to see the transformation. Especially now that all of the tools and debris had been removed. The cool mint-julep-colored walls were accented by darker pillars set throughout the space. A counter circled the entire area, and a drop ceiling with hidden lighting gave the room a soft, inviting atmosphere.

"It's wonderful."

He smiled. "We finished the extra bathroom in the back this morning. All that's left is to get your furnishings in here."

"I suppose my mother will want to take care of that when she gets back." She took a breath. "So, where's your next job?"

"I was hoping to get something in the area. But it didn't work out. Our next gig is in New Jersey. We start next week."

"Oh." She turned to leave.

"Chauncie."

She stopped. Drew walked up behind her and held her shoulders. "What we have, Chauncie, has nothing to do with working together." He leaned down and kissed the back of her neck. "If I was a million miles away—I would still love you."

She spun around, her eyes wide, her heart pumping. "Love me?"

He looked down into her eyes and felt himself sinking. "Yes, love you. I love you."

She tried to wrap her arms around his broad back but they wouldn't reach, so she did the best she could, squeezing her body against his.

"Maybe we'll discuss it. Tonight. At my place, after a long, hot bath, a delicious meal and—well, we'll figure out the rest." He lowered his head, curved his fingers in her hair and pulled her close. "And maybe I'll even tell you that I love you again."

"Hmmm, not if I beat you to it," she moaned against his mouth.


Della stood in the opened doorway, a soft smile curving her mouth. Ruthie had kept her updated on Chauncie's progress during her absence, and she wasn't anything less than thrilled. As she'd walked through the shop, she could feel its vibrancy, almost a new energy. And everyone had something positive to say about Chauncie. She'd taken a quick look at the books in her office and found everything to be in tip-top shape. Not to mention that they had a pick-up service for the deposits, something she'd promised herself she'd do for years.

Now, standing there watching her daughter being embraced, and obviously in love, she knew that she'd done the right thing; putting her in charge of the shop had forced her to take on some responsibility. And putting her in the path of Drew Lennox had healed his wounded heart and stolen her daughter's.

She smiled, turned, and walked back into the shop. Funny how things happen, *just like that*!

# The Awakening

# Francis Ray

# Chapter One

Gabe Jackson didn't like rushing and he didn't like being late. Thanks to the message he'd listened to an hour ago on his answering machine from Shelton, his younger brother, Gabe was both. And in one of the worst possible places—the crowded concourse of Newark Airport. Hurrying around a slow-moving family, Gabe passed Gate 17. Gate 23 was his destination.

A glance at his Rolex told him Flight 675 from Atlanta, Georgia, had landed ten minutes ago. There was no guarantee that Jessica Ames would still be waiting at the gate despite Shelton's instructions to meet her there.

Gabe blew out a disgusted sigh. Although he hadn't dated in months, it had been his experience that women generally did what they wanted, and although they could keep you waiting for hours, if the man were a single minute late, he'd have hell to pay. He was now eleven and counting.

He hurried past Gate 20, thinking it was a good thing he kept in shape by jogging every morning. The things he did for his only sibling.

Gabe certainly could have thought of a more pleasant way to meet his future sister-in-law for the first time. He hoped she wasn't snooty. More than a few of the rich young women he had met thought the world should bow at their well-shod feet.

Whatever the outcome of their meeting, he'd have more of a handle on why Shelton had given him that strange answer when Gabe asked when he had found time to fall in love or court a woman with his busy schedule.

*Gate 23.* Gabe quickly scanned the waiting area and saw only one woman alone. Her slim arms were wrapped tightly around her waist, and her eyes searched the crowd as anxiously as his did. His gaze skimmed past her, dismissing her completely.

Shelton liked his women sexy, elegant, and vibrant. The drab-looking woman had on a mud-brown suit that did nothing for her smooth, almond complexion. In fact, if she hadn't been standing where the sunlight poured through the windows on an unusually sunny October day in New Jersey, or hadn't looked so tense, he might not have noticed her at all. Talk about someone blending into the wall.

As seconds passed, Gabe's hope that Jessica Ames had patiently waited plummeted. Muttering under his breath, he turned to leave.

For some odd reason his gaze went back to the nondescript woman in brown. She was watching him, her lower lip tucked between her teeth. The moment he met her gaze, she glanced away in obvious embarrassment.

It had been so long since Gabe had encountered a shy woman that he simply stared. From the Louis Vuitton case at her feet, her handbag by the same designer, the long, brown cashmere coat slung carelessly on the back of a seat, it appeared she wasn't hurting for money.

Although someone should have told her that brown wasn't her color. Not even his mother wore deep pleated skirts to mid-calf. And her French roll-styled hair was definitely for a much older woman.

Poor thing, he thought. She must be waiting for someone to pick her up. She had apparently stayed put, whereas Jessica Ames had taken off to God knows where. He wasn't looking forward to tracking her down. Knowing he didn't have a choice, he went to find a phone to have her paged.

A short distance away, his steps slowed, then stopped completely as he recalled Shelton's answer to his question. "Some women don't require as much to woo and win, especially when there are other considerations and compensations to be considered.''

Whirling, Gabe rushed back to Gate 23. The woman in brown hadn't moved. She waited, just as Shelton had said she would.

Gabe's certainty that she was Jessica Ames grew with each heartbeat, and so did his apprehension. He didn't like to think his brother was so cruel or so callous as to hurt any woman, but particularly one who seemed so vulnerable or ill-equipped to bounce back.

Gabe was a realist and he knew some people, unlike his devoted parents, married for reasons other than love, but he couldn't help wondering if she knew how Shelton felt or if he had pulled a fast one. It wasn't difficult to imagine his handsome, smooth-talking brother getting over on this luster-less woman.

Although she wasn't Shelton's type, she had something else to attract his ambitious brother. If this was Jessica Ames, her father was senior partner of the prestigious Ames & Koch law firm based in Atlanta that he worked for. And Shelton wanted to become a full partner.

Although he loved his brother, who was five years younger, Gabe wasn't blind to his many faults. He was a climber, in society and business. He wanted to succeed and he was well on his way to doing so by being in charge of opening a new branch of the firm in New York. If Gabe didn't miss his guess, the woman standing several feet away was an integral part of Shelton's plan in obtaining that partnership.

Besides, Gabe thought, if Shelton really loved her, he'd have been there to meet her after six weeks' absence. He'd kiss her breathless, then whisk her off someplace where they could be alone. He wouldn't have been so thoughtless as to leave a message on Gabe's answering machine, then be out of his office and unavailable. If was almost as if she were an afterthought.

Same old Shelton. Always thinking what he had to do or say was more important than what anyone else did. He couldn't have chosen a better career than corporate law. He'd do well swimming with the sharks. Gabe had once swum the same dangerous waters until he took a hard look at his life and hadn't liked what he saw.

Pushing away the memory, he walked up to the woman. All he could hope for was that she knew what she was letting herself in for. "Excuse me, are you Jessica Ames?"

She jerked her head toward him, her eyes widening. He was surprised at how beautiful they were despite being rimmed by the ugliest brown frames he had ever seen. Obviously she had noticed him watching her before and she took a hesitant step back.

Belatedly Gabe remembered the aviator shades he had forgotten to remove, and slipped them on top of his head.

There wasn't much else he could do to reassure her. The closely cropped beard and mustache, his mother was fond of telling him, made him look like a hoodlum.

He smiled in reassurance. "Sorry, I didn't mean to startle you. I'm Gabe Jackson, Shelton's brother. He couldn't make it."

Jessica glanced from the large, blunt-tipped fingers on the hand extended toward her, then back to the broad-shouldered mocha-skinned man in front of her. He wore a gently worn black leather bomber jacket, paint-splattered jeans, and a smile that probably let him get away with anything he wanted.

He looked wholly dangerous in a way only a woman could understand. It didn't take much imagination on her part to see him astride a big motorcycle, his hands gripping the handlebars as he revved the motor, daring fate, daring a woman to climb on behind him.

He frowned, deepening the grooves in his forehead. "You are Jessica Ames, aren't you?"

Hastily she extended her hand. It wasn't like her to be so whimsical. "Yes. I'm sorry. It's just that I was expecting Shelton, and you don't look anything like him."

The grin returned. White teeth flashed in his darkly handsome face. "So he likes to point out." He reached for her train case. "I know this isn't all you brought for two weeks in New York."

Picking up her long coat, she tried to smile, hoping he didn't remember her staring at him. At least he couldn't possibly know she had been speculating on the color of his eyes. Black, deep and velvet and as lethal as the rest of him. "The rest of my luggage is at baggage claim."

"For a while I thought you might be there, too, or wandering around the airport."

She shook her head. "No matter how much I travel, airports tend to make me nervous. That's why I wanted to meet Shelton at Newark Airport, since passengers coming into LaGuardia or Kennedy can only be met by the public at the baggage claim area."

"Smart thinking." Gabe's hand closed lightly over her elbow. "Let's go get the rest of your luggage."

She fell into step beside him, noting he was several inches taller than Shelton and broader, but moved with an easy strength in paint-splattered athletic shoes. Shelton favored Bally as his footwear of choice. "Is Shelton meeting me at my aunt's apartment?"

Gabe assisted her onto the gliding steps before answering. "Afraid not. He'll be tied up until late tonight."

"Oh," she answered and looked away.

Gabe glanced down at the slender woman by his side. She had to be unhappy that Shelton wasn't anxious to see her. "He's pretty busy opening the new office."

"I know. My father is quite proud of him."

"How about you?"

Her head came up, surprise clearly evident on her face, as if she hadn't expected the question. "Of course."

Gabe nodded. "You just wish it didn't keep him away from you so much."

She focused ahead. "Shelton's work is very important to him."

It was on the tip of Gabe's tongue to ask if she was important to Shelton when they reached the end of the walkway. Continuing to the baggage claim area, it occurred to him that Jessica didn't act like a woman anxious to see her man. From the stiffness of her body next to his, he knew she was still tense, and for some reason he didn't think it was totally due to the busy airport.

With every piece of Louis Vuitton luggage Gabe pulled off the conveyor, Jessica's irritation and embarrassment grew. She had tried to tell her mother that she didn't need that much, but Henrietta Ames had been insistent. She even had the maid include Jessica's makeup case, which she hadn't opened in months.

Her mother wanted to make sure she was prepared when Shelton took her out. Jessica had tried to tell her that wasn't likely to happen.

She knew Shelton's priority was opening the new branch of the law firm in New York. His interest in Jessica had been fleeting at best. He had been kind enough to take her out several times during the two months he was in Atlanta, but it hadn't even begun to get serious.

Her parents believed differently. All they thought she had to do was accept Shelton's invitation to come to New York, and she'd have a big diamond engagement ring on her finger when she returned home.

Shelton might be "fond" of her, as he often told her parents, but his heart belonged to the law office. She knew that. Most of what he talked about when they were together was the law firm and how much he admired her father. It was embarrassing the way her parents started throwing hints about what a fine catch he was. As if he were the last chance for their dull only child to snag a man.

Jessica was aware she wasn't attractive or athletic, and no matter what she wore, she tended to look dowdy. She had reconciled herself to that long ago. She didn't mind being nondescript or being by herself. She was used to both.

She valued her work at the women's shelter, and in January she was returning to graduate school to work on her Master's in education with an emphasis on counseling. She knew where she was going and it didn't include marrying someone who was "fond" of her, no matter what pressure her parents put on her.

Reminding her mother that Shelton's calls had been infrequent and hurried since he returned to New York hadn't dimmed her hopes of an engagement. She had simply had the maid take more clothes out of the closet. The wife of a corporate lawyer had to understand that business sometimes had to come first, but that in no way meant he didn't love his wife and family.

Jessica hadn't said another word. To do so would have shown her own doubts about how much her father loved his family. If that was how love was shown, she wanted no part of it. Only no one was listening.

"Five pieces. I'd say you came prepared," Gabe told her.

Jessica came out of her musing and flushed. If anyone knew how little Shelton thought of her or how unnecessary the mountain of baggage was, it was the man standing easily in front of her, his hands on his trim waist, a teasing smile on his mobile lips. She moistened her own.

There was no reason for her to notice his mouth. "You've been very kind. I can get a skycap and take care of things from here. Thank you."

Gabe stared at the small hand extended toward his, noted the unpolished oval nails, then lifted his gaze to Jessica's plain face. The smile was forced. "I hope you aren't going to insult me by suggesting I leave you."

Her hand wavered. "You must be busy."

"Not that busy." The moment the words were out of his mouth, hers tightened. "I'm self-employed. I make my own schedule," he quickly explained.

"Need any help with those bags?" asked a hopeful skycap, his hand wrapped around the handle of a luggage carrier.

"Thanks," Gabe said, grateful for the intervention, and he took Jessica's extended hand. He accepted the slight leap in his pulse rate due to nerves, and the slight jerk in her hand due to the same thing.

She lifted those large, solemn brown eyes to him. "I don't want to be a nuisance. I don't mind renting a car or grabbing a cab to Manhattan."

"I do. Driving in New York takes skill, nerve, and practice.

A weekday is no time to start developing either. And taking a cab unless necessary is sheer lunacy,'' Gabe said, leading her toward the exit, wondering where the crazy urge to hug her to him and reassure her that she wasn't a bother had come from.

''I may have been wrong about something,'' Jessica said, following him out the door.

''What?''

''You and Shelton are alike in some ways.''

Gabe felt annoyance sweep through him, and without slowing his stride, glanced down at her. There was no way he'd stoop to what his baby brother was planning to do, or treat a woman the way he had. ''How?''

''Once you make up your mind about something, nothing else matters.''

Gabe simply kept walking. He didn't think she had given him a compliment.

# Chapter Two

Jessica hadn't meant to anger Gabe. But one look at the tight set of his mouth and she knew she had.

She was almost certain it wasn't because he had forgotten his trunk was full and he and the skycap were having a difficult time putting her luggage in the backseat of his Mercedes. She thought it more likely had something to do with her comparison of him to Shelton.

At the time she had thought she was stating the truth. Now, watching him help the skycap instead of standing back and deeming the task menial and beneath him as her father or his associates would have done, she wasn't so sure. In any case, she absolutely hated people being upset with her and she usually bent over backward to avoid it from happening. That particular attribute had gotten her into her present situation.

The back door of the car slammed. "What's bothering you now?"

She frowned. "What are you talking about?"

He nodded toward her purse. "You're clutching it."

Surprised that he had paid that much attention to her, she felt even more miserable. All he had been was kind to her and she had hurt his feelings. "You're very astute."

"A man in my business has to be," he said, and opened the passenger door.

"What business is that?" she asked, hoping they could start over.

"Shelton didn't tell you?"

She shrugged slim shoulders. "He talked mostly about the law firm."

"Figures." Closing the door, Gabe walked back to the trunk and opened it. "Please come here."

Curious, she watched his head disappear behind the raised trunk and did as he instructed. She was still looking at him when he gestured toward the open trunk.

"That is what I do."

Jessica turned. A soft gasp of wonder slipped unnoticed past her lips. Without conscious thought, she moved closer to the oil painting of a black woman in a blue silk robe, her slender body bent over that of a smiling chubby baby in a wooden cradle. The baby's fingers were curled around one of the woman's. The picture was one of complete love.

"You did this?" she asked, her finger gently touching the clasped hand of mother and child on the canvas.

Many people had admired Gabe's work before, but no one's reaction had affected him more deeply. "Yes."

She glanced back up at him, her eyes shining with moisture, her face soft. "How does it feel to create something so beautiful, to know that a part of you will live on long after you're gone, and give pleasure to everyone who sees your work?"

The question caught Gabe off guard as much as the desire he suddenly felt to touch her face, to hold her in his arms. Until now, no one else had understood his desire to leave something tangible behind. His hands clenched instead. "Humble, scared, grateful."

Her attention refocused on the painting. "Is this for sale?"

"No. It's a surprise gift to the woman's husband. They're friends of mine," Gabe explained. "I'm supposed to deliver it tonight."

Jessica straightened and pushed her glasses back in place. "I'm glad the portrait is going to someone who will appreciate and cherish it. A lot of things in life aren't. Thanks for taking the time to share your work with me."

"My pleasure," he said, meaning it. "Maybe you can come by my studio before you leave."

The idea was so intriguing that Jessica almost said yes before realizing he was probably just being nice again. Men, especially ones as sexy and handsome as Gabe, never had time for her unless there was an ulterior motive. Somehow she didn't want to chance finding out Gabe was like all the other men before him.

Smothering her disappointment, she said, "I'd like that if I have time. Shall we go?"

Gabe had never been around a woman who confused him more. On the slow, bumper-to-bumper drive back on the George Washington Bridge after delivering the portrait to his friends in New Jersey, he wasn't able to get Jessica out of his mind.

One moment she had tears in her eyes looking at his painting, the next she was stiff and unapproachable. But he couldn't erase the image of the careful way she had touched the clasped hand and finger of mother and child.

Or the brief flash of hurt that crossed her expressive features when the maid at her aunt's apartment told her that her Aunt Irene had gone skiing with some friends. The maid wasn't sure when she would be back. Jessica was to make herself at home and her aunt would call later.

The thoughtlessness of her aunt and that of Shelton coming so close together had to bother her. Yet she had discounted both as if she had expected no less. Gabe's fingers flexed on the steering wheel as the black luxury car broke free of the bridge.

He'd attempted several times without success to reach Shelton after leaving Jessica earlier in the day. His secretary, then later his answering service, kept repeating he was unavailable. Gabe knew he wasn't with a woman unless it was business-related. Shelton might be a louse, but he was a loyal louse. Even so, sometimes Gabe could shake him.

Up ahead was the familiar turn to his brownstone on Striver's Row. If he continued, he could take 96th Street and be on the East Side with Jessica in twenty-five minutes. He rolled tired shoulders.

Since dawn he'd been up painting. She wasn't his problem.

Clearly she had wanted to get rid of him. He looked at the digital clock in the dash. Eight-forty-one.

The car passed his turn and kept going. It wouldn't hurt to check on her.

No one should spend their first night in New York alone.

Jessica couldn't have been more surprised to see Gabe through the peephole than if it had been Denzel Washington. Frowning, she unlatched and opened the door. "Did you forget something?"

One hand dug into the front pockets of his tailored slacks, but his gaze never faltered. "No. I thought I'd drop by and see if you were all right."

She stared at him a long moment, unsure if she had heard him correctly. People tended to forget her even when she was still in the room with them, but especially if she was out of sight. Her aunt and Shelton were perfect examples. "I beg your pardon?"

His hand zipped out of his pocket. "No one should spend their first night in New York alone."

Pleasure, slow as a sunrise, began to spread through her and reflect itself in her growing smile. "Actually I've been to New York several times."

"Oh." His gaze and feet shifted. "In that case, I guess I better let you get back to doing whatever it was you were doing."

He actually appeared embarrassed. The thought of her having such an effect on such a commanding figure was so incongruent that her smile burst into laughter. His shoulders stiffened beneath his leaf-green herringbone jacket. Nodding brusquely, he whirled and started down the wide, carpeted hallway at a fast clip.

He was several feet away before she realized he probably thought she had been laughing at him. She ran to catch up with him. "Wait. Please wait."

He did, but he didn't appear overjoyed by the prospect. "Yes?"

"I think you misunderstood me," she told him, searching

his eyes for some softening. "I'd like it very much if you'd come back inside and have dinner with me. I've never had to eat dinner alone in New York and I'd like not to start."

Her hands were clasped to her chest, her eyes behind her glasses were bright with expectation. The tightness in his stomach eased. "Sure."

Her smile blossomed. "I'll get another place setting."

By the time he was inside the apartment and had closed the door, she was rushing out of the kitchen with silverware, china, and a wineglass. He went to help.

"Slow down." Relieving her of everything, he quickly arranged the elegant place setting atop a white banana-silk place-mat with a matching silk organza napkin.

Looking up from placing the stemware etched in twenty-two-karat gold on the table, he found her staring at him. "Did I do it wrong?"

"I was just trying to imagine my father or one of his friends helping set the table, and I couldn't."

"Maybe they aren't as hungry as I am."

"I think it's more than that. Please have a seat."

He did, and in a matter of moments he was eating freshly grilled salmon. "My compliments to the chef."

She dipped her head in acknowledgment. "Thank you."

"You cooked this?"

She laughed, a low, sweet sound that made her expressive face come alive. Despite the lack of makeup, she was almost pretty. Large brown eyes sparkled in the light from the glass candelabrum. Gabe found himself laughing easily with her and thinking models would kill for her cheekbones.

"Since you picked me up from the airport and carried all my luggage up here, I'll consider your outburst a backhanded compliment," she said easily.

"Please do." He took another bite. "How did you learn to cook this well?"

"My mother." The smile slowly slid from her face. "It's part of my training, but I'm afraid she's doomed to disappointment."

"Training for what?"

Her head came up sharply, as if she had unintentionally revealed too much. Her head dipped briefly as she pushed her salmon around on the richly colored china featuring exotic butterflies and delicate gold blossoms. "It's too boring to talk about. I'd rather hear about you and your painting. You seem to have done well for yourself."

He decided to let her change the subject. Maybe if she knew him better, he could help her with whatever it was that caused her to look so down and retreat from him. "What you see is from my other life a little over two years ago as a stockbroker when I was pulling down six figures a year plus bonuses."

He placed his fork on his plate and gave her his full attention. "I've bought relatively few things since I decided to paint full time. Frankly, my art is not supporting itself yet."

"You gave all that up to paint? Why?"

Gabe had seen the same astonishment in the faces of other people, but this time he didn't see the derision. Somehow he had known he wouldn't. "Because I lost two close friends in less than six months. One to a car accident, the other to a massive coronary." His hand tightened around the stem of the wineglass.

"The three of us had big plans and dreams for the future. For them, that day never came. I decided I didn't want that to happen to me."

Her hand lightly touched his jacketed arm. "Walking away took more courage than staying."

"Most people think it was a cop-out."

"Not to anyone who has seen your work. You obviously did well as a stockbroker, but people were probably waiting in line to take your place once you left." Her fingers tightened. "Your paintings come from the heart and they can come only from *your* heart. Therein lies the difference."

His large hand covered hers. "Thanks."

Awkwardly she pulled her hand free and picked up her wineglass and took a sip. It didn't help to steady her nerves or to stop the strange sensation quivering through her.

Somehow she still felt the lingering touch of his hand on hers, of her hand on him. She had been right. Gabe made a woman want to risk everything and tempt fate.

Too bad she hadn't the foggiest notion of how to do either.

# Chapter Three

The next morning Gabe repeatedly rang Shelton's apartment doorbell, then pounded on the door when there was no response. It was half past seven and Shelton seldom left for his office until after eight. His baby brother had some explaining to do.

The door abruptly opened. Shelton stood with a towel wrapped around his narrow waist, water beaded on his well-conditioned brown body. "What's all the rush?"

Stepping past him, Gabe entered the immaculate apartment, done completely in stark white with splashes of black for accent. Glass and chrome gleamed everywhere. The apartment always reminded Gabe of a showroom, not a home.

"Where were you all day yesterday and last night?" Gabe fired.

Shelton swung the door closed. "Taking care of business. What do you think?"

"You couldn't have found one minute to call the woman you claim you're going to marry?" Gabe asked, the anger that had been simmering all night coming to a boil.

The frown on Shelton's boyishly handsome face cleared. "You always were a sucker for the lost ones. You dragged home so many stray animals and people, Mom always said she sometimes hated to see you come home."

Gabe planted his hands on his hips. "Jessica is not lost. She's a grown woman who you should show some consideration and attention."

"I got it covered, Gabe," Shelton said dismissively, turning toward his bedroom. "Jessica understands. She knows business comes first."

"Did she tell you this or is it your assumption?" Gabe asked, following Shelton into the luxurious bathroom. Greenery cascaded from high arches, and mirrors reflected the men's images and that of the immense sunken whirlpool tub and glass-enclosed shower.

Shelton picked up the electric shaver from the marble counter top. "Look, Gabe, I know since you left the corporate world you tend to think less of those of us who stayed. Jessica has been trained to be the wife of a corporate executive."

"She's not a puppy," Gabe snapped.

"Gee. I should have known not to ask you to meet her, but I needed someone to look after her while I was busy. I still do."

"You mean you're not going to see her today either?" Gabe asked, wondering how his brother could be so callous. "Then why in the hell did you invite her to New York?"

Looking as exasperated as his brother, Shelton laid the shaver aside. "I thought I'd have it together, but there are a few glitches that I need to straighten out before the office opens in thirteen days." His face hardened with resolve. "But it will open on schedule."

Gabe didn't doubt it for a minute. Nothing stood in Shelton's way when he wanted something. That was the reason he was so worried. "In the meantime, you expect Jessica to spend her time alone in her aunt's apartment?"

"Irene is there with her," he returned easily.

"Irene went skiing and she left a message with the maid saying she didn't know when she was returning. Seems she had something better to do, too," Gabe said, not even trying to hide his annoyance at the absent aunt and Shelton.

"What!" Shelton exclaimed. "How could she do this to me?"

Gabe shook his head. Did Shelton ever think of anyone besides himself? "How indeed?"

Shelton's eyes narrowed on his brother. "I need you now

more than ever with Irene gone. You have to help me on this, big brother. Keep Jessica occupied until I have time to ask her to marry me. Her parents have secretly given me their blessing.''

Something tightened in Gabe's gut. ''How does Jessica feel about this?''

''She'll be grateful. She's no raving beauty,'' Shelton scoffed.

Although Gabe had thought the same thing, hearing the words out loud made him want to shake his egotistical brother until his capped teeth rattled.

Apparently taking Gabe's silence for agreement, Shelton continued, ''I know personally she hasn't had a real date in years. Her male cousins were her escorts to her prom, her debutante parties, and her sorority functions. I'm her last chance for a marriage and she knows it. Her parents know it also, and they approve of my intentions.''

Gabe needed to know one thing. ''Do you care anything about her or is she a means to an end?''

''I wouldn't condemn myself to live with someone I didn't care anything about. She's reserved, intelligent, and manageable. I haven't even tried to make a move on her,'' Shelton related. ''I don't want my future wife to have even a hint of gossip linked to her name. After we're married, I promise I'll take care of her and respect her.''

''In exchange for an eventual partnership in her father's law firm,'' Gabe stated, certain of the answer.

Shelton winked and smiled. ''Senior partnership. Her old man can't live forever.''

Gabe looked down at the black marble floor, then back up at the man he had carried on his back as a child when he was too tired to walk, had given the tire off his own bike until his could be repaired, had fought bullies to keep him safe. ''I don't know you anymore.''

''Gabe, don't get sanctimonious on me,'' Shelton pleaded, his hand gripping his brother's upper forearm. ''You know I always keep my word. I won't be a bad husband to Jessica. Just help me out and keep her entertained for a few days.''

"On one condition."

Suspicion narrowed Shelton's black eyes. "What?"

"That you're up front with her and you let her make the decision; no coercion from you or her parents," he said, flatly ignoring something twisting inside him. "The choice has to be hers."

Shelton laughed his relief. "Whew. You had me worried. No sweat. Jessica knows what a catch I am."

Gabe shook his dark head in derision. "No wonder you've never liked wearing a hat. It would be impossible to find one to fit over that big ego of yours."

Grinning, Shelton playfully punched his older brother on his wide shoulder. "It's a good thing I love you."

"Likewise," Gabe said, then his eyes narrowed, his voice carrying a hint of steel. "Don't hurt her, Shelton."

"Why would I want to hurt the woman I'm going to marry?" he asked. "To show you, I'll send her some flowers."

Gabe nodded. It was a start. "A phone call and a visit would be better."

Shelton picked up the shaver and flicked it on. "I'll try to call, but I'm booked solid. Tell Jessica hello for me and I'll see her as soon as I can."

"I may help, but I'm not your messenger boy." Turning, Gabe left the room, feeling his brother's stare all the way.

Jessica awoke the next morning without much enthusiasm for getting out of bed. As she had told Gabe, she had been to New York before and although she thought the city fascinating, she didn't particularly enjoy the prospect of seeing it again by herself.

It was a sure bet that Shelton wouldn't be around to go with her. Not that she wanted him to, she thought, throwing back the goose-down comforter and getting out of bed. Now, his brother was a different matter and also entirely unlikely.

Pulling off her flannel nightgown, she adjusted the water in the shower and stepped beneath the tepid stream. Gabe was only being nice and she'd probably never see him again. The thought saddened her and the feeling stayed with her through getting dressed and eating breakfast.

Two hours later she still hadn't shaken her melancholy and was seriously considering booking the next flight home to Atlanta. Her parents would have to accept the fact sooner or later that she and Shelton weren't getting married. She had wanted to ignore Shelton's invitation, and had only accepted because her parents had insisted that she do so.

Sighing, she picked up a magazine. There was something to be said for moving out of your parents' home once you completed college. At least they couldn't nag you all the time.

She tossed the fashion magazine aside seconds later. It hurt to think that her parents thought so little of her ability to get a man on her own that they thought they had to practically throw her at Shelton. All right, she admitted, she hadn't been doing so hot in that area, but her parents were supposed to believe in her when no one else did.

Restless, Jessica pushed to her feet and stared at the New York skyline from her aunt's windows. She had known from childhood that her father had wanted a son to carry on the firm after he retired, and no matter what she thought of Shelton, he was reported to be a good lawyer.

The fact that he was in charge of opening the branch in New York was a clear indication and testimony of her father's faith in him. If George Ames couldn't have a son, a son-in-law was the next best thing.

He and her mother were both doomed to disappointment. Love was the only reason she was getting married and when she did, the man she chose wouldn't treat her as an afterthought. He wouldn't forget she existed unless he wanted something from her the way Shelton did.

The chime of the doorbell interrupted her thoughts. Waving away the maid, who had come from the study, Jessica went to the door. She had met many of Irene's friends. Her mother's older sister had quite a few colorful acquaintances. Hopefully it was someone Jessica knew and they wouldn't mind staying a little while to help her stave off boredom.

The idea was dismissed two steps later. She and Irene's

female friends, cultivated during her aunt's twenty years in New York, during which she had gone through three wealthy husbands, didn't have much in common. Most of them were into fashion, men, seeing and being seen, and remaining on the A-list. Things Jessica had little use for.

Her spirits taking a nosedive, she slowly opened the door. "Gabe!"

"Good morning, Jessica," he said easily, trying not to be delighted by the quick pleasure he saw radiating in her big chocolate-brown eyes. He couldn't quite manage it.

"Come in. Have you had breakfast?" she asked, taking his arm and pulling him inside.

"Unfortunately, yes, if you were going to cook for me," he told her lightly, thinking the lilac-colored sweater she wore suited her complexion better, although it was two sizes too big and hung past her hips.

She folded her arms across her chest. "Cheese and ham soufflé."

"You really know how to wound a bachelor," he told her, enjoying the light of humor dancing in her eyes.

Her arms slowly came to her side. "Maybe another time?"

"Count on it." There was no mistaking the wish in her soft voice. She was lonely and it was Shelton's fault. Gabe wasn't about to let her spend the remaining days of her visit waiting for his brother to call or drop by. She deserved better. "In the meantime I stopped by to see if you wanted to ride with me to the Hudson Valley. I have to deliver a portrait."

She didn't have to think. "I'd love to. I'll get my coat." Jessica dashed for the bedroom in an undignified manner that would have horrified her mother. She didn't care. She wanted to go with Gabe and she wasn't giving him a chance to change his mind.

"Get a scarf and gloves. The temperature is dropping outside," he told her retreating back, then shook his head. He didn't know if she'd heard him or not.

However, on returning, she was struggling to find the other sleeve opening on her long cashmere coat while continuing toward him. Brown leather gloves dangled from her coat pocket. An oversized paisley scarf hung around her neck.

Enjoying her enthusiasm, Gabe helped her with her coat. "You didn't give me a chance to tell you we'll be gone most of the day. Is that all right?"

"That's fine." With her coat on, she draped the scarf over her head and fingered her glasses back in place. "I have nothing scheduled. Is it another portrait?"

"In a way. Since you're from the South, you probably know that many old Southern churches deep in the rural country have a yearly homecoming celebration where all the old members return from wherever life has taken them. After service they eat dinner on the grounds because the churches are too small to hold everyone," he explained, following her to the door.

"Nathan Page, my client, is a retired minister who grew up going to homecomings in Louisiana. He commissioned me to paint such a scene using old family photographs."

She stopped pulling on her glove. "You re-created history. Can I see it?" she asked, then rushed on before he could answer. "No, I'll wait. I want to see his expression when he sees what a great job you've done."

He was touched. "You have that much confidence in me?"

"I've seen your work." Opening the door, she called over her shoulder to the maid. "Marla, I'll be gone all day."

"Yes, Miss Ames," answered the servant as she came across the living room. "Good morning, sir."

"Good morning," Gabe answered the elderly woman and followed a fast-retreating Jessica out the door.

Deep in thought, Gabe scratched his short-cropped beard as he followed her to the elevator. He couldn't help wondering how his brother could think her dull or reserved. Or how it was possible that he didn't want to be with a woman who obviously enjoyed life, if only someone took the time to show her how.

# Chapter Four

The big luxury car ate up the road like a hungry cat slurps milk—with finesse and pleasure. The heavily wooded and rolling countryside was postcard-pretty. Stately Colonial red-brick homes sat behind white wooden fences. Horses, their tails high, their shiny coats glistening in the noonday sun, ran for the sheer joy of being alive.

Gabe knew the feeling.

He'd never felt freer than he did these days. His checking account might not have as many digits as it had two years ago, but he wouldn't go back for three times the money.

Some things were worth taking a chance for and came without a price tag.

For some reason, he glanced at his silent passenger. Instinct and observation told him that Shelton was so caught up in what he saw, he hadn't taken time to look any further. Jessica was quiet, as she was now, and people probably tended to dismiss her. That was a mistake.

She was intelligent, sensitive, and compassionate. Which meant she had two more qualities than his baby brother possessed. She also had a smile that was pure sunshine. There was definitely more to her than was initially apparent.

For the past thirty minutes she had been silent, her gaze lingering first here, then there, her enjoyment evident by the slight upward curve of her unpainted lips. Delicate fingers occasionally tapped on her knee in perfect sync to the jazz music flowing from the CD.

A gust of wind sent a swirl of leaves across the road. The myriad colors ranged from deep golds to smoldering reds. Nature had outdone herself and the endless battle to keep the leaves raked from yards would last for months.

Two preteens, judging from their size and height, were already finding that out in the immense yard up ahead. Even as they worked, the brisk wind sent more leaves drifting to the ground.

Jessica nodded toward them as the car drew closer. "I wonder how long before they start playing?"

The words had barely left her mouth, when the smallest of the two did a back flip into the middle of a pile that came to his waist. The other somersaulted into his pile.

Gabe glanced into his rearview mirror and chuckled. "You called it. Sounds like you spoke from personal experience. Have you pulled some leaf-raking duties yourself?"

"A time or two."

"You can't make a statement like that and leave a guy hanging. How about some details?" Gabe asked, genuinely interested, wanting to know the woman behind the quiet, composed exterior.

Jessica looked at him in that strange way she had sometimes, as if she were trying to figure him out. "The countryside is beautiful. Why spoil it with details about my boring life?"

"Everybody's life is boring to them."

"Well, mine actu—Don't hit Rocky!" she shouted, sitting up straight in her seat.

Gabe had already seen the squirrel dart out onto the highway and gently braked. "Rocky? Don't tell me you're a fan of Rocky and Bullwinkle."

"Don't forget Boris and Natasha, and the Fractured Fairytales," she admitted with a wry twist of her mouth. "I think my tolerance of cartoons is the main reason the children like having me around."

"Children?"

"I teach preschool to the three- and four-year-olds at the women's shelter where I volunteer," she said.

"There is no way you can tell me that's boring." Gabe looked at her. "Some of my friends have children that age and the only time they stop moving is when they're asleep."

"No, *they're* never boring, but working with them is the best and worst part of my job," she admitted slowly.

"How so?"

She sent him that strange look again, but continued, "A few women who come to the shelter are homeless, but the majority are there because of abusive relationships. The women have gone through a horrific amount of physical and emotional pain and suffering." Her hands clenched in her lap as she continued speaking.

"They have difficulty understanding why the man who says he loves them treats them so cruelly. It's so much worse for the children I work with. Their young world is in chaos. They want to go home, sleep in their own bed, and not be surrounded by strange people and unfamiliar surroundings. They can't."

Anger crept into her tightly controlled voice. "So many of them think being there or the situation at home is their fault. They shouldn't have to suffer because their mother chose the wrong man to fall in love with."

His hand closed around her clenched fist. "So you watch cartoons with them and let them know they're safe, and for that moment in time at least, they have control over some aspect of their lives."

"I want to do so much more," she said fiercely. "I'm enrolling in graduate school in January to begin work on my Master's in Education with an emphasis on guidance counseling."

Something wasn't right here. Shelton would want a wife at his beck and call. Slowly Gabe removed his hand. "In Atlanta?"

She nodded. "That way I can still work at the shelter. Mrs. Lewis, a retired schoolteacher, is taking my place while I'm here."

"I suppose you've discussed this with your parents?" he

asked, delicately probing further as he pulled into the Pages' driveway.

"I'm not sure 'discussed' is the correct word," she told him, slipping her scarf over her head.

Gabe slowed down to a crawl and hoped the effusive, elderly couple didn't see him drive up and come out to greet him. "Would you care to explain that?"

"I told them and, as usual, they completely ignored my plans and kept talking about what they wanted me to do." She dug in her coat pocket and pulled on her gloves. "They mean well and I'm ninety-six percent sure they love me, but they won't believe I won't do as they say until I come home loaded with my textbooks. It's the only thing that has worked in the past."

Gabe stopped behind the couple's RV and cut the motor. Although he had a pretty good idea, he asked anyway, "What is it they want you to do?"

"To settle, to be less than I can." She pulled her coat over her shoulders. "I've seen too many people ruin their lives that way to allow the same thing to happen to me." She looked straight at him. "Like you, I'm going to follow my dream, regardless of what others think I should do."

"Are you sure?" he asked.

"I'm aware you don't know me very well, but I've always been a methodical person. I don't think I've ever done an impulsive thing in my life," she said softly. "Yes, I'm sure. Nothing is going to change my mind."

*Least of all my brother*, Gabe thought as he read the determination in her face, the set of her small shoulders. Shelton, you're going to lose this time. But Jessica would win. Gabe felt himself smiling at the prospect. "Then I wish you luck."

"Thanks." She returned the smile with interest, then reached for the door handle. "Come on and let's get the portrait inside. I can't wait to see what you've done."

The twenty-by-thirty portrait was as spectacular as Jessica had known it would be. There were a dozen animated black people sitting on colorful quilts or standing around talking, with a

white-steepled church in the background. Their facial expressions were so lifelike, she felt they'd respond to her if she
spoke to them.

Judging from the awestruck way Reverend Page stared at
the portrait Gabe had placed on the easel he had brought with
him, the elderly man agreed with her. His frail hand trembled
as he pointed out various relatives. When he reached his de-
ceased parents, his eyes misted and his arm tightened around
his diminutive wife.

He insisted on calling his brother, who lived nearby. In a
little over an hour the house was filled with friends and relatives who had come to see the portrait. There was nothing
but praise for Gabe's work. With each accolade, her pride in
him grew.

Standing in the midst of a small group of people, she
glanced up and found Gabe watching her from across the
room. The troubled expression on his bearded face cleared
when she smiled at him.

Sipping her coffee, she still found it difficult to believe that
with all the attention Gabe was receiving, he didn't forget her.
She had been to numerous social functions, but she couldn't
ever remember someone keeping an eye on her to make sure
she was all right the way Gabe was. More often than not,
people lost interest in her as soon as the social pleasantries
were completed.

Not Gabe. He had introduced her as his friend. Not as the
friend of his brother. Apparently, he didn't use the term
lightly. She didn't even try to discount how pleased she was
by the distinction of his phrasing. If the crazy idea occasionally slipped into her mind that she'd like for him to be much
more, she wasn't foolish enough to dwell on it.

Some dreams were possible, others were inconceivable.
Friendship was better than nothing, especially if the friend
was Gabe.


The lush scent of roses greeted Jessica the moment she opened
her aunt's apartment door. On the glass cocktail table were

two dozen deep red roses arranged among various cut flowers in a round crystal vase. She sneezed.

"Bless you," Gabe said, closing the door behind them. So Shelton had gotten around to sending flowers. Too little, too late.

Jessica sneezed again.

"Bless you." He frowned down at her. "Are you coming down with a cold?"

She shook her head and pointed at the floral arrangements. "Snapdragons. I'm allergic to them."

"Wh—"

Another sneeze cut him off. "Please take them out of here or I'll sneeze myself silly." As if to prove her point, she sneezed again.

Unsure of what to do with them, Gabe picked up the bouquet. She sneezed again. "Move away from the door and I'll set them outside."

Nodding, holding her finger beneath her nose, she did as he instructed. She sneezed again.

Coming back into the room, he handed her the card. "Will you be all right?"

"I'm not sure." She opened the envelope and read the message. "They're from your brother."

Gabe felt he'd be disloyal not to speak up in his brother's behalf. "I'm sure he didn't know about your allergies."

She sneezed again.

"Miss Ames, you're back," the maid said and glanced around. "Where are your beautiful flowers?"

"In the hallway. I'm allergic to the snapdragons in them," Jessica explained, waiting for the next sneeze.

"Oh, what a shame. They are so lovely," she said.

Jessica sneezed again. "Then please take them with my blessings." She looked at Gabe. "Do you think you could stand to be with me for another hour or so until the air clears in here?"

He glanced at his watch. "It's only a little past seven. We can catch a movie."

"Marla, please see that the flowers are gone by the time I

get back,'' she said, trying to hold back another sneeze.

''Right away, Miss Ames,'' the woman promised. ''I'll turn the ventilation on.''

''Thank you.''

His arm around Jessica, Gabe led her back the way they had come. Poor Shelton, he was certainly batting zero.

Outside in the cool night air, Gabe stared down into her face. ''Feeling better?''

''Much.''

The corner of his mouth quirked. ''Allergic to snapdragons, huh?''

''Very.''

''So I won't make the same mistake, are there any other flowers to steer clear of?'' he inquired.

Jessica's heart stopped, then raced wildly in her chest. He could send her a weed and she'd be happy. ''That's about it.''

''So my meticulous brother managed to send you the only flowers you're allergic to?''

She nodded.

''When Shelton makes a mistake, it's a doozie.'' Taking her hand, he started down the street.

Jessica shivered, her heart rate going crazy. The sexiest man in the universe was actually holding her hand. Thank you, Shelton, for inviting me to New York, she thought. Forgive me for all the unkind things I thought of you.

The street light changed to 'Walk.' Gabe released her hand, his arms curving naturally around her waist, drawing her closer to him. Jessica went willingly and without a moment's hesitation, a dreamy smile on her face.

# Chapter Five

Elbows propped on her knees, the palms of her hands cupping her face, Jessica stared at the silent white phone in the living room. Sunlight had finally pushed away the smog that had covered the city most of the morning and it now shone through the wall of windows behind her.

She didn't particularly care. Her entire attention was focused on the phone since the clock on the mantel ticked past twelve and Gabe hadn't called.

In the past two days he had always called or dropped by by now.

They'd talked about his work, her plans. She hadn't realized how much she enjoyed those times with him until they stopped.

Sighing, she glanced at her tiny gold wristwatch. Two minutes after one. He had told her he'd be busy completing a family portrait, but how long did it take to make one simple phone call?

Her shoulders jerked upright in her snake-print silk top as inspiration struck. Picking up the phone, she dialed information. Seconds later she was speaking to Shelton's secretary.

As Jessica had expected, the woman didn't hesitate to give her Gabe's address and phone number. Hanging up the phone, she decided there were certain advantages to being the boss's daughter.

Staring at the information, she came to a quick decision.

Gabe had invited her to see his studio. Today was as good a time as any.

With a smile, she raced to the bedroom. Pulling on the stone-colored sueded silk jacket that matched her pants, she grabbed her coat and her purse. Passing the dresser, she happened to glance at the mirror.

Her steps slowed. Her smile faded. Not for the first time in her life she wished that she could have had a nodding acquaintance with pretty.

Her features were proportioned, but ordinary. The eyeglasses for her myopia didn't help. The only thing she had going for her was her unblemished, clear brown skin. Her shoulder-length black hair refused to hold a curl or stay styled the way she combed it, and had been a problem since she was in junior high.

Her salvation had been styling gel that kept her hair in place, or so she had thought. The French twist she had worn for years because of its neatness and practicality now seemed too severe for her oval face. The bangs covering her high forehead helped a little, but she needed something more.

Leaning closer to the mirror, she studied her reflection critically. Maybe if she wore makeup other than a lip gloss it might soften her face and bring out her dark brown eyes. They were kind of pretty at times. But here again, she never seemed to have the patience to apply it just like the fashion consultant did.

More time was spent trying to get the smeared mascara from beneath her eyelids than doing the whole makeup routine. Eyeliner was impossible, and dangerous. Afterwards she usually resembled a raccoon or a little girl turned loose in her mother's makeup kit.

She glanced at the closed train case on the dresser. Perhaps she should try again.

Becoming aware of what she was doing and thinking, she straightened and started for the front door. Gabe liked her the way she was. She hadn't tried to impress a man since Kendall Lawson in the eighth grade.

She had almost broken her neck in the high heels and she

looked ridiculous in the frilly blue dress for the eighth grade dance. Kendall had laughed so hard he rolled on the floor.

She wasn't putting herself through that again. Gabe had to take her the way she was. Telling the maid she was leaving, Jessica went downstairs and hailed a cab. Friends accepted each other the way they were.

Jessica told herself the same thing in varying ways right up until she emerged from the cab in front of Gabe's brownstone and saw a beautiful black woman clinging around his neck. A woman who obviously had no problem with her makeup or her hair. Her short black hair was as stylish as the black leather miniskirt, which barely reached below her hips.

Everything Jessica had tried to convince herself of in the past thirty minutes was shattered. She wished she were pretty. Most of all she wished she were pretty for Gabe. Hands clenched, she turned to leave.

Smiling, Gabe pulled his newest client's arms from around his neck, took her elbow, and started down the steps again. He never thought giving someone a discount would get such a reaction.

"You're more than welcome. I—" He broke off as he saw a woman, head bowed, slowly walking away from him. He recognized Jessica and the long brown cashmere coat instantly.

He frowned, wondering why she was leaving without saying hello. As far as he knew, she didn't have any other reason to be in Harlem except to see him.

"I'm just so glad you're going to do my portrait, Mr. Jackson. My fiancé is going to be so pleased."

Gabe glanced at the excited Loraine and everything clicked. "I'm sure he will. If you'll excuse me, I see a friend of mine I want to speak with. I'll call to set up an appointment," he told the woman as he backed away, then he turned and sprinted.

He easily caught up with Jessica. But since he wasn't sure what to say, he just fell into step beside her. He had intentionally not called or gone by today because he had woken up smiling, thinking about her, and anticipating the call. A sure sign of a man getting in over his head.

He didn't want a relationship. Certainly not one with a woman his brother thought he was going to marry. Gabe hadn't had time for anything serious with a woman since he decided to paint full-time. Painting had been his life and he hadn't felt the need for anything else. Until now.

It wasn't lost on him that Jessica hadn't gone by Shelton's office or house. Gabe knew it as surely as he knew his own name, as surely as he knew his feelings for the woman walking with her head bowed down were steadily growing deeper. He never wanted to see her upset or sad again. She asked for so little in life and gave so much.

"Hello," he ventured.

"Hello," she returned.

At least she's still speaking to me, he thought. "Did you come to visit my studio?"

"Yes, but I saw you were busy." Her voice was tight.

"Yes, Loraine's my newest client. I'm glad I only gave her a ten-percent discount instead of twenty. She might have squeezed the life out of me. I feel sorry for her fiancé."

Slowly Jessica came to a halt and finally met his gaze. "Her fiancé?"

"It's her wedding gift to him."

"I—" She glanced away. How could she tell him she had been hurt and envious?

Gentle hands on her shoulders turned her around to face him. "Since I'm free, would you like to come back to the house and see the studio?"

She wanted to, too much. "I don't want to keep you from working."

"You won't." Taking her hand in his, he started back.

For his studio, Gabe had converted a bedroom on the second floor in the brownstone that caught the first rays of the morning sun. The large, rectangular room was surprisingly neat. On an easel was a covered work-in-progress. The walls were pristine white and unadorned except for one. That was what drew Jessica.

She slowly walked from picture to picture, her respect for Gabe's talent growing with each one. There was a portrait of Billie Holiday in a gold dress, her trademark white gardenia in her hair; another of Louis Armstrong, his trumpet wailing while people crowded on the dance floor; happy children playing in the arch of water from an open fire hydrant; four black men playing dominoes on a crate in the front yard of a framed house. But the one that caught and tugged at her heart the most was that of a young woman with a letter clutched in her hand, tears streaming down her cheek.

''What's in the letter?'' Jessica asked, feeling an instant empathy with the woman.

''Her future.''

Jessica faced Gabe. ''What?''

He stood beside her and gazed at the picture of the black woman in the faded dress seated at the scarred table, the windows bare of curtains behind her. One pane was covered with an oilcloth.

''People tend to see what they're feeling at the moment. Tears can come from more than fear or despair or pain. There are other emotions like joy, hope, excitement.''

''Which is it for her?''

''That's for you, the viewer, to decide.''

''Gabe,'' she said exasperated.

He laughed at the mutinous expression on her face, wanting more than anything at the moment to be able to hug her. He couldn't. Shelton had to have his chance. But if you mess up, little brother . . . ''You know artists have their quirks. Come on, I'll fix us lunch.''

They were cleaning up the bright yellow-and-red kitchen after eating corned beef and rye sandwiches when the phone rang. Throwing the towel he had been drying the dishes with over his shoulder, Gabe reached for the red wall phone.

''Hello. Hi, Shelly, thanks for the reminder. Hold on.'' Pressing the mouthpiece to his white-shirted chest, he spoke to Jessica, "I have an appointment to get a haircut. It only takes about thirty minutes. Do you mind?"

"No," she said, letting the dishwater out of the sink and trying to keep the disappointment out of her voice. "I've taken up enough of your time."

He smiled indulgently. "I meant, do you mind going with me?"

"Oh," she answered.

"Well?"

"Not at all."

He raised the mouthpiece to his lips. "I'll be there." Hanging up the phone, he picked up the last glass to dry. "The receptionist knows how busy I get painting so she gives me a call to make sure I keep my standing appointment. I think you'll like the salon."

"I'm sure I will," she answered, really not caring as long as she could still be with Gabe.


'Like' was putting it mildly, Jessica thought as she got her first view of Rosie's Curl and Weave. Jessica had been in some stylish salons before, but none compared with the subdued elegance of Rosie's place. From the moment they stepped onto the pastel blue-and-pink marble floor of the spacious, airy salon and were greeted by the receptionist who took their coats, she was impressed.

The relaxed, unhurried atmosphere reminded her of the European spas she and her mother had visited. She wasn't surprised to find the facility offered a day spa and an entire array of beauty treatments to pamper their clientele.

Only two of the chairs lining the white walls were empty. Women and men were being serviced with everything from weaves to permanents. Finished, they could view themselves in the huge mirrors in front of their chairs. Light came from the recessed lighting and elegant globes separating each booth.

A young woman wearing a black smock came up to them. "Good evening, Mr. Jackson. Anthony is ready for you." She smiled at Jessica. "Do you have an appointment or are you with Mr. Jackson?"

"She's with me, Dakasha," Gabe said and faced Jessica. "You're sure you don't mind?"

"No. I'll just look through some magazines."

"This way, Mr. Jackson."

Jessica took a seat. As time passed, her gaze flicked from one woman to the other. Each hairstyle caused her to wish she could do something different with her own. Surely she wasn't the only woman in the world with unmanageable hair.

A fashionably dressed woman with short braids passed. On the back of her head the braids were swept upward into an intricate French twist. Stylish and elegant. Jessica's fingers touched her own French roll. In her opinion, there was no comparison.

"Thinking about changing your hairstyle?"

Snatching her hand down, she jumped up. "It was just a thought. You finished quickly."

Gabe knew when someone wanted to change the subject. "Unlike most barbers, Anthony doesn't stop cutting my hair when he's talking. Let's get our coats."

"All right."

While the receptionist was getting their coats, Gabe couldn't help noticing that Jessica kept sneaking glances at the other women in the salon. He picked up the shop's business card and handed it to her. "If you ever change your mind."

Silently Jessica accepted the card and her coat and then said, "No one would notice."

Turning up the collar of her coat, Gabe stared down at her unhappy face. "So what? Do it for yourself."

"My mother doesn't like braids," she confessed once they were outside.

"She wouldn't be wearing them. You would."

"You make it sound so easy."

He stared down into her troubled face. "Sometimes you have to ask yourself what is more important, what others think or what you think? Somehow, I thought you had already asked that question and found the answer."

"This isn't the same as grad school."

"Isn't it?" he asked. "You have to stand on your own and know what you want about every aspect of life; otherwise someone is going to make the decision for you."

For some reason her parents' pushing her toward Shelton flashed into her mind. She had tried to tell them it wasn't going to happen, but had eventually caved in when the pressure became too much. "I don't like for people to be upset with me."

His mouth hardened. "Then get ready for your life to be run by others."

"I'll speak up for myself when I have to," she told him, a hint of anger in her voice. "The braids just aren't that important."

"If you say so, Jessica. It's your life." Taking her by the arm, they continued down the street.

Jessica didn't know why, but she felt sad. As if she had somehow failed Gabe.

Gabe didn't feel the elation he had earlier. He had thought Jessica wouldn't bow to the pressures of Shelton and her parents, but now he wasn't so sure.

"I can take a cab home from here," she said.

"Why would you want to do that?"

"I kind of think you're upset with me," she said.

"I'll get over it," he said. "In your trips to New York did you ever tour Harlem?"

"No."

"Then you're long overdue."

"Gabe?"

"Yes?"

"If something is really important to me, no matter how upset my parents get, I won't back down. I promise."

He squeezed her hand, not knowing if she realized her hand was trembling in his and that her quiet voice didn't sound the least bit sure. He only knew it disturbed him that she was frightened and he was going to do something about it.

"I want to show you what people were able to accomplish because they had faith in themselves and the determination to succeed," he told her. "I want to show you the Harlem I know."

# Chapter Six

Gabe showed her a Harlem she hadn't known existed, with clean, well-maintained homes, businesses, and streets. As New Yorkers, the residents still didn't make eye contact with strangers, but those who knew Gabe welcomed her warmly.

They drove past the legendary Apollo Theatre, then stopped by Sylvia's restaurant for some soul food. Words failed her when she saw the magnificent Cathedral of St. John the Divine. After one hundred years of construction, the edifice was only two-thirds finished, but when completed it would be the largest cathedral in the world.

On Monday she saw the original site of the renowned Cotton Club, where such musical greats as Lena Horne and Cab Calloway got their start. The Schomburg Center for Research into Black Culture took the rest of the day. Tuesday they went to the open air African market on 116th. She purchased so much that they had to get a cab from there and go back to the apartment.

With the passing of each day, he showed her how people with courage and faith in themselves had succeeded when others failed. She recalled hearing that only the strong survive, and it was certainly true of people of color. That night she called her parents and told them she was going to graduate school and Shelton wasn't a part of her future. Despite their protests, she was firm.

When she told Gabe Wednesday morning on the phone about notifying her parents that she was definitely going to grad school, he let out a wild cheer. He suggested they should go out and celebrate.

Aware of the short time left, she invited him to dinner at the apartment instead. He could bring the wine.

While she was at the market, Shelton called. Dutifully she had returned his call and was told he was in a conference and couldn't be disturbed. Her delight in his being unavailable didn't bother her at all.

Simply, there was nothing she had to say to him, she thought as she went about preparing dinner. Her parents had probably called him and dropped some broad hints. The poor man probably felt pressured to make some overtures.

She wished she had enough spunk to tell him not to bother. She held her tongue because she didn't want to be rude to Gabe's brother, and she owed him for inviting her to New York, even if it was to make points with her father.

She had just finished lighting the candles when the doorbell rang. Smoothing her hands over her long, midnight-blue velvet dress, she answered the door.

"Hello, Gabe. Come in."

"Hello," he greeted her, handing her a bottle of vintage wine. "Something smells almost as good as you look."

She blushed and took the wine out of his hand. "You must be starved. We can go in to dinner now."

Taking her arm, Gabe led her to the dining room and placed the wine in a waiting ice bucket. He had learned Jessica didn't take compliments well. It angered him because it was a sure sign that she hadn't received many in the past. He personally planned to rectify the situation.

They dined on sautéed veal cutlets with wild mushrooms and for dessert they had a fruit napoleon with raspberry sauce. Gabe insisted on helping with the dishes. Jessica refused. He challenged her to a game of five-card-draw poker. The winner would decide who did the dishes.

"I don't know how to play poker," she told him.

"Perfect."

*    *    *

Locating the cards in her aunt's game room was the easy part—learning how to play was another thing altogether. Gabe couldn't believe she hadn't learned in college. She politely informed him poker wasn't considered appropriate for ladies at Vassar.

"And now?" he asked, a teasing light in his beautiful black eyes.

Jessica pushed her glasses farther up on her nose. "Deal the cards."

She lost three games in a row. Gabe's stack of pennies was growing, hers dwindling. She stared at the three cards in her hand, determined to win this time.

The peal of the doorbell interrupted her concentration. The sound came again. Sighing, she laid her cards down. "Marla has the night off."

"Be sure to check before you open the door," Gabe cautioned.

Gazing through the peephole, her mouth gaped, then thinned in annoyance. *Shelton.* Reluctantly, she opened the door.

Shelton smiled down at her. "Hello, sweetheart, how are you?"

Her brow arched at the endearment he had never used before. "Fine. Is there something I can help you with?"

He tweaked her nose and stepped past her, removing his long charcoal topcoat as he did. "I never knew you were such a kidder."

She resisted the urge to roll her eyes and tried to remember his part in getting her to New York. "Neither did I."

"Gabe, I didn't expect to see you here," Shelton said.

"I might say the same thing about you," Gabe returned, and leaned back against the silk upholstery cushion.

Shelton frowned. "I beg your pardon?"

"Have a seat, Shelton," Jessica invited, seeing he wasn't going anyplace. She sat back down on the sofa beside Gabe and picked up her cards.

Shelton, who had been about to hand her his coat, sat down in an armchair and drew it into his lap, studying the other two people intently. "What are my two favorite people up to?"

"Gabe is teaching me to play five-card-draw poker," Jessica explained, trying to concentrate on her cards instead of being annoyed at her unwanted visitor. She didn't want to share Gabe with anyone.

"Chess is much more stimulating," Shelton said.

Jessica glared over the top of her cards. "This is stimulating *and* fun."

Gabe tried to smother his laughter at the perplexed look on his brother's face. Obviously he had expected a more—what were the words he had used?—yes, "manageable and grateful" Jessica.

He didn't know squat about Jessica and was too full of himself to learn. Gabe had tried to warn him again this past weekend, but as usual Shelton hadn't had time to listen. Now it was every man for himself.

"Something the matter, Shelton?" Gabe asked mildly. ·

"No. Ah, Jessica, fix me a scotch," he requested, sitting back in his chair. "You know how I like it."

Her hands clenched. She laid the cards on the heavy glass table and turned to Gabe. "Do you want anything?"

"No, thank you."

Smiling, she rose gracefully and went to the bar in the far corner of the room. As soon as she lifted the heavy crystal decanter, Shelton jumped up and sat next to his brother. "What did you do to her? I've never seen her act this way."

"Maybe you didn't take time to look."

"Gabe, I haven't got time for this."

"For Jessica either. If anyone has done anything to her, it's you. You invited her to New York and haven't called in ten days."

"I called today and she was out. I sent flowers." Shelton glanced around the room. "Where are they?"

"Maybe you should ask her."

"I'm asking you."

"Your drink." Jessica held the squat crystal glass out to him.

"Thank you," he said, all smile and charm. Jessica's dour expression didn't change.

"I'll hang up your coat."

"You're such a treasure. Thanks."

"You're welcome."

Shelton lifted the heavy glass to his mouth, all the time watching Jessica. When he thought she was out of hearing distance, he turned to his brother. "I don't know what is going on, but I want you to leave. The office opens in three days and I'd like to make an official announcement then."

"What announcement?" Gabe asked calmly, although he was anything but.

"You know damn well what announcement."

"Got the ring yet?"

Shelton actually appeared embarrassed. "Actually no. I haven't had—"

"Time," Gabe finished. "Do you know anything about Jessica? What her plans are, what she likes, her favorite color, food? Anything?"

"What difference does it make? I'm marrying her, aren't I?"

"Are you?" The softly spoken words were a direct challenge.

"Yes, I—" Shelton began to mutter beneath his breath and snatched his pager from his pocket. "Morrison. Damn! Where's the phone?"

"Behind you."

Jessica retook her seat and gathered her cards. If Shelton was like her father, he'd be gone in less than five minutes. She glanced at Gabe.

"Three minutes tops," he whispered.

She laughed. They were thinking the same thing.

Shelton, who had been deep in conversation, glanced up sharply at the sound and frowned. His frown deepened as they appeared to ignore him and went back to playing cards. The receiver rattled in the cradle as he hung up. "I have to leave."

Jessica jumped up. "I'll get your coat."

Shelton stared at her, then faced his brother. "What did you do to her?"

"Why do you keep asking me that?"

"Because I know you. You saw Jessica as one of your lost souls and you changed her somehow. I want her back the way she was," Shelton hissed between clenched teeth.

"Here's your coat."

He was all smiles when he turned and took the coat and tossed it casually over his arm. "Thank you, dear. I really hate that business has kept us apart. Did you get my flowers?"

"Yes. Thank you."

The wattage of his smile increased. "Where are they? In your bedroom?" he asked in a stage whisper, his voice low and husky.

Her black eyebrows lifted in obvious displeasure at the inference. "Actually, I don't know where they are. I gave them to the maid."

"You did what?" he shouted.

"They had snapdragons in them and they made me sneeze."

"Snapdragons? I told my secretary to send roses!" he snapped.

"She did, but among the roses were other flowers," Jessica explained. "Actually, the arrangement was very pretty. Please thank your secretary for me."

Shelton stiffened. His gaze narrowed. "I'm sure your father has had his secretary send you and your mother flowers on numerous occasions."

"That he does, and I always call to thank her and send her a gift for her birthday and Christmas," Jessica returned mildly.

Her calm explanation removed the lines from Shelton's brow. "I'm sorry if I appeared a little short. My patience hasn't been the best lately. I'm working long hours to get the office opened as scheduled."

Jessica smiled her forgiveness. "I know. Father is very proud of you and counting on you to do just that. We all have the utmost confidence in your business abilities."

Shelton's shoulders straightened in his double-breasted gray wool suit. "That's nice to hear."

She took him by the arm and steered him toward the door. "I'm sure you have things that need your attention. I wouldn't dream of keeping you."

"Yes," he said, stopping at the door and staring at her, the frown returning to his handsome face. "The party is Saturday and I want you looking your best. Why don't you get a new hairstyle and have your nails done? They have some fabulous salons in Manhattan that can do wonders."

Instead of being hurt or incensed as she would have in the past, she thought of Rosie's Curl and Weave on 125th Street. A smile blossomed on her lips. "Shelton, that sounds like a marvelous idea. I know just the place."

He patted her on the shoulder. "Good. I guess I better be going."

"Good night, Shelton," Gabe called.

His baby brother's eyes narrowed. "Good night, Gabe. I'll call you later tonight."

"Somehow I thought you might," Gabe said.

Impatient for him to be gone, Jessica opened the front door. "Good night, Shelton. I'll see you at the party."

"I promised your parents I'd pick you up," he said. "They're going straight to the hotel, where they have a room. The party is also being held there."

Her shoulders dropped, her lack of enthusiasm evident. "If you insist."

Shelton shot his smiling brother another mutinous look. Clearly, they were going to have a talk before the night was over. "I'll pick you up around five. I want to be there before the guests start arriving at six."

"Of course. I'll be ready."

Her quiet acquiescence pleased him. He showed his pleasure by patting her on the arm again. "Good girl. Good night."

Jessica closed the door, her teeth clenched. "You'd think I was a dog. Perhaps I should have barked."

A whoop of laughter from Gabe had her whirling in that

direction. He was laughing so hard she feared he might roll onto the floor. She'd forgotten he always paid attention to her and what she said. Unease pricked her.

People had laughed *at* her rather than *with* her more times than she wanted to remember. A picture of Kendall at the eighth-grade dance came to her. "I didn't mean to insult your brother."

Gabe stopped long enough to wipe the tears from his eyes. "If you didn't, you're not the woman I've grown to admire. Shelton was being a jerk and we both know it."

"I'm sorry."

"He deserved it. There's nothing to be sorry for."

Shaking her head, she retook her seat. "Not about that. About doubting you were laughing at me instead of with me."

His smile was tender. "You should be. Now, let's get back to this game so I can beat you again."

She did as he suggested, her tongue poking out her cheek as she studied the three cards. "Not this time. I raise you another two pennies. Another card, please."

"I'll take another card, and raise you by five pennies."

"I'll see you and raise five. Another card please." She squealed on seeing the Queen of Hearts. *Perfect.* "Gotcha," she said, laying out a royal flush.

"Guess I'm a pretty good teacher."

"The best," she said, raking up the small pile of pennies. Being with Gabe had taught her to believe in herself. "Can I ask a favor?"

"Sure."

"Do you think you could take me to Rosie's if I can get an appointment for Friday?"

"No problem, and I can almost guarantee you can get in. The owner is a friend of mine and I used to be his broker." He started gathering up the cards. "You're going to get a new hairdo?"

"Yes, but not the way Shelton thinks."

The corner of Gabe's mouth quirked. "You're going to get the braids."

"And the reddest nail polish they have for my manicure."
He knew she had it in her. "This I want to see."


"Yes, Shelton," Gabe said as soon as he picked up the phone.
At eleven-thirty P.M. it was a safe bet who was calling.

"I want you to stop seeing Jessica," his brother ordered.

Gabe had expected as much. "I can't do that."

"You only took her out because I asked you to, so why
are you being obstinate?"

"I picked her up at the airport because you asked me to. I
took her out because she's a nice woman and I thought you
gave her a dirty deal," Gabe corrected.

"It comes down to the same thing, and I did not give her
a dirty deal. Jessica knows what to expect," Shelton said,
exasperation in his clipped voice.

"You haven't spent enough time with Jessica to know what
she wants."

"Maybe not in New York, but we went out lots in Atlanta."

"Did you talk?"

"Of course we talked."

"So you know where she works."

"At a shelter," Shelton said triumphantly.

"Doing what?"

After a pause Shelton said, "Helping people."

Gabe had to give the lawyer in his brother points for being
quick. "She teaches preschool children and she plans to ob-
tain her Master's."

"She'll have to give all that up once we're married. She'll
be much too busy."

"You're forgetting something."

"What?"

"You haven't asked her and she hasn't said yes."

"She will. You saw how easily she agreed to have her hair
done. She'll do anything I ask her."

"You really believe that?"

"I'm considered a very good catch. Jessica is no fool."

"On that, we finally agree on something. Good night, Shelton. I have an appointment early in the morning.'' Gabe hung up the phone, then placed his entwined fingers behind his head and stared up at the ceiling. Little brother, you're in for the shock of your life and I can't think of anyone who deserves it more.

# Chapter Seven

Jessica was nervous. What if it didn't work? What if she remained an ugly duckling instead of turning into a graceful swan?

"We're ready for you, Miss Ames."

She glanced at Gabe, her hand tightening in his. "Here goes."

"I'll stop by to check on your progress since the braiding is going to take a long time," Gabe told her, wishing he could take some of her anxiety away.

She nodded. "I'd like that." She took a deep breath and slowly released his hand and started after the assistant.

A few steps away, she stopped and came back to Gabe. There was something she had to say. "I'm not getting this done for Shelton."

His chest felt tight. "I know."

Smiling brilliantly, she turned and followed the assistant. "I hope this works."

"What?" the assistant asked.

"Making me over," she admitted.

"You have good bone structure and fantastic skin. You just need some help bringing it out." Smiling, she opened the door to the shampoo area. "You couldn't have picked a better place. We're going to pamper you sinfully today."

Jessica soon found out the woman wasn't exaggerating. After her shampoo, she was shown to a quiet room where she was given a bone-melting massage, then served hot tea before she had her facial. She didn't have to think twice when asked about her nail color during her manicure and pedicure.

"The redder the better."

The staff soon caught on that they were in the process of a transformation. They got into the spirit of things. Three cosmetologists and the manager conferred on the best style of braids for her hair. A soft page boy for the front and sides, and for the back a triple twist in a figure eight for a dynamic impact.

Gabe came by about that time, saw the excitement in Jessica's eyes and smiled all the way back to his brownstone. He liked Jessica the way she was, but if a new hairstyle gave her more confidence, he was all for it.

Lunch was quick; the braiding was not. The time would have seemed unbearable if not for the friendliness of the braider, and the fact that by then the fashion consultant had done her magic with her makeup.

Jessica couldn't see herself because the beautician was standing behind her working, but she still remembered how good she looked with her make-up on. Since she was near the mirror, she had removed her glasses and put them in her purse.

Her anxiety grew for the woman to finish so she could see the end results.

"All done."

Slowly the chair revolved until she saw her reflection in the mirror. Trembling fingers with Exotic Red nail polish touched quivering Plum Red-colored lips. She hadn't known her cheekbones could be that dramatic or her eyes could look so mysterious. And her lips . . . they actually looked lush and inviting. She leaned closer so as not to miss one detail. She had already decided she was getting contacts as soon as possible.

"Oh my goodness. It worked," she breathed excitedly.

"You look terrific," said the salon manager as she walked up. "I knew you'd be sensational. When you start receiving all the compliments, please mention Rosie's."

Jessica glanced at the polished woman in her late fifties and smiled. "Thanks seems so inadequate."

"You haven't seen the bill yet."

Laughing gaily, Jessica rose from the chair. "Whatever it is, it's a bargain." Opening her purse, she handed the braider a tip. "Thank you."

"Thank you. It was a pleasure in more ways than one," she said, sliding the fifty-dollar bill into her pocket.

"You mind if I give you a little more advice?" asked the salon manager, her voice softly modulated.

"Please do," Jessica said.

"Get rid of the browns or accent them with oranges or yellow or other bright colors. They're draining you." She studied Jessica with a connoisseur's eyes. "I think you'd look great in red."

Since the woman talking was wearing a melon suit that was dramatic and flattering, Jessica readily took the advice. "Any suggestions of where to look for the clothes? I'd like to impress a friend."

The manager gave her the name of a shop. "Ask for Yvette."

"I will." She extended her hand. "If I lived in New York, you'd have another customer. Thanks again." She paid the bill and was fumbling in her purse for some change to call Gabe when she heard her name.

"Jessica?"

Instantly she recognized the hesitant voice. Taking a deep breath, she slowly turned, hoping neither of them would be disappointed.

"Jessica," Gabe whispered her name in awe and wonder. His black eyes that had always fascinated her roamed over her face as if the sight were something new and exotic he had just discovered, and the discovery was just for him.

She felt heated. She felt wonderful. Not even the quivering of her stomach could dampen her elation. To have Gabe look at her with desire was something she hadn't let herself believe could happen. She wished she had on something more flattering than the chocolate-brown tailored pantsuit.

Most of all she wished she could say she loved him. Loved him so much it hurt not to be able to tell him. Basically she was shy, but she'd find a way of letting him know. She hadn't met the man of her dreams only to let him get away.

Gabe's unsteady fingers touched those incredible cheekbones of Jessica's, then swept upward to her braids that barely skimmed her shoulders. Her brown skin glowed and her eyes sparkled as if she had suddenly discovered the secrets of the universe.

Knowing he shouldn't, but unable to help himself, he brushed his lips across hers, tasted something sweet and uniquely her, and felt her trembling breath brush over his own lips. Desire struck him hard and fast, but tempered with the emotion was a deep tenderness and unspeakable joy for her.

He loved her, wanted to cherish her and keep her happy always. He loved this changeling of a woman who was finally growing into her own.

A woman his brother wanted to marry.

Wishing he could tell her his feelings, but knowing he owed Shelton his chance, Gabe stepped back. But not too far back. When Shelton struck out, Gabe planned to be standing nearby.

Unsteady from Gabe's light kiss still pulsating through her body, Jessica did a slow pirouette. "I take it you like my hair."

"You're beautiful, but then you've always been beautiful to me," he told her honestly.

"Oh, Gabe," she said, her voice as wobbly as her lips. "If you make me cry and mess up my mascara, I'll never forgive you."

The pads of his thumbs brushed away the moisture in her eyes. "Since I'd like to take you out tonight, I'll behave."

She smiled, her heart soaring. "First, I have to do some shopping."

Gabe usually hated shopping, but the thought of *not* going with Jessica never even crossed his mind. She was glowing, her energy and enthusiasm contagious. Her first stop was an optical shop for contact lenses. Next, they went to a boutique.

"Nothing brown," she told the saleswoman on entering the posh shop in upper Manhattan.

From the number of packages she later handed him, she had found what she was looking for. When asked what she bought, she sent him a saucy look and said, "You'll see."

The slumbering sensuality in her eyes had his blood pounding through his veins. He wanted very much to lower his mouth and taste her lips again and keep right on tasting. The urge had steadily been growing all afternoon.

He couldn't. Not yet.

"Shoes are next."

She might not have wanted him to see her other purchases, but the shoes were a different matter. Red, high-heeled, and sexy. She had great ankles. The red patent leather evening sandals by an Italian designer had a tiny padlocked ankle strap that could only be opened with a key. When she handed him the key so she wouldn't lose it, he thought his heart would stop.

He was in trouble. Jessica was sending out signals a blind man could see. He'd have to do a delicate balancing act to keep from hurting her. Too bad her aunt wasn't due back until next week. He needed a buffer. It was going to be a long evening.

Gabe's reaction to seeing her in the fitted red silk chemise gown was everything she had hoped and prayed for. The hour she had spent on her makeup, and all the aborted efforts with her contact lenses had been worth the effort.

He couldn't seem to take his eyes off her then nor during their candlelit dinner in the quaint restaurant. Darned if he wasn't staring hungrily at her lips. When they danced, his heart beat as erratically as hers. Yet, when they were back at her aunt's apartment, he stopped at the door.

"Aren't you coming in for a drink?"

"No. You have a big day tomorrow. You need your rest," he said, sliding his hand into his pocket.

"Are you coming to the party?"

"No. I need to catch up on some work."

"Oh," she said, biting her lip.

"Here," he said, the key to her shoes in his hand.

Hurt and embarrassed, she lifted the key from his palm, making sure she touched him as little as possible. Love wasn't supposed to hurt. "Good night."

"I enjoyed our evening together. You looked sensational."

"Apparently not sensational enough. Good-bye, Gabe."

The palm of his hand caught the closing door. "I'll see you before you leave."

She wished for the courage to tell him that wasn't necessary. "If you want."

"Lady, you have no idea of what I want, but you will before you leave New York, that I promise." Whirling, he stalked away.

The sensual undertone in Gabe's voice sliced through her misery. He was angry, but she no longer doubted he wanted her. "If you break your promise I'll never speak to you again," she yelled, ignoring years of training again.

He turned, the lines of strain clearing from his face. "I won't. Good night, Jessica."

"Good night, Gabe." Stepping into the apartment, she closed the door, trying to figure out what Gabe had meant. He wanted her, yet he didn't even try to kiss her again. Even Shelton had kissed her twice on the cheek. She'd just have to wait. She trusted Gabe. That thought was the only thing that got her through the long, lonely night.

"My goodness! What did you do to yourself?" A wide-eyed, disapproving Shelton asked the moment Jessica walked into the living room.

"Just as you suggested," Jessica said, handing him the floor-length matching cape to her figure-revealing red beaded halter gown.

Automatically, he took the cape and held it for her. She turned. Breath hissed through his teeth. "This thing hardly has a back! I said nothing about braids or this kind of dress."

"I know. It's what I wanted, Shelton. Your opinion didn't enter into the situation." Drawing the cape around her shoulders, she pulled on her long red gloves and went to stand by the door. "We should leave or we'll be late."

"This is all Gabe's fault," he muttered beneath his breath as he opened the door.

Jessica heard him and decided to ignore the remark. She hadn't expected Shelton to like her makeover, but she hadn't expected him to be this annoyed. If this was his reaction, there was no telling about her parents.

The elderly Ameses were both speechless. As she had for Gabe, she pirouetted in the red gown, then raised her hands. "It's the new me."

Before her parents could say anything, her father's elderly partner, Oscar Koch entered the room. "Jessica, is that you?"

"Yes, sir," she answered affectionately. She had always liked the robust, no-nonsense man.

"Goodness, young lady. Where have you been hiding this other you?" he asked, his brown eyes twinkling.

She laughed. "I don't know, but I'm glad I let her out." She turned to her mother. "How about you?"

"What can I say except we should have sent you to New York by yourself years ago?" Smiling, Henrietta Ames took her daughter's hands in hers. "You look fabulous, even with the braids, doesn't she, George?"

"I suppose," her ultra-conservative, normally outspoken father said slowly.

"Coming from you, Dad, I'll take that as a compliment." Guests began to arrive. "Looks like we're on." Taking her parents by the arm, they went to greet them.

The party was a resounding success and so was Jessica's new look. However, the more compliments she received, the more Shelton glowered at her. Finally, she had had enough and took him aside. "What is your problem?"

"You."

"Me?"

"You've changed, Jessica. I thought you'd make the perfect wife, but I was wrong."

Her mouth worked for a long time before she could get the words out. "You thought what?"

"Keep your voice down," he warned, glancing around the crowded room as people turned toward them. "Your parents and I discussed everything. But that was before Gabe entered the picture. He changed you."

"Did you tell Gabe you wanted to marry me?"

"Of course. I asked him to keep you company." His mouth narrowed into a tight line. "Instead of doing just that, he somehow managed to change you. I'm sorry, but you won't do as my wife."

She laughed in his face. "I'm not and you're right. I'd do much better as a sister-in-law, if I can get your brother to ask me. Maybe I'll have to ask him."

"What?"

"Lower your voice, Shelton. You wouldn't want to create a scene." Patting his cheek, she then tweaked his nose for good measure. "Excuse me, I need to call someone." She started for the door just as it opened and Gabe walked in.

The smile started in her heart and bloomed on her face. "Gabe! I was going to call you."

"Then I'm glad I saved you the trouble." Gabe figured he had wasted enough time. "Did you turn down his proposal yet?"

"Yes," Jessica told him, her heart thudding again. He was dressed the way he was the first time they met. In a black leather jacket, jeans minus the paint, and aviator glasses. He looked hard and dangerous and gorgeous. She wanted to curl up in his lap and purr. This time, she was more than ready to tempt fate and go with him wherever he asked.

"Good, then I think it's time we went someplace and talked," he said, his gaze roaming boldly over her. "By the way, you look incredible."

"So do you," she said.

His gaze heated. "Let's go."

"Now, hold on a minute, Gabe," Shelton said, grabbing his brother by the arm as he turned to leave. "Do you mean to tell me while you were supposed to be watching my girl, you stole her from me?"

"I never was your girl, Shelton, so there was nothing for Gabe to steal," Jessica said indignantly.

Gabe's arm curved around her bare shoulder. "I gave you every opportunity to win her and I'll always be grateful you didn't. If you want to blame someone, blame your overinflated ego."

"What is going on here?" asked Mr. Ames, pushing his way through the gathering crowd with his wife by his side.

"My own brother stole Jessica from me," Shelton fumed.

"You can't steal what you never had," Gabe pointed out, drawing her possessively closer. "Besides, you'll make a much better brother-in-law than a husband."

"Wait a minute," Jessica said, pushing out of Gabe's arms, her hands on her slim hips, happiness soaring through her. Seems she didn't have to ask him to marry her, but there was something else she desperately wanted, needed, and she wasn't waiting another minute. "I'm not about to consider marrying a man who barely kissed me."

"I thought you'd never ask." He took her in his arms, his mouth finding hers, shaping itself effortlessly and beautifully. There was no hesitancy, no fumbling, just sweetness and fire.

Finally Gabe lifted his head, his breathing unsteady. "I love you with all my heart. Will you marry me?"

It took a second before Jessica could draw in enough breath to speak. "You talked me into it."

His lips found hers again.

Shelton folded his arms, glaring at the two. "If he thinks I'm going to be the best man, he has another think coming."

Gabe ignored his brother and apparently everyone else in the room did also. They were too busy watching this real-life drama unfold. "Please don't leave tomorrow. Stay and spend some time with me."

"I'd like to see anyone try to stop me."

"That's my girl. Get your coat and we can get out of here."

Jessica took off in a flash, grinning, her gown drawn up to her knees.

"Jessica, don't run," her mother admonished. She never slowed.

Gabe turned to her puzzled parents. "As you may have guessed, I'm Gabe Jackson, Shelton's older brother. I know this entire situation is a little crazy, but please know one thing: I love your daughter very much and I'd never do anything to hurt her."

Their expression didn't alter.

Gabe smiled. "It's the beard. My mother always said it made me look like a hoodlum. For the past thirteen days I've been with or spoken to Jessica every day. And did she appear the least bit reluctant to leave with me?"

"No, in fact, I've never seen her happier," her mother confided, slowly relaxing.

"I could have made her happy, too, given the chance," Shelton growled for good measure.

"You would have tried and failed and Jessica would have been the one to pay," Gabe said softly to his brother. "Do you remember all the things you said you wanted when you were growing up, only to get tired of them and stick them in the back of your closet and forget about them? I couldn't let you do that to Jessica. I love her."

Shelton snatched his arms to his sides. "I still want to punch you in the nose."

"For Jessica it would be worth it."

More than one woman aahed, Jessica's mother included.

"You're not playing fair." Shelton knew when he had lost. "It's a good thing I love you."

"Likewise." As if they were connected somehow, he turned to see Jessica struggling to get her cape on. He rushed over to help.

"What does your brother do, Shelton?" Mrs. Ames asked.

"He paints."

"Paints?" Mr. Ames repeated loudly, then shared a look of pure horror with his wife. Recently they had had the trim on their one-hundred-year-old mansion expertly restored.

"Portraits," Shelton clarified, watching Jessica and Gabe make a hurried exit out the door.

The frown on Mrs. Ames's perfectly arched brow lessened only slightly. "Is he solvent?"

The door closed behind the fleeing couple. Oddly, Shelton wasn't as ticked off as he wanted to be. Partly because Gabe was right. He hadn't exactly been looking forward to marriage with Jessica, but he fully planned on becoming a partner one day with her father's firm.

"Shelton, is he solvent?"

He glanced at his former-future in-laws. At least Gabe had kept Jessica all in the family. Actually this could work out better.

"My brother's not bringing down the high figures he once did as a stockbroker, but that's about to change. He's been commissioned by some very influential people to do their portraits. In the meantime, knowing Gabe, he has more pots of money in various funds than a leprechaun."

"Influential people?" Mrs. Ames asked, her eyes sparkling with interest.

"Funds?" Mr. Ames questioned, his interest equally piqued.

"Why don't we join our guests and I'll tell you?" Shelton said, a genuine smile on his handsome face for the first time that evening.

# Epilogue

It was the longest and happiest day of Gabe Jackson's life. A sunny June day with the scent of magnolia in the air and the faint chirp of blue jays. He couldn't seem to get the smile off his face, nor did he try. Each time someone patted him on the back and congratulated him on marrying such a beautiful and vivacious young woman, he almost felt like thanking Shelton all over again.

"You think she's ever going to throw that bouquet or is she just teasing the horde of women waiting to catch it?"

Gabe, a silly grin on his darkly handsome face, winked at his wife, who winked back. "Shelton, your guess is as good as mine. Jessica has a mind of her own."

A manicured hand settled on his shoulder. "You're right about that. She's nothing like I thought she was."

"She's everything I thought and more," Gabe said softly.

Shelton chuckled. "Spoken like a man in love. That's one of the main reasons I forgave you, you know. I may not believe in it, but I know you do."

Gabe glanced at his brother. "When the right woman comes along, you will. And I'll tell you something else. You won't mind leaving the office and going home to her."

"Yeah, right," Shelton said, his disbelief obvious.

Shaking his head, Gabe turned to hear his bride of an hour ask the clamoring women if they were ready. Their shouts of "yes" shook the Rose Ballroom of the Grand Hotel in downtown Atlanta.

Jessica grinned, obviously giddy with happiness and simply beautiful in an elegant off-the-shoulder gown of ivory silk with beaded chantilly lace bordering the wide skirt. It was clearly her day.

She sent Gabe a secret look. "Just checking."

Turning her back on the crowd, she tossed the bouquet. Women squealed and jumped. The jubilant woman held her trophy of miniature red and pink roses aloft.

"It's time to throw Jessica's garter," advised Mrs. Apple-white, the bridal consultant.

"You'll make sure my best man is there, won't you?" Gabe asked, grabbing Shelton by the arm before he could make his getaway.

"Have I ever let you down, Mr. Jackson?"

"No, and thanks." Gabe made his way toward Jessica. From six months' experience with the forceful consultant, he knew he could count on her. Yet at times, between her, Jessica's mother, and his mother, he had considered eloping. Since Jessica was in grad school, he was probably more a part of planning the wedding than most men.

He was glad she was taking off the summer and was going to enroll in the fall at New York University near their home. Planning the wedding the first of June had been perfect. For the rest of the summer, he had his wife to himself. He was more than ready.

"I believe you have something I have to take off?" he said teasingly, his fingers brushing across her smooth cheek.

She leaned within an inch of his ear. "I know you have some things I want to take off."

Resisting the urge to drag her into his arms and kiss her until they reached meltdown, he went down on one knee and reached for her foot to the applause of the women. Her white leather shoe settled on his tuxedoed thigh. Slowly she raised the hem of her dress. Gabe chastised himself, but he was unable to stop thinking she'd be taking the dress off shortly and he'd finally make her his.

His fingers trembling, he pulled the blue garter from her leg. Damn fine legs, too. To think he'd fallen in love with a woman before he'd seen her legs. He hadn't needed to. Her heart and soul were enough.

As he drew the garter over her ankle his heart rate kicked up. There was a tiny lock on the shoes, just like her red ones, and he had the key. Jessica had sent it to him just before the wedding.

Love shining in his eyes, he looked up, knowing she would be watching him. "I love you."

"Impossible as it may be, I know." Her trembling hand tenderly touched his face. He kissed her palm. Neither noticed the camera flash.

Garter in hand, Gabe stood. "Here goes." The dainty blue garter sailed straight to Shelton, who instinctively caught it, then dropped it. The men beside him were only too happy to return it to him.

Amid the laughter and teasing, Gabe and Jessica said their good-byes and made their way to the private elevator of the hotel. His hungry lips crushed down on hers. She melted into him.

The elevator pinged open on the top floor. They kept on kissing.

"I think this is your floor."

Gabe lifted his head to see an elderly couple smiling at them. "Yes, thanks." Picking Jessica up in his arms he strode to the door of the bridal suite. It took two tries to get the key in the lock because Jessica was biting and blowing in his ear.

Finally, they were in. He sat her down immediately and drew her arms away from him. He swallowed. "Do you need any help changing?"

"No."

Nodding, Gabe watched her go into the bedroom and close the doors behind her. His hands were sweaty. His throat dry. He had never wanted any woman like this or been so scared he'd mess up.

Jessica had such an expression of love and trust and, yes, pride, whenever she looked at him. He'd eat shredded glass rather than risk that changing. When she came over to his place last week to bring her things, the awesome responsibility he was about to undertake hit him.

He was going to be responsible for her the rest of his life—to love, to cherish, to honor in sickness and in health, on good days and bad days. He had looked up and she had been watching him.

There wasn't a shadow of doubt on her beautiful face or in her eyes. He had searched his heart and soul and found none as well. Wherever life took him, Jessica would be at his side and would be a part of him.

That's why he didn't want to mess up her wedding night. Both of them had wanted to wait and it had been hard. Now the time was here and he was nervous.

His hand jammed into his pocket. The key. She needed it to take off her shoes.

He knocked on the door. "Jessica."

"Come in."

"You for . . ." His words trailed off. She stood by the bed in something white, lacy, and decadent. He was profoundly glad he hadn't known during the ceremony that beneath her gown she had on a merry widow. "I-I knocked."

"I know."

His gaze roamed hungrily over her. "The key."

"Yes." She sat down on the bed and crossed shapely legs in sheer stockings and a garter belt.

He swallowed, then slowly walked toward her when he wanted to run. Kneeling, he took one shoe on his knee, removed the lock, then repeated the process and took off her other shoe. The light fragrance she wore stirred his senses more.

Her hand touched his face. "I love you, Gabe."

His control slipped a notch. His arms went around her crushing her to him. "Don't be frightened."

She laughed, and laughed again at his strange look. She kissed him quickly on the mouth. "Frightened! I'd fight anyone or anything that tried to take me away from you, from this. I don't know what life holds, but I know with you I have the freedom to be me, not what someone expects me to be."

Love shone in her misty brown eyes. "You are my freedom, Gabe. You are my life, my love. Who could be frightened of that?"

"Oh, Jessica." His mouth found hers again, no longer hesitant. He drew her down on the bed, kissing her greedily. She met him boldly, her hands and lips as eager to touch, to taste, to savor, as his. Each caress was more desirable than the last.

Clothes were cast aside in heated urgency. Gazing into her eyes, he made her his, watched the surprise and momentary discomfort break across her expressive face, then watched the slow spiral of pleasure.

She came to him with all the innocence and fire he knew she possessed. She held nothing back. Neither did he. They both gave and in return received.

Much later, Gabe drew Jessica to his side, his hand tenderly stroking her. "Like I always said, you're incredible."

"If I would have known how incredible *this* would be, you would have had to fight me off."

Chuckling, he rolled her beneath him and kissed her. "Welcome to my world, Jessica Jackson. I'll love you through eternity."

"And I'm going to love you right back, Gabe Jackson." Her lips touched his and it was a long time before either had enough breath to speak again.

# Special Delivery

# Rochelle Alers

This novella celebrates:

My sister, Louise Dennis
stylist, esthetician extraordinaire,

and Deirdre Lee
an up-and-coming diva

Some people pretend to be rich, but have nothing.
Others pretend to be poor, but own a fortune.

Proverbs 13:7

Zahara Jenkins lay on a chair in the room set up in Rosie's Curl and Weave expressly for facials, listening to the soothing sound of taped music coming through hidden speakers; she inhaled the sensual fragrance of vanilla, jasmine, patchouli, and bergamot from burning candles positioned on several tables in the pristine, modern space, and luxuriated in the breath of warm steam caressing her face and opening her pores under the mask of a rich cream derived from the fruit of an avocado. The softly blowing steam against the circles of cotton, soaked in a cool cucumber solution and placed over her eyes, was a stimulating and invigorating contrast.

She had come to look forward to her monthly full day of beauty at the trendy, upscale beauty salon located on Harlem, New York's 125th Street. It was her time to relax, be pampered, and escape from life's everyday mundane activities. Rosie's Curl and Weave was built directly across the street from the building where she worked as assistant manager for a neighborhood bank. Her employment history with the Ansonia National Bank began at their headquarters on Manhattan's Upper West Side when she was thirty, but after five years in what employees referred to as "corporate," she was transferred to a neighborhood branch. The bank's president and board of directors decided the 125th Street branch needed an African-American female presence.

Zahara enjoyed interacting with the residents and merchants in the Harlem community. It had taken six months before she recognized most bank customers on sight, and whenever she strolled the streets of the wide avenue, she was warmly greeted by passing pedestrians and motorists. And since she'd come to work in the predominantly African-American neighborhood, she felt if as she had become a part of a large, extended family. The last time she'd felt that way was when she attended Hampton University as an undergraduate student. The students who attended Hampton were a startling departure from the ones in the all-white Vermont community where she'd grown up with her parents and younger brother. Her father, now a retired IBM executive, had moved his then-pregnant wife and small daughter to the quaint New England town in Vermont thirty years before.

She and her brother had grown up without the stigma of overt racism, but that hadn't stopped Zahara from feeling disconnected from her race. Her parents always sent their two children to Mount Vernon, New York, to summer with their grandparents. It was in Mount Vernon that they played and interacted with children and adults who looked like them, talked like them, and ate what they ate. Each return to the Westchester County suburb was always a homecoming for her and her brother Russell. The summers with her paternal and maternal grandparents had such an indelible impact on her young life that she spent all of the school year waiting for the end of classes so she could return.

Working at the bank's corporate office was akin to living in Vermont—it was comfortable and staid, but coming to 125th Street was like spending four years at Hampton or the summers in Mount Vernon.

A smile curved her lips as she settled into a more comfortable position. She had inherited the large house in Mount Vernon from her maternal grandparents and she worked in Harlem. She had finally come home.

"How you doing?" asked the low, sultry voice of the esthetician.

Zahara smiled. "I'm falling asleep." Her slow drawl mirrored her relaxed state.

"Don't get too relaxed 'cause you still have to get your nails, toes, and hair done."

Zahara moaned softly under her breath, then gave herself up to the expert ministration of the skilled esthetician. The woman's strong fingers massaged her shoulders, the back of her neck, and her upper chest to stimulate the upward flow of blood to her face. The services she sought at Rosie's for this Saturday were more vital than usual because of the dinner party she was to attend later that evening.

Thinking of the upcoming festivities elicited a rush of anticipated pleasure. She had been invited to a black-tie affair at the home of the bank's president to celebrate Ansonia National's soon-to-be-announced merger with another small, but very prestigious, upstate bank. It had taken her several weeks to select the suitable dress and accessories for the affair. She smiled again. She had the appropriate attire and proper escort to accompany her to an event such as this.

She had begun a regimen of dating seriously after she left college, but each encounter left her wondering if something was wrong with her choice in men. Her family and friends all said she aimed too high. She believed that being able to trust a man was the most significant component in any successful relationship. And she had had only one serious relationship in her adult life, but it had ended three years ago. The man she'd been infatuated with relocated to South Africa when his export company opened a Johannesburg office, ending what she eventually concluded was a union based solely on image. Physically they had complemented each other: both were tall, slender, well-dressed, and upwardly mobile. She now hoped her string of dead-end liaisons was finally over with James Sheldon.

She met James Sheldon at the Schomburg Center for Research into Black Culture during a Black History Month celebration and was instantly taken with the quiet poise of the Wall Street systems analyst. They'd dated a half dozen times over the past two months, and each encounter found them enjoying the other's company more and more. Once she received the invitation for the dinner party she'd asked James to accompany her and he had consented without delay.

"Heard you have a big affair tonight," the esthetician remarked as she wiped the mask off Zahara's face with squares of moist cotton.

"It's a dinner party," Zahara confirmed.

"Where?"

"Short Hills."

"That's up where you live, isn't it?"

"No. You're probably thinking of Scarsdale. Short Hills is in New Jersey."

Kimm Gilmore shrugged her shoulders under the tunic of her white uniform. "Scarsdale or Short Hills. It's still too rich for this round-the-way girl."

Zahara wanted to openly admit that at times it was too rich for her, too. There were occasions she resented some wealthy people who felt they were entitled based solely on the number of commas attached to their bank balances. What she had learned to do was to treat every customer who came into her branch as an equal. The man who coveted his one-thousand-dollar account was as important to her as the one whose balance approached the one-million-dollar figure.

"I know you have your outfit already," Kimm continued.

"I got it a couple of weeks ago."

"It is nice, girl?"

Zahara smiled. "Very nice."

"Don't you worry about a thing. Leave it to Kimm. I'm gonna make you look so-o-o good that when you come back next month I wanna hear that you hurt somebody."

"I'm not out to hurt anybody . . ."

"Well, you should. If I had your body, I'd work it, girl-friend. After this last baby I'm ready to sign myself into the liposuction clinic. Now, how did my hips go from a thirty-eight to a forty-six with two kids?" She waved a hand. "I just about lost it when Malik said he wants one more baby. I told him not here. Not with this woman. I told that man what was going to happen to my body, but would he listen? Oh, no-o-o. It's not as if he had to go to a psychic to see the future. All he had to do was look at my mother and my sisters. He had to see that we're built like 747s.''

''Exercise, Kimm. I get up at five to work out before I come to work.''

Kimm concentrated on removing a clogged pore under her client's lower lip. ''You can get up at five because you don't have chick nor child. I have a husband who has become more of a baby since I had my babies. Sorry, girlfriend. I'm rolling over and catching some much-needed sleep at five A.M.''

Zahara hadn't wanted to get up at five in the morning to drive blurry-eyed to the gym, but at thirty-five she wanted to get a jump on her slowly changing figure. The moment she noted a hint of excess flesh on her inner thighs, she increased her allotted workout time. At five-eight she was tall, but like Kimm she had a black woman's body wherein her thighs and hips were certain to become her problem areas. She didn't mind them spreading a little as long as they remained firm.

Kimm waxed her eyebrows, then applied a rich, oil-based moisturizer to her clean face. A clock on a table chimed the noon hour and Zahara smiled. She was on schedule. She anticipated another two to three hours for a manicure, pedicure, and a blow and curl. If she left Rosie's at three, then she would have plenty of time to take the train back to Mount Vernon and prepare for the evening.

She retrieved her handbag, tipped Kimm, then made her way across the rear of the shop to the area set aside for manicures and pedicures.

Rosie's was always bustling with activity; however, Saturdays were like rush hour at Grand Central Station. Walking into Rosie's Curl and Weave enveloped one with a sense of endless expansiveness. The white walls made the salon appear even larger, while the pastel colors of blues and pinks on the marble-tiled floors offered a cool, airy ambiance. The daily operation was absolute precision. Each stylist shared a number of assistants who were responsible for shampooing, coloring, cleaning up, and restocking supplies. The assistants moved quickly and silently, their black smocks fluttering around their bodies like the ebony-hued wings of a butterfly.

Maria was waiting for Zahara. "I have your color ready for you," the manicurist replied with a wide grin, holding up a bottle of sandy beige-hued nail polish.

Zahara shook her head as she settled down on the pedicure chair. "I need a red today."

The young woman arched her professionally waxed eyebrows, lowered her chin, and glanced up from under her lashes. "Red?" Since she had become Zahara Jenkins's permanent manicurist, she never knew her to wear a color other than the soft beige shade. She attributed the choice in shade to her position at the bank.

"Ruby red."

Her mouth formed an attractive moue. "Ouch. I'm afraid of you." Maria searched her tray for a deep gold-red. "Fingers and toes?"

Zahara nodded. "Fingers and toes." She had a standing weekly appointment on Wednesdays for a manicure, Thursdays for a wash and blow, and sometimes a touch-up, and every other Thursday for a pedicure. There were times when she felt as if she spent a great deal of her time at Rosie's, but maintaining her appearance was important to her. As important as her career.

She had inherited her fastidiousness from her maternal grandmother. Her grandmother never worked a day in her life, yet had attended her local beauty salon every week of her adult life. She had accompanied her Nana to the beauty salon the summer she turned ten, and had become as addicted to their services as the older woman.

"You must have a big date," Maria inquired, filling the black porcelain sink with warm water and easing Zahara's bare feet from a pair of worn loafers and into the soapy solution.

"A formal dinner party," she supplied.

"Nice. Where are you . . . ?" The cellular telephone in Zahara's leather bag chimed softly, preempting whatever Maria was going to say.

Zahara retrieved the bag and answered the small, palm-size phone. "Hello."

"Hi, Zee, this is James."

She felt her heart lurch. Closing her eyes, she mumbled a prayer. Why was James calling her on her cell phone? What was so important that he hadn't waited to call her at home? She didn't have long to wait for an answer.

"What's up, James?"

"Zee—I'm sorry, but . . ."

Her large eyes narrowed. "You're sorry about what, James?"

"It's Yvette."

She swallowed painfully. "Yvette? Who . . . is . . . *Yvette*?" she questioned between clenched teeth.

"Well—well, she's my ex-wife."

The mention of an ex-wife rendered her speechless. James had told her that he'd never married. *Liar!* He'd lied to her. If he'd lied about not having been married, then what else was he hiding?

Counting slowly to ten, she composed herself. She refused to discuss his ex-wife. "Are you calling to say you can't make it tonight?"

"Well—yes. But . . ."

Zahara never heard the rest of his excuse as she pressed a button, ending the call. Placing a hand over her forehead, she slumped back against the pedicure chair. He'd waited six hours before he was to pick her up to tell her he couldn't make it.

*Dog!*

No, she thought, shaking her head. He wasn't as good as a dog. She'd found dogs to be loyal and trusting companions.

*Snake!* James Sheldon was lower than a snake's belly.

How could he? she fumed inwardly. James with the sexy DJ voice; James with the Wharton School of Business MBA; James Sheldon—Mr. *GQ*; James the bald-faced liar!

Spurred on more by anger than disappointment, Zahara quickly dialed a number, counting off the rings. There was a break in the connection, then the distinctive sound of a recorded message with a cheerful male voice saying he'd return the call if the caller left a message.

"This is Zahara. Please call me as soon as you pick up this message. It's a nine-one-one. I need a date for tonight. I promise to return the favor."

She dialed three other numbers, leaving the same message. Sighing, she felt some of her tension easing. One out of four should yield success. If the affair had been other than a formal one, she would have considered going alone. Closing her flip-top phone, she glanced over at her regular stylist staring at her. It was apparent she had overheard her frantic telephone calls.

Deirdre Lee flashed an uneasy smile. "I wasn't eavesdropping, if you know what I mean. But I couldn't help overhearing that you need a date for tonight."

Closing her eyes, she nodded slowly. "I've just been stood up."

"Oh, no!"

"Oh, yes, Dee Dee!"

Tiny, talented Deirdre rested her hands on her narrow hips, shook her head, and clucked her tongue. "He must be some kind of a loser," she snorted under her breath. "But I think I can help you out."

Zahara's eyes narrowed. "Help me out how?"

"I can hook you up with someone if you need a date for tonight."

What had initially been anger was now humiliation. She'd been stood up, she couldn't contact any of the men she'd called, and a twenty-two-year-old hairstylist had offered to hook her up. She shuddered to think of Dee Dee's choice of a suitable date.

Deirdre took Zahara's hesitation for an affirmative. "I'll call him," she said quickly. "He's supposed to bring something by the shop anyway, so I'll have you meet him. His name is Adam Vaughn. Don't worry, Zahara. I know he's your *type*."

*Just what is my type?* she asked herself. Men who thought only of themselves? Men who were habitual liars? Men who presented themselves as the "together brother" until it was time to commit?

Why couldn't she find a man like her father and brother? Her father and mother loved each other unselfishly and dedicated themselves to making the other happy and fulfilled. Her brother married his college sweetheart a month after he'd signed an NBA contract with the Miami Heat, and had proven himself as a faithful, supportive husband and father.

Nodding, she closed her eyes. "Okay, Dee Dee. I'll consider him only if he doesn't have an eye in the middle of his forehead like a Cyclops."

"Cy—who?" A look of bewilderment shadowed her features. "Never mind. You won't be sorry," Dee Dee said, smiling broadly and displaying a perfect set of white teeth in her round dark-brown face.

*I hate men!* The three words reverberated in Zahara's head as she pushed the phone into the cavernous depths of her oversized handbag. Now she knew why some women made it a practice to utilize an escort service. They rented a date for a function—no strings attached. The men were prepared to play a role for whatever the occasion, didn't stand up their dates, and when the night was over it was truly over.

She refused to give James Sheldon another thought as she settled back on the chair and let Maria take care of her feet. Half an hour later, her bare feet ensconced in a pair of paper slip-ons, and her toes painted a shimmering red, Zahara shifted to a chair for her manicure. Maria worked quickly, efficiently, and soon her beautifully tapered fingernails wore a matching shade.

At one-ten she sat at Dee Dee's station, staring back at her reflection from the mirrored wall. A face she'd seen thousands of times suddenly looked strange. Her complexion was flawless after the hydrating European facial. A healthy sheen of red undertones shimmered under her medium-brown skin. Her face was narrow, cheekbones high and pronounced, eyes large and alert, nose short and rounded, and her mouth generous and lush. She'd always thought of her features as uneven, but had to admit that the overall effect was exotically attractive enough to garner any man's rapt attention. She had learned to apply her makeup to highlight her best features—her eyes and mouth. And she had also learned to camouflage the dark circles under her eyes with a concealer whenever she hadn't had enough sleep.

Dee Dee placed both hands on her shoulders over the protective cape and met Zahara's gaze in the mirror. "Do you want the same style or something a little different?"

"How different?"

Lifting the thick dark strands off her client's neck, the stylist smiled. "How about a cut?"

"How short?"

"Not too short. I'd like to try stacking your hair and have it fall naturally around the nape of your neck. You can either have it blown out or wrapped. If I wrap it, then I'll just bump the ends."

"Can you get me out of here by three?"

Dee Dee glanced at the watch on her wrist. "I can get you out of here by two-thirty."

Zahara nodded, saying, "Then do it."

Dee Dee had just begun sectioning Zahara's hair in preparation for applying a relaxer to her new growth when she spied the person she'd been waiting for. Gesturing with a hand covered with a latex glove, she beckoned to a tall man pushing a handcart stacked with four large corrugated cartons.

"Hi, Adam. This is Zahara Jenkins. She's the one I told you about."

Dee Dee's voice seemed to reverberate off the walls of the spacious salon, and it was then Zahara realized that all conversation had stopped the moment Adam Vaughn walked into Rosie's.

She stared at Adam staring back at her in the reflection of the mirror. *I don't believe this*, she wailed silently. *He's a deliveryman!* If everyone hadn't been staring at her and Adam, she was certain she would've bolted from the chair.

Her gaze traveled downward, taking in the thick toes on his work boots. Her gaze reversed itself, moving slowly upward. She took in the bagginess of his navy-blue twill, industrial-styled jumpsuit, a two- or three-day growth of whiskers on his cheeks which hadn't quite caught up with the thickness of his mustache, and a battered navy-blue baseball cap bearing the New York Yankees logo covering his head. She couldn't make out the eyes hidden behind a pair of oval, wire-rimmed sunglasses or the condition of his hands under a pair of work gloves.

*Please don't let him have dirty fingernails*, she prayed silently. Somewhere, somehow, she managed what could possibly pass for a smile. "Hello."

Adam inclined his head. "Hello. Let me take these supplies in the back, then we'll talk."

Closing her eyes, Zahara wanted to tell him not to come back. That he should keep walking—right through the back door. But she needed a date. She'd made four telephone calls and an hour later none of the men she'd called had returned her frantic plea. And the clock was ticking. She had to be on the road by six if she was to make it to New Jersey by seven-thirty. The cocktail hour was scheduled for seven, but she had always made it a practice to arrive half an hour into the appointed time. That way she would allow herself one drink before and one during dinner.

"What do you think of him?" Dee Dee asked close to her ear.

"He's tall enough." It was the only positive thing she could think of.

"Don't you think he has a nice voice?"

"Oh, yes. His voice is nice." And it was. It was deep and well-modulated. *Please let him use the right verb tenses*, Zahara continued in silent supplication.

The steady hum of conversation started up again, but quickly subsided the moment Adam returned to Dee Dee's station, and not wanting everyone in Rosie's to overhear her plight, Zahara stood up.

"Perhaps we should talk in the back," she suggested.

Adam nodded and extended a gloved hand. His fingers cupped her elbow as he led her past stylists, shampoo girls, several manicurists, and every client sitting, standing, and staring at their retreat.

Zahara felt the strength of his fingers as they tightened on her upper arm, felt the heat from his tall body, and inhaled the faint scent of cologne mingling with clean male sweat. It was apparent that he showered daily, even if he hadn't shaved in days.

He led her to a small space near a storeroom and dropped his hand. Crossing his arms over his chest, he angled his head. "Deirdre says you need a date for tonight."

Tilting her chin, Zahara stared at his mustached mouth. Upon closer inspection she saw that it was beautifully formed. "I don't need a date as much as I need an escort."

Adam nodded. "An escort. What type of an affair?"

"Formal. Black tie. Will that pose a problem for you?"

He stared at her from behind the dark lenses, unmoving. "No." The single word was firm, emphatic. The words "beautiful" and "snobby" sprang into Adam's mind as he stared down at the woman who looked down her nose at him even though he eclipsed her by at least seven inches.

"What time do you want me to pick you up?" he questioned.

"I'll pick you up, if that's all right with you," she countered.

"It's not all right. I will pick *you* up. Where do you live and where are we going?"

Zahara felt a shiver of annoyance sweep up her spine. He had some nerve telling her what he would do—but then, she couldn't afford to alienate him. She needed him. If the affair had been other than a formal one she would've gone alone. But not this one. It was too important for her to miss, and she didn't want to appear socially deficient, showing up without an escort.

"I live in Mount Vernon, and the dinner party is in New Jersey."

"Give me your address and the one where we're going."

"Do you have a pen and paper?"

Adam shifted his eyebrows slightly. "Tell me the address. I'll memorize it."

Her annoyance became panic. Einstein in the jumpsuit would memorize the address, then would probably transpose the numbers and have to drive around for hours trying to find her house.

"Well?" he drawled.

Inhaling, she closed her eyes and recited her address and that of the bank's president. "In case you get lost, I'll also give you my telephone number."

"I won't get lost," he insisted. "What time should I pick you up?"

"Six."

"Then six it is." With a barely perceptible nod of his head, he grasped the handles of the handcart, turned, and walked to the front of the salon, leaving Zahara staring at his wide shoulders.

Waiting a full minute, she followed and returned to Dee Dee's station. Meanwhile the stylist and Adam stood at the receptionist's desk, her head barely reaching the middle of Adam's chest as she gestured animatedly with him. He smiled at what she was saying, then leaned down and kissed her cheek. Raising his head, he glanced in Zahara's direction, then turned and walked out of Rosie's, pushing the empty handcart.

Dee Dee rushed back to Zahara, a wide grin creasing her youthful face. "Well—what do you think of him?"

"He'll do for the night." There was no mistaking the lack of excitement in her voice. And if Adam Vaughn lost the jumpsuit and baseball cap, showered, shaved, and put on a pair of shoes, he definitely would do. She didn't think she had to worry too much about his grammar. He hadn't said much, but at least he'd used the proper tenses for his verbs.

Zahara's black silk-covered sling-strap sandal touched the first stair of the curving staircase at the same time the front doorbell chimed. She didn't have to glance at a clock to know Adam Vaughn was early; at least fifteen minutes early. She smiled. Mr. Industrial Jumpsuit had managed to get over the first hurdle. He'd found her house and he was early.

Holding up the slim skirt of her dress with one hand, she navigated the stairs, crossed the living room, and made her way through a golden-lit entry to the front door. Peering through a light-colored pane of stained glass, she spied a large, dark shape. She opened the door and came face-to-face with a man who looked nothing like the one she'd met at Rosie's.

The jumpsuit, work boots, battered baseball cap, gloves, and sunglasses were missing; in their place was an elegantly tailored tuxedo, dress shirt with a wing collar, white bow tie, silver-and-black paisley-print vest, and black patent leather dress slippers.

Adam's hair was cut close to his scalp, and in the diffused glow from the outdoor lanterns she could make out a sprinkling of gray at his temples. His cheeks were clean-shaven and his mustache was trimmed, offering her a glimpse of his very sensual mouth. She couldn't see the color of his large eyes, but his apparent shock at seeing her in formal dress matched her own.

*Nice,* Adam mused. *Very, very, nice.* At first he'd balked at Deirdre's plea to help out her client when Zahara's date had stood her up, followed by a mental flagellation once he'd met the damsel in distress. But standing on the front steps to a stately English Tudor house and staring down at its owner was truly worth his going through with his promise to attend the dinner party with her.

The golden light from a Tiffany lamp on a drop-leaf table highlighted the slender curves of the woman attired in black. His gaze swept from her face to her chest. Zahara Jenkins had selected a dress in chiffon and silk crepe de chine. A finely woven lace bustier provided the only hint of modesty under the sheer bodice. But that didn't stop Adam's penetrating gaze from registering the soft swell of flesh rising above the deep V of the bustier or the brown flesh of her well-conditioned arms through the revealing long sleeves. She wore no jewelry other than a pair of large multifaceted onyx earrings suspended from brilliant pear-shaped diamonds.

He moved closer and his eyes widened in appreciation. She was tall, a lot taller than he'd first thought. And with her heels she stood close to the six-foot mark. *She's the epitome of confidence and elegance*, he added in his silent appraisal.

"These are for you." He extended his right hand, offering Zahara a bouquet of flowers wrapped in layers of colored cellophane.

The sound of his deep, rich voice broke the spell, and Zahara blinked at the bouquet in his hand as if it were a venomous reptile. "Thank you, Adam. You didn't have to . . ."

"I wanted to," he interrupted. He smiled, rewarding her with the display of a deep dimple in his right cheek.

She took the flowers, stood aside, and motioned to him with her free hand. "Please come in."

He took two steps, closed the door behind him, and suddenly the small space was dwarfed by his height and the breadth of his shoulders. Zahara felt as if all of the air in the entryway had been sucked out of the space. Adam Vaughn was tall—almost as tall as her six-foot, seven-inch brother—and broad. But from what she could discern, there wasn't an ounce of excess flesh on his muscular frame. Even in formal dress he appeared hard—rock solid.

His gaze swept over the furnishings in the entry. Tasteful elegance were the two words that came to mind. And the two words were fitting for Zahara Jenkins as well. Despite her snobbiness, she was elegant. He noticed her evening bag on the drop-leaf table beside a velvet silk-lined wrap.

Zahara turned, glancing over her shoulder. "Please have a seat in the living room while I put these in some water."

Adam followed, watching as she headed through a narrow hall off the living room, but he didn't sit. He made his way over to a piano and ran his fingers over the surface of the polished wood. The aged dark wood shone like soft black velvet under the glow of the living room's massive chandelier. His footsteps were muffled by a priceless Aubusson rug on the parquet flooring as he walked over to a fireplace. A faint smell of burnt wood lingered with the distinctive odor of beeswax, indicating a recent fire had roared in the enormous space.

He studied the smiling images of the people in the photographs lining the mantel, recognizing an adolescent Zahara with a man and woman whom he assumed were her parents. Peering closer he identified the youthful face of Russell Jen-

kins before his gaze moved on to an older Russell in his
basketball jersey. Biting down on his lower lip, he nodded.
Zahara was the sister of one of the NBA's most talented and
popular players. Clasping his hands behind his back, he examined the other photographs, knowing he was going to enjoy
his date and the evening.

It had been a long time since a woman intrigued him. He
had had his ups and downs over the past ten years, but lately
everything was on an upward spiral. Everything but his love
life. It was only in that arena that he was cautious—overly
cautious. He'd fallen in love once, fallen hard, and the pain
still lingered. Within a six-month period he'd lost his mother
and father, while his ex-wife had gone through with her promise to divorce him. It took him nearly two years to recover
and turn his life around, and by the time he'd turned thirty-
three he'd become a very different person. He'd changed ca-
reers, set up his own business, and now at thirty-eight he was
satisfied with his accomplishments.

He saw a few women occasionally, yet none of them elicited a longing that made him want to commit again. There
were times when he thought of remarrying and fathering children, but as soon as the notion entered his head he dismissed
it. He didn't want to go through loving and losing again.

"The flowers are incredibly beautiful." Adam turned and
stared at Zahara holding a vase filled with the snowy white
blooms. A mysterious smile curved her crimson-colored lips.
"Who told you calla lilies are a personal favorite of mine?"

He returned her smile. "Calla lilies and peonies. The florist
didn't have any peonies, so I settled for the lilies."

Taking a half dozen steps, she placed the crystal vase on a
rosewood side table. Each step drew Adam's gaze to linger
on the provocative slit in the front of her dress. Her legs,
encased in sheer black nylon, were perfectly formed with slender ankles and curvy calves. He shook his head, wondering
how a man could stand up a woman who looked like Zahara
Jenkins.

Zahara closed the distance between them and stared up at
Adam Vaughn. She still found it difficult to believe his star-

tling transformation. He seemed so comfortable, almost relaxed, in formal attire. It was as if he'd been born to wear
formal dress. Whoever had rented him the tuxedo had fitted
him perfectly. Her gaze locked with his and for the first time
she realized his large eyes were not at all dark. They weren't
hazel, but a sooty gray that appeared well-suited to the alizarin
brown hues in his lean, masculine face.

"Do you bring all of your dates flowers the first time you
take them out?"

He unclasped his hands from behind his back and crossed
his arms over his massive chest, cupping his elbows. "No.
You're the exception because you quickly reminded me at
Rosie's that I'm not your date but an *escort*."

A wave of heat shimmered in her face as she lowered her
gaze. "*Touché*, Adam."

He glanced down at the thin gold watch on his left wrist.
"It's six o'clock. We'd better get going."

She nodded, still feeling the biting sting of her own words
coming out of his mouth. *I don't need a date as much as I
need an escort.* And that was what she had to remind herself.
Adam Vaughn was her escort for the evening.

She pressed a button on a wall, turning off the lighted chandelier, but she left several table lamps on. She felt the heat
from Adam's body as he followed close behind her. Picking
up her evening purse, wrap, and keys, she opened the front
door and stepped out into the warm spring evening. The win-
ter had been unusually mild in the Northeast, and the day
spring put in its appearance the temperature had broken records when it climbed into the upper sixties. It was now the
middle of April and the heat had not abated.

Adam waited for her to lock the door, then held out his
hand. He was not disappointed when she placed her hand in
his as he led her to the driveway and his parked car. He
opened the passenger-side door to a shiny black, two-seater,
Mercedes-Benz sports coupe. His eyebrows shifted as Zahara
lifted the skirt to her dress while she slid gracefully onto the
leather seat.

Closing the door, he circled the car, smiling at the same

time he removed the jacket to his tuxedo. She may have been covered from neckline to ankle, but he was certain Zahara's dress was going to garner a lot of attention before the night was over. He placed the jacket on the space behind the seats and slid in behind the wheel. He waited a few seconds before he turned on the ignition, savoring the haunting scent of vanilla and musk wafting sensually from the tall, slender woman sitting beside him. Not only did she look good, but she also smelled good.

Zahara snapped her seat belt in place at the same time Adam shifted into gear and maneuvered the low-slung car out of her driveway. She stared straight ahead, watching darkness descend on the Westchester community as houses, trees, and cars rushed past. Adam drove quickly, expertly, while staying just under the speed limit. *Nice car. Like the tuxedo, it's probably rented for the evening*, she reflected in amusement.

What had begun as panic six hours before had settled into a state of confident relaxation, and she knew instinctively that Adam Vaughn was certain to be an exemplary escort.

"You never answered my question earlier. Who told you I liked lilies and peonies?" she asked once he got on the parkway.

"Deirdre. She told me the reason you picked her as your stylist was because you liked the lilies and peonies in the dried flower arrangement at her booth."

Zahara chuckled softly. "It turned out to be a wonderful sign because Dee Dee is a fabulous stylist."

Adam gave her a quick glance before turning his attention back to the road ahead of him. "I like your hairstyle. It's very becoming."

There was a momentary silence before she found her voice. "Thank you, Adam."

She had been more than pleased with the results of Dee Dee's latest artistic endeavor. Her thick hair was cut in layers where it fell around her neck and ears as if it had taken on a life of its own. Dee Dee had parted it on the right and whenever she lowered her head the straightened strands flowed over the crown of her head to the left side of her face.

It was Adam's turn to chuckle. "You're quite welcome. I wanted to tell you how beautiful you looked, but I didn't want to infringe on my role as your *escort*."

Staring numbly at his solemn expression, she felt her spine stiffen until she noticed a hint of a smile curve his mouth. "I suppose you want me to tell you how exquisite you look?" she countered with a wide grin.

"Not at all. I just don't want to embarrass you, Zahara."

"Oh, but you're not," she protested quickly. Glancing out the side window, she composed her words carefully. "I must admit I had my reservations when I first met you. Well—I didn't expect a deliveryman to . . ."

"To what?" he questioned when she didn't finish her statement.

"Adam. Don't." There was no mistaking the humiliation in her voice.

His hands tightened on the steering wheel. "Don't what? Don't remind you that even deliverymen know that black tie means wearing a tuxedo or dinner jacket? That a formal affair calls for a shower, shave, and clean nails?"

His mocking tone irritated her at the same time she was annoyed at the transparency of her thoughts. He had registered her reaction to his jumpsuit and work boots immediately. Adam Vaughn might earn his living delivering merchandise, but he was no fool.

Gathering what was left of her pride, she offered him a smile. "What can I say except that I'm sorry?"

Adam smiled, the dimple in his right cheek winking at her. "Sorry is enough." His deep voice was soft, comforting. "Tell me a little about yourself," he suggested after a comfortable silence. There was a hint of laughter in his tone, indicating his prior annoyance had vanished.

Shifting to her left, Zahara stared at his bold profile. Adam was very easy on the eyes with his high forehead, and strong nose and chin. And despite the obvious bulk of his large body, his face was lean with high, pronounced cheekbones.

"There's not much to tell."

He gave her a skeptical glance. "You're Russell Jenkins's sister, aren't you?"

"No. He's my brother. I'm five years older than Russell."

Again he smiled. "How old are you?"

"Thirty-five," she said without hesitating. "And you?"

"Thirty-eight."

"Any brothers or sisters?"

Adam shook his head. "No. I'm an only child. My parents were married for more than twenty years, and they thought they would never have a child. What my mother thought was menopause at forty-four turned out to be a baby. They were surprised and very embarrassed."

"How was it growing up an only child?"

He shrugged a muscular shoulder. "Very lonely."

Suddenly Zahara wanted to know more about the man she would spend the next four to five hours with. "Do you have any children?"

Adam pushed a button for cruise control and removed his right foot from the gas pedal. "No. I'm not married."

"Not being married while making babies doesn't seem to bother some men nowadays."

"I'm not one of those men, Zahara. I'd like to be married when I father children. How about you? Were you ever married?"

She knew the conversation was becoming very personal, but it didn't matter. She would see Adam only for the night. "No."

"Have you ever come close?"

"No. How about yourself?"

Adam's eyebrows slanted in a frown as he berated himself for bringing up the subject. "I was married once. It ended after a couple of years."

"I'm sorry," she whispered.

"Don't be. It was either divorce or annihilation." What he couldn't tell Zahara was that it was he who was destined for complete ruin. "Whose party are we attending?" he continued, deciding to change the subject.

"The president of Ansonia National Bank." She disclosed

the upcoming announcement of the bank's merger.

"Sounds like big doings," he remarked.

"It should be advantageous to all involved. Stockholders and employees."

"Will that mean a promotion for you?"

Zahara shook her head. "Not right away. I was just promoted to assistant manager at the 125th Street branch six months ago."

"Very nice. Maybe I'll think about transferring my account to your bank."

"Are you dissatisfied with your bank?"

"Not really. Perhaps I'll stop in one of these days and let you convince me why I should move my account to Ansonia."

She flashed a sexy sidelong grin. "Who do you work for?"

"Mazao Health Foods."

"The same Mazao products that are sold at Rosie's?"

"Yes, ma'am. Have you ever tried some of the soups or juices?" She shook her head. "Then I'll make certain to send you a few samples."

"I'm not into diet foods."

"They're not diet foods. They're made with only natural ingredients without the high levels of sugar, sodium, and fat in many prepackaged foods found on supermarket shelves."

"What does 'Mazao' mean?"

"It's Swahili for fruits and vegetables."

"Oh, how appropriate."

Their lively conversation shifted from nutrition to sports as they crossed the George Washington Bridge and left the environs of New York City for New Jersey.

They debated good-naturedly about whether the Knicks could win a much-sought-after championship this season, while Adam insisted that the New York Yankees were certain World Series winners with their new and improved pitching staff. It was nearly seven-twenty when they entered the town limits for Short Hills.

Zahara pulled down the visor on her side and studied her face in the lighted vanity mirror. She dusted her nose with a layer of loose powder from a tiny jeweled compact and applied a fresh coat of red color to her lips. Adam had slowed the car as he took surreptitious glances at her profile as she primped, seemingly ignoring his presence.

Returning the visor to its position, she turned and smiled at him until the blazing light from a large house on a hill caught her attention. "How did you find this place without getting lost?"

"Any deliveryman worth his salt is never without a map. I looked up the town and street address and mapped out my route."

Adam maneuvered into a curving driveway where a number of valets waited to park cars. He put the Mercedes in park and stepped out when the valet opened the door. Within a span of a minute he'd retrieved his jacket, slipped his arms into the sleeves, and circled the car to open the door for Zahara.

He extended his hand and caught her delicate fingers. Using a minimum of exertion, he helped her out of the low-slung vehicle. He took her wrap and placed it over her shoulders, then held out his left arm.

Zahara felt the unleashed power in his forearm through the fabric of his jacket and unconsciously moved closer to his tall body. She didn't know why, but for the first time in her life she felt totally protected. There was something about Adam Vaughn that made her feel more feminine, more fragile, and as they neared the entrance to the sprawling mansion they shared a smile.

The room set up for the cocktails was ablaze with light from three massive chandeliers. A woman standing outside the room took Zahara's wrap moments before Adam's right hand cradled the small of her back. Tilting her chin, she stared up at the face of the man she had spent the past hour with. In the full light his masculine beauty was breathtaking. His luminous dark-gray eyes narrowed as he returned her intense stare. The heat of his gaze ignited a longing she hadn't felt in years. A longing that reminded her that she was physically attracted to him.

"Are you two going to admire each other all night, or join the rest of us?"

Zahara spun around, a wide grin on her face at the sound of the familiar female voice. "Marlena!"

Marlena rested her hands on her hips, her gaze never straying from Adam. "Oh, you do remember me."

Zahara caught Adam's arm. "Adam Vaughn, Marlena Robinson. She's responsible for auditing Ansonia's loan department."

Marlena fluttered her lashes wildly while wrinkling her nose. "Hello, Adam. In case Ms. Jenkins didn't tell you, we also *were* best friends."

"Don't listen to her. We *are* best friends."

Marlena rolled her eyes upward. "Since Ms. Jenkins moved uptown we don't get to see her anymore."

"Adam! She's lying. We get together once a month to play the card game bidwhist."

Adam smiled at the petite woman who claimed smooth dark skin that complemented her elaborately braided hair. "May I get you ladies something to drink?"

Marlena handed him an empty champagne flute. "I'll have another glass of champagne, please."

"Zahara?"

"I'll have a dry white wine, thank you."

Both women watched him turn and walk toward the bar. As soon as he was out of earshot, Marlena grabbed Zahara's arm. "Where did you find him? Girl-l-l-l! He's some kinda fine."

Zahara didn't know whether to tell all of the truth or just a portion of it. She decided on the latter. "My hairdresser introduced me to him."

"Girlfriend, stop it!" There was an expression of disbelief on Marlena's face. "You got to be lying."

"I'm not lying," she admitted between her teeth, as she noticed a tall, blond woman making her way toward her. Alicia Wheaton was the main reason she'd asked for a transfer out of the corporate office. She didn't know what it was, but they disliked each other from the moment they were introduced.

Alicia smiled a cold smile that did not quite reach her cornflower-blue eyes. "Zahara. You're looking wonderful."

"So do you," she countered with a facetious grin. Alicia came from a family of bankers, and had secured her position with Ansonia not because of what she knew, but because of who she knew.

"Lovely dress," Alicia continued. "Armani, isn't it?"

"Why, yes," Zahara exclaimed with more enthusiasm than she actually felt.

Whatever Alicia intended to say died on her lips the instant she spied Adam. Her jaw dropped as she stared at him. Zahara waited until he'd given Marlena her flute of champagne, then wound her arm through his. Rising on tiptoe, she pressed her mouth to his. "Thank you, darling," she whispered against the brush of his thick, silky mustache as she took her own flute.

Caught off-guard by Zahara's unexpected display of affection, Adam curved an arm around her waist and held her tightly against his side. He didn't know what had transpired between the three women, but he suspected all did not bode well between Zahara and the tall, attractive, fragile-looking blonde.

Lowering his head, he pressed his lips to her fragrant hair. "Any time, my love."

Zahara and Marlena stared at each other, praying not to dissolve into laughter while Alicia's enraptured gaze was fixed on Adam.

Zahara wanted to slight Alicia and not introduce her to Adam, but social correctness superseded her personal feelings. "Adam, this is Alicia Wheaton. Alicia, Adam Vaughn."

Alicia flashed a teasing smile and extended her right hand, her wrist hanging limply. Tilting his head at an angle, Adam took her proffered hand gently. "My pleasure, Ms. Wheaton."

Alicia's smile widened. "The pleasure is mine, *Adam*." His

name came out in a soft purr. "Are you also in money management?"

Zahara felt her breath catch in her throat and a flood of heat suffuse her face with Alicia's query. Her tortured gaze met Adam's as he stared at her. How could she tell her peers he was a deliveryman? That all he needed was a pair of capable hands and a strong back to earn a paycheck?

"No, he isn't," she said quickly, not giving Adam the opportunity to answer Alicia's query. "He's in merchandising. Adam is responsible for marketing health food products," she said smoothly, registering the slight tensing of his body before it returned to its relaxed state.

"How nice," Alicia murmured.

"Yes, it is," Zahara replied with again a little too much enthusiasm. Pressing closer to Adam, she gave him an adoring smile. He lowered his head and brushed his mouth lightly over hers.

The brightness in Alicia's face faded as quickly as the act of extinguishing an electric light. "It was nice meeting you, Adam," she threw over her shoulder as she turned and walked away.

"That was priceless," Marlena whispered. "I bet she won't get in your face again tonight. There isn't a man Alicia thinks she can't pull," she explained to Adam.

Turning slightly, he stared at a retreating Alicia. "It wouldn't matter, because she's not my type."

"I hear you, my brother," Marlena crooned. "Let me go find my *man* and I'll be back."

Zahara waited until Marlena walked away, then turned to smile at Adam. "Thanks for helping me out."

He tightened his hold on her waist. "Do you still need rescuing? Because I think I can accommodate you again."

Lowering her lashes, she shook her head. "I don't think so, Mr. Vaughn."

The remainder of the night passed by in slow motion for Zahara. She introduced Adam to people she had worked with in the corporate offices and to the manager at the 125th Street branch and his wife.

The sixty invited guests were seated at six round tables in a formal dining room and were served by more than a dozen silent, efficient waiters. Zahara noted that Adam ate only vegetables while drinking seltzer, and she wondered whether he was a vegetarian. Speeches were given throughout dinner with the intention of saving time for several hours of dancing.

After dessert everyone filed into a ballroom where a band played popular tunes from the past fifty years. The lights in the ballroom dimmed and Zahara found herself in Adam's arms during a slow number as he hummed softly against her ear.

His arm slipped lower on her waist as he pulled her hips against his middle. Every soft curve of her body branded his through the fabric of his clothes. He'd watched her interact with her colleagues and had secretly admired the way she carried herself. There was no hint of snobbiness or pretension. She was intelligent and very secure. He'd found her to be an attentive *date*, and not once had she neglected to introduce him to anyone she knew. He had also noticed that she didn't watch him to see which fork he would pick up whenever a new course was served.

The fingers of his right hand were splayed over her hip, eliciting a rush of breath from her parted lips. The heat, the hardness of his solid body, the hypnotic fragrance of his cologne swept Zahara into a maelstrom of physical longing. She groaned inwardly as her breasts grew heavy, swelling against his chest. Did he know? Did he know what he was doing to her? Did he know what she was feeling?

"Adam?" His name came out in a shuddering moan.

"Yes."

"Please take me home."

Adam felt her trembling. He loosened his hold on her slender body. "It's okay," he whispered near her ear. "Relax. That's it. Breathe deep. In and out. In and out."

Following his own advice, Adam felt the hardness easing in his groin. Shifting his head, his mouth grazed her earlobe. "How are you feeling now?"

Raising her head, Zahara smiled up at him. "Better. Thank you."

His hands went from her waist to cradle her face between his palms. "Are you ready?" She nodded. Hand in hand, he led her through the slow-moving couples swaying to the beat of the sensual rhythm. "Wait for me and I'll get your wrap."

Adam and Zahara slipped out unnoticed, and as she sat beside him in the sports car, she relived the feel of his body pressed to hers all over again.

*Three years.* It had been that long since she'd shared her body with a man. Was she feeling what she was beginning to feel for Adam because she'd been celibate for so long? Or was it because she was actually attracted to him?

She shook her head. She couldn't be. He was a delivery-man! The men she usually dated were educated professionals. Closing her eyes, she settled back on the leather seat and tried sorting out her emotions.

Zahara hadn't realized she had fallen asleep until Adam shook her gently. "You're home."

Blinking to clear her vision, she stared at him. His eyes appeared abnormally large in the glow from the lighted dashboard. Running a hand through her hair, she pushed it behind her right ear. "I'm sorry about falling asleep on you."

"Don't worry about it. It would've been worse if I'd fallen asleep."

"You're right about that." Giving him a tired smile, she said, "How can I ever thank you for a wonderful evening?"

His penetrating gaze traveled over her face and searched her eyes. "Go out with me again."

She became instantly wide awake. It wasn't supposed to happen that way. They were to see each other once—just for one night.

"When?" She hardly recognized her own voice.

Adam shrugged a shoulder. "Whenever you're free."

He was making it easy for her. It would be at her discretion. She gave him a gentle smile. "Okay. I'll call you."

Reaching over to his right, the back of his hand grazing her breast, he opened the glove compartment and withdrew a pencil and paper. He flicked on the overhead dome light and quickly wrote down his phone number and handed the single sheet of paper to her.

"It's my home number."

Zahara folded the paper and slipped it into her purse. She sat staring out the window as Adam got out of the car. She was still staring out into the blackness when he opened the passenger-side door and extended his hand.

"If you don't want to get out you can always come home with me."

His softly spoken invitation spurred her into action as she turned and placed a sandaled foot on the ground. Adam pulled her to her feet in one smooth motion. He held her hand as he led her up the path to her door. Leaning down from his impressive height, he kissed her cheek.

"Good night, and thank you for a wonderful evening, Zahara."

Turning to face him, she shook her head. "I'm the one who should be thanking you. I'll call you," she promised.

Adam waited until she turned the key in the lock. He pushed open the door, then waited for her to close and lock it. He stared at the colorful panes of stained glass. "If you don't call me, Zahara Jenkins, then I'll call you," he said softly to the closed door.

Whistling softly, he strolled back to his car. It had been a long time since a woman had gotten under his skin. And that was what Zahara had done. She had gotten under his skin where he couldn't scratch the itch. Only she could do that.

Zahara spent the night mentally recalling the time she'd shared with Adam Vaughn. There were times when she thought she heard his voice, could detect the fragrance of his cologne, and when she slept, she dreamt of dancing with him. She relived the solid crush of his body pressed to hers, her breasts heavy against his broad chest, his fingers splayed over her hip, and the solid bulge between his thighs molded to her burning, throbbing flesh.

Turning over and punching her pillow, she tried for a more comfortable position. It was after one in the morning and she hadn't had more than two hours of sleep.

"Adam, Adam," she whispered in the silence of her bedroom. "Why are you doing this to me?"

She knew the answer even before she asked the question. He wasn't doing anything to her. She was doing it to herself. She had set up barriers to keep men at a distance if they didn't meet her superficial criteria for what she deemed as successful. Flinging aside the sheet and lightweight blanket, she turned on the bedside lamp and pulled her knees to her chest.

What was it about Adam Vaughn other than his gorgeous body and face that wouldn't permit her a peaceful night's sleep? She replayed her conversations with him and could not come up with anything on the negative side of the ledger. He was gentle, unpretentious, and conspicuously attentive and protective. Everyone at the dinner party knew he was her escort. Whenever she said something to him, he'd lean in close to listen intently, and whenever she introduced him to someone he'd always touch her body. Whether it was her hand, shoulder, or her waist, the possessiveness of his gentle graze was apparent. And she had liked him touching her. There were times when she'd found herself leaning against him just to enjoy the solidity of his large body.

Her head came up as the realization swept over her. He made her feel safe. He was the first man, aside from her father, who had made her feel as if he would protect her at any cost. It wasn't his size, but his manner. Adam Vaughn was a man she knew she could trust—with her life, if the situation called for it.

Turning off the lamp, she slid down to the mattress and pillow. She'd made her decision. She would call him. She would see him again.

Zahara walked into Rosie's on Wednesday, stopping at the receptionist's desk. "I have an appointment with Maria at six."

The receptionist checked the large calendar. "She's ready for you. How was your date with Adam?"

Grimacing, she inhaled, then slowly let out her breath. The Rosie's Curl and Weave inquisition was about to begin, and she wondered how many more times she would have to give the same answer. "It was very nice, Ramona."

The receptionist picked at a decoratively airbrushed acrylic nail. "You going out with him again?"

"I don't know," she lied smoothly.

Ramona sucked her teeth loudly while shaking her head. "You know what they say. If you're slow, you blow."

"I'll keep that in mind," Zahara replied, smiling.

"How did it work out with Adam?" an operator called out as she made her way past her booth to the manicure section.

"It was nice," she repeated what she'd told Ramona.

"Being nice is never fun, Miss Banker. You'd better take a cue from Tina Turner. It's always better when it's a little nice and *rough*." She growled the last word.

Zahara shook her head while grinning. "I'll see what I can do about that."

She sat opposite Maria. A knowing smile on the manicurist's face reminded her of a cat who had just finished licking drops of rich stolen cream off its delicate whiskers.

"What!" she hissed at the younger woman.

Leaning in closer, Maria whispered, "How was he?"

"He who?" She decided not to make it easy for Maria.

"Adam Vaughn, of course."

"He was a gentleman."

Maria waved a hand. "I know he's a gentleman. But what did you guys do?"

"We went to a dinner party. We ate and danced, then he took me home before he went home."

The manicurist looked disappointed. "That's it?"

"Of course that's it. What did you expect?"

"Bummer," Maria said under her breath as she moistened a strip of cotton with nail polish remover.

\* \* \*

Zahara sat down on an empty seat on the Metro-North train and stared out the window as the train pulled out of the 125th Street station. She had put off calling Adam for three days. Walking into Rosie's and having everyone ask her about him made her aware of him all over again.

Pulling the cellular phone from her leather bag, she dialed the number she had spent the past three days memorizing. His phone rang twice before an answering machine switched on. She waited for the recorded message to end.

"Adam, this is Zahara," she said quickly before she could change her mind. "It's Wednesday. Please call me when you get the chance. I'll be in after nine." She recited her home telephone number, then pressed a button and ended the call.

She did it! She had committed to seeing Adam Vaughn again.


Adam walked into his apartment and saw the blinking red light on his answering machine. Each night he'd come home hoping the blinking light meant that Zahara had called him. The calls were from women, but not the woman he wanted to talk to. He'd listened to the messages before erasing them without returning the calls.

He pressed the PLAY button, listening to the first message as he slipped off his jacket. He kicked off his shoes and pulled the hem of his shirt from his slacks at the same time the next message clicked on. His hands stilled as he listened to the voice he'd spent days waiting for. It was the first time he noticed the sensual, breathless quality. She said his name as if it were a caress.

He replayed her number, then wrote it down on the pad next to the phone before glancing at his watch. It was nine-forty. He wanted to take a shower, but that would have to wait. Calling Zahara was now a priority.

Picking up the receiver, he dialed her number. She answered after the third ring.

"Hello."

"Hi. This is Adam."

There was a slight pause. "Thanks for getting back to me."

There came another pause. "When do you want to get together?"

"How about Friday night?" he said quickly. There was no
hesitating, no need to play head games with her.

"What time Friday?"

A satisfied smile smoothed out the lines of fatigue ringing
his generous mouth. It was apparent that Zahara was also not
into head games. He'd discovered that a lot of women liked
playing hard to get. Not only did it turn him off, but he'd
made it a practice not to see them again after their first encounter.

"I can pick you up after work. We'll have dinner before I
take you to a jazz spot. If you don't like jazz, then we can
always do something else."

"Jazz will be fine, Adam."

"What time do you usually get off?"

"Five."

His smile broadened. "Then I'll meet you in front of the
bank at five."

"I'll see you then."

"Zahara?"

"Yes."

"Thank you."

Her soft laugh came through the wire. "You're welcome."

He heard the click as she hung up. Lowering his head, he
let out his breath slowly. He had to plan something special.
As special as the woman who had slipped under the wall he'd
erected to keep from loving again.

Zahara wound her way through the throng of customers filing
into the bank for the branch's late-night evening hours, hoping
to avoid an elderly gentleman who was inclined to engage her
in lengthy conversations whenever he came in. *Four more
steps and I'm out the door,* she mused, taking long, measured
strides.

"Miss Jenkins!"

She muttered a soft curse. She couldn't escape. Spinning
around, she flashed a friendly smile. "Good evening."

The wizened Harlem resident approached and grasped her left hand. "I just want to thank you for helping me out the other day."

She patted the hand clutching hers. "It's all right, Mr. Fletcher. Linking up your savings account with your checking will give you a line of credit and should alleviate all of your overdraft worries."

"You've helped me so much, Miss Jenkins."

"It's my job to help our customers." She glanced up at the clock over the door. It was five after five. "I'm sorry, Mr. Fletcher, but I have to meet someone."

"Will I see you come Monday?"

"Yes, you will. Have a wonderful weekend."

Still clutching her hand, he peered at the red silk dress and black jacket skimming the curves of her tall, slender body. "You look very nice. You got a date?"

A slow, secret smile trembled over her lips. "Yes. I have a date." Adam was her date, as she was his. Less than a week before, she'd berated him for suggesting he was her date, and now she looked forward to seeing him again with an anticipation she hadn't felt in years. Dee Dee had coiffed her hair the day before and the dress she had elected to wear had taken her more than an hour to select.

Most of the gossip about her going out with Adam had subsided when she went to Rosie's to have her hair done the day before. Dee Dee's only comment was that Adam said he'd enjoyed going out with her.

"Where are you going to meet your young man?"

Zahara steered Mr. Fletcher toward the door. "He's waiting outside for me." Holding the door open, she let the older man precede her as they stepped out into the late-afternoon sunlight. She held her breath when she spied Adam standing near the curb. Staring wordlessly across at him, her heart pounding with an inner excitement, she rewarded him with a sensual smile.

The trembling smile on Zahara's lush mouth caused Adam's breath to falter before it started up again in a slow, measured rhythm. He took in everything about her in one sweeping glance. He'd spent the week trying to remember what she'd looked like and had failed miserably. The prolonged anticipation of waiting to see her again had been unbearable after he'd confirmed meeting her Friday. But seeing the red silk dress with the mandarin collar under a black jacket, watching her coiffed hair swing forward as she leaned over to listen to the elderly man, brought back the surreal image of her beautiful face and gentle manner. She gestured toward him and he moved from his leaning position against a parking meter to approach her.

The man clinging possessively to her arm glanced up at Adam. Eyes faded with age in a lined mahogany-colored face surveyed him closely. "Are you Miss Jenkins's young man?"

Adam nodded, extending his right hand. "Yes, I am. Adam Vaughn, Mr. . . ."

"Mr. Fletcher, sonny." He took the proffered hand. "You take good care of Miss Jenkins, do you hear me, sonny?"

Adam hid a smile. "I hear you, Mr. Fletcher. I give you my word that I'll take real good care of her."

Appearing quite satisfied with Adam's response, the elderly man's head bobbed up and down in slow motion. "She's worth more than all of the money inside that bank."

Zahara's gaze met Adam's and her heart softened with the tenderness shining from the depths of his radiant dark-gray eyes.

"You're right about that, Mr. Fletcher," he said in a deep, rumbling whisper.

"Well, I'll let you two kids go. Enjoy yourselves."

"Thank you." Adam and Zahara had spoken in unison.

Adam watched the older man make his way slowly toward Adam Clayton Powell, Jr. Boulevard. "Should I be jealous?" he asked quietly.

Zahara's jaw dropped slightly before she was able to form a comeback. "You're kidding, aren't you?"

Shifting, he arched an eyebrow at the same time his serious gaze fused with hers. "Should I consider Mr. Fletcher a worthy rival?" he quizzed in a dangerously soft tone, ignoring her inquiry.

"He's an old man. Old enough to be my grandfather."

"There's nothing going on between the two of you?"

Zahara noticed the beginnings of a smile deepening the dimple in his lean jaw, and suddenly she wished they were anywhere but on 125th Street and Malcolm X Boulevard, or in front of the building where she worked. She hadn't thought of Adam Vaughn as a tease.

"You're going to pay for that, Adam."

"Pay how, Miss Jenkins?"

"Oh, I'll think of something."

He flashed his sensual smile. "I can't wait."

"You may come to regret those three words."

"I seriously doubt that." Adam's teasing smile vanished, and in its place was a silent expectation that stoked an awareness both were helpless to resist.

Zahara conceded they were attracted to each other, but more than attraction was an entrancement she could not deny. His masculine appeal was devastating, from his casual attire of dark brown slacks, brown loafers, cream-colored silk shirt, and lightweight khaki jacket, to his neatly brushed hair and freshly shaven jaw. He wasn't wearing a tie and it was apparent to her they weren't going to dine in an establishment that required a jacket and tie.

Grasping her hand, he smiled again. "You look very nice."

A warm glow of heat stung her cheeks with his compliment. "Thank you. Where are we going for dinner?"

"To a place that's private and very, very intimate."

"The Terrace?"

"I'm not telling."

"Aren't you going to give me a clue?"

Adam shook his head. "Nope."

He steered her toward the East Side, which meant he wasn't taking her to the Terrace or the very popular soul food restaurant called Sylvia's. They reached Fifth Avenue and turned left uptown, and by the time they'd walked another three blocks Zahara's curiosity threatened to overwhelm her. Adam led her down a block lined with brownstone buildings and three-story townhouses. He stopped in front of a townhouse in the middle of the quiet, spotless, tree-lined street and pushed open a door to the vestibule. Within minutes she found herself standing in the entry of a first-floor apartment at the rear of the building.

Adam extended his arm outward while bowing from the waist. "Welcome to Café Vaughn." Her apparent shock was mirrored on her face. He had taken her to his apartment.

Her startled gaze swept around a large room with brick walls, pale, glossy wood floors, a massive fireplace, and streamlined functional furnishings covered in off-white Haitian cotton fabrics and saddle tan leather.

Four steps led to a raised alcove enclosed with a panelled partition rising to half the room's height. Two delicate crystal vases on tables in differing heights held fresh flowers in varying hues from snowy white to deep rosy pinks.

Massive potted trees flanked a wall of sliding glass doors; dropping her handbag on a chair, she made her way to the glass wall, noticing the rear apartment merged into a garden and patio.

The heat from Adam seeped into her as he moved closer, and she closed her eyes, enjoying his warmth. Unconsciously she leaned back against the solid wall of his broad chest. She shivered visibly when his moist breath swept over the back of her neck, and she wanted to turn and run, run out of the apartment and away from whatever it was that made Adam Vaughn so hard for her to resist. His large hands caressed the silk covering her shoulders, increasing the heat building up in her body.

Adam lowered his head, his lips brushing the thick, sweet, fragrant strands of her straightened hair. His touching her was what he'd wanted to do for seconds, minutes, hours, days. He wanted Zahara to know what he was feeling by utilizing touch.

Curving one arm around her waist, he pulled her hips to his middle. She groaned softly, eliciting a smile from him. He felt rather than saw her return his smile.

"Did you invite me here to seduce me, Adam Vaughn?"

A deep chuckle rumbled in his broad chest. "Initially that was my intent," he confessed.

"Did you change your mind?"

He nodded. "I decided I wanted you to get to know me better and vice versa."

Both her hands covered his, her fingers tightening with a gentle squeeze. "Know me how?"

Turning her in his embrace, Adam stared down at her composed features. Her eyes were wide in anticipation, her soft lips slightly parted in a measured waiting. His lids lowered over his expressive eyes. "I know how you feel, look, and smell. But the only thing that's missing is how you taste."

Lowering his head slowly, deliberately, he covered her mouth with his in a whisper of a kiss that snatched her breath from her lungs. Adam was the first man she'd kissed who favored a mustache and the feel of it was startling and exhilarating. She felt the building pressure as he deepened the kiss, and without warning her lips parted, allowing him access to the passion she'd curbed for years.

Her arms moved up his hard chest and curved around his shoulders as she pressed closer, wanting to become one with him. Everything that Adam Vaughn was made of melded with her as she gave herself up to the man and the moment.

The thick brush of his silken mustache was masterful and masculine. She moaned again when his hand moved over the silk covering her back, then continued downward to splay over a hip.

Feelings she did not know existed spiraled out of control. Again she asked herself what it was about Adam Vaughn's caress and kiss that touched a core of Zahara Rachel Jenkins that no other man had been able to do with total possession.

He was nothing—absolutely *nothing* like the other men she'd socially interacted with, yet he had the power to move her as no other man had.

Was it because he was so masculine and sensual? Was it because he wasn't pretentious? Or was it because he was very secure just being blue-collar working class?

And after their first encounter, hadn't she wanted to know

what it would be like to kiss him? To feel his arms around her again?

*Yes!*

She wanted to know that *and* more. The memory of Adam Vaughn haunted her dreams and waking moments because she'd constantly told herself that she would only date men who were college educated, white collar, and upwardly mobile. She'd consciously rejected any man who did not come to her "correct." And under the column of *correct* was a long list of prerequisites. But after spending five-and-a-half hours with Adam Vaughn, he had just shattered those prerequisites.

Pulling back slightly, she relived the burning aftermath of Adam's fiery possession. Smiling, she kissed his chin, cheek, earlobe. Her soft mouth was like the petal of a newly opened flower, showered with morning dew and overflowing with the sweet nectar she'd willingly shared with the man holding her possessively to his heart.

Adam tightened his hold on her waist, lifting Zahara effortlessly off her feet. He recaptured her mouth until there was a dreamy intimacy to the joining. His kiss told her what he could not openly verbalize. That he'd found his other half. That she had crawled under the barrier he'd set up to keep all women at a distance. That he wanted to see her—every day, and that he would willingly offer up all he possessed to keep her in his life.

He'd stopped trying to analyze what it was about her that would not permit him a peaceful night's sleep. Why he'd resorted to stress-relieving activities to control his mind and body whenever the image of her hauntingly beautiful face surfaced. All he knew was that he wanted her—all of her!

He was one thing and that was patient. He would wait her out. And he was also very confident. He knew he eventually would claim her as his own.

Using Herculean strength, Adam held Zahara aloft with one arm while his other hand swept under the nape of her neck, his fingers threading through thick strands of hair. She shuddered, went limp, and buried her face against his strong neck.

He smiled when she whimpered like a small child. He'd found her erogenous zone.

"Adam."

"Hmm-mm?" He loathed opening his eyes or letting her go.

"No more. Please." Her voice came from far away, resembling the sound of a muted horn. He complied quickly, lowering her feet to the floor, but he was slower releasing her as his hands came away in slow motion.

Zahara stared numbly at Adam, unaware of the tempting package she presented: chest rising and falling under the cover of silk, eyes wide, pupils dilated with arousal, lips parted, moist and slightly swollen. The halting cadence of her breathing shouted mutely how much his kiss had affected her.

Adam felt everything she felt—and more. He was just better at concealing the changes taking place in his body. A teasing smile trembled over his mouth. He'd kissed her and she had responded in kind. They were off to a wonderful start.

"I've invited you to eat and so far I've been the only one sampling," he teased with a devastatingly irresistible grin.

She returned his smile. "And I'll have you know I forfeited lunch today, because I wanted to save my appetite for dinner."

"I'll make it up to you," he promised. Sliding open the glass doors, he guided her out to the patio. Streams of late afternoon sunlight filtered through the leaves of a flowering dogwood tree, which reached up past a second-story veranda. Smaller trees and flowering plants were cradled in massive terra-cotta pots placed at strategic positions around a wrought-iron fence enclosing the townhouse's property.

Gazing up, Zahara surveyed the lush privacy of the courtyard. "It's like an oasis in the middle of the city."

"The first-floor tenant gets the patio, the second the veranda, and the third-floor the rooftop."

Her enthralled gaze met Adam's. "I much prefer the patio."

He nodded. "That's the reason I took the first-floor apartment even though it's smaller than the ones on the upper floors. After I give you something to alleviate your immediate hunger, I'll show you around my humble abode. I can't have you fainting on me. Besides, there isn't enough of you that you can afford to miss a meal.''

She gave him an I-know-you've-got-to-be-kidding look. ''Do I look anorexic to you?''

''I wouldn't call you anorexic, but you're still no heavyweight if I can lift you with one arm.''

''That's because you probably outweigh me by at least seventy-five pounds.''

''Try more than a hundred, Zahara.'' Without elaborating further, he turned and walked back into the apartment.

She sat down on a cushioned wrought-iron chaise, thinking Adam Vaughn's place was anything but humble. In fact it was quite luxuriant for a deliveryman's salary. Rents weren't cheap in Manhattan—not even in Harlem where luxury apartments were at a premium.

She hadn't missed the exquisite quality of the fabric covering a sofa and love seat, the beautifully aged leather on an armchair, or the weight of the wrought-iron chaise that matched a round table and four chairs. It was apparent Adam had excellent taste in home furnishings. And now that she'd seen him casually dressed, she knew his taste in clothes was also impeccable.

She found Adam Vaughn to be an enigma. Especially for someone whose livelihood was delivering merchandise.

He emerged from the apartment ten minutes later pushing a serving cart. He'd removed his jacket and her gaze was fixed on his muscular forearms under the short-sleeved, cream-colored silk shirt. Her mouth went suddenly dry as she surveyed his well-toned physique. He had to stand at least six-four and weigh well over two hundred pounds, but he was put together like the marble statues of the ancient gods she'd observed in museums during her travels in Europe. Closing her eyes, she felt a wave of throbbing, pulsing heat settle into her core as she tried imagining Adam completely nude.

She opened her eyes and observed him as he quickly and expertly set the wrought-iron table with china, silver, serving pieces, stemware, damask napkins, and an icy pitcher filled with a red concoction, a platter with hors d'oeuvres, and another with a chunk of blue-veined cheese.

"I'll be right back," he promised. "The bread should be warm enough now."

As she stood up and removed her own jacket, Adam returned carrying a wicker basket covered with a linen cloth. He placed the basket on the table, then extended his right hand. "Come."

The single word touched a vibrant chord inside Zahara as she moved over to the table. The command was a caress, stroking and hypnotic. She wanted to *come* to him—hiding nothing, and giving him what she'd never given another man. She would come to him as a female who had become a woman. With Adam there would be no pretense, only the simple truth. And the simple truth was that after seeing him only twice, she liked him, liked him much more than she wanted to.

She ached to reach over and touch him as boldly as he'd touched her. She wanted to run her fingertips over the planes of his muscular body, sculpting as if she were an artist.

What she did instead was place her hand in his and permit him to seat her. She felt the heat from his body as he lingered over her head before he circled the table and sat opposite her.

His large capable hands filled two flutes with the red liquid, handing one to her. Raising his glass aloft, his gaze bored into hers. The slanting rays of the sun left his face in half-shadows. However, his eyes gleamed with a strange, mysterious glow.

"I'd like to propose a toast to a lasting and open friendship."

Zahara smiled a slow smile, biting down on her lower lip. He'd said friendship, and not relationship. She was relieved because what she didn't want was for their liaison to move too quickly. She needed time—a lot of time—to sort out her feelings for him.

Raising her own glass, she said softly, "And to a friendship that's not only open, but honest."

"Amen," Adam murmured under his breath as he took a sip of the cold drink.

She took several sips of the bubbling icy liquid, rolling it around on her tongue before swallowing. It was delicious. "What's in this?"

"It's a powdered fruit drink packaged by Mazao. I added club soda instead of water, along with a small amount of white rum."

She took another sip. "It's wonderful." And it was. It was a fruity combination with a distinctive cherry flavor. "I noticed you didn't drink anything alcoholic or eat any meat at the dinner party, and I thought perhaps you were a teetotaler and a vegetarian."

"I'm neither," Adam admitted as he filled a small dish with portions of thinly sliced cheese, smoked salmon and spinach pinwheels, and a slice of warm, freshly baked bread, handing it to her. He filled a dish for himself, then stared across the table at the questioning expression on her face.

"There was a time in my life when I had a serious weight problem," he continued. "So serious it wrecked my marriage and nearly destroyed me in the process. I told you my parents were middle-aged when I came along, and I'm the first one to admit that they were very indulgent. Whatever I wanted I got, even though my folks weren't well-to-do.

"My father worked for the post office for thirty years and retired as a supervisor, while my mother gave Harlem Hospital twenty-five years of service in their admitting office before she retired. We took vacations, I went to sleep-away camp for a couple of summers, and had the best orthodontic care available in those days.

"I was always tall, but I didn't start putting on the weight until my late twenties. My dad was diagnosed with lung and bone cancer and it took him two years to die. I spent every spare moment I had with him, carrying him to the bathroom when he couldn't make it out of the bed, or bathing him when he was too weak to stand up. My ex-wife complained about my overeating and that I was neglecting her, and after a while we grew further and further apart.

"My dad's pain and suffering ended when he died in my arms early one morning. The life seemed to go out of my mother the moment he drew his last breath. Within six months she was gone. The doctor claimed she died of natural causes, but I knew it was because of a broken heart.

"My wife had left me and sued for divorce, accusing me of abandonment. I didn't contest it, while I withdrew into myself. I continued eating—everything. One day I passed out on the street and woke up in Harlem Hospital's emergency room. My blood pressure had spiked where I was a prime candidate for a stroke. The emergency room doctor prescribed something to bring down my blood pressure, then suggested I see my own doctor.

"I tried every diet known to man as my weight fluctuated between three hundred and three-fifty for several years. I'd declined attending family reunions because I was too ashamed to let anyone see me looking like a walking condominium."

"How did you lose the weight?" Zahara questioned. "I must admit that you have a fantastic-looking body."

Adam acknowledged her compliment with a nod. "I had help from a cousin who was trained as a dietitian before she became an herbalist. She came up with a health drink that contains all of the daily requirements for vitamins and minerals in two eight-ounce shakes."

"Do you still drink the shakes?"

"Only when I've overdone it the day before. I had to learn how to eat all over again." He tapped his temple with his forefinger. "It begins up here. I had to change my approach to eating. I suppose you can call it behavior modification, but I can assure you it works. I don't weigh or measure my food, but I'm aware of what I can eat and what I can't eat.

"After I lost the first fifty pounds, I joined a gym and began working out. I learned to meditate and became involved with *T'ai Chi* to find my own center of balance in my life. I even used *feng shui* to set up my apartment."

Her gaze was fused to his. "I take it life is good for you now."

"Very good," he confirmed. *And it just got better since I've met you*, he added silently.

Zahara nodded as she speared a portion of the delicate pinwheel hors d'oeuvre covered with flaky phyllo dough and bit into it. The salmon, spinach, and a soft creamy cheese literally melted on her tongue.

"How do you like working for your cousin?"

He shifted an eyebrow. "We've worked out an arrangement. She takes care of manufacturing and I'm responsible for distribution." What he did not say was that his cousin worked for *him*. He was sole owner of Mazao Health Foods, Inc.

Adam had toasted to an open and honest friendship with Zahara, but he knew he could not disclose his position at Mazao—not yet. Not until she could accept him for himself, and not the means through which he earned his salary.

"Are your folks alive?" he asked, deciding to change the topic.

"Very much alive and kicking. They live in a retirement community near Charleston, South Carolina. It took them a year to adjust to living in the South after spending nearly twenty years in Vermont."

Adam's fork was poised in midair. "Vermont? Don't tell me you actually grew up in Vermont."

Zahara laughed at his stunned expression. She spent the next half hour detailing exploits of the years she lived in a New England town where she interacted with only one other black child, not counting her brother. She also told of Russell's athletic prowess and how basketball coaches from every major and minor college in the country offered him full scholarships to sign with them. Russell decided on Georgetown. He'd graduated with a degree in pre-law and was a first-round draft pick by the Miami Heat.

"Speaking of the Heat," Adam stated as a slight smile deepened the dimple in his right cheek, "they're coming to the Garden tomorrow night."

"And?"

"Would you like to go with me?"

"Do you have tickets?"

"I can get tickets."

"From a scalper?" she teased.

"No!" He managed to look insulted. "I have a friend who has season tickets."

"Don't bother your friend. My brother usually leaves a couple for me at the box office. You're welcome to come with me tomorrow night."

"Are you asking me out, Miss Jenkins?"

"Why, yes, Mr. Vaughn."

Tilting his head at an angle, he winked at her. "Then you've got yourself a *date*."


"Listen up, brothers. For our Friday Night Motown Revue we are taking special requests. And the first one is for "My Girl." Now that means that you brothers select your special lady, hold her real close, and tell her what she wants to hear." The band's lead vocalist shook his head, gesturing wildly at a table near the stage. "Sit yo' butt down, Darryl! That honey you're reaching for belongs to me." He waited for the noise to fade away when the capacity-packed crowd roared in laughter. "Now if you don't dance with your special honey, then that means she's available for the next brother."

Reaching across the small round table, Adam grasped Zahara's hand and pulled her slowly to her feet. Within seconds his arm circled possessively around her waist as he led her out to the dance floor.

"Now Brother Vaughn has the right idea," the singer continued. "He's not taking any chances by leaving his lady sitting where someone with a wandering eye can scoop the pretty thang right up." He winked at Zahara. "How ya doin', sugah?"

"Just sing the song, Hakim," Adam drawled, affecting a frown.

There was another round of laughter, then the bass guitarist began a refrain of the three familiar notes of the popular Temptations song, and suddenly the dance floor was crowded with couples.

Zahara wound her arms around Adam's neck, following his strong lead. A satisfied smile curved her mouth at the same time she inhaled the scent of sandalwood on his warm flesh. She heard a deep rumble of laughter start deep in his chest before it bubbled up and out.

"What's so funny?"

"Hakim. He puts up a fuss when another man goes after his woman, yet he forgets all about that when he tries coming on to my lady."

Pulling back slightly, she gave him a bewildered stare. "*Your* lady?"

"If you're with me, in my arms, then you're *my* lady. Besides, you did let me kiss you."

"Oh, it's like that?" There was a trace of laughter in her query.

"It is," he replied, deadpan.

"I think not, *Brother* Vaughn. Not after only one kiss."

He pulled her closer, his nose nuzzling an ear. "What would I have to do to make you my lady?"

"It would have to be more than a little ole kiss." Her words were muffled against the unyielding wall of his chest.

"Do you care to be specific?"

"I plead the Fifth."

"Coward! Chicken!" he crooned.

Both were smiling as they moved fluidly together as if they'd spent years dancing with each other.

The jazz club occupied the third floor of a brownstone building that also claimed a first-floor coed health club and a second-story restaurant.

Adam had admitted spending a great deal of free time in the brownstone building, either at the gym or in the jazz club on Thursday or Friday nights when they featured live entertainment. What made the clubs so accessible was that they were around the corner from where he lived.

Dinner had been a wonderful experience. They had dined on a salad of crisp field greens with a balsamic vinegar dressing, Mazao-produced cream of celery soap, thinly sliced butterflied lamb broiled on a stove-top grill and an accompaniment of grilled vegetables.

She was as impressed with Adam's culinary skills as she was with his apartment. Sliding doors concealed a spacious kitchen and dining area from the living room, while the raised alcove set off a sitting area and the space where he had elected to place a king-size iron bed. Green paint with a hint of yellow provided a relaxing backdrop for the bed and a massive bleached pine armoire. A stack of books rested on a bedside table, bearing author names she recognized as mystery writers.

Moving closer as they danced, she smiled up at him staring down at her. She couldn't remember the last time she'd truly enjoyed herself with a man.

He pressed his mouth to her forehead. "Tired?"

"A little," she admitted. And when she thought of it, she was. She'd been up before five, worked out, returned home to eat breakfast, then showered and dressed for her commute into Manhattan.

Adam went still as he visually examined the woman in his arms. His penetrating gaze caressed her velvety brown skin, hair as dark as a cloud, and her large, almond-shaped, dark liquid eyes that were deep enough for him to drown in. Resisting the impulse to kiss her passionately, he buried his face against her hair. He waited for the number to end, then led her to the elevator that took them to the first floor and street level.

They stood in the lobby of the health club. "Do you want to wait here or come with me to pick up my car?"

"Where is it?"

"Parked in a garage a couple of blocks away."

She flashed a tired smile. "I'll come with you."

Hand in hand, they left the brownstone building and strolled the Harlem neighborhood like so many lovers were doing on the warm spring night.

They arrived at the garage, which took up half a city block. Adam rang a bell for the night attendant, who appeared at the door, yawning and scratching his head as if he'd just been awakened from a peaceful slumber.

"Evening, Mr. Vaughn. I'll bring your car around directly."

Zahara shivered as a cool breeze swept her dress around her legs. Adam moved closer, folding her against his body and providing additional heat. "I'll have you home in no time," he whispered against her ear.

"I have to pick up my car," she informed him.

"Where is it?"

"At the Mount Vernon Metro-North commuter lot."

"We'll pick up your car, then I'll follow you home."

Turning in his embrace, she tried making out his features. "Do you have to work tomorrow?"

"Only in the morning."

"If that's the case, then I'll meet you in front of the Barnes and Noble bookstore on Thirty-third and Seventh."

"You don't want me to drive up and pick you up?"

"No. My brother will bring me back. Whenever he's in town he stays over with me."

"What time should I meet you?"

"Seven. I usually come in early to get in some shopping before I pick up the tickets."

The door to the parking garage slid up and the sleek shape of the black Mercedes-Benz appeared. Adam opened the passenger door and waited until Zahara was settled before he took the seat the attendant had vacated. He fastened his seat belt, adjusted the heat, shifted into gear, then headed north.

Zahara settled back against the leather seat, closed her eyes, and listened to the soft sounds of a radio station playing cool jazz. Except for the music, there was a comfortable silence she did not want to shatter.

After a while she opened her eyes and stared out into the darkness of the night. What had begun as a chance meeting with Adam had turned into something she would not have expected or predicted. But whatever it was she felt for him astounded her with a sense of fulfillment. She would see him tomorrow and that realization left her reeling with anticipated excitement at the same time her heart swelled with an enthusiasm she hadn't felt in three years.

• • •

Adam made it to Mount Vernon in record time, waited for
her to pick up her car in the nearly empty commuter parking
lot, then followed close behind until she maneuvered her late
model Nissan into the attached garage.

He got out of his car and met her at the front door. Cradling
her face between his large hands, he lowered his head and
brushed his mouth over hers.

"Thank you for a wonderful evening."

"You're very welcome," she whispered, her breath mingling with his. Rising on tiptoe, she kissed him. "Good night.
I'll see you tomorrow."

Pushing several strands of hair behind her left ear, he returned her kiss, then ran his tongue over his lower lip, tasting
her again. He would have to wait to see her again, but this
time it would be less than twenty-four hours.

"Good night, Zahara."

And as he'd done a week before, he waited for her to lock
her door before he went back to his car to begin his return
trip to Manhattan. This trip would be different from the one
before because he now had the memory of the taste and feel
of her sweet mouth to keep him company.

Zahara doubted whether she would be able to speak above a
whisper the next day. The game between the New York
Knicks and the Miami Heat had gone into double overtime
and everyone in the uncontrolled excitement in the Garden
had reached a fever-pitched frenzy. The Knicks managed to
win by one point—a three-point shot had sailed through the
net at the exact moment the final buzzer rang.

She stood on the corner of Eighth Avenue with Adam, her
face pressed against his shoulder. The late afternoon temper-
atures had dropped nearly fifteen degrees, and the denim
jacket she'd paired with her jeans and an orange cotton mock
turtleneck was not sufficient for the forty-eight-degree night-
time temperature.

"What time is it?" she asked him for the second time
within twenty minutes.

"It's ten twenty-five."

Shivering, she wrapped her arms around his waist inside his windbreaker. "The driver's due here in five minutes." Adam tightened his grip on her body, offering more of his body's heat.

As if on cue, a sleek limousine slid up along the curb at the same time a door to the service entrance at Madison Square Garden opened and Russell Jenkins emerged. He waved to his sister, who was huddled close to a man built like a football linebacker. The few times she attended the games alone, she normally waited for him in one of the sports bars in Pennsylvania Station. But when he'd called her soon after he'd checked into his hotel earlier that afternoon, she informed him that she would be waiting for him outside the service entrance.

Zahara left the protective warmth of Adam's body for the familiarity of her brother's. Rising on tiptoe, she kissed his cheek. "Even though you tried to destroy *us*, I still love you."

"You'd better," Russell teased, ruffling her hair. He handed a garment bag and a matching leather tote to the driver before extending his right hand to Adam. "Russell Jenkins."

Adam took the proffered hand. "Adam Vaughn."

Russell's friendly gaze returned to his sister. "I don't know about the two of you, but I'm starved. Hop in and we'll decide where we're going to eat on the way uptown."

Adam held back. "Thanks for the offer, but I'm going to have to take a rain check."

He'd enjoyed the game and Zahara's company, but one thing he didn't want to do was intrude on the time she had with her brother. And seeing her interact with Russell Jenkins evoked a foreign emotion of melancholy. It had been a long time since he'd felt lonely. He had told Zahara his life was on track, in alignment, but that was only a half-truth. His business was solvent, his health was excellent, and whenever he needed female companionship, all he had to do was make a telephone call. But now it was different, because after seeing Zahara for the third time, he realized what was missing in his life. A wife and family.

He'd married once, because he wanted to do the right thing. Janice had told him she was pregnant. He'd found this hard to believe because both were using protection whenever they slept together. But he did not doubt her claim, and married her within the month. After two months Janice disclosed she wasn't pregnant and that her period was probably late. He'd fallen for the oldest trick in the book for a woman to get a man to marry her. She later confessed she had tricked him because she was afraid of losing him. Her fears were not unfounded because eventually she did lose him and whatever love he'd felt for her.

But he knew instinctively that Zahara was very different. When she'd related her childhood exploits growing up in Vermont, he had sensed an inner strength she'd been given by her parents to survive in an environment where they were an anomaly. Despite this, she had grown up secure, and it was apparent Russell Jenkins was also quite secure. He had always admired Russell's basketball skills and the younger man's choice in a wife. In a time when young African-American athletes were signing million-dollar contracts, too often they shared their money and their lives with women who were not of their racial group. Russell had grown up dating girls who looked nothing like his mother or his sister, yet when graduating college he married a woman who did resemble them.

Russell's startled gaze shifted from his sister, then back to Adam. "I—I thought the two of you . . ."

"It's all right, Russ." Zahara's voice held a hidden warning that he picked up on immediately.

"Can't I at least drop you off somewhere, Adam?"

"No, thanks."

Zahara caught Adam's hand. "Don't be stubborn. We'll drop you off at home and that will be that." There was a finality in the statement that dared him to challenge her.

Adam winked at Russell. "Was she always this bossy?"

Russell nodded. "She had me browbeat until I realized I was taller than she was and therefore a lot stronger."

She snorted delicately. "You two can stand here and chew the fat all you want. I'm freezing."

The driver held the door open for her as she climbed into the automobile's warm, dark interior. Adam climbed in, followed by Russell who had elected to sit facing the couple.

"Where to, Mr. Jenkins?"

"We'll be making a stop before we get to Mount Vernon. We will drop Mr. Vaughn off first."

Adam gave the driver his address. He considered himself lucky to have spent two consecutive days with Zahara. He recalled the feeling of pride that had swept over him when he spied her strolling down Seventh Avenue, head held high, in a pair of jeans that outlined every lithe curve of her body. He hadn't missed the admiring glances several men gave her as she passed them. Her walk was loose with just enough sway in her hips to be deemed sexy.

Once they entered Madison Square Garden, all of her inhibitions were stripped away. She whistled loudly between her fingers, applauded, booed, and shouted with the best of them. The score between the two teams seesawed back and forth every quarter, and there were times when Zahara held his hand so tightly he was certain her fingernails had left little half-moons on his wrist. And when the final basket was good and the partial Garden crowd erupted in their usual victory shouting and dancing, she was in his arms, kissing him passionately. He hadn't kissed her back, but she had permitted him to see another side of the very proper bank executive.

Stretching out his long legs, Russell let out a long, ragged sigh. "I'm glad that game is in the record books."

"With your thirty-two points you played a helluva game," Adam remarked.

Russell whistled, shaking his head. "Man, it was awesome. There was a point when the tension was so high I thought we were going to mix it up right there on the court."

Zahara leaned against the velour softness of the seat, closed her eyes, and listened to the lively conversation between her brother and Adam as they delved into the science of professional basketball. If Russell had not decided to make basketball his career she knew she would not have permitted herself to become involved in the sport.

The focus of their conversation shifted to Adam, and she became suddenly alert. He told Russell he worked for Mazao Health Foods, extolling the nutritional value of their products.

Russell's expression became very animated. "It's wonderful to see the entrepreneurial spirit in full effect. I don't know whether my sister told you, but I invested in a sports camp in the Port Saint Lucie area with three other guys who are also professional athletes. One is a teammate of mine and the other two play for the Florida Marlins and Miami Dolphins.

"We offer instructional training for baseball, basketball, and football. We get a lot of rich kids whose parents want them out of their hair for a few weeks out of the year, but we also get a lot of kids from the urban areas during the summer months. We try to teach discipline and teamwork in conjunction with a healthy lifestyle."

The topic of their conversation changed back to basketball as they argued good-naturedly about teams and players. Adam glanced over at Zahara, his expression softening as she looped her arm through his and rested her head on his shoulder. He covered her hand with his, enjoying the delicate softness of her slender fingers.

After a while a cloaking, comfortable silence filled the automobile as it moved smoothly through the streets of Manhattan on its way northward.

Zahara checked the dining room table for the final time, making certain she hadn't missed anything. It was the last Sunday in May and her turn to host the monthly bidwhist gathering. She visually accounted for everything: plates, napkins, silver, stemware. It was all there.

The doorbell rang and she made her way to the front door for the delivery of foodstuffs she had ordered the week before. She usually prepared her own menu for the quartet of women, but decided at the last moment to have the food catered. Opening the door, she smiled at the youthful-looking deliveryman holding a large covered aluminum tray.

"I have a delivery for Miss Jenkins."

"I'm Ms. Jenkins. Come this way, please."

At exactly one-twenty, three-quarters of the bidwhist quartet filed out of the taxi and stood at the entrance to the stately English Tudor house. Zahara opened the door to the frantic chiming of the doorbell, smiling at her three best friends.

Marlena Robinson ignored the air kisses the other women gave Zahara as she stood, both hands on her hips, one foot tapping impatiently. "I want to hear all about *himmmm*."

"Yes!" Taylor and Eden chanted in unison.

"Ev-er-ree-thang," Marlena continued, enunciating every syllable.

Zahara managed to give Marlena a look which mirrored apparent bewilderment. "Who are you talking about?"

Marlena held up a hand. "Oh, no, Sister Girlfriend. I know you're not goin' there. There's no way you're goin' to get out of telling us what's happening between you and one very luscious-looking brother named Adam Vaughn."

"I want to hear *all* about it," Eden Hampton drawled, making her way past Zahara.

Tall, reed-thin Taylor Kelly snapped her fingers over her head. "Me, too."

Marlena kissed Zahara's cheek. "You know our rules. We keep no secrets from one another."

"I have no secrets."

Marlena flashed a Cheshire-cat grin. "If that's the case, then I want to know every juicy detail."

Zahara closed the door, rolling her eyes. There weren't too many details to disclose. She'd been seeing Adam for six weeks, and six weeks was long enough to realize that she'd fallen in love with him.

She followed her friends into the dining room and saw them standing at the buffet table, their mouths gaping. "What's the matter?"

"Where's the fried chicken and potato salad?" Eden questioned. There was no mistaking the disappointment in her voice.

"And the greens and cornbread?" Taylor echoed.

Resting her hands on her hips over an oversized T-shirt

falling halfway down her firm thighs, Zahara shook her head. "I didn't feel like cooking and decided to have the lunch catered."

Marlena crossed her arms under her breasts. "We spent the entire time on the train talking about eating your soul food."

"I—I don't believe you," Zahara sputtered. "If you want soul food, then go to Sylvia's."

"You can say that, Miss Uptown Girl, because you work how many blocks from Sylvia's?" Eden snapped.

"Miss Robinson and Miss Hampton, there's nothing stopping you from leaving Brooklyn to come uptown to eat at Sylvia's," Zahara argued quietly. And you, Miss Kelly, aka Miss Greenwich Village, the same goes for you. Y'all live right in the City while . . ."

"All right!" the three women screamed in unison.

"You've made your point," Marlena mumbled. She peered closely at a bowl filled with a cracked wheat and parsley salad, then up at Zahara. "Tabouleh?" Zahara nodded. "Stuffed grape leaves?" She nodded again. "Sliced lamb with garlic, Greek salad, and pastitsio . . ."

"A pre-celebratory dinner for your upcoming trip to the Greek Isles."

Marlena clapped a hand over her mouth in embarrassment. She and her travel agent boyfriend were scheduled to fly to Greece in another two weeks for a fourteen-day Mediterranean cruise. She dropped her hands, extending her arms, and she wasn't disappointed when Zahara hugged her.

"Thank you, girlfriend."

Zahara patted the shorter woman's back. "You're welcome, girlfriend."

Eden Hampton's slanting eyes narrowed slightly. "Madam Hostess. What's for dessert?"

"I broke down and made a sour cream pound cake," Zahara admitted.

Taylor, Eden, and Marlena turned their gazes upward, mumbling their own personal thank yous. Zahara laughed, shaking her head. Her friends were unique as a group and as individuals.

Thirty-year-old Taylor Kelly used her stunning looks to her advantage whenever she modeled part-time to supplement the erratic payments she earned as a free-lance writer for children's books and magazines. Tall, with waist-length naturally curling black hair and brilliant hazel eyes in a gold-brown face, Taylor tried marriage twice before she realized she'd achieved more success and satisfaction as a writer than a wife.

Eden Hampton claimed her own brand of exotic beauty. Zahara met Eden at Columbia University when they'd enrolled in different graduate programs. Eden earned her Master's in Public Health Administration at the same time Zahara earned a Master's in Business Administration. She was medium height and claimed flawless, satin-black skin. Her slanting catlike eyes, short straight nose and thin lips made one wonder what bloodlines she claimed, other than her obvious African heritage. She was the oldest in the group, thirty-six, and happily married to an orthopedic surgeon.

Zahara met Marlena Robinson when she came to work for Ansonia National. Marlena took her to lunch to welcome her to the corporate office, and the two women bonded instantly. Marlena married her college boyfriend, but annulled the marriage six months before they would have celebrated their first anniversary. She never divulged the reason, and respecting her privacy, Zahara never asked. Marlena dated a lot of men, yet if they appeared to get too serious she ended the relationship. The only exception seemed to be the travel agent.

Taylor affected her patent model pout. "What are we drinking? Ouzo?"

Zahara pointed to a large punch bowl on the large, oval dining room table. "I decided to serve something different." It was the same drink Adam had served her the first time she'd gone to his apartment. She duplicated his recipe, but substituted a pale, bubbly champagne for the white rum.

The Tuesday following her basketball game date with Adam, she arrived home to discover a large carton sitting on her front steps. There was no mailing label affixed to the box, and after she opened the carton to find a generous sampling of Mazao products, she realized Adam had made the delivery.

Single-size portions of soups, fruit drinks, shakes, and rice mixes, along with a specially sealed box of frozen entrees provided her with an ample supply of quick, simple, and nutritious meals within minutes.

"Tell us what's going on with you and your new man," Eden said after she'd filled her plate and sat down at the lace-covered dining room table.

"Yeah. What's up with you and your *man*," Taylor crooned in a low, sultry voice. "And what does the brother do for a living?"

Zahara sat down, trying to hide a smile. "He's not my man."

"And why not?" Marlena asked, also sitting with the others.

She shrugged a shoulder. "I just wouldn't call him my man—not yet anyway."

"O-kay. But what does he do for a living? Or better yet, does he have a job?" Eden asked, repeating Taylor's query. "Maybe Miss Zee is hiding her man because he has something to hide, if you know what I mean, Sister Girlfriends."

"I think not, Miss Wannabe Covert Operative," Zahara countered, glaring at Eden. "He works for a health food company, and is responsible for distribution." It was only a half-lie. Adam stated his cousin was responsible for manufacturing while he handled distribution. And she had to stick to the version she had given at the dinner party, because Marlena had been in attendance and overheard her less-than-honest account.

"So he does have a *job*," Eden said facetiously. "But what has to happen before he can be your man?" she insisted.

Raising a flute filled with champagne punch to her lips, Zahara took a generous swallow. Eden's eyes narrowed in concentration. "Oh. I know what it is. He's . . . what's his name?"

"Adam," Marlena supplied quickly.

"Thank you, Marlena," Eden continued, her head bobbing up and down slowly. "I think Miss Thang here doesn't think of Adam as *her man* because they have yet to do you-know-what together.''

Taylor arched her professionally waxed eyebrows. ''Are you talking about them sleeping together?''

Marlena gave Taylor a stunned look. ''I think you're hanging out with too many kids and not enough adults. Of course we're talking about them sleeping together!''

''There's no need for you to get hos-tile.''

Marlena ignored Taylor as she turned her attention back to Zahara. ''What gives, girlfriend? Why are you holding out?''

''It has nothing to do with holding out. I've only known him for six weeks.''

''Six weeks,'' Taylor repeated, after she'd popped a stuffed grape leaf in her mouth. ''I married both my husbands after dating them a month.''

Eden wagged her head. ''And that's why you've been divorced twice.''

''I got rid of them because they didn't come correct,'' Taylor argued.

''Hold on a minute,'' Marlena shouted. ''All of us have been married at one time or another. All of us except Zahara. We're not here to talk about brothers coming correct. We just want to know about Adam,'' she added with a wide grin.

''There's not much to tell,'' Zahara stated. ''We see each other at least once a week . . .''

''And . . . ?'' the three women said when she didn't finish her statement.

She waved a hand. ''We go out to dinner, take in a movie, visit jazz clubs, and go to basketball and baseball games. That's it.''

Marlena waved her hand back and forth over her head. ''Don't believe her. They've got to be doing more than just going out together. Ladies, you've got to see the brother.'' Pushing back her chair, she stood up. ''He's pow, pow, and pow-pow.'' She gestured over her shoulders, chest and hips. ''He stands about six-four, maybe six-five, and tips the scale somewhere between two and a quarter and two-fifty. He has all of his hair. It's cut close to his scalp with a little gray at the temples.''

''Sexy,'' Eden crooned.

''Very sexy,'' Marlena confirmed. ''It's the eyes and mouth that leave you gasping for breath.''

''What about his mouth and eyes, Sister Girlfriend?'' Taylor urged.

''Oooo-wee! Swee-eet.''

Zahara covered her mouth with a napkin as she doubled over in laughter.

''Oh, Sister Girlfriend,'' Marlena stated, pointing at Zahara, ''you laugh because you know it's the truth.''

''What color are his eyes, Marlena?'' Eden queried.

''Hazel.''

''They're dark gray.'' Zahara stopped laughing long enough to correct Marlena.

''I stand corrected,'' Marlena conceded. ''But let me continue. He wears a mustache . . .''

''Stop! You know I have a serious weakness for mustaches,'' Taylor crooned, flashing her brilliant eyes.

''Wait, wait. Let me finish.'' Marlena tossed a profusion of braided extensions over her shoulder. ''You've got to check out the walk. I couldn't decide whether it was a Denzel Washington swagger or a Laurence Fishburne slow drag. He looked *real* good—coming and going, if you know what I mean.''

''Damn, Zahara!'' Eden exclaimed. ''Are you certain you have blood in your veins? Why haven't you sampled the brother?''

Placing a manicured hand over her T-shirt-covered chest, Zahara closed her eyes. ''I don't want to complicate what we have.'' She opened her eyes, staring at the women staring back at her. ''It's the first time I don't feel pressured in taking a relationship to a level of intimacy. What I have with Adam is simple and very comfortable. He's the first man I've dated whom I can truly admit is a friend.''

A pregnant silence enveloped the large formal room, swallowing up everyone, and Zahara wanted to scream that she loved Adam. She loved everything about him: his gentleness, patience, masculine sensuality, and most importantly his not wanting or expecting more from her than she was willing to offer him. His kisses and caresses ignited and stoked a fire she thought long dead, and there were times when she wanted to strip off her clothes and bare her body for his total possession. But she hadn't—not yet. What she wanted was a sign from Adam that he wanted her as much as she had come to want him.

However, she was honest enough with herself to admit her reluctance to sleep with Adam was due to her own hangup about his job, because he did not have the professional pedigree of the men from her past. What he had was a *job*, but not a *career*.

"Then I must admit that what you have with Adam is very special," Marlena remarked wistfully, sitting down and breaking the comfortable silence. "You have a lot to offer him if he's smart enough to recognize it. You're attractive, bright, healthy, and educated. You're the assistant vice president for what is now considered an elite bank, earn a damn good salary, own a home filled with priceless family heirlooms, and last, but not least, is that fact that you're the sister of one of the most talented, brilliant, and wealthiest athletes in the world today."

Taylor raised her champagne. "Here's to Russell Jenkins and his Sister Girlfriend wife and babies."

Zahara blinked back a flood of tears, raising her own flute. "And I toast my Sister Girlfriends who truly have become my sisters in blood as well as in spirit."

She always enjoyed getting together with her girlfriends, but this time she felt a thread of sadness. And the sadness had come from the barriers she had erected. Adam was perfect, in every way, except he lacked the professional credentials she required in the men she dated.

Marlena stood up again. "Let's not get maudlin. Where's the music? Put on the Sistah anthem." She spun around and dipped a hip. "Shoop, shoop . . ."

Zahara rose to place a stack of CDs on the carousel. She was partial to music from movie sound tracks, and it had become a ritual whenever she hosted the bidwhist luncheon to play the music from *Waiting to Exhale*, *Boomerang*, and *Set It Off*.

Zahara found her mind wandering as the weeklong seminar wound down to a close. She'd spent the week living out of a suitcase in a midtown Manhattan hotel. She missed taking her nightly bath in her own bathtub, sleeping in her own bed, and most of all, she missed Adam. She had called him from her hotel room the first night she checked in, but hadn't spoken to him since. They had agreed he would pick her up on Friday and they would have dinner together before he drove her home to Mount Vernon.

Surreptitiously retrieving her cellular phone from her handbag, she palmed it and walked out of the carpeted meeting room to the hall. She dialed the number to Mazao and asked for Adam once the pleasant, well-modulated voice of the receptionist answered.

"I'm sorry, but Mr. Vaughn just stepped out for a moment. May I take a message?"

She thought about calling back, but changed her mind. "Kindly let Mr. Vaughn know that Miss Jenkins will be out of her meeting at four."

"Do you want to leave a number where he can reach you?"

She left her cell-phone number, then hung up. Not wanting to return to the meeting, she made her way to the lounge. Standing in front of a floor-to-ceiling mirror, she stared at her reflection. Her next scheduled full day of beauty had come at the right time. After five days of living in air-conditioned rooms and breathing recycled air, she was more than ready for a hydrating facial and a massage. And after five days of six-hour sessions dealing with the restructuring of the newly merged Ansonia Central Trust Company, she was ready for a mini-vacation.

She had just run a large-tooth comb through her hair when the telephone in her handbag chimed softly. She answered on the second ring. "Zahara."

"How are you?" came the deep voice she'd come to love along with everything else about Adam Vaughn.

"I'm ready for a vacation."

He chuckled softly. "Where are you?"

"I'm still at the hotel."

"Are you ready to leave?"

"I am, even if the others aren't."

"Do you have another seminar?"

"No. There's supposed to be a farewell cocktail party around six for our upstate people. I'm bailing out now."

There was pause. "Give me at least an hour."

She managed a tired smile. "I'll be waiting in the lobby."

"I'll see you in a little while, baby."

Zahara listened to the dial tone as she repeated his endearment. *Baby*. He had never called her by anything but her name. She would've resented any other man calling her "baby," but somehow its coming from Adam made it okay.

Her step was lighter as she returned to the meeting room to listen to the concluding remarks from the various presenters sitting at the head table.

Adam walked into the hotel lobby and spied Zahara immediately even though she couldn't see him from where she sat waiting; her luggage rested on the carpeted floor beside the overstuffed chair. She was dressed for success in a subtly tweeded black-and-white linen jacket, slim black linen skirt, and a white V-neck silk blouse. Her high-heel black-and-white leather spectator pumps rounded off her winning look. He'd registered the fatigue and resignation in her voice when she told him she was going to pass on the cocktail party. A rush of protectiveness swept over him, and at that moment he wanted to hold her and let her know everything would be all right; she was safe, and she was loved.

He crossed the lobby and she turned her head, as if sensing his presence. A slow smile deepened the dimple in his cheek at the same time her expression of weariness faded. In a motion too quick to discern, he pulled her to her feet, clasping her body tightly to his.

Zahara felt Adam's warm, moist breath against her face, and her heart skidded with excitement. She was conscious of his thighs pressing against hers, his chest molded to her breasts, and the touch of his fingers at the nape of her neck sending heated shivers through her. Her gaze fused with his, screaming mutely, *I love you.*

"I've missed you," she said instead.

"And I you," Adam whispered. His head dipped and he took possession of her mouth like a man dying of thirst. He was used to seeing her on an average of once a week, but not talking to her every day had tested the limits of his patience.

Zahara's lips quivered in unspoken desire as he drank deeply, temporarily assuaging an aching need to possess not just a small portion, but all of her.

Pulling back slightly, he surveyed her face, seeing fatigue and tension. "How was your week?"

She gave him a tired smile. "Intense."

"What do you have planned for the weekend?"

"I have an appointment at Rosie's Curl and Weave tomorrow morning."

He arched an eyebrow. "That's it?"

Zahara nodded. "That's it. Why?"

"After a rather *intense* week I've decided to offer you a gift of a weekend at a private B&B. You'll be served breakfast in bed, lunch in a patio garden, and exotic dinners by candlelight. All with first-class service."

Her expression brightened in anticipation. "Where?"

"You'll see." His lids lowered, concealing the amusement shimmering in their dark-gray depths.

"Why are you always so mysterious?"

"Don't you like surprises?"

Her expressive face changed, becoming somber, and there was no way she could conceal her fatigue and disappointment. She had given a twenty-minute presentation on her views for the future of her neighborhood branch, and another four hours defending her proposal. What Adam did not know was that she was not in a teasing mood.

"Not really."

Adam hesitated, measuring her reaction. It had been more than six weeks since he saw Zahara Jenkins for the first time, and at that time she unknowingly had turned his world upside down. He'd learned to trust a woman again, but more than that, he'd learned to love again. Their relationship was comfortable and undemanding. He knew she enjoyed his company as much as he enjoyed hers. They saw each other on Fridays, even though he wanted more than just one day a week. He wanted more because he wanted all of her—every day.

Leaning over, he whispered against her ear, "I'm taking you home with me." Pulling back, he stared down at her, his eyes smoldering with banked passion. "And I don't intend to let you out of my sight for the next two days."

She stood completely still, returning his stare. "No, Adam. I can't. Not tonight."

His eyes widened until she could see their clear depths. "Why not?"

"I'm exhausted from my presentation and—"

"Don't you think I realize that?" he interrupted. "I called your hotel room Tuesday, Wednesday, and Thursday nights, and each time the desk clerk told me you had your DO NOT DISTURB button activated. I'm more than aware that you spent a week cooped up in a room where the only focus was how to make more money, and I'm also aware of how exhausting it can be to try to get your point across to others who have their own agendas about how they want to see a company managed.

"I'm not asking you to come home with me so I can make love to you." His expression softened as he moved even closer. "I want you to come home with me so I can love you. Let go of your executive persona and let me take care of you—just this one time," he pleaded softly.

His plea that he wanted to love her was her undoing. All of the tension, anxiety, and disappointment of the past week erupted and she collapsed against his unyielding strength. He wanted to love her, she needed him to love her, and she didn't know when it had happened, but she suddenly realized she *needed* Adam Vaughn. She needed not only his protection, but all of him.

Tightening her grip under his massive shoulders, she raised

her chin and smiled through the moisture welling up in her eyes. "Take me home, Adam," she whispered tearfully. "I *need* to go home with you."

Zahara sat on the middle of Adam's king-size bed, her back braced against his chest. It had taken the taxi driver more than an hour in bumper-to-bumper traffic to go from midtown Manhattan to East Harlem. It was a Friday night in June and anyone who could afford it sought to escape the heat of the city for the weekend. En route the cabbie turned off the air-conditioning to counter overheating his taxi.

She had arrived at Adam's apartment, sans her shoes and jacket, and when she followed him into the comfortably air-cooled living room all she thought of was a bath. It had taken her less than a quarter of an hour to unpack her bags and hang up her clothes before she retreated to the spacious bathroom and stepped into the bathtub filled with a profusion of silken, scented bath gel. She then changed into a tank top and a pair of shorts before succumbing to his entreaty that he give her a massage.

Adam's strong fingers kneaded the tight muscles in her neck and upper back. Leaning forward, he pressed his mouth to a bare shoulder under the body-hugging tank top. The thick, silken brush of the hair on his upper lip elicited a noticeable shiver of awareness.

"Tell me about your proposal," he crooned against her ear. The moist, warm heat of his breath brought on another shiver.

Closing her eyes, Zahara lowered her chin to her chest. "It was so easy that it's almost too simplistic. I proposed they use the 125th Street branch as a training center for every new downstate employee. Ansonia Central Trust's new claim is they're the bank for the twenty-first century, yet they want to continue in their business-as-usual mode. I told them that my branch is perfect as a training center because of the racial, cultural, and ethnic mix of the neighborhood. Harlem is no longer ninety-nine percent African-American, but is home to and serves more than sixty nationalities. I have the demographics to prove my claim."

"Would you have the space to accommodate all of the new employees?"

"We would if we rotate. In other words, no 125th Street employee, or any other branch with similar demographics would be permanent. You come to us for training, then are transferred out. The world is changing rapidly, and this country, state, and city are changing just as rapidly. Someone who lives in an affluent community in Westchester or Nassau County and becomes an Ansonia employee may never interact with someone from Raipur, India, or Dakar, Senegal. But they will if they're trained at our branch. People of color are no longer the minority in terms of numbers, and those who aren't of color and refuse to acknowledge this fact must learn tolerance. And what better way to learn it if not to serve these people when they come into our branch?"

"Did they reject it outright?"

"No." She sucked in her breath, then let it out slowly as Adam's thumb moved up her spine. "We argued back and forth for four hours before it was tabled. It just made me so angry that they're not willing to set up a pilot program in another neighborhood even if they choose not to try it in Harlem."

Flickering flames from wicks floating in oil in three hand-blown lamps in vibrant colors of green, blue, and purple lit the bedroom alcove with soft, romantic light. The candles, the soft music flowing from a speaker hidden in a wall, and the calming fragrance of dried lavender in a crystal bowl on a table in the sitting area created a mood of total relaxation. A smile curved her lips. She was pleased Adam had insisted she come home with him.

"They'll come to their senses after they think about it."

"I hope you're right."

Adam stopped his ministrations and turned her around to face him, her thighs straddling his. "I know I'm right. How can they resist someone as beautiful and intelligent as you?"

Resting her forehead against his, she smiled demurely. "Easily."

He gathered her closer, his large hands pressing her hips

intimately to his groin. "Wrong. I can't resist you, baby. From the first time you opened your front door and I saw you dressed in that very wicked black dress, I knew I was caught in your spell. I totally ignored the fact that you'd looked down your nose at me in Rosie's . . ."

"I didn't look down my nose at you, Adam," she protested softly.

"Yes, you did. But that didn't matter, because I was willing to endure your snobbiness if it meant seeing you again."

She looped her arms around his neck and placed a tender kiss at the corner of his strong mouth. "I'm not a snob and you know it."

"I know nothing of the sort. All I know is that I love you, Zahara Jenkins."

She covered his mouth with her fingertips. "Adam . . ."

"Don't," he cut in, pulling her hand away. "You don't have to love me . . ."

"But I do. I do love you."

His gaze widened, and in the muted glow of the flickering candles, his eyes seemed silver in contrast to his golden sun-browned face. "When?" He didn't know why he'd asked the question, but he needed to know.

"The first night you brought me here," she whispered reverently. "The first time you kissed me."

Running his fingers sensuously along the nape of her neck, Adam closed his eyes and listened to the halting sound of Zahara's breathing. He had told her the truth. He hadn't invited her home with him to make love to her, but that was what he wanted to do at the moment. He wanted to be inside her.

Closing her eyes, Zahara slumped limply against Adam's chest as she tried swallowing back the whimpers threatening to erupt from her throat. Every nerve in her body trembled and screamed for release.

"Adam."

"Yes, darling?" His own respiration increased and his chest rose and fell heavily as he tried controlling the hardness swelling beneath her hips.

Heat and a trembling desire settled between her thighs, leaving a rush of moisture in its wake. "I want—I need you," she gasped as the pulsing increased with every breath she drew.

"How?" He wanted to make certain she wanted what he wanted. What he didn't want was to take advantage of her vulnerability. He didn't want her to confuse her needing him with physically wanting him.

"I want you to make love to me."

Her voice had dropped an octave, and Adam registered the passion shaking her body. Gently removing her arms from his neck, he reached down and pulled his T-shirt over his head, then placed her palms over his chest near his heart. The steady, strong pumping of his heart reached out and captured hers as they pounded in a rhythmic tempo, increasing until it became a frenzied velocity that matched their rising passions.

Everything seemed to happen in slow motion as Adam undressed himself before he undressed Zahara. Once naked, each gazed on the other's body in rapt wonder.

The beauty of Adam's well-toned physique was displayed in golden brilliance in the candlelight as Zahara's gaze moved sensually over the width of his smooth, muscled chest, and lower to the defined muscles in his flat belly, and still lower to his thick, powerful legs and thighs. She was certain Adam was aware of her reluctance to stare at the thick, swollen flesh throbbing between his thighs as she quickly reversed her gaze to linger on his face.

He lowered her to the bed, his arms cradling her gently as he settled his body between her outstretched legs. "I won't hurt you," he crooned over and over. His hands began a gentle exploration of soft flesh, his mouth following the same route, both leaving her body burning and trembling with a screaming lust that threatened to drown her whole. He worshiped her velvet body, flesh against flesh. He stopped long enough to take a plastic packet from the drawer of a bedside table and ease the latex contents over his swollen sex, then entered her pulsing wet body with an aching slowness that threatened to send both over the edge of fulfillment before they were ready. It became flesh to flesh, man to woman, lover to lover.

Zahara welcomed the heavy crush of Adam's body as he slowly, methodically loved her, his hardness setting a deliberate thrusting and withdrawing rhythmic pace. Everything about him was different from the other men she had known; different from his extended gentle foreplay, and to his need to arouse her where she could take her own pleasure before he embraced his own.

And her pleasure came—hurtling her beyond herself as she arched at the same time her breath caught in her throat, not permitting her to scream out the passion gripping her trembling limbs. But she did scream. She screamed out his name over and over until it became a soft, hiccupping sigh of sated ecstasy.

"I love you," Adam gasped as his own breathing slowed to normal. "I love you," he repeated over and over in a hoarse litany.

Gathering her closely, he reversed their positions, pulled a sheet over their moist bodies, and then they slept the sleep of sated lovers.

It was near midnight when Zahara awoke to darkness and the solid press of a hard male body molded along the length of hers. She shifted slightly, turning away from him, and Adam's arm tightened around her waist. The cadence of his respiration changed before resuming its former rhythm. She lay still, reliving the passion she had shared with the man holding her close to his heart.

Her sleeping with Adam had changed her, him, and their relationship. They were friends, but they were also lovers. She stretched a leg and felt an unaccustomed tightness in her upper thigh. It ached a little, but it was a good ache as she remembered the vigorous intensity of Adam Vaughn's lovemaking. Snuggling against his warmth, she closed her eyes and drifted back to sleep. She did not want to think of a future with Adam because that was not an option for her. She would share her love with him, and if it ended, she knew she would always have the memories.

Zahara lay facedown on the table, arms at her side as she gave herself over to the expert ministration of the masseur. Kiyoshi Tamiko increased the pressure to her inner thigh, causing her to catch her breath.

"Did I hurt you?"

"Only a little," she admitted.

"You're not as tight today as you usually are," he commented.

What she wanted to tell Kiyoshi was that Adam Vaughn was responsible for her lack of tension. She and Adam had made love a second time earlier that morning. They'd shared a shower before eating breakfast on the patio while watching the sun rise. They returned to bed and talked for hours, then made love again. The second shower ended with them splashing each other like little children before she reminded Adam that she had to leave for Rosie's.

She'd dressed casually in a pair of jeans, T-shirt, and sandals. Adam was equally casual in a pair of jeans, navy-blue golf shirt, and a pair of running shoes. He walked her to Rosie's, but didn't bother to go in with her. He promised he'd be back to pick her up at three that afternoon.

Zahara completed her session with the masseur, but had to wait for Kimm Gilmore to finish up with a customer before she lay on the chair for her hydrating facial.

If Kimm wasn't her usual chatty self, then Maria was. The manicurist kept up a steady stream of conversation as she pampered her hands and feet.

Peering closely at her client's hands, she gently pushed back the cuticles. "You have wonderful fingers, Zahara. They're long, slender, and your nails are beautifully shaped. Why is it you don't wear rings?"

Zahara shook her head. "I don't know. And it's not as if I don't own any. I inherited all of one grandmother's jewelry, but I can't wear her rings because they're too big and I've never considered having them resized."

"What size are you?"

"Six."

"What style are they?" Maria asked.

"Most of the pieces are art deco. A few are from the Victorian era. I must admit they're magnificent."

Maria glanced up, smiling. "Do they look like the jewelry the people wore in the movie *Titanic*?"

"One ring is. It was my great-grandmother's."

"Girl, what are you waiting for? If it was me I'd wear a ring on every finger."

Maria sighed audibly before the topic shifted fluidly from jewelry to movies. Zahara listened as the young woman recounted the plot of every movie she'd seen over the past month. Her ears were still ringing from Maria's incessant chatter when she sat in Deirdre Lee's chair.

The stylist gave her a warm smile as she snapped the cape around her neck. "How's Adam?" she whispered near her ear.

Zahara smiled at their reflection in the mirror. "Wonderful," she mouthed softly so as not to be overheard by the other operators and their clients.

After her first date with Adam, most of the gossip at Rosie's about their liaison had died down considerably, and she didn't want to do or say anything to reactivate it.

Dee Dee winked at her. "Good for the two of you."

"He's picking me up at three."

"I'll have you out in plenty of time."

The next two hours passed quickly for Zahara as she took time out to drink a cup of herbal tea before Dee Dee bumped the ends of her hair, and at exactly three o'clock she stepped out onto 125th Street to find Adam standing at the corner waiting for her.

His admiring gaze took in her flawless skin and softly curled hair. "You look beautiful. And to show you how selfless I am, I'm going to take you out and show you off."

She looped her arm through his as they wound their way down the crowded avenue filled with afternoon shoppers. "Where are we going?"

"Tavern on the Green."

She stopped, pulling at his arm. "How did you get reservations for Tavern on the Green when there's always a two- to three-week wait?"

"I made reservations a month ago."

"A month ago? What if I'd stopped seeing you a month ago?"

"You didn't, did you? Let's go home and get dressed. Our reservations are for six-thirty."

Zahara fell in step with Adam as he pulled her gently along with him. "What's your rush? We have three-and-a-half hours."

He smiled down at her. "I'd like to give us plenty of time in case we become distracted by other *things*."

"What other *things* are you talking about, Adam Vaughn?"

He released her hand and curved his arm around her waist. "You're a very intelligent woman, Miss Jenkins. I believe you know what I'm talking about."

"I don't think so, Mr. Vaughn. Perhaps you can give me a hint."

"I'll have to show you," he teased.

Both were laughing as their gazes met. They registered the laughter and also the love they were unable to disguise or conceal from each other.

The summer had passed quickly for Zahara, too quickly. Her love for Adam deepened and she couldn't remember not loving him. And they never seemed to get enough of each other. She had taken to sleeping at his Harlem apartment during the week, while he shared her Mount Vernon home on the weekends.

He made her laugh when she didn't feel like laughing, and both had taken a week's vacation from their jobs to spend it together in a chalet in the Maine woods.

She was never bored with Adam, and she was always amazed by the amount of knowledge he'd gleaned from reading two or three daily newspapers or from watching an all-news television station. She shared his interest in sports, health foods, and jazz, yet she still hadn't introduced him to her bidwhist girlfriends, even though the three other women hounded her incessantly about intimate details of their relationship.

He woke her one Sunday morning in early September and entered her body before the last vestiges of sleep fled completely. Her pulsing flesh closed around his hardness, igniting a rush of passion that sucked them in where they became one. What had surprised Zahara was the absence of foreplay as Adam rode out his passions until the storm building within him broke, and left her gasping from the unrestrained primitive joining.

Holding her tight enough to stop her drawing a normal breath, Adam stared down at her moist face with an expression that made her think of him as a stranger. "Marry me, Zahara."

Her large eyes widened in shock at the same time a cold chill rendered her speechless. *No!* her head screamed. She hadn't wanted it to come to this. Not now. It was too soon. She had just fallen in love with him, gotten used to the fact that she was involved with a deliveryman, and he wanted to complicate everything by proposing marriage.

Pulling away, Adam lay down beside Zahara, throwing a muscular arm over his forehead. Closing his eyes, he listened to the sound of her irregular breathing. He hadn't meant to blurt out his proposal, but he could hold it in no longer. He wanted a wife; he wanted children; he wanted Zahara in his life—permanently.

Zahara stared at her lover, her heart turning over in sorrow. She wanted to tell him she couldn't marry him. There were too many dissimilarities. She had greater earning power, was better educated, and she was afraid these differences would eventually become points of contention between them. Would he come to resent her earning more money than he? Would the resentment result in an eroding of his self-esteem and his overeating again? Could she afford to take that chance? *No, you can't*, the voice of wisdom whispered to her.

Pushing herself up on an elbow, she stared at him. She

found Adam to be more attractive than when she had first met him. His hair was grayer and it was the first time she had noticed a few strands of gray in his mustache. The summer sun had darkened his skin, which made his luminous eyes appear lighter than usual.

Running her fingertips along his shoulder, she smiled. "Can you give me time to consider your precious offer?"

His eyes opened and he stared at her. There was no mistaking the pain of rejection in their depths. The seconds ticked off to a full minute. A slight smile curved his mouth. "Yes, Zahara. I'll give you time." He sat up, supporting his back against several pillows covered in pale blue organdy with an antique yellow lace trim. "I'll make it easy for you. So as not to complicate or compromise your feelings, I'll stay away from you until you reach a decision—one way or the other."

Not giving her an opportunity to discuss it further, he rolled over and left the bed, leaving her staring at his magnificent naked body.

She lay in bed while he showered, fighting back tears. She was still in bed when he returned to the bedroom, fully dressed. He walked over to the bed in what she had come to recognize as a fluid catlike gait, leaned over and pressed his mouth to hers.

"I love you," he whispered, then turned and walked out of the room as quietly as he had entered.

Zahara listened intently to the sound of his car as he started up the engine. She lay in the same position long after the sound of the departing automobile faded, and it was then that her tears fell and she cried until her eyes were swollen. She called the branch manager on Monday, telling him she didn't feel well and that she was taking a couple of days off. And when she returned to work on Wednesday she was back in control. She had picked up the pieces of her life and continued what she'd been doing before Adam Vaughn changed what she had become.

Zahara walked into the restaurant she had frequented many times during the five years she'd spent at the bank's corporate office, unbuttoning the jacket to her wool suit. She spied Marlena immediately. Sliding into the leather booth, she smiled at Marlena sitting opposite her.

"What's up?" Marlena asked without any preliminaries.

She ignored her friend's inquiry as she signaled the waiter. "I'll have a dry white wine please." He nodded, walking away.

"What's up, Zahara?" she repeated. "You call me, frantic, saying you want to meet when we'd just met the day before."

Closing her eyes, she pressed her back against the leather seat. "I didn't want to say anything in front of Eden and Taylor."

Marlena placed her hands over Zahara's. "Does this have anything to do with Adam?"

She nodded, opening her eyes. Then she told her best friend about her relationship with Adam, leaving nothing out. She watched Marlena's expression change from shock to anger.

"I don't believe you, *Miss Thang*! You don't want to commit to the man because he's blue collar?" Averting her gaze, she didn't see Zahara nod. "You truly piss me off, Zahara." Her head snapped around and she glared at her across the table. "I didn't think you'd be so superficial."

"Me! Superficial?"

"Yes, you, Zahara. What's wrong with you? You meet a man any woman would scratch another woman's eyes out for, and you're balking because he doesn't have a college education or wear designer suits to his office. Girlfriend, you really disappoint me. My mother married my daddy even though she had a master's in social work, while he slung garbage cans for a living. He protected his wife and his family. Whenever we needed him, he was there for us. That's all a woman can ask for from a husband and the father of her children, because when they put you six feet under, all of the titles and degrees don't mean a damn thing."

"I know you're right, girlfriend. I just needed to hear it from someone else."

"How long ago did he ask you to marry him?"

Zahara took a sip of the wine the waiter had placed on the table. "September third."

"You mean to tell me you've waited a month and you still haven't gotten back to him?" Biting down on her lower lip, Zahara nodded. "Oh damn, girlfriend," Marlena groaned. "We're going to have something to eat because you look as if you're going to blow away in strong wind, then we'll talk some more."

Adam paced the length of the patio, ignoring the chill of the autumn night air settling on his bare arms. It had been a month since he'd proposed marriage to Zahara and each day found him waiting—waiting for her to give him an answer. He knew he could take her rejection because it was better than no answer at all.

He didn't want to go back into the apartment because he didn't want to be reminded of the things he had shared with Zahara when they'd worked side by side in the kitchen, or shared a shower, or the times when she lay beside him on the large bed in the alcove. There were times when he imagined smelling her haunting vanilla-musk perfume, or heard the sound of her beautifully modulated voice.

She haunted his days and his nights; she had crawled under his skin and captured his heart . . .

The chiming of the doorbell interrupted his turbulent thoughts. Walking through the apartment, he made his way to the vestibule. He peered through the glass in the door and spied a man holding a bouquet of flowers.

"I have a delivery for Adam Vaughn."

Adam opened the door, reaching into the pocket of his slacks at the same time. "Thanks," he murmured, handing the man a bill.

"Thank you, sir."

After closing the door, he retraced his steps, wondering who had sent him flowers. He had another month before he celebrated his thirty-ninth birthday.

He took the bouquet into the kitchen and plucked the envelope off the cellophone wrapping. Withdrawing the enclosed card, he read it once, twice, and then a third time before whispering a prayer of thanks.

Sinking down slowly on a chair, he read the card aloud: "My precious Adam—I'm not certain what you've planned for the rest of your life, but I hope you will include me in your future. Love always, Zahara."

He exhaled a long sigh of relief. She had accepted him; she would become his wife and the mother of his children. Walking over to a wall phone, he picked up the receiver.

"Deirdre, this is Adam," he announced after the break in the connection. "I need you to find out something for me."

The moment Zahara walked into Rosie's Curl and Weave for her Thursday night hair appointment, she berated herself for being a fool. She'd sent Adam a bouquet of calla lilies and peonies with an accompanying card accepting his marriage proposal. The next day would be a week and she still hadn't heard from him. She had listened to Marlena and sent him the flowers when what she had wanted to do was call him with her answer.

She hung up her all-weather coat and suit jacket, then made her way past the reception desk to Dee Dee's station. She sat down and smiled at the stylist as she draped the cape over her shoulders.

"How's the banking business?"

Zahara smiled at Dee Dee in the mirror's reflection. "Wonderful. They just approved a proposal of mine."

Dee Dee raised her hand and the two women affected a high-five fingertip handshake. "You go, girl." Lifting the heavy strands of Zahara's hair, the stylist stared at Zahara in the reflection of the mirror. "It's time for another cut."

"Just trim it. I need more hair on my neck now that it's getting cold."

"A trim it is," Dee Dee conceded. "Tamika will shampoo you."

Zahara walked over to the sink where Tamika stood waiting for her. She sat down, sliding until her neck was fitted comfortably along the sink. Closing her eyes, she gave herself over to the strong fingers of the girl massaging her scalp with a thick, oil-based fragrant shampoo.

After the shampoo and an instant conditioner, she found herself back at her operator's station. She was grateful Dee Dee hadn't asked her about Adam, because she didn't want to lie to the young woman.

Dee Dee appeared preoccupied as she trimmed the ends of Zahara's hair before blowing it dry, utilizing a large round brush. She curled the ends with her bumper curler, then combed it into a becoming style that flattered her client's face. "How about a little oil sheen?" she questioned, smoothing several strands in place.

"Just a little."

Dee Dee picked up a can of oil sheen and shook it. "This one is empty. I'll be right back."

The operator walked out of her line of vision in the mirror, and the image was replaced with that of the man who had stolen her heart. Zahara never noticed the fading human chatter as she stared mutely at Adam staring back at her.

He wore the same jumpsuit he'd worn the first time she met him, but this time he didn't have on work gloves or a hat. Placing a hand on the back of her chair, he turned her slowly to face him. Her eyelids fluttered wildly as she tried focusing on his face and the name stitched into the patch over the navy-blue garment.

She missed the mysterious smile curving his sexy mouth as she silently mouthed the words, Mazao Health Foods, Inc. Adam Vaughn, Pres. He wasn't a deliveryman, but the president of the company!

"I have a special delivery for a Miss Zahara Jenkins." Extending a hand he'd held behind his back, he handed her a small bouquet of pure white calla lilies. "I couldn't find peonies, so I suppose the lilies will have to do," he crooned softly.

Zahara took the bouquet, noticing the crowd of people moving closer to her and Adam. "Thank you. They're beautiful."

"So are you," Adam countered, reaching into the breast

pocket of the jumpsuit. "I'd like for you to have this, too."
He gave her a small box wrapped in gold foil with a black
velvet ribbon.

"Open it!" shouted Maria. The manicurist had come from
the back to watch the scenario between Adam and Zahara.

She hoped no one noticed her fingers trembling as she un-
did the bow and peeled the paper off the box. However, she
was certain everyone could hear the runaway pounding of her
heart when she lifted the top on a black velvet box to reveal
the brilliance of an emerald-cut diamond framed by sparkling
baguettes on a circle of yellow gold. A chorus of gasps reverberated throughout the large shop.

Adam's face swam dizzily before Zahara's eyes as she
handed him the box. Going down on one knee, he removed
the ring and slipped it on the third finger of her left hand.

Attractive lines fanned out around his eyes when he smiled
at her tearstained face. "Will you marry me, Zahara Jenkins?" The floodgates broke and she buried her face against
his strong neck and wept uncontrollably.

"Girl, you'd better tell that man yes so we can break out
the champagne," Maria shouted over the applause that had
erupted.

"It better be champagne, Maria, and not that bogus wine
cooler you tried passing off as the good stuff," an operator
shouted.

She rolled her eyes at the operator. "Excuse me, Missy.
I'll have you know Adam bought the champagne."

"Well?" Adam drawled.

"Yes, yes, yes," Zahara said seconds before she sealed her
promise with a passionate kiss.

Adam pulled her limp body from the chair and swung her
around as if she were a child. Zahara's freshly coiffed hair
fell forward as she tightened her grip on his neck.

"You planned all of this," she whispered in his ear after
he'd carried her toward the empty reception area.

"Not without help." He lowered her to the blue-and-pink
floor at the same time a cork popped loudly. "Maria got your
ring size, and Cousin Deirdre helped out when she told me

what time you'd be in to get your hair done."

Taking the handkerchief he offered her, she blotted her cheeks. "So, Dee Dee's your cousin. What else are you hiding from me?"

"Not much else."

Her gaze narrowed as she pointed a finger at the patch on his jumpsuit. "What did you do before you set up Mazao Health Foods?"

"I taught school," he admitted, wincing slightly.

"What subject?"

"Physics."

"High school?"

He shook his head. "College."

She placed her trembling fingers over her mouth and shook her head. "Oh, Adam. I thought . . ."

"You thought I was an uneducated, thirty-eight-year-old deliveryman, didn't you?" Her fingers curled into a fist against her mouth; she nodded. "I saw the way you looked at me the first time I came in here. I don't know if you're aware of it, but your eyes give you away. It was then that I decided to teach you a lesson. I made Deirdre swear not to tell you anything about me, because I wanted you to want me for who I am, and not for what I do."

"If you're president of your own company, then why were you delivering merchandise?"

"One of my drivers broke his ankle, and it was going to be six weeks before he could return to work. Instead of hiring a temp driver who probably would never make the deliveries on schedule, I filled in for him. Just because I'd earned a doctorate in physics, that still doesn't make me any better than the guy who pushes a handcart."

Moving closer, she ran her hands up his chest. "Will you forgive me for being superficial?"

"Only if you spend the rest of your life with me."

Smiling, she rose on tiptoe and pressed her mouth to his. "You've got yourself a deal."

Adam returned her kiss. "How about a glass of champagne before we leave?"

"I'd love one. We can't let them have all of the fun."

The overhead light caught the brilliance of the perfection of the diamond on her finger as she walked beside Adam to share her joy with everyone. She never knew the first time she'd walked into Rosie's Curl and Weave that one day she would fix her hair, mend her heart, and find her true love.

# About the Authors

## Felicia Mason

Felicia Mason is a motivational speaker and an award-winning journalist and author. Her novels include *Rhapsody, Seduction, For the Love of You* and *Body and Soul*. In 1997, *For the Love of You* was named one of *Glamour* magazine readers' "Favorite Love Stories." Mason is a two-time winner of the Bestselling Multicultural Title Award from Waldenbooks. Her work has also received a Reviewer's Choice Award from *Romantic Times* and the Best Contemporary Ethnic Novel Award from *Affaire de Coeur*. Her recent releases include a novella in the *Man of the House* Father's Day anthology from Pinnacle Books in June, and her fifth novel, *Foolish Heart*, available in November from Pinnacle Books. Felicia Mason can be reached at P.O. Box 1438, Yorktown, VA 23692.

## Rochelle Alers

Native New Yorker Rochelle Alers draws inspiration for her novels from her love of traveling, art, music, gourmet foods, and meditation. A prolific writer, she has written and published more than a dozen novels and several anthologies.

# Donna Hill

Donna Hill began her writing career in 1987 with the short story, "The Long Walk." From there it was on to an array of writing successes, culminating with her first novel, *Rooms of the Heart*. Since that time, Donna has written several books, including *Temptation*, *Scandalous*, *Deception*, *Intimate Betrayal* and *A Private Affair*. Her novels have received literary praise and have earned her a legion of devoted fans. Donna has been featured in *Essence* magazine, *Publishers Weekly*, and *USA Today*, among others. She has also made numerous radio and cable appearances across the country, including Lifetime Television and B.E.T. Donna currently resides in Brooklyn, NY and works by day as a Public Relations Associate for the Queens Borough Public Library System.

# Francis Ray

Francis Ray is a native Texan who lives in Dallas with her husband and daughter. A graduate of Texas Women's University, she is a School Nurse Practitioner for the Dallas Public School system. After publishing sixteen short stories, she sold her first book, *Fallen Angel*, in 1991. Since then she has written several books, including *Forever Yours*, *Undeniable*, *Only Hers*, *Incognito* and *Silken Betrayal*. Her books have earned her critical praise and have hit bestseller lists, including *Blackboard* and *Essence*. Francis is also the recipient of the *Romantic Times* Career Achievement Award for Multicultural Romance.